THE
WAYWARD
HAUNT

THE WAYWARD HAUNT
CAS E CROWE

THE WAYWARD HAUNT

CAS E CROWE

IDRA

JUBRIS

GALVAC

TARAHIK

BRENDLASH

ESSIDA

GOSHENIENE

VALDAVAR

PROLOGUE

G hosts haunt dreams.

I didn't believe it myself at first, but it's true.

Over the course of my life, I'd seen wraiths in the waking world—shadowy figures that crept in sinister places, hideous and senseless in their madness. Others drifted like harmless fog, unaware they were dead. Anything could hold the essence of a ghost: a bloodstain, a knife, the chilling deep waters of a river or lake. For me, ghosts were a daily encumbrance.

That was why I felt safe only when I slept.

Until the black-veined woman haunted my dreams.

It happened the same way every night. I remembered nothing about how the dream started, or how I ended up in a freezing, barren wasteland. Fog swirled above, blocking out whatever passed for sky. Heavy wind whipped down the slopes, sucking heat from my body. There was no other soul in sight. I was cold, lost, and alone.

Ahead, a maelstrom of clouds drew near.

No. Not her. Not again.

Tendrils branched out from the sweeping darkness. Skeletal and wraith-like, they swatted and pinched. Strange purplish welts popped across my exposed skin.

Help!

But my mouth couldn't master the word. The moisture in my throat had frozen.

The churning clouds parted like a stage curtain, the air resonating with cruel laughter as the black-veined woman emerged. She reminded me of a reviled queen—one who'd clawed herself from an icy grave. Spidery veins protruded from her chalk-white skin. Black hair floated down her back, reminding me of weeds in water. What made my heart skip beats were her eyes. They were charcoal black. Staring into them was like looking into the depths of an abyss.

She moved toward me without taking strides. "Where is it, Zaya?"

My head spiralled toward vertigo. I couldn't breathe. Her voice was otherworldly and piercing.

I don't know. Please. I need air.

Rage flared in her eyes. Black bled outward until no white was left. "You know where it's hidden. It's deep in your mind."

I don't. I swear.

A hopeless, watery feeling sloshed in my stomach. Like every other night, no matter what I said, it wouldn't help.

She wrenched me off the ground by the throat. A wicked smile curled her lips. "Then I will dig for the truth."

Her fingers jabbed into my skull. Blinding pain obscured my vision. She clawed and tore, her fingers driving deeper into my head.

I screamed and screamed.

CHAPTER ONE

A grinding shudder woke me.

For a few addled seconds, I had no idea where I was. Then the drowsiness cleared. Thessio—the prison guard on my most-hated list—rattled the barred door and hurled abuse. "Wake up, dissent scum."

When I didn't argue like I usually did, he sneered and moved on to the next cell. The wardens did that from time to time—rammed their batons against our cells to give them something to do. There wasn't a huge amount of entertainment to be found in the panopticon after hours. Tonight, I was grateful for the interruption. It saved me from the nightmare.

I sat upright and hugged my knees. Strands of my dark hair stuck to my face in matted tangles, my scalp itchy with sweat. Later, the frigid air would cool my perspiration and lower my body temperature. The risk of hypothermia would be high. I'd seen it happen to prisoners before.

Calm down, Zaya. Breathe.

My head throbbed but was intact. No one had tried to chisel my brain like a jackhammer. The black-veined woman was a nightmare. Nothing more.

Then why had it seemed real?

A flame that was equal parts fear and confusion ignited in my mind. I slammed my fist into the wall, barely flinching when the impact split the skin across my grazed knuckles. I'd seen spooks before and should have known if this was a figment of my imagination or a wraith communicating from beyond. Most of the ghosts I encountered in the Gosheniene labour camp were confused, wandering spirits, muttering trivial nonsense to themselves, oblivious of my presence. I made sure to avoid the places where the harmful ones lurked. Since the black-veined woman plagued my dreams though, something had changed. The ghosts sought me out. They hovered outside my cell at night or watched me shovel in the mines. They never said anything, just observed with their milky grey eyes.

I rested against the cold bricks, shivering. My eyelids struggled against the haze of sleep that tried to pull me under.

I wish I had the ability to conjure warmth, not the dead.

A beam of flashlight slipped across my cell. I squinted as the light came to a stop on my face. My cell door rattled. Thessio was back, only this time he'd brought friends—an extra half-dozen guards. "Dissent scum. You're wanted."

Wanted?

That wasn't a good sign. It meant I'd done something wrong. Again.

I wrapped my coat tightly around me and slipped off my metal sleeping shelf. My boots, which I wore to conserve warmth, had fit great two years ago but were now a size too small. The blisters on my heels stung as I moved to the door. I blinked back the pain, refusing to show weakness.

Thessio surveyed me in turn, judging, calculating, tense. He pointed a crooked finger at me through the bars. I'd broken it a year ago and took great satisfaction knowing it never truly healed. "Don't you try anything funny," he warned, then typed into the numeric keypad. The door swung open, his guards moving quickly to intercept me.

Where would I go, idiots?

Thanks to several failed escape attempts, I knew the layout of panopticon C like a mouse knows a maze. And I knew that tonight there was no chance of pulling off a breakout, not when surveillance had been doubled in the observation tower. Which meant something untoward had happened, or was about to.

Thessio cuffed my hands and gave me *that* look—the one that said he expected me to do something dangerous.

I smiled sweetly. "Afraid I'll hurt you again?"

He smacked me across the back of the head. Pain stabbed down my scalp. My vision see-sawed up and down.

I shook it off, squaring my shoulders. "That was like being hit by a wet tissue."

Never mind that I could taste the bitter, metallic blood in my mouth.

The head warden gripped my shoulder. "Shut up and move."

I shouldn't have antagonised him. Thessio enjoyed prodding inmates with stun guns when he was in a foul mood. My smartass attitude should have seen me sent to the underground punishment cells long ago, but other than the occasional slap, the worst punishment I received from Thessio was the isolation ward—torture by boredom. Yawn.

It was no secret he despised me; his tightly wound anger made his temples bulge whenever I was present. But for reasons I didn't know, he let me get away with the wild stunts I'd pulled in panopticon C. That leniency didn't extend to the mines or re-education though, which were monitored by different jailers. Inside the filthy, wet tunnels of the mountain, I kept my head down and shovelled crithanium stone. In re-education, I was the perfect model of a subdued zealot. That was how I survived—behaving and plotting escape in the background.

Thessio took my arm in his iron grip and corralled me along the steel platform. The extra guards followed at a distance, stun guns ready. Some of the men were practically salivating at the thought of using the weapons.

Whatever this is, please don't intervene with my plan.

My scheme had been in the works for weeks now. I'd never seen what was beyond the prison walls, but re-education had allowed me to study enough maps to get a sense of where I'd go. Five nights from now, I'd break out of Gosheniene and cross the Oldric Mountains. It would be a long journey to Yuchicana, the nearest city, but there I'd be able to blend in. I'd find a job, earn some cash, and buy my way to a new province. Maybe, with some luck, I'd find a witch doctor who could cure me of the ghosts.

Please… please let this mean they haven't discovered my plan.

But praying was useless. If God had existed, he'd abandoned the world long ago.

Thessio's fingers bit painfully into my shoulder. "Stop dawdling, scum."

I picked up my pace, my blisters making every footstep agony. Goosebumps that had nothing to do with the chilly air broke out on my arms.

Who wants me? And why can't it wait till morning?

Inmates never left the prison in the evenings unless they worked the graveyard shift in the mines. It was past midnight, which meant that wasn't our destination.

I pushed my fear aside and gave the head warden my best cocky grin. "Are you breaking me out?'

He laughed—the irritated, humourless kind. "No. After two years, my prayers are finally answered. You're being removed."

A greasy sensation churned down my throat. "Removed" was a subtle way of saying "You're being lowered into the underground punishment cells."

No. No, no, no, no.

It was worse than I'd imagined. I was being led to my execution.

Thessio tilted his head back and laughed. "Justice is served."

CHAPTER TWO

My jailers steered me into the formidable grey cell block. I fiddled with my manacles, but they were unwelcomingly tight—tighter than they'd ever been. The extra guards watched me like hawks fixated on a mouse. Putting it simply, there was no getting out of this.

I slipped closer to Thessio. "Removed? Would you mind elaborating?"

The cold satisfaction in his eyes robbed me of breath. "It means you're a goner... about to meet your maker... bitten the dust. Kapoof. Gone. Now keep moving."

His fist smacked my spine. I toyed with the idea of strangling him with my manacles, but that would be a waste of energy.

Better to keep my strength for later, when I really need it.

The building was dim after hours, but enough moonlight flowed in to see the top of the fifty-storey panopticon. It was a network of iron platforms and aluminium scaffolds, the cells arranged around the open space in multiple tiers so each prisoner could be monitored. Tonight, curious onlookers watched from doors obstructed by steel bars. They knew where I was being led. They skulked back into the darkness, their fear reinforcing the danger I faced.

Below ground, the panopticon descended into the earth where no light reached—to the punishment cells. Tonight, the high-pitched snarls from the yawning deep shook the building's foundations. It sounded as though a pack of wolves was feasting on a maimed animal. Knots of tension pulsed in my lower back. In the centre of the panopticon was the observation tower. Made of black galvanised metal, the tower was virtually impossible to see when clouds coasted the night sky. That was its purpose, of course; the jailers didn't want the prisoners to know who was being observed at any time. But the moonlight this evening provided just enough visibility to see a hanging cage lowered from the tower. Sickness coiled in my stomach. The prisoner inside looked closer to an animal. His sunken face was smeared with dirt, his hair matted and unkempt. He bared his stubbed teeth, yelling what must have been a frenzied prayer in a forgotten language.

My feet froze. I didn't want to witness this, but I couldn't look away. The cage descended into the punishment cells. The creatures below emitted a roar that sounded like a thousand gunshots fired at once. Nothing could drown out their preternatural cries, or the screams of the man as he was immediately feasted on.

Lycanthors.

Every night I'd heard their scratchy growls resonate from the punishment cells, but this was the first time I'd heard them eat in action. I'd never seen one and prayed to providence I never would. Lycanthors were known for their everlasting, ageless hunger. They weren't picky; they were happy to devour anything meaty in their path.

My throat burning from nausea, I looked away. Most of the time, the firing squad executed prisoners. There was only one reason this man had been lowered into the punishment cells: he'd rejected allegiance to the Council of Founding Sovereigns.

Thessio gripped my arm so hard I thought he'd break the bone.

Despite wanting to vomit my insides out, I cracked a smile. "Scared?"

Because I am. I'm scared shitless.

The glare Thessio gave me was sharp and cruel. "Not as frightened as you'll be. If I have my way, you'll be next in that cage. Now keep moving. And keep your mouth shut."

The jailers marched me across a series of gantries and down a passage I'd never been to before. The overhead light had burned out, the walls veiled in shadow. Thanks to the war, there was never enough power to go around.

We stopped at a heavy maximum-security door. I inhaled a long breath, trying to avert the dizziness that crept into my brain. This wasn't your average prison door. It was airtight so not even an explosion could blast it open. Which was the point. This door was here to prevent radiation from leaking into the room beyond. Now that my eyes had adjusted, I recognised the galvanised air pipes that ran across the ceiling, pumping extra oxygen. The person behind this door was... human.

I am in serious trouble.

Thessio hunched his shoulders to block my view and punched numbers into the keypad. Security was different at Gosheniene. It was powered by magic and never went out. Judging by the amount of numbers Thessio typed, the code was complex.

"Inside," he barked when the door buzzed open.

The jailers hauled me into the room. No, not a room. More like a hotel suite, opulent to the max. I swallowed surprise. It was a working oval office with three doors: the west door led to a private chamber with the usual bedroom accessories, including wardrobe, dresser, and nightstand; the north door opened to a dining room set for one; and the east door led to a plush parlour room. Everything was richly decorated in marble and wood furniture. Flames crackled in a fireplace, the air rippling with delicious warmth. I wanted to lie on the rug, curl up like a cat, and doze into a dreamless sleep.

In the centre of the office, a man observed two holographic displays of the world as it had been and what it was now, the globes strikingly different. No one knew for certain what had caused the fires, storms, tsunamis, and earthquakes to restructure the continents. Scientists were in a mixed mind that either an asteroid hit the Earth or Mother Nature pressed the reset button, sending the world into a new age. It was too long ago for either theory to be considered definite, though.

The man's face was stoic and devoid of warmth. Nothing differentiated humans and casters in appearance, save for the fact that humans always carried a small air inhaler on them and had to wear a radiation-resistant suit when travelling out of the Free Zones. But this room was uniquely designed to keep radiation out, and this man strolled leisurely around as though he owned the place. He was impeccably dressed in a tailored suit, his thinning pepper-grey hair neatly parted at the side. My palms turned sweaty. The symbol of the Infinite Eye was embroidered on his left armband—a triangle with a hexagon-shaped eye in the centre.

He's a council dignitary. Someone high up who works for the seven sovereigns.

Two Haxsan Guard soldiers flanked him when he sat on the cushioned sofa. Another three were stationed at each door, their faces grave and unmoving. In their black ballistic body armour, they looked lethal and dangerous. One wrong move and they'd have me disabled, or worse, dead. Their grip tightened on their weapons so hard, I wondered if it hurt. I stared incredulously. I hated how these casters moved, stood, and acted like they had no mind of their own, ready to sacrifice themselves for this human's survival, as though their own lives didn't matter compared to his.

Conditioned zealots. And idiots.

Thessio bowed his bald head, which was shiny from sweat. "Prisoner C317 as requested, sir." He bowed several more times and slipped back among the jailers. I rolled my eyes. It wouldn't be long till he bobbed a curtsy.

The dignitary surveyed me with an amused glint. "She doesn't look dangerous." His eyes shifted to the head warden. "She's a filthy, emaciated girl. Hardly worth anyone's time. Barnes, remove the handcuffs. They're not required."

Thessio gaped. "But, sir, she's a prisoner. And I assure you, she's a trickster and a charlatan."

"Are you questioning my authority?"

The head warden sucked in a breath. "No, sir. Not at all."

Thessio tossed me a dirty look but unlocked my shackles. In the firelight, my wrists were cut red raw, the skin bruised and inflamed. A groan of distress worked its way from my throat. Whenever I moved, wincing pain shot up my arms.

The dignitary watched me with a polished smile. "My name is Romadus Ablott. I have been sent to Gosheniene to assess you."

My throat went dry.

Assess me? For what?

I filtered through the recent troubles I'd caused. I'd broken into and entered the armoury, stolen a Taser—Thessio had regrettably taken it back—

been involved in a punch-up with a fellow prisoner, and taken extra rations to prisoners who'd been denied food. On top of everything else I'd done in panopticon C over the past two years, did this now warrant my execution?

Fear crawled up my skin.

Yes. It does.

Romadus looked over the dossier in his hands. It had my photograph, taken last month after I'd gotten into a brawl with a prisoner in the mines, showing the nasty bruise on my head and a cut on my lip, which had now healed. But still, it wasn't my finest photo.

"Zaya, is it?" His voice was clipped and low. He looked me up and down and gave a subtle shake of his head.

My insides constricted. I wasn't a beautifully made-up countess from the Free Zones, but that was no way to give me the critical once-over. My clothes had seen better days and my hair needed a wash, but all things considering, I wasn't too bad-looking. I had long dark brown curls that shone auburn in the sunlight—not that I experienced the sun often—coral lips, skin so fair the moon was probably jealous, and tiny freckles only visible if you got close. I was about five foot seven and, thanks to working in the mines, athletically built and toned, which was more than any girl from the Free Zones could boast, thank you very much. Not that it mattered now.

Romadus studied me, his eyes probing and intent. "This dossier does not list a last name. What is it?"

I remained tight-lipped.

I'd like to know myself.

Thessio's nostrils flared. "C317 doesn't have a last name, sir. We call her Wayward, after the reform school she was raised in. She says she has no memories of her life before the school, but I'm certain she's lying."

The dignitary tilted his head. "Lying? How do you know?"

Hatred filled Thessio's face. "She's caused nothing but problems from the moment she stepped into panopticon C. I'm surprised this worthless scum hasn't committed the same crime that brought her to Gosheniene in the first place."

My anger paralysed me for a moment. I wanted to claw my fingernails into Thessio's eyes. What he said was true. I had no recollection of my past.

Everything was a black hole with no memories, names, or family to fill it. I was ten years old when I'd woken inside the stale walls of Brendlash Orphanage—or, to be precise, Brendlash Orphanage and Reform School for Wayward Youth. They tended not to put that last part on the brochure. I had no clue who I was or where I'd been. The doctor who'd attended to me had said my memories would return in time, but they never did. I was diagnosed with amnesia, despite having no sign of trauma or a head wound. All I had was a name. Zaya.

But the crime I'd committed?

That was not true.

Romadus chuckled at my silence. He took a fancy silver pen from his jacket and began writing. I craned my neck to watch. Under surname, he wrote *Wayward*.

Zaya Wayward. Well… it's an improvement from "dissent scum."

His gaze locked with mine. "You turned nineteen on the tenth of January. Is that correct?"

What is this, twenty questions?

I secretly assessed the office for danger. The Haxsan Guard soldiers remained rigid but vigilant. I couldn't see them breathe under their thick armour, but I sensed their mounting tension. They were here in case I started something unpleasant, which was laughable. I couldn't take out thirteen grown men. And if I were to pull a trick, I'd make sure it was discreet.

I glared at Romadus, clenching my jaw. "If you're going to lower me into the punishment cells, I'd rather we skip the interview and get it over with."

Prisoners were allowed a final meal before they were thrown into the earth—probably so it would take longer to die if the lycanthors didn't finish them first. I'd be locked in a room with a warden to monitor me while I ate and drank. The jailer wouldn't be difficult to take out. A single hit to the temple and he or she would be on the ground. I'd steal their weapons and slip through the ventilation shaft. A few more days to settle the details of my escape would have been ideal, but time was against me. I had to leave tonight.

An amused leer played on Romadus's lips. "I don't know what your head warden insinuated, but I'm not here to sanction your execution. I'm a minister from the council and am here to give your orders. You are the property of the

Council of Founding Sovereigns and have been called to serve."

My breathing turned short. The lavish room started to feel like another prison.

Council property?

Serve?

Frustration set hard around Thessio's mouth. "Sir, I must protest. This girl is dissent scum. Whoever surrendered her to the orphanage was too ashamed to identify her with a surname. What does that tell you? It says her parents sided with the United League of Dissent. She's one of them. A dissent rebel."

Stay composed.

But what I really wanted to do was punch Thessio's teeth out.

The head warden's eyes darted to his colleagues, but none of the jailers offered to help. They shuffled and looked at their feet. Thessio glowed beet red. "Sir. I was lenient on her because that's what the council ordered, but she's a murderer, sir."

Rage, deep and dark, filled my blood. "I am not."

Thessio turned on me, wild with impatience. "Really? Adaline White froze to death on her own, did she?"

I tried not to flinch. It had been a long time since I'd heard that name. But I couldn't reveal what had killed Adaline that night, just like I hadn't been able to tell the judge. It happened on my seventeenth birthday. The worst winter storm struck the Brendlash Province just after 8:00 p.m. Miles from any village, and isolated in the barren wilderness of the Brendlands, it hadn't taken long for the orphanage's power to shut off, the central heating we depended on gone. No one knew what had occurred that evening in room 216. The council guard, the judge, my criminal psychologist—they'd all endeavoured to pry the truth from me, but it wasn't something easily explained. I'd woken in the middle of the night, sensing down to the marrow in my bones that something wasn't right. My bedroom door was open, as was the door adjacent to mine across the passage—room 216. Adaline's room. That had been odd. Children weren't supposed to be out of bed at night, and I was positive I'd closed my door before I'd gone to sleep. I tossed my sheets aside and tiptoed across the hall into Adaline's room. The cold air plummeted. It felt as though someone had opened a freezer. Adaline had to be an icicle in the sub-zero temperature.

At her bedside, I reached down to shake her awake. "Ada, come on. Get up. It's too cold in here."

Nothing.

"Ada? Ada?"

My fingers touched something chillingly firm. For a second, my sharp intake of air lodged in my throat before I recognised what I was staring at. I screamed. I didn't know how long I stood there, bawling and crying. Someone rushed into the room and gathered me into their arms, tugging me to safety.

Away from the dead girl shelled in ice.

Out in the hallway, *she* was there. The black-veined woman. Her smile was laced with malicious pleasure. She sank through the floorboards like oil, her laughter peeling across the walls in a sinister echo.

No one else saw or heard the black-veined woman, of course. I couldn't tell the authorities that a ghost had killed Adaline. People had demanded justice for the dead girl. The judge granted their wish. That was how I'd ended up in the lifeless, colourless world of Gosheniene Internment Camp.

I shook my head, driving away the memory.

Thessio's lips pulled into a triumphant grin. "See? Her silence confirms her guilt. Deep inside, she's twisted and rotten. I told you, she's a dissent rebel through and through. She should be lowered into the punishment cells and left for the lycanthors. Read her file. Next page, sir."

Romadus flipped the dossier. He exhaled a breath. "Theft, assault, eight attempted escapes in the past two years… and you've hospitalised every warden in panopticon C."

Despite my fear, I couldn't deter a smirk. It was impressive when he listed it that way.

Romadus crossed his long legs. "I have to admit, I didn't fully understand why the council wanted an alleged murderer assigned to the Tarahik Military Base, but now that I've read these misdemeanours, it makes perfect sense."

A strange urge to laugh formed in my throat. "Military base?"

Is this a joke?

Romadus waved a folded parchment lazily in the air. "Yes. I have the order here. You have been conscripted into the Haxsan Guard. Congratulations."

He said it with little enthusiasm.

My heart thumped so hard it was a miracle it didn't crack my ribs. I'd heard stories about the Tarahik Military Base and its academy, one of the most prestigious defence colleges for casters. It was located deep in the Tarzor Plains and was a large castle—and by large, I meant a hulking, gothic, impregnable fortress, complete with underground dungeons and hidden chambers. It didn't matter if you were a wealthy caster living among humans in the Free Zones or were combing for scraps in the provinces; at nineteen, all casters went to military school—unless you were imprisoned in a labour camp… or so I'd thought. At the bases, cadets trained, graduated, and joined the Haxsan Guard—the council's armed forces. The Haxsan Guard were committed to serving and protecting humankind from the dangerous, destructive Earth we'd inhabited. Without casters, humans were simply no match for our world with its unpredictable weather, radiation, and severe climate. But I never thought Earth was threatening or toxic. Not for casters, anyway. Radiation didn't affect us. Nor did the fragile atmosphere. To me, Earth was fresh and clean and something to be explored.

Something dark flitted across Thessio's face. "But she's a murderer. Worthless ULD spawn that deserves to rot. She belongs in the ground with the lycanthors."

Romadus dismissed the claim with a firm shake of his head. "Caster children make mistakes when they develop their powers. It's why Miss Wayward wasn't given the death sentence… and why you were ordered to make sure she remained unharmed, Mr Barnes."

Thessio blanched at the accusatory tone.

Romadus peered curiously at me. "The dossier says that your ability is freezing. That would be a frightening addition to the Haxsan Guard."

My stomach did a queasy somersault. "No, that's inaccurate."

Romadus's lips lifted into a poorly disguised smile. "Is it? Please enlighten me. What is your magic?"

"I… I never specialised."

Seeing the dead wasn't something I'd ever admit to. I'd read the history books and understood the brutal measures the council took to eradicate necromancy. Any caster who possessed the magic was executed. Necromancy had been purged from the world. At least, that was what the council and the humans believed.

Romadus laughed. "Are you telling me you're human? What a remarkable discovery. A human who can survive beyond the Free Zones? I must have you examined at once."

A shudder passed through me. Centuries ago, after the reshaping of the Earth, our human ancestors were infected by the influnix virus. The infected evolved into casters. All casters excelled in a distinctive magic: telekinesis, alchemy, elemental control, precognition—whatever it was, it was unique to that caster. No one knew why certain powers resulted in certain people. It was inherent, developed in the body through puberty, but wasn't genetic. We could survive the Earth. Humans could not. They lived in the Free Zones, large pockets of lands protected by celestial shields designed to keep radiation out, while the rest of us casters who lacked the wealth and fortune to live among them were forced to work in the provinces.

I blinked back angry tears. I'd fallen into Romadus's trap.

The dignitary's slim fingers tightened together. "Don't lie to me, Miss Wayward. If you were human, radiation would have sucked the life from your frail body the moment you left the Free Zones. Judging by your scruffiness, I'm confident you've never set foot in a Free Zone. Admit it. You killed that poor girl, but you didn't mean to." He leaned forward, his gaze scrutinising. "The Haxsan Guard is a second chance."

Thessio's face crumpled with distaste. "She doesn't deserve a second chance. Not after everything she's done to my men."

Romadus's spine straightened, his expression firm but irritated. "The council believes with the right training, Zaya could be a useful member to the Haxsan Guard. The war against the United League of Dissent has cost us many soldiers. Support for Morgomoth continues to grow in the provinces. Every day, the ULD are closer to overthrowing the council and destroying the celestial shields that protect the Free Zones. The council cannot be picky about who it recruits."

My quasi-stability drifted away like a bottle at sea. Before I could get a grasp on myself, the words spilled freely. "Morgomoth is dead. If the council wish to end the war, they shouldn't ostracize casters from the provinces. It's no wonder they joined the ULD in the first place. They found a voice with Morgomoth."

There was a collective intake of breath from everyone in the room. I wanted to smack myself. Why hadn't I kept my mouth shut?

Thessio bellowed a throaty laugh. "See? I told you she was dissent spawn. She can't be trusted."

Romadus's focus settled on me. "You are misguided in defending those casters, Miss Wayward. I see re-education has failed to reach you, so let me set things straight. Morgomoth's intention was to destroy the Free Zones and purge the world of humans. He was a madman who had to be stopped. Unfortunately, his execution made him a martyr. Now, his followers want to obliterate the Free Zones, which is no doubt a tempting offer to casters struggling in the provinces. Morgomoth might be dead, but his ideology is not."

My face twisted into a scowl. "His followers want to destroy the Free Zones because the council have enslaved them. You force them to work against their will and without pay."

Romadus rose from his chair. Tension lines appeared around his pinched lips. "Casters serve humans. That is the way it has always been." Spittle flew from his mouth. "What these traitorous casters really desire is the wealth of the Free Zones. The United League of Dissent cannot be reasoned with—something you'll learn when you serve the Haxsan Guard. Tarahik awaits you."

Without needing a response, he marched to the door.

Thessio swore viciously. "You can't be serious. She'll betray the base."

Romadus stopped at the threshold. One of his Haxsan Guard soldiers helped him into a radiation-resistant suit, which looked easier to slip on than I would have thought. The dignitary clucked his tongue and laughed. "There won't be an opportunity for that, Mr Barnes. Soldiers are tightly monitored in the Haxsan Guard. And there's the oath."

My stomach plummeted.

Please do not be a blood oath.

Blood magic was impossible to break.

Romadus must have seen the colour drain from my complexion, because his face lit with an appraising smile. "Captain Arden will be here to collect you at dawn. I suggest you try and make a good impression."

He swept out of the room, his lightning-swift guards quick in pursuit.

Dawn?

My eyes shifted to the clock.

I had minutes to escape.

CHAPTER THREE

My chest crushed under layers of panic. I was dragged wordlessly from the plush oval room into a passage—not the one we'd come through—passing several unmarked doors and into the custody of the brawny-chested, shaven-headed Dera. She didn't like me any more than Thessio did. When I'd first arrived at Gosheniene, it took me a week to figure out if the warden was a man or woman, something she didn't appreciate when I asked.

She crossed her muscular arms, which were dark and hairy like a gorilla's, her catty eyes slitted. "Look what the storm blew in. What's she done this time, Thess? Does it warrant the punishment cells?"

Thessio scoffed. "No. She's been conscripted."

Dera's brazen smile dropped. "What?"

Honestly, you'd think they'd sold tickets to my execution.

The wardens led me from one lonely hallway to another. It was a huge compliment to be assigned with so many guards, but also a real pain in the ass. And it had never happened before.

What are the jailers afraid of?

My mind wandered back to Thessio's comment. *"I was lenient on her because that's what the council ordered."*

But what did that mean?

Had the council kept me here for two years simply to extract me to a base when I reached nineteen? An icy sensation floated down my neck. The full implication of what was about to occur hit me. Being shipped off to Tarahik was bizarre and completely abnormal. Only the wealthy and privileged casters from the Free Zones went to that base. Soldiers who showed potential became officers and worked their way up the ranks. They were the knights, bishops, queens, and kings on the chessboard. Casters from the provinces—people like me—went to less-refined bases, the pawns first to be sacrificed.

None of it made sense. And it pissed me off not knowing why.

Thessio's fingers burned into my arm. "You're straggling! Keep moving."

My feet hurt, asshole.

The back of my boots rubbed against my heels, popping blisters.

But that was the least of my worries, because through the windows, morning light ascended above the mountain. I was out of time. Dawn had arrived.

We crossed the front entry of the panopticon into the yard, immediately embraced by cold, damp air. Snow swirled through the open door, delicate as sand. Wind lashed at my clothes, blowing freezing precipitation onto my skin. My fingers went stiff. I struggled to bend them at the knuckles.

Thessio's bravado drained from his face. "What is this? A snowstorm in the middle of March? This wasn't on the weather radar."

Dera blew warm air into her hands and danced on her toes. "It's rare, but it has been known to happen."

Despite the cold drilling into every fibre of me, I raised my eyes devilishly. "You're welcome to go back inside. I can wait here on my own."

The morning shift in the mines wouldn't start for another hour. The grounds were empty except for Thessio and Dera. The other jailers had returned to the panopticon, unwilling to brace the cold. If providence gave me a last chance to flee, now was it.

Thessio sputtered out a laugh. "The hell you will. Do you think I'm stupid?"

"Yes."

He shot me a filthy stare. Whatever he was about to say next was swallowed by the *whoomph, whoomph, whoomph* of rotor blades. A carrier-hornet appeared in the turbulent sky, pitching toward us as though its pilot deliberately sped in to blow us off the earth. My chest constricted at the sight. I'd tried many times to escape Gosheniene. Now I was leaving—just not in the way I'd imagined.

The aircraft's landing gear deployed. The jet settled smoothly, the blades beating in time with my pumping heart. The aircraft was much larger than I'd anticipated. It had swept-back wings and cannons mounted on the grey hull. The door was large enough that in a conflict, it probably stationed five door gunners at a time.

The loading ramp lowered, and two soldiers disembarked. The tallest of the pair—he might have been six-seven—strolled purposefully toward us, shoulders relaxed and arms loose by his sides. My throat made a strangled noise. I wasn't the sort of person to go googly-eyed, but he was insanely good-looking—in a bad way. The kind of guy who was every girl's prerequisite crush before sadly giving up and moving on. His black hair hung messily over his ears, like poets from the bohemian age. Dark stubble covered his chin to his jaw, showing off the perfect evenness of his face. He'd spent time outdoors, because he had a tan I could only dream of, and his fitted flight suit hinted at an athletic build and strong muscles.

But this very attractive, chiselled Greek god was irrelevant. He was the obstacle that hindered my escape.

The young man assessed my jailers. I got the impression that in that single moment, he'd worked out their characters and didn't peg them as threats. He was highly intuitive, then, studying his surroundings and ready for any peril. He probably took his opponents out with his eyes closed.

Thessio stretched his hand in greeting. "Captain Arden. I'm Thessio Barnes, the head warden for panopticon C. Welcome to Gosheniene."

I stared, trying not to gape.

Captain?

Surely he was too young for that rank. He couldn't have been any older than midtwenties.

Captain Arden eyed the warden's outstretched hand but didn't take it. "We nearly didn't make it, Mr Barnes." His tone was direct but not unpleasant. "We spotted dissent rebels in the Gossen Mountains. Why are there rebels in close range to Gosheniene?"

Thessio looked like he'd caught a mouthful of chilli. "I'll make sure they're hunted down and detained, sir. I assure you the sentinels on watch will be punished. There is no excuse for dissent rebels being that close to Gosheniene." His voice dripped with panic. Seeming to realise his competence was at stake, he handed my dossier to Arden. "Prisoner C317. You'll need to watch yourself with this one."

The young captain skimmed the page. His eyes fell on mine. Something in the way he stared made the blood thrum in my temples. Was he... evaluating me?

His broad hands tensed. "Right. Cuff her."

The other soldier—he had shaggy red hair and a smattering of freckles—bounded back into the aircraft, probably to find a pair of shackles.

Anger shoved aside my mortification. "Cuff me? I haven't done anything wrong."

The captain stared, unfazed. "Said the girl who hospitalised seven grown men." He pointed to the dossier, where it listed exactly what I'd done to the jailers. "You're dangerous, and while you're in my custody, you will be detained."

Without giving me an opportunity to protest, he turned his attention to the warden. "Mr Barnes, may I have a word."

It wasn't a request but an order.

The captain confidently led Thessio into the panopticon and shut the door, only it didn't quite catch. Dera remained close, but I managed to inch my way back a few steps and peek through the gap.

Captain Arden's voice was pitched low and urgent. "The general wants to know if it's been found."

Thessio's shoulders visibly tightened. "Found? We've searched the mines and the prison twice. What more do you people want? It's not here. Maybe if your general told me exactly what it looked like, we'd have better luck. But as it is, everything we're going on is guesswork."

"Then try harder, Mr Barnes. You do not want to disappoint General Kravis. He's not the kind of man you want for an enemy."

Either Captain Arden was super quick and saw me staring, or he'd sensed my eyes on him. He grabbed Thessio's arm and marched the warden out of sight.

Somewhere, an engine revved, grabbing my full attention. The large compound gates at the front of the camp swung open and a lorry entered. The vehicle parked at the sentinels' office, where a jailer emerged. He checked the driver, the registration and, after a brief inspection of the back, signalled the all-clear. Two men jumped out from the lorry and began unloading boxes—probably unwanted food left over from the Free Zones. Judging by the size of the truck, it would take time to fully unload. But more importantly, the jailer on duty had left the gates open.

I calculated my options. It would be risky, but if I timed it right, I could make a run for it. Dera was in no way a clever woman. She'd never see it coming.

The soldier with scruffy red hair returned with handcuffs, only these weren't like the shackles used in the camp. These were solid bar cuffs, five inches long and reinforced with magic. My wrists had been shackled in this indestructible metal once before, back when I was transferred to Gosheniene. They were for the dangerous and insane. If you struggled, the sorcery stung like a swarm of hostile bees.

The soldier wore a lopsided smirk. "I'm Private Crawley," he announced. He was a couple of years older than me, but it was evident by the way he exuded superiority that he was a caster from a Free Zone who hadn't so much as seen a battle, let alone experienced one. He raised the handcuffs to my eyes. Heat chafed my face. "You try and pull free and these melt your bones. Understand?"

I nodded, wondering what it would take to snap his thin neck.

He began the process of looping the cuffs over my wrists. The skin above my upper lip dampened. It was now or never. Before Crawley could lock the handcuffs in place, I kicked in an offensive manoeuvre into his stomach. His cry of pain was the sweetest sound. I slammed my fist hard into his nose, the strike pitching him violently in the snow. The back of his head hit ice. His face blanked.

Dera scrambled to intercept me. She reminded me of a grizzly, her movement bearlike and heavy. I dove onto Crawley's slumped body, seized the private's cast-shooter from his holster, and fired a warning shot at Dera's feet.

For a second, her eyes pierced mine with silent menace, trying to glean a hint into my thoughts. Then she sprang. I ducked under her arm and slammed the barrel into her head, the impact met by a wet clomp. Dera sagged to the ground, her face empty and her eyes unfocused.

The only thought that pounded in my head was reaching the gates. I ran in broken steps across the snow, swinging my arms to propel myself faster. My feet felt like they ran on hot coals. Blood trickled past my heels, pooling under my feet.

Don't slow down.

Ten metres.

Nine metres.

Beyond the gates, the blur of white trees came into view.

Five metres.

Four metres.

I could see white crags.

Three metres.

My breath came out in short, erratic pants. I was nearly there.

Gunfire blasted. A gush of gold light struck the ground ahead, sending a pillar of snow into the air. The impact split the earth. I was too close to avoid the devastation and plunged into the gaping hole. A half second later, my legs were buried in the snow's freezing embrace. I cursed every profanity I knew. In the commotion, I'd dropped Crawley's cast-shooter. It was buried in the snow.

A cry tore from my throat. The gunshot had grazed my arm, the burn rising into an oozing, dribbling bubble. I scooped snow over the wound, afraid I'd pass out if I stared at it too long.

Dera stood over me, massaging her injured head. She breathed hard, her body pulsing with fury. "Get up."

That line of logic wouldn't get either of us anywhere. "I'm stuck, idiot."

Returning my glare, she gripped the collar of my coat and tugged me out of the snow. Her fingers dug into my neck, a silent warning that if I did anything like kick or scream, she'd grind my bones.

Thessio stormed toward us, his cast-shooter aimed solely on me. The barrel still smoked.

So you're the bastard who fired the shot.

He must have heard the commotion, stepped outside, and botched my escape. Over the years, the prison guard had shown immense restraint, but this time I'd gone too far. Protocol be damned, Thessio was going to kill me. I saw it in his eyes.

Dera took a moment to register that she too was in firing range. She raised her hands in an imploring gesture. "Don't shoot."

But the head warden didn't care. His finger curled around the trigger. I braced myself for the barrage of bullets.

At the last second, something dark lunged at Thessio. It took me a moment to realise that Captain Arden had thrown his arm around the warden and pummelled him into the ground. An explosion erupted. A flash of gunfire burned my eyes. The shot missed, blasting a hole in the perimeter wall behind me. Sparks rained down, the snow in the immediate vicinity coated in ash.

Captain Arden tore the cast-shooter away from Thessio. The head warden remained on the ground, howling like an injured animal. A lump protruded where his shoulder should have been. The bone had dislodged.

Thessio spat ruddy saliva onto the snow. "You'll regret striking me down."

The captain plucked him easily from the ground. "You had no right. She no longer belongs to Gosheniene." Contempt edged his words.

The knotted tension in my shoulders released, but if I thought the young man with the striking good looks was my saviour, I was wrong. "Get her on board," he shouted at Crawley, who'd barely resurfaced from unconsciousness.

The private scuttled toward me and seized my wrists. My limbs were heavy with exhaustion. Even if I escaped his hold, I wouldn't have the energy to flee. Crawley locked the handcuffs in place and dragged me toward the plane. His nose bled, and a red welt had sprung over his check.

Geez, I hit him hard.

Thessio watched me pass. This would be the last time I'd see him, so yeah, I did the mature thing and shot him the finger. He leapt for me like a raging pit bull.

"Leave it." The captain held him back, struggling to keep him restrained.

Arden's eyes snapped to mine. They were lethal around the edges. My head burned as if with fever, but I stared back, defiant. That look lasted for an eternity, only broken when I turned away. But Captain Arden wasn't done yet. I felt his eyes follow me onto the aircraft. I couldn't understand the depth of his loathing.

CHAPTER FOUR

I'd never been in a plane—at least, I couldn't remember if I had. The carrier-hornet's main cabin was an all-metal interior, probably used to airlift troops, weapons, and cargo to difficult terrain. Today it was empty except for a line of jump seats and support struts. Despite how vacant it appeared, the air was suffocating. I inhaled a dramatic sniff. It smelt as though the hornet had slowly digested the torment of soldiers' past. A shiver crept through me. There was a presence in the cabin that made icy fear crawl across my bones. Cold spots hinted that activity occurred on a deeper level. I shrugged the feeling away. I had no business with these ghosts. They were sad, not harmful, and their reasons for haunting the cabin were none of my business.

An open palm smacked me hard between the shoulder blades. "In the cockpit. Now," Crawley's disgruntled voice snapped in my ear.

We entered what appeared to be a futuristic flight deck. Everywhere I looked there were multifunction screens and navigation displays. Massive dome-shaped windows provided an unrestricted view of the landscape. Towering over the communication console, holographic scanners illustrated difficult terrain that remained invisible to the eye. The entire flight deck was a network of control panels, dials, toggles, and switches, each beeping and tinging in time with the cadenced drone of the engines.

How could anyone possibly know what these all do?

At one of the stations, a young man was bent over a display screen, his thin fingers typing complicated calculations. He was closer to Captain Arden's age but had a shorter build and was sturdier in the shoulders. His blond-brown hair was cropped and tidy. When he turned, I immediately braced myself for a threat. To my surprise, his lips curled into a pleasant half-smile. "Hi. I'm Marek."

My aggression took a sober turn.

Why is he being... nice?

He slapped a hand to his forehead. "Oh, man. Sorry, I'm Sergeant Spiers. I always forget to add that part." He gave a boyish shrug. Flecks of gold lit in his green eyes, his flustered grin enhanced by cute dimples.

Not hot, but pleasant to look at.

He stepped forward to shake my hand. "I'm recently promoted. I'm Jad's... I mean Captain Arden's co-pilot." His eyes fell on my restraints and his smile dropped. "Oh."

Crawley grunted from the doorway. "Watch her. Carefully. The bitch hit me in the face. I'm getting the first aid kit." He shot a spiteful glance in my direction and disappeared into the main cabin.

I was hankering for a fight but had an inkling Crawley would shriek like a chicken if I apprehended him. It would hardly be worth the energy.

Marek dipped his head to catch my eye. "Did you do that to his face?"

I snorted. Unbelievable. These guys were soldiers. A punch from a girl shouldn't have been a traumatic experience. "I'm sure he's suffered worse."

Marek's eyes sparkled. I wondered if he secretly enjoyed seeing Crawley beat on by a girl. "You'd be surprised. Privates like Crawley have a talent for avoiding confrontation. This way please, Miss...."

"It's Zaya."

He nodded. "Then follow me, Miss Zaya."

He steered me to a seat at the back of the cockpit.

From my assessment, Marek was a humble, modest guy. If I played my cards right, I was confident I could get answers out of him. "When you say 'privates like Crawley,' what do you mean?"

The friendly lines around the sergeant's mouth disappeared. He inhaled a steady breath. "Soldiers from wealthy families buy themselves out of duty.

Crawley might look tough, but apart from training, he's never held a cast-shooter in his life. Before Tarahik, he hadn't even stepped foot outside a Free Zone."

My body turned rigid. This did not add up with what I'd been told. Casters at Tarahik were meant to be gods—indestructible, brutal, impossible to defeat. That matched Captain Arden's image to the bone. I was positive you wouldn't be able to crack a joke at his expense without having your innards spilled in a creatively horrid way. Marek? I'd been acquainted with him for two minutes and knew he had the emotional capacity of a teddy bear. But Crawley? It was evident he was upper class by the way he expected everyone to obey him like an obedient lapdog. He was the diamond of casters—shiny and polished. When it came to battle, he'd flee the scene like a hunted criminal. And if Marek was telling the truth—which I had no reason to doubt—there were meant to be more soldiers like Crawley. All my views were erased, replaced with reservations and doubt.

I sat down, immediately jolted by searing pain.

What the fu—

Heat coursed through my wrists, running up my arms to the top of my scruffy head. My stomach twisted with nausea. It was like someone had dipped me into a pool of bubbling larva.

Marek's gaze dropped to my blistered wrists. He grimaced. "Don't make sudden movement, okay? Crawley switched the shackles' Taser to the highest level. The magic will burn right through you if you struggle."

I bit my lip to keep the profanities at bay. "Great. Thanks for the explanation. Would you mind switching it off?"

A hint of regret flashed across his face. "Only Crawley has the key to do that." He leant forward and fumbled with the harness, gently tightening it around my shoulders. "I'll strap you in. Just don't move."

The throb in my wrists subsided, but keeping perfectly still for the next however many hours it took to get to Tarahik would be a true bitch to deal with. "I haven't done anything wrong," I protested. "I shouldn't be shackled."

Marek met my eyes. "The captain doesn't restrain people without a reason."

My mind, still stunned, took a moment to register that he wasn't on my side after all. He came across as nice, even charming, but he didn't trust me. And why would he? Soldiers were taught to be wary of outsiders.

Marek focused on my harness, averting his eyes from mine.

I couldn't prevent a bitter laugh. "You know, if you remove the handcuffs, I could do this myself."

The co-pilot smiled like we'd shared a private joke. "Nice try, but Captain Arden wouldn't be pleased if I did that." He strapped the last buckle in. "It won't be long till we take off. Yell out if you need anything."

He returned to the flight deck, typing promptly into a screen.

Need him? For what? Entertainment? To see the in-flight menu?

I tried to arch forward to see what he was doing, but the jab in my wrists warned me it was a bad idea. I sat back with an annoyed grunt. The waiting was terrible. What was Captain Arden doing out there? Searching the entire camp for this "thing" his general wanted? Didn't he realise Gosheniene was a big place?

Don't think about him. He's a jerk.

But my mind wandered away without any direction from me. I clutched the details I knew about him as though they were prized crithanium. He was a captain. That hinted he was wealthy—likely from a Free Zone. He was young for his rank, which meant he was clever, possessed aptitude, and kept a cool head in a crisis. His confidence alluded to the fact that he knew he was handsome. Dark and brooding, he probably had a string of girls pining for him at the base. Pathetic. I hated men like that.

"Hey, Marek?" I tossed my shoulders back, annoyed it was all the movement I could achieve. "That jackass you call Captain, you said his name was Jad, right?"

Marek swivelled around. His cheeks took on colour because at that moment, Captain Arden strolled in. I'd seen loathing before—experienced it a hundred times in the camp—but that was nothing compared to the way Jad looked at me now. Why, for the love of casters, did he have to overhear me at that precise moment? The media lights that blazed through the cockpit shadowed the hard edges of his face, displaying the full force of his resentment.

Common sense told me to keep my mouth shut, but my contempt prevailed. "I'd give you the finger, but some idiot put me in shackles."

His face morphed into scowl. His eyes flicked guardedly to his co-pilot. "Don't talk to her."

Marek nodded and returned to his typing, head down.

I laughed. "What do you think we were doing, Captain? Devising a strategy to commandeer the plane?"

Jad tilted his head skyward, as though to say *why me?* He whirled around. "Do you want me to gag you?"

I didn't answer.

"No? Then keep your mouth shut."

My anger rose like mercury in a thermometer. "You can throw me out of the plane for all I care."

At least that gets me out of this shit. And away from the ghosts.

He jerked away from me, my remark catching him off guard. It had surprised me too. Like any prisoner, I had dark days. Sure, I said things in the heat of the moment that I regretted, but this time my comment had been extreme. Even for someone with my temperament.

Jad closed his eyes for half a second, then, without another glance at me, marched to the front of the cockpit.

A series of short, resonant vibrations rumbled through the floor. The engines shuddered and bucked, sparking into life. Outside, the rotor blades seemed to lurch in the terrible, howling winds. A storm was brewing on the horizon. Black clouds coasted over the skyline, the sharp cracks of thunder momentarily drowning out the engines.

Can we seriously fly in this?

The hull shrieked as something heavy bounced over the hornet's roof. Both the captain and his co-pilot didn't seem fazed. They made final checks on the instruments and examined the holographic scanner. The display illustrated what appeared to be a roiling storm of snow and lightning... and something not natural to the Earth.

I craned my neck. "What is that?"

Jad met my stare in the windscreen's reflection. "Nothing to concern yourself with."

He flipped a series of toggles, conversation ended.

Crawley returned with his nose bandaged. His grinning idiot face looked like a perfect target for another punch. He must have thought I wouldn't hear him over the heavy thrum of the engines, because he bent forward and spoke into the captain's ear. "Did you get a whiff of her? Sweat and filth. She smells worse than the boys in the trenches. I thought Macaslan said she'd be clean."

Jad offered a subtle shake of his head. "She's lived in Gosheniene for two years. What do you expect? She could scrub as hard as she liked. It wouldn't stop her smelling of garbage."

My finger's dug into the chair's armrests. A spasm shot through my wrists, my shackles warning me not to get too angry.

Don't make a scene. It isn't worth it.

But Crawley's next words did nothing to temper the hurricane inside me.

He snorted with contempt. "What is the council thinking by sending her to Tarahik? Unless she's target practice, it's insulting that they're allowing her into the base."

The captain fixed his steel-like gaze on the private. "She won't be at Tarahik for long. Casters like her... they never last."

I flinched at the hurtful truth as my confidence deflated like a slashed tyre. Casters like me rarely survived long in the Haxsan Guard. Did that mean I was being sent to Tarahik as a sacrificial lamb? If, by some miracle, I did survive my decade of service, what waited for me in the provinces wasn't much better. I'd board in a farmyard and work to earn my keep. Unprotected from the severe weather, bombings, or ULD snatchers that frequented the provinces, life promised to be difficult and unpleasant.

The disdain in Crawley's voice went up a notch. "Look at her. She's ghastly. The only men who would touch her are the desperate ones. It's sad."

My body went hot with rage. I raised my voice over the engines. "And the only women who would touch you, Private Crawley, are the ones you'd have to pay for. Sad indeed."

Three sets of eyes turned on me. Crawley's cheeks turned the colour of boiling lobster. Marek glanced away, the corners of his lips lifting in a satisfied smile. But it was Jad's burning stare that made my anger fall into the pit of my stomach. His hands were taut on the controls, his lips pressed tight. But there was something else in that spiteful gaze too: curiosity... and caution, like he'd just realised what a true threat I could be.

CHAPTER FIVE

The take-off was more terrifying than I'd imagined. Winds tore at the carrier-hornet, the rain streaming down windscreens to thicken into slush. My gut gave a queasy shudder as the vessel rode the waves of the storm. Something metallic wailed beneath the floor. It took me a second to realise it was the engines straining.

I chewed my lip. "Is it safe to fly in this?"

Jad exhaled a sharp breath. "Carrier-hornets are designed to withstand the pressure of storms. It's galactic storms we have to worry about, and none are forecast."

The tips of my fingers tingled with frustration. "Really? Because that thing I saw before on the scanner… that looked a lot like—"

"That was nothing," he snapped. "Just rocks blown by the winds. The storms are fierce in this province."

The tone in his voice made me want to slap him, but I could feel his eyes on me through the reflection in the window and kept a cool head. Tarahik wasn't my choice, but it was a far better alternative to what I was leaving behind, and the last thing I wanted was to give the captain a reason to drop me back there.

Jad and Marek were unperturbed by the weather, their hands playing over the controls with ease. I studied the soldiers and their easy-going nature, attempting to unravel their puzzling relationship. They didn't speak often, but when they did, there was a banter between them that hinted they were friends long before they served in the Haxsan Guard. I wondered what their story was.

Crawley had gone to sleep in the chair next to mine. His head drooped from side to side in time with the aircraft's dips and jolts. In an odd way, it reminded me of a laughing clown in a sideshow alley. If it were in my capacity, I'd throw something into his open mouth. How different he was to the two men piloting the aircraft. Not that I was on their side, but it seemed unfair that Crawley slept while they did the hard work. I was certain the private was meant to be monitoring me. Again, I questioned what power his family held in the council court if he wasn't afraid to slack off on his duties. Or be rebuked for them.

A relieved laugh carried from Marek. "The clouds are parting."

He was right. From the window, there was a clear view of the valley. My head spun from the height. Gosheniene's mountain had never looked more hostile or dangerous. Thick, glacial clouds drifted through the trees, encasing the valley in ice. The mouth to the mountain was practically a massive crater in the earth. I could picture how dank the tunnels would be this time of morning. Poor ventilation meant the cold air would be saturated with the scent of damp earth, clogging noses and assaulting heads with fierce migraines. In the mountain, you were accompanied by a constant sense of suffocation. I wouldn't miss it.

Jad's head whipped around, his eyes stinging. "Don't get too comfortable. The storm spans eight provinces. It'll get worse the farther we ascend."

A strange buzzing filled my ears as the carrier-hornet's altitude changed. My teeth smacked together, my ears popping. My rational mind struggled to comprehend how the clouds darkened so drastically in such little time, churning around the aircraft as though the storm endeavoured to rip the carrier-hornet apart. I'd never experienced turbulence before and prayed it wouldn't last. Each lurch, quake, and drop made my stomach ache, as if doused with acid.

If only I could move my arms, make myself more comfortable.

I focused on the clouds outside. Every so often, though I knew it couldn't be possible, pale, translucent faces appeared in the misty swirls.

I shook my head, clearing the image from my eyes.

It's not real. Just a trick of the storm.

Wispy fingers tapped the glass. A surge of panic coursed through me. They were staring through the window now, their eyes melting into black pools and bleeding down their cheeks to drip off their chins. It reminded me of thick, fatty oil. Their mouths lodged wide into screams.

I cried out and frantically tried to undo my harness. The agonising burn in my wrists slammed me back in the chair. My heartbeat thundered in my ears; my body enveloped in throbbing pain.

When I glanced back at the window, the faces were gone.

Jad tossed a glance over his shoulder, his face contorted with confusion. "You were instructed to remain still. What part of that don't you understand?"

"I had cramps in my legs," I lied.

"Then stretch your legs, not your arms."

The bitter, sharp taste of rage filled my mouth. He was lucky I was shackled.

The electrical jolt caused the wound in my upper arm to bleed again. The blood trickled thick and fast, soaking into the line of my coat to pool beneath my elbow. Pain scraped along my skin like a knife's edge. Weak and dizzy, black dots crept over my field of vision.

No. Don't fall asleep. She'll be there.

She was always waiting… watching… wanting in the dark.

I was trapped in that half-groggy, half-awake stage when something strange occurred. I peeled my eyes open and found myself floating on water.

I must be dreaming. This can't be real.

Sun dapples bobbed peacefully on the surface beside me. Warmth spread through my body, the sun bearing down from a cloudless sky. My lips lifted into a grin. This was a serenity I'd never experienced before. But then the water lapped at my cheeks, spilling over my nose and into my mouth. I was submerged, my clothes and boots making my legs too heavy to tread water. No matter how often the voice in my head screamed for me to kick to the surface, I couldn't.

Blood pounded in my ears as a large patch of darkness floated from the watery abyss below. Terror settled deep in my chest.

It's her. The black-veined woman.

Her neck twisted around like a corkscrew. Her fish-eaten cheeks pulled back in a grisly smile.

I cried for help, but of course I only succeeded in swallowing water.

Her pale hands reached for me. Veins snaked in and out of her skin, threading into a grotesque entanglement. I kicked and thrashed, but the current held me in place. She drifted closer. Her mouldy, black-crusted lips opened into a scream.

A sting in my arm startled me awake.

I lashed out with a fierce cry, driving my foot into someone's knee. Water burst from my mouth in incredible volume. It tasted like seawater.

No. Not possible. It was a nightmare. I wasn't there. What happened wasn't real.

"For the love of casters!" Crawley barked. He was on the floor, his long legs twisted in a gangly mess. He wiped away the water I'd spat in his face. "That's it. I'm not dealing with her any longer." He dropped the plastic syringe and stormed into the cabin.

I blinked the vertigo out of my eyes. My handcuffs were gone, lying discarded on Crawley's empty seat. My boots had also been replaced. I wriggled my toes. Someone had wrapped bandages around my feet.

How long had I been dreaming?

A concerned face wandered into my line of vision. It took me a second to realise it was Captain Arden. Without so much as a gentle warning, he grabbed my jaw and tipped my head, flashing a penlight in my right eye.

"Excuse me." I slapped his hand away. "Are you trying to blind me?"

He shone the penlight in my left eye. "You passed out. You've been unconscious for three hours. I need to do some routine checks."

"Three hours! And you're only checking on me now?"

Callous bastard.

He inched closer. "I thought you were asleep. I assigned Crawley to do this, but you saw how well that worked out."

From this angle, the captain's eyes were much darker than I'd first perceived, almost black. I couldn't see where the pupil ended and the iris began. His hands were covered in white scars, most likely from years of service to the Haxsan Guard, but his tanned face was perfectly smooth and unblemished. "This is going to hurt." He picked up the syringe and jabbed it into my wound.

I bit back the pain, mortified that a small tear leaked out.

Jad either pretended not to notice or didn't care. "You should have told me the flame from the cast-shooter struck you. It's a second-degree burn, so it'll heal, but it looks like a curse inside the bullet erupted with the shot. It's entered your bloodstream."

Yeah. No shit.

The sleeve of my coat had been cut to allow better access to the injury. The wound had a white, leathery texture, the skin around it inflamed.

Another scar to add to my collection.

Jad skilfully bandaged my arm, his long fingers working with precision. In the cool air conditioning, I caught a whiff of soap and spicy cologne. "I just gave you an antibiotic potion for the curse. You'll start to feel more yourself in a minute or two." His lips teetered toward a smile. "Not that I'm sure I want to see that."

It was a nice smile. I got the sense he didn't show it often.

"Afraid I'll hijack your plane, Captain?" I made sure to sound condescending.

He snorted. "I'd like to see you try."

My face transformed into a pitiless scowl. His lack of confidence was insulting.

Jad snatched up the first aid kit, his good humour gone. "You were saying things in your sleep. Crying and telling someone to go away. You sounded... afraid."

I didn't meet his eyes. The salty taste of water lingered in my mouth, burning the back of my throat and forcing me to relive the nightmare. "Sometimes I have bad dreams. It's nothing."

"We all have bad dreams. You were having night terrors."

My anger resurfaced. "What are you, my counsellor now? I said I was fine."

End of conversation.

I didn't want to process what the nightmare meant. The black-veined woman was leaking into other dreams now, spreading her poison. It frightened me more than I wanted to admit.

Jad shifted his stance, his face thoughtful but intense. "I read your dossier. After everything you've been through, you're not fine. You're troubled. I've seen it before."

I didn't say anything.

"What you did at the camp," he continued, "running to the gates. What was that back there?"

Is he serious?

I looked at him stonily. "It's called trying to escape."

"No. It's called being an idiot, and if you pull a stunt like that at Tarahik, the council won't be forgiving. They'll drop you straight back in Gosheniene. We don't have time for deserters."

"And what do you care if I break out or not?" My cheeks were flushed and my voice sounded strangled. "You don't like me. I heard you talking to Crawley. You believe taking me to the base is a mistake."

He gave me a contemptuous look, as though I were a child on the verge of a temper tantrum. "I care about my orders, which are getting you to Tarahik. After that, you can do what you please. You're not my responsibility once this hornet lands. I'm just warning you of the consequences if you do anything rash." His tone was particularly harsh because it revealed the truth. He didn't give a damn about me, not really. Thessio could have shot me dead and the only thing Jad would have cared about were the repercussions from his commander. No wonder he'd healed my injuries. There was no moral obligation here. What he'd done had been for himself.

His eyes glistened with determination. "I'm curious. Had you escaped Gosheniene, where would you have gone?"

I stared out the window. *Screw him.*

He crossed his arms. "I thought so. You wouldn't have stood a chance out there. Gosheniene is surrounded by landmines."

I stared, wishing my eyes would burn him like acid. "Well, aren't you a Mr Know-it-all."

Perhaps sensing he wasn't going to get another syllable out of me, he strode back to his seat. "Get some rest. We still have a few hours before we arrive at the base."

Marek looked eternally grateful to see him, but like a light blinking out, the relief disappeared just as fast. "The weather's changing ahead."

Jad surveyed the holographic scanner. His eyebrows narrowed into a frown, his sudden intake of breath alerting me that something was terribly wrong. It was satisfying to see that irritating confidence squeezed out of him like pulp from a lemon, but if the captain was afraid, that meant we were in serious trouble. The idea that we were in jeopardy turned into a vexing torment in my gut.

Jad strapped on his harness and immediately took control of the aircraft. "It's developing fast."

"What is?" I cried. "What's wrong?"

"Galactic storm?" Marek snapped out of his panic-stricken daze long enough to look at Jad for confirmation.

The captain nodded.

Rage ripped from my throat. "Damn idiot. I told you I saw something on the scanner."

Jad didn't look at me, but his voice cracked with aggression. "That was back at Gosheniene. We're hours away from there."

A siren blared, warning that peril was imminent.

My mind raced. A galactic storm! We'd be like a paper airplane in cyclonic winds. Casters were told to bunker down when these terrifying phenomena occurred. The storms were caused by stellar explosions near the Earth's atmosphere, playing havoc with our magnetic field. They advanced with alarming speed, distorting radio waves and making compasses erratic. Their destruction was known to knock out power grids and devastate communication systems in the provinces, while the Free Zones were protected by celestial shields and barely saw a disturbance. I'd heard that humans stepped out of their houses to watch the spectacular aurora displays. They marvelled at the storm's beauty while we suffered under its destruction.

Outside, the clouds darkened from a deep plum shade to tar black. Menacing crackles of thunder drowned out the *thwump thwump thwump* of the rotor blades.

I bit on the inside of my cheek. "Excuse me, but don't pilots tend to avoid galactic storms?"

Jad's shoulders stiffened.

Marek peered over his shoulder, his face lacking conviction. "Jad's the best pilot at Tarahik. You have nothing to fear."

The plane dropped. My insides pivoted into my mouth, and I had to swallow to keep the sick down. Tremors juddered through the cockpit. A cacophony of warning beeps split the air as the radar displays blinked on and off. When I looked out the window, the rotors appeared to be bending in the blustery winds. They reminded me of banana skins, limp and stripped back.

Crawley appeared in the doorway, his face pinched and ashen. "What the hell is going on?"

Jad didn't take his eyes off the instruments. "Strap yourself in. Now."

The private dropped heavily into a chair, the farthest he could find from me.

I balled my sweaty palms together. Chain lightning burst between the clouds like camera flashes. The storm's floodgates opened, the sky breaking into a torrent of icy precipitation. It sounded like thousands of bullets hit and scraped the hornet all at once.

Marek peered up from his navigational display with a pressing look at his captain. "There's a safer route just over the Falnic Islands. We could land there. It'll divert us only by a few hours."

Jad shook his head. "That's ULD territory. Dissent rebels will shoot us out of the sky before we could land. Flying through this storm provides the best cover."

"Flying through the storm?" I repeated. "That's suicide."

He banked the aircraft to the right suddenly to avoid a flash of forked lightning.

My harness strained, biting into my shoulders. "Did you buy your pilot's licence?" I screamed.

The captain glared at me through the reflection in the window. "I know what I'm doing."

"Know what you're doing? How could you possibly know where you're going?"

The monstrous storm had become a vortex of whipped-up rain, hurricane winds, and jagged lightning. Something large hurtled past, followed by a streak of burning light. I felt the bloom of its heat even through the window.

"Meteoroid fragments." Jad watched the shower of light plunge into the ground below. "They start to burn when they enter the Earth's atmosphere. It's nothing to worry about... unless they hit us." He double-checked his harness. "All going well, we should reach Tarahik by 3:00 p.m."

I gave a harsh, disbelieving laugh. "That's not far away at all."

The digital clock on the display said 2:43 p.m. I could survive seventeen minutes, so long as Jad didn't fly us into a meteor.

He shot me a lazy grin. "That's 3:00 p.m. Tarahik time. It's still four hours away."

I slammed my head back and swore. I really hated Captain Arden.

CHAPTER SIX

Galactic storms usually disappeared as quickly as they came, but this one proved to be the exception. It pursued us for hours. The carrier-hornet bucked and bounced in the heavy turbulence. The tension in the cockpit rose to a crescendo each time Jad was forced to swerve past large chunks of meteorites and space dust. My heart raced, my knuckles white on the armrests. I expected the hornet to be blasted into twisted chunks of metal at any moment.

A *ting* chimed through the cockpit. Jad communicated with someone on the radio, his voice low and cryptic. There was too much static in the transmission, and with the storm thrashing the plane like we were a dinghy at sea, there wasn't a chance to overhear what was said. I studied the captain for clues. I'd always been good with body language, but Jad's rigid posture gave nothing away besides showing that he was stressed and probably in need of a relaxing shower.

"We've been assigned a runway," he shouted over the fierce rumbles of thunder.

I looked out at the maelstrom of clouds. Two meteorites smashed into fragmented pieces, showering our windows with small rocks and dust. The plane pitched on the impact. If I hadn't been strapped in, I'd be a caster pancake on the ceiling by now.

Jad straightened in his chair. "Sorry… didn't see that one."

A laugh that sounded on the verge of hysteria bubbled out of my throat. "Didn't see it? It was huge."

The captain swung his upper body around to give me a severe glare. "Once we approach Tarahik, the winds will slow down. Nothing passes the celestial shield, including storms."

"Just focus on where you're going." I inhaled a huge breath, hoping it would alleviate the sick roiling in my stomach. We barely missed another, much larger meteorite.

Best pilot ever. Sure.

Jad saluted me with a roguish smile. I got the sense he rather enjoyed my discomfort.

I knew it. I'm flying with a cowboy.

Skilfully, he lowered the aircraft toward a line of strobe lights that blinked in the distance. I squinted. Maybe the lightning was playing tricks, because built in the sharp vertical peaks of the mountain ahead, a massive castle appeared like a ghostly contour in the mist. Surely it couldn't be real? A structure like that in such difficult terrain could not have been built without magic.

Marek nodded in the direction of the edifice. "Welcome to Tarahik."

The aircraft descended rapidly out of the clouds. With the brunt of the storm behind us, I was able to see the landscape clearly. My mouth gaped. Gosheniene had been an imposing structure, but Tarahik took daunting to the extreme. It was a castle with tall black windows, gothic buttresses, and towers that cut into the storm like the tips of blades. It was sprawling and magnificent but modernised with aluminium and steel—protection against the severe weather patterns that frequented the ranges.

The nose of the jet dipped at the same moment the sky lit up in a blaze of orange and gold fire. A rush of electrically charged power hit the plane, so extreme I feared the wings had blasted off. The lights along the control panel flickered, reinforcing my panic.

I tasted a fresh sheen of perspiration above my lip. "What was that?"

Did lightning strike us?

Jad focused on his navigational equipment, which seemed to be spinning out of control in frantic confusion. "That was the celestial shield. The invisible boundary surrounds the base and keeps dissent rebels out. Any unauthorised entries are obliterated by magic. It's the same shield that monitors the Free Zones. We're safe in here."

I craned my neck to get a better look outside. A blue aura domed the mountain. It reminded me of a snow globe, only instead of gentle, wispy snow, the castle was hit by a deluge of rain. The celestial shield rippled from our impact, as though the hornet had been a rock projected through water. Colours shimmered across the shield's domed surface before it blended with the sky again.

Shock overrode my alarm. "It camouflages."

The captain tossed an exasperated look over his shoulder. "It would defeat the purpose if the dissent rebels saw it."

The revelation made my stomach clench. This was bad. If the celestial shield impeded the rebels from entering Tarahik, that meant it stopped deserters leaving too.

There will be a way out, Zaya. Stay calm. Tarahik would have been built with escape tunnels in case of invasion. You'll find one. It'll be okay.

But my confidence plummeted the closer we approached the castle. Hardened aircraft shelters, underground hangars, and landing pads had been dug into the side of the mountain. At the base of the castle, where the ranges dropped vertically into the sea, warships and aircraft carriers were docked. My hands squeezed into fists. The reality of escaping was fast becoming a joke. This place was a fortress.

The landing gear engaged with a heavy clunk. Jad masterfully set down on the runway, the rear thrusters roaring into action to slow us down. I exhaled, grateful we were no longer airborne. My legs itched to move. The mere thought of food made my stomach sound as if it had its own storm raging inside; apart from a bowl of tasteless gruel the night before, it had been nearly twenty-four hours since I'd eaten.

Find food, then a way to escape.

Normally I was decent at instigating a plan, but the long flight, my never-ending concern over the black-veined woman, and my injury had taken their toll. I couldn't scrape together a coherent arrangement in my head.

The hornet taxied into an underground hangar. Cargo pallets, armoured vehicles, and stationed shuttle planes flashed by, another sign Tarahik was an organised and equipped stronghold. Movement caught my eye to the right. Soldiers, pilots, engineers, and technicians scrambled toward an assembly of fire-crusaders, preparing the fighter jets for take-off. I shivered, recalling the night a low-lying formation of the jets tore across the skies above Gosheniene. I later learnt they'd been deployed to bomb rebel threats to the south. It had gone on all night. There'd been no escaping the sounds of ruptured earth and shattering metal, or the screams that followed. The worst part was the people who'd arrived in the morning looking for food and shelter, the women half dressed, the children still sleepy, the men struggling in vain with suitcases and baggage. The sentinels turned the women and children away but kept the men and forced them to dig in the mountain.

Were these soldiers about to do the same thing to another town now? It was scary how efficiently the men and women worked. In the short time it took Jad to taxi the hornet to a stop and switch the engines off, the fighter jets were armed, fuelled, and ready for flight.

Marek stared, mouth ajar. "Must be an exercise."

Jad shook his head, impatient. "Air traffic control would have warned us if a combat exercise was scheduled." His face was lit by the instrumentation, his brow tightly furrowed. "Stay with the plane." He unbuckled his harness and darted into the cabin.

His command was met with a shared groan of annoyance.

This is just cruel.

Marek watched his captain move swiftly down the boarding ramp. "Where are you going?"

Jad didn't answer.

Looking defeated, Marek slouched in his chair and closed his eyes. Perhaps he intended to take a power nap. He must have been tired after flying the plane for so long.

Crawley swore and slammed his fist onto the armrest. In another life, he'd get on beautifully with Thessio.

What I should have done was follow orders, but both boys had their backs turned to me.

They're not the brightest stars in the sky, that's for sure.

I unclipped my harness and inched away. Something was happening in the hangar. If luck was on my side, it could be the distraction I needed to escape. Checking over my shoulder, I descended the boarding ramp. Immediately my senses were assaulted by muggy fumes and oil. I spotted an exit, but the hangar was so heavily strewn with soldiers, it wouldn't be possible to make it out without being seen.

No one knows me. No one cares who I am. I'll blend in.

I dared a tentative peek at the captain. He was conversing with the pilots. Even from this distance, his body appeared as taut as wire.

Now or never.

I made a beeline for the exit.

A laugh sputtered behind me. "You're terrible at following orders, aren't you?"

I whirled around, my heart somersaulting into my ribs.

Marek gave me a "poor newbie" shake of his head. "Not a good idea, Zaya."

Damn. Damn. Damn.

I squared my shoulders, desperate to hide my rattled expression. "Didn't you read my dossier? I have a reputation to uphold."

He looked like he was trying not to laugh. "You're going to be a headache for Jad, I can tell."

A headache? If I didn't escape this place, I'd make sure I was the worst frigging migraine Captain Arden had ever experienced.

"Shouldn't you find out what's bothering your captain?" I suggested sweetly.

"No point. He's on his way back."

I spun around.

Oh shit.

Jad had indeed returned. His pace picked up when he saw me. "I thought I said to stay on the hornet?"

I shrugged. "Sorry. Must have misheard you."

He didn't look like he believed me.

Marek tilted his head in the direction of the pilots. "What's happening over there? It looks serious."

The captain wiped his arm across his damp forehead. He was sweating, and I didn't think it was because of the heat or the exhausts. "Lycanthors have been spotted outside the celestial shield. I'm going back out."

The sergeant squeezed the bridge of his nose. "Back out? That storm is getting more intense, not less. It's madness going out there. Are you even thinking?"

Jad shot him a stern gaze. It was an expression that said *don't challenge me*. Marek's face went slack with defeat. "Make sure you come back."

The captain gave a subtle nod and loaded a fresh magazine in his cast-shooter. It was a large full-powered assault rifle, fitted with a telescopic scope for firing accuracy. Long, sleek, and powerful, it was truly a magnificent weapon.

Where can I steal one?

Jad saw my weird fascination for the cast-shooter and transferred it onto his other shoulder. It was possible that eyeing off his weapon like it was a nice tantalising hamburger had made him think twice about having it near me.

"Get her to the castle," he told Marek, his voice simmering with rage. He tore away from me with cool detachment and headed in the direction of the fighter jets.

"Nice to meet you too," I shouted, ignoring the stabbing pinch of rejection in my chest. People had been rude to me at Gosheniene and I'd managed to endure it, so why did the captain's attitude grate on me so much?

Marek's emerald eyes were fixed on his friend, brimming with worry.

I was still intrigued by their relationship. Jad didn't strike me as the sort of guy who assimilated with others, especially with someone as good-natured and kind as Marek. "Your captain needs a lesson in manners."

The sergeant's lip twitched. "So do you."

I laughed. "Yeah, but I'm a slave from the mines of Gosheniene. My lack of civility is explainable. Jad's a captain. His manners should be exemplary."

"And with most people, his behaviour usually is."

I fell silent.

If Jad's rude conduct was unusual, then there was only one reason why he'd direct such hostility toward me. "He thinks I'm dissent scum, doesn't he?"

Marek's eyes dropped to the ground. "No… well, yes… but that's only because he read your dossier."

"It isn't true." I tried to sound convincing, but my voice betrayed me. My clammy hands trembled at my sides. "My parents weren't dissent rebels."

Marek crossed his arms, but not in an unkind way. "It doesn't matter if they were. You're not them. I have a talent for guessing a person's character… and I have a good feeling about you."

I groaned inwardly. Marek was a nice guy but terribly naïve. He certainly wouldn't think highly of me if he understood I was neither loyal to the Haxsan Guard nor the council. "I think you're being too optimistic."

He gave a low whistle. "Not so. I'm an omnilinguist. I can read any language, including body language. Sometimes I can read feelings too, though not very well. It's a work in progress." He drew in a rocky breath. "I'll admit, Jad and I had our doubts about you. Internment camps tend to produce dissent sympathisers, but I can see you're a good person. You are right, though." His lips shifted into a coy smile. "I am too optimistic. Jad's told me it'll be my downfall."

My pulse raced. Marek could read body language? Was that how he knew I was about to do a runner out of the hangar?

Nice or not, he was a danger to me.

His grin dissolved. "Come on. Commander Macaslan is expecting you."

He led me deeper into the underground hangar. There was no possibility of escape now. I'd have to find a way out later.

The hangar was essentially a vast subterranean cavern. Giant stalactites drooped from the ceiling, reminding me of sharp pointed teeth. Artificial light illuminated rows of combat planes and long-range bombers that were undergoing various stages of maintenance and repair. I felt skittish knowing that millions of rocks were above us. Most structures were reinforced with magic, but magic or not, this was not a place I'd like to be in during an earthquake.

A group of soldiers scrambled past us, each equipped with cast-shooters and silver blades strapped to their calves and forearms.

Why do they need blades?

I paced impatiently by Marek's side. "What's so concerning about lycanthors outside the base? I didn't think anything could pass the shield?"

The sergeant did a quick survey of our surroundings, making sure no one was within earshot. "There's talk that the ULD are getting stronger, gaining more numbers. Now that the ULD and lycanthors are allies, approaching such a heavily armed base like Tarahik means they're no longer intimidated."

Heat surged across my face, the anger boiling in my cheeks. "Or maybe the lycanthors are fighting back, sick of being locked away and left to die in punishment cells."

Sure, the creatures got fed well, but it had to be boring living in total darkness and confinement. Monsters or not, their necessity for freedom didn't make them so different to casters or humans. The United League of Dissent understood that. That was why they were able to make allies out of the lycanthors. The council would never be able to ascertain loyalty like that, not when the Seven Sovereigns publicly denounced lycanthors, treating them as primitive, unintelligent animals that should have long ago been extinct.

The sergeant let out a throaty cough. "You'd be wise to keep comments like that to yourself. Tarahik has punishment cells too, you know. And that's the last place you want to end up." His words were underscored with weariness.

I should have let it go, but my dark feelings got the better of me, exploding to the surface. "Jad hates lycanthors, doesn't he?"

You didn't have to be an omnilinguist to understand the captain's body language—the violent shade of colour in his eyes, the tightly wounded expression. He'd gone out there with the intention to kill.

Marek only nodded.

My struggle to know more about the captain became an all-out war inside me. "You and Jad seem close. Have you known each other long?"

The sergeant closed his eyes for a second. I think he knew I wasn't going to stop poking the fire. "Jad's like a brother to me. We grew up together in an orphanage in Ludovitch."

Surprise engulfed me so quickly, it took a moment to respond. "I thought you were both from the Free Zones?"

"We were, once. My parents and siblings died in the Mazdaprine bombings when I was nine. I was miserable until I met Jad. He brought me back to life. I owe him. That's why I signed up when he volunteered to retrieve you from Gosheniene."

My eyes flashed wide. "Volunteered?"

That didn't match the story I'd been told. Captain Arden had made it clear he'd been following orders when he salvaged me from the camp. What possible reason could he have had to lie?

Marek nudged my arm softly. "Not such a bad guy after all, huh?"

I laughed bitterly. "I don't know about that. He's difficult to work out. What's his story? Other than being a complete douchebag, of course."

The sergeant's good humour crumbled and his sweet-tempered face turned pensive. "Jad's mother died when he was ten. He never told me the cause. His father was murdered a few years later."

That put a freeze in my step. "Murdered?"

Marek's shoulders drooped. "Yes… by lycanthors."

CHAPTER SEVEN

M arek never said any more on the topic of lycanthors, or Jad for that matter. I dropped the subject, guessing it was deeply personal and Marek had reached his limit of divulging information. I sped up to match his stride as we entered a vaulted colonnade, the walkway stretching to a sealed black door. Torches were set on brackets, flickering monstrous shadows across the walls. Gnarled tree roots overlayed the ceiling, black and rotten in the intermittent light. A salty, nervous taste filled my mouth. Some of the colonnades had been submerged in the wet earth, like the mountain had slowly devoured this section of the castle.

Marek scooted closer to me. "Impressive, isn't it? This is one of the original entrances to Tarahik. It used to be grand once. The nobility would arrive through here from the gardens. There are pictures of it in the museum on level four, if you're interested."

I stopped abruptly. "Gardens?"

A mischievous smile curled his lips. "This entry wasn't always underground. After it was abandoned, the castle sank into the mountain for centuries. Magic is the only thing holding it together."

I studied the sergeant to see if he was kidding. No. He'd been serious.

So the castle was supported by an underground base, which in turn was protected by a celestial shield, which was bordered on three sides by vast overrun forest. Not forgetting the vertical cliff face that plunged into the open sea either, I was starting to feel incredibly claustrophobic.

We reached the intimidating black door. Figures of angels had been carved into the woodwork, aged and damaged from time, their faces appearing more demonic than serene. Their noses were flattened, their cheeks swollen and split from the rotting wood. If Hell had an entryway, well… this was it.

I jumped at Marek's voice, right at my shoulder. "Someone will be waiting for you on the other side. Good luck, Zaya."

"Wait. You're not coming with me?" I hated how lonely and desperate I sounded. For once, I wanted someone to guide me, point me in the right direction. But Tarahik was no different to Gosheniene. No knight in shining armour would rescue me, no handsome prince, no guardian angel. It was up to me, just like it always had been.

"This is something you must do alone." His gaze dropped to the ground. When he looked back at me, his eyes were filled with deep concern. "Zaya, I feel I should warn you. There are things in the castle that aren't…." He hesitated. I didn't think it was because he struggled for words.

"Aren't what?"

He shook his head in warning. "Just… be careful in there, okay?"

With that, he walked back in the direction of the hangar.

Okay. There's no reason to be afraid. It's just a crumbling building held together with magic. It doesn't matter that Marek totally freaked out on me.

But my head was plagued with doubt.

The massive door dwarfed me, like it had grown twice its size in Marek's absence. I looked back at his retreating figure, wishing I could run after him to safety.

"I'm not going to be afraid," I vowed in a whisper.

I'm going to open that door and strut inside with confidence.

But I didn't have to, because when I turned around, the door had somehow opened, revealing a huge majestic foyer.

It had been built to impress with its high arched ceiling and stained-glass windows, and must have been magnificent once but, like the door, had fallen to age and disrepair. The lingering scent of decay seemed to bleed from every surface. Cobwebs hung from the beamed ceiling, looking like creepy stitched doilies. The floorboards were warped in places, showing how uneasily the castle had settled. Above a grand but dusty staircase were the remains of a chandelier, unused in decades. It gave me the impression of a tiered wedding cake tipped upside down. I shivered. Portraits nailed crooked on the walls displayed stiff, unsmiling faces. I couldn't help but feel they were watching me, as if they were in on a secret I was yet to discover.

I stepped inside. In the centre of the hall was an impressive monument of four horsemen riding abreast. They wore dark riding cloaks, their faces concealed by hoods. If I tipped my head at the right angle, I could just make out their gaping mouths, which were open in a cavernous scream. I squirmed. Each horseman carried a weapon: the first held a scythe, the next a sword, the third an axe, and the last a mace. It was a sculpture more suited to a graveyard.

It certainly makes for an interesting conversation piece.

I eyed my dim surroundings. Marek said someone would be here, but the hall was empty. And yet, there was something off about this place. Every creak, scrape, and groan made me think the castle stirred uneasily, as though it were a living, breathing organism and I was walking right into its stomach. I wondered how many people had come and gone in the centuries that Tarahik stood. More frightening, how many remained—a ghostly imprint entrenched deep in the building's foundations.

A crack in the staircase gave me a start. A girl stood on the landing. Maybe she'd been out in the storm, because her long, wet, and tangled hair hung past her shoulders, making a curtain on either side of her face. Her naked arms appeared almost blue in the chill air. She watched me with wild eyes, eerily reminding me of a rabid animal on the verge of attack.

No. No, no, no.

I shook my head. This couldn't be happening. The girl wasn't corporeal.

I squeezed my eyes shut, then opened them.

She was still there.

And I recognised her. "Adaline?"

Her ghostly manifestation looked like a photograph bleached by sunlight. She moved across the mezzanine without taking her eyes off me, her feet dragging horribly. Her wet nightdress dripped on the floor, each fat drop amplified by the open foyer. Now that she hovered in stronger light, I realised her hair—which I'd mistaken for blonde—glistened with frost. Anyone would have thought she'd died in a winter storm.

That wasn't the truth, of course. What happened to her was beyond understanding—and cruel.

I struggled to get my voice past a whisper. "I'm sorry… for what happened to you."

She didn't answer.

Somewhere, a clock chimed, ticking in time with my frantic heartbeat. "What do you want?"

Adaline raised her slender hand, pointing to a remote hallway off the landing. A narrow ray of moonlight lay on its floor, but otherwise the hall was shrouded in darkness.

"I… I don't understand."

She continued to stare with those hollow, waxen eyes.

A door near the stairs swung open with a resounding creak, sending a spasm of terror into my blood. A woman who looked to be around a hundred staggered from the doorway. Her eyes were bloodshot, her skin heavily lined and spotted. I caught a whiff of alcohol in the air. She looked like she'd raided the liquor cabinet one too many times. "You're the Wayward girl, right?"

I was too wired to answer. I shifted my gaze back to the stairs. Adaline had vanished.

The woman stood with her hands on her hips. Her dull eyes gave me a once-over. "I'm Millie Flitcroft. I'm Commander Macaslan's personal assistant."

And resident drunk.

A frown appeared between Millie's bushy eyebrows. "What's the matter? Are you a mute?"

I shook my head, then remembered the point of her question. "No."

"Thank the casters for that." Millie pushed back her straggly hair to get a better look at me. "Good gracious, girl, did you see a ghost or something? You're as white as a sheet."

Her choice of words unsettled me.

"Ooooh." She clapped. "It's started, hasn't it? The castle is playing tricks."

Tricks? "I beg your pardon?"

Millie skipped around me like an elated schoolgirl. "The castle plays games, dear."

I inched away. The woman had clearly lost her marbles.

Her smile deepened, displaying a row of yellowed teeth. Her long nose with its overgrown hairs reminded me of a root vegetable about to sprout. She didn't understand personal space because she bounced closer, her toes flush with mine—and oh boy, the breath on her. That smell could do more damage than nerve gas. My gag reflex was about to get a serious workout.

I forced some distance between us. "Listen... the commander is expecting me, so if you could tell me where I need to go—"

"Ooooh, touchy little sprite, aren't you? Impatient too. All right, all right. I'll take you to the commander." She scratched her head. A moth flew from her hair. "Yes, I remember now. That's why I'm here. Come along. Chop chop. It's rude to keep the commander waiting."

I groaned inwardly.

Resident drunk and suffering from Alzheimer's too.

Millie's eyes did a dramatic sweep of the foyer. "Where's your luggage? You haven't hidden it, have you? Mr Sweeney will want to take it to your room, and he doesn't like playing games. He prefers things in an orderly fashion. He's not like the castle. He doesn't have time for tricks."

I feigned patience. "I don't have belongings."

"What? You forget to pack?" She made a *tsk tsk* noise. "Well, come on, then. Follow me, and don't stray. Until you're accepted by the commander, the castle won't trust you."

"Won't trust me?"

I don't trust it.

Millie inched her skirt above her knees—a sight I really could have done without—and trotted up the stairs.

Questions popped into my mind. What did she mean, the castle played tricks? Was Millie saying the castle was alive? Had Adaline been a hallucination, conjured like a marionette to terrify me? Could Tarahik read my deepest and private thoughts? Worse—did the castle know about the black-veined woman?

The wooden stairs whined under my weight. On the landing, I examined the spot where Adaline had stood. A wave of cold air enveloped me. I glanced down the hall to peer beyond the dark. I could make out cracked walls and a floor covered in fallen plaster but nothing else. "What's down there?"

Millie scrunched her nose. "Nothing. Just a few abandoned bedrooms and a balcony that overlooks the woods. No one comes into this part of the castle anymore. It's restricted. Too dangerous, you see. The only thing holding anything together is—"

"Magic. Yeah, I've heard. If this place is restricted, then why are we down here?"

Millie's eyes glittered. "Tonight is the initiation ceremony... a great celebration the gentry attend. The commander didn't want a prisoner from the mines to be seen."

I detected the faintest smile on her lips.

I raised my head proudly. "Nor personal assistants, it seems."

Her smile dropped.

"Why hasn't the castle been restored?" I continued. "The council has money to fix a place like this."

Millie laughed, but it lacked humour. "Tarahik has been restored on the upper levels. The war has bankrupted the council. And the Seven Sovereigns don't want to invest in this castle when they can make a fortune in weapons development. Now come along. Oh... I almost forgot. You're likely to see many things that will disturb you. It's best to keep them to yourself."

A tingly feeling crawled over my skin. "What kind of things?"

A mysterious smile twisted her lips. For such a frail, brainless drunk, Millie moved with precision, avoiding every rickety floorboard. Restricted or not, she must have been down here hundreds of times. "You'll see soon enough."

She waved her hand, indicating I was to fall into step behind her.

CHAPTER EIGHT

Millie led me up spiralling staircases and down long passages. There were parlour rooms, gaming rooms, study rooms, and libraries, each more opulent and spacious than the last. The farther we progressed through the castle, the larger and more expansive the halls became—and yes, I spotted things that didn't bode well for any visitor. Beneath a closed door, an oily stain materialised. It stretched into the shape of a disembodied hand to seize my ankle. I shrieked like a frenzied barn owl and stumbled backward, my knee colliding with a table hard. A vase that would have cost more than a farmer earned in a decade smashed into irreparable fragments.

"Shit." I fought the note of panic in my tone but lost. "What the frig was that?"

Millie cocked her head to the side like a curious dog. "*What* was *what*?"

"There was a hand… and the vase… I broke it—"

But when I glanced at the door, the hand had vanished. There wasn't even a stain to suggest it had been there. The vase was intact on the table, no evidence it had been damaged.

Millie paced serenely down the hall. "The castle is wary of you, dear. Tarahik is safeguarded by a series of enchantments. Once you meet the commander and she accepts you, the castle will protect you like the other soldiers. Now, this way please. Time is of the essence."

I hurried after her, hardly daring to look around. On the landing of another grand staircase, we passed an iron maiden. I swear a set of brown eyes watched me from the inside, but like it had been with the hand, when I peered over my shoulder, it was gone.

Is the castle deliberately causing me to hallucinate?

It must have been an odourless hex pumped through the ventilation system. I'd seen the method employed in Gosheniene. When prisoners were taken into the interrogation cells for questioning, the airborne hex created terrifying hallucinations, forcing its victims to disclose information—or so I'd been told. I'd never actually witnessed that part, just heard the screams. But why would Tarahik need to operate the same curse? I wanted to ask, but something about the way Millie stared resolutely ahead made me think twice.

The strange woman turned sharply up a narrow flight of stairs. I followed, my head foggy and leaden. It was incredible how the castle drastically changed from wing to wing, some parts in various states of decay, others ornamented and exquisite. There was nothing tasteful about this staircase, though. If anything, it felt like I was being led into a dungeon. Coldness seeped from the stone floor. A frigid draft sent a wave of goosebumps up my arms. Even the air smelt damp.

The commander wouldn't be up here.

I watched the back of Millie's head, wishing I could read whatever creepy ideas she had in store. "Are you sure you're leading me to the right place?"

Millie croaked, like she'd choked on her own laughter. "Yes... fairly certain."

We reached the landing and stopped at a grey door peeled of paint. The peelings on the floor reminded me of dead insects shrivelled and fossilised. Millie grabbed a torch from a bracket and fumbled with a set of keys.

Something about the way she looked at me made my heart plunge straight into my gut. "Don't be afraid." Her eyes were big and wide, and the small undertone of excitement in her voice hinted that she hoped for exactly that.

Crazy bitch.

She opened the door. My first torchlight glimpse did not reveal a cell but a huge tower of interweaving staircases and granite columns. Worse, not one of the staircases had handrails. One slip and you'd be lost to the cavernous dark below. Millie's torch cast elongated shadows along the walls. My stomach roiled. Every surface was adorned in bones. Skulls set in geometric patterns smiled gap-toothed grins at me. Garlands of bones draped enormous candelabras. There were even mausoleums decorated with painted skeletons. In a bizarre way, they reminded me of creepy gingerbread houses.

"What is this place?" My voice rolled into the vast echoing tower.

The torchlight provided a sallow cast to Millie's skin. "This is the original ossuary, dearest. Over ninety thousand bones are kept here. Some belong to victims of the influnix virus, others to war and dark curses. In the old days, the corpses were burnt and dismembered to stop the dead returning. Silly superstitions."

I swallowed, my throat dry. "Why would the commander live in this part of the castle?" Not only was it macabre, but it didn't strike me as the sort of thing a person of authority should do.

Millie chuckled low under her breath. "Because the ossuary is the last place an assailant would expect to find her, silly." She shook her head, like it was obvious. "Commander Macaslan is wanted by the United League of Dissent. In case of an invasion, it makes sense to have her chambers in a part of the castle no one would expect."

I frowned. "But if everyone in the castle knows she's here, aren't you afraid someone might betray her location?"

"No. The oath prevents betrayal."

I felt a wild urge to run back the way I'd come. I didn't understand the magic that coursed through the castle, but I had an image of it running the same way blood flowed through the body, keeping everything inside contained and functioning. Everyone was a part of Tarahik. They belonged to Tarahik. No one could leave it.

A whirlwind of panic swept through my head when I looked down. Perhaps it was a blessing I couldn't see beyond the dark. "How high is this tower?"

Millie's lips curved into a puckish smile. "It's high. I hope you're not afraid of heights… or the dark."

I gave a harsh laugh. "I hope you're not afraid of falling… or being pushed."

Her impish grin dissolved.

We began our ascent. Some of the steps were tall—almost double the size of a normal step—while others were short enough to nick your toe. Millie skipped up the stairs with renewed energy. Perhaps she'd forgotten about the great gaping hole beneath us. Maybe she didn't care if she fell. At her age, Millie probably didn't purchase under-ripe tomatoes.

"Keep up. Keep up," she pestered in a sing-song voice.

At the top of the tower, the stairs widened out to a square pavilion where a lonely door waited. It was the kind of door you'd expect to lead to a dry and weathered basement.

Millie rapped twice.

"Who is it?" a voice called, stern and strict.

"Millie Flitcroft, madam. I've brought the Wayward girl."

"Show her in."

We entered an office that was, like the rest of the castle, Victorian and candle lit. The light fixtures were in the shape of flowers but covered in dust. Rain had soaked into the ceiling, leaving patches of damp. Even the rose-coloured wallpaper was sodden in places, giving the impression of running blood. I wrung my hands together to stop them trembling. Again, I had that nagging sensation that the castle was alive. The office furniture was comfortable but worn. Someone had tried to liven the place with cherry curtains and a burgundy rug.

In the centre was a mahogany desk where a proud woman sat, hands clasped in front of her, a few wrinkles on her neck the only thing to betray her age. Even though she was seated, she looked tall and impossibly thin. In a strange way, she was exactly like the castle—elegant but falling to disrepair. She wore a lace blouse gathered at the neck, and several gold rings on her fingers that sparkled with coloured gems. Her white-blonde hair was tugged so tight to the back of her head that I wondered how she didn't have a headache.

Beside her, a man spoke zealously into her ear, his voice pitched low. He looked to be a caster in his late forties with raven black hair and a strong, commanding jaw. He wore the typical battle dress of the Haxsan Guard—black armour magically enhanced to ward off curses.

His face crumpled in despair, his voice rising several octaves. "Ma'am, please. I implore you to see reason. This is the third attack by lycanthors in the past month. Vulcan Stormouth and his forces are getting stronger. I'm sorry to pain you, but it must be said. That ice witch of his is only—"

"Not now, Colonel." The woman waved his objection away.

"Ma'am," he persevered. "Captain Arden failed to recover it. Our time is running—"

He broke off when he saw me, his temples pulsing under his skin.

I snorted through my nose. *Well, sorry to breathe in the same air.*

The woman smiled coolly at me, the expression in her eyes difficult to define. A prisoner learnt to study faces, the way the mouth moved, the change of colour in the complexion, whether the eyes widened or narrowed. At Gosheniene, all this helped glean hints into the wardens' moods. But here, the aptitude to read her face failed me. I wasn't sure if her smile was friendly or cruel.

"Millie," she shrilled, her voice loud enough to rattle the marrow in my bones.

Millie flinched. "Yes, ma'am?"

"Wait outside."

"Certainly, ma'am." Millie scuttled out of the room like a chastised schoolgirl.

The woman silently assessed me. She lit a cigarette and balanced the silver holder expertly between her fingers. I swallowed back a cough. She was making the air toxic.

Is everyone in this castle self-medicating?

Smoke wafted out of her thin mouth. "So you're the prisoner from Gosheniene. Welcome to Tarahik." She sounded like she'd rather have me thrown out for untidiness than greet me to the base.

I was sweaty, sore, and in desperate need of a shower, and I'd seen a ghost from my past and witnessed horrifying hallucinations in the space of a few minutes, but I arched my neck defiantly, refusing to be intimidated. "I am."

Her hawklike gaze flashed with dislike. "I am Commander Macaslan. I'm responsible for the soldiers and cadets at this base." She turned to the man at her side. "This is Colonel Harper. He oversees military leadership and performance. He also supervises cadet training."

Even though Commander Macaslan was unquestionably in charge, Colonel Harper presided over the office like a lawyer in a court case, ready to take control at a moment's notice. His eyes were blue like mine, only his were the colour of the ocean—calm one second and thunderstorm dark the next. He must have been into parlour tricks. Either that or he was an earth wielder, because he levitated a pebble. The rock circled around his fingers the same way a planet orbits the Sun.

Displacement behaviour perhaps?

Or maybe Colonel Harper was the type of man who needed to occupy his mind. He was all hard angles and grim expressions, and no matter how much of an earth wielder he was, I couldn't imagine him frolicking with nature.

Commander Macaslan looked me up and down. Her expression twitched, as if there was a horrible smell beneath her nose. One minute in her presence and we hated each other already.

Her pale nostrils flared. "I want you to understand that this is a delicate situation. It's not customary for the council to extract a prisoner from an internment camp and sanction her enrolment at a base. I've read the report sent from the council." She patted a document on her desk. "It says you are wild, headstrong… and unpredictable at best. During your flight, Captain Arden radioed ahead and described how you caused a scene at the camp. I'm warning you, Miss Wayward. Troublemakers are not tolerated at Tarahik."

I couldn't wipe the crooked smile from my face. "And with all due respect, Commander, had Captain Arden not intervened, I would have fled and there wouldn't have been a scene."

It wasn't entirely true, but she didn't need to know that.

Her eyes glittered. "Let's get this straight. There are casters at this base who will not be pleased to find a slave in attendance… even less so the spawn of dissent scum."

Anger burned across my face. "My parents weren't dissent rebels."

Her condescending grin deepened. "Believe what you will, but to avoid any… unpleasant situations, we have created a cover story. You will go by the name of Zaya Wayward because if anyone tries to discover any information on the Wayward family, there will, of course, be nothing to find. Your family were wealthy and donated a significant amount to the council's cause. All of your relatives are dead, murdered by dissent rebels. You were the sole survivor and were brought up in an orphanage in Wilksonsville. If anyone asks, that is your background. Understand?"

A cheeky thought popped in my head. "And what if a young man mistakes me for a wealthy heiress?"

Macaslan looked at me through slitted eyelids. "You will correct him." She took another drag of her cigarette. "There are three rules at Tarahik that must be obeyed. Follow the daily routine assigned to you, do not wander the castle after curfew, and do not at any time enter Shadow's Wood."

A grin split my face. "Shadow's Wood? Are you trying to make it sound sinister?"

"No. I'm trying to prevent people from wandering in there and meeting a gruesome end."

The clever retort I had flew out of my head. "What do you mean?"

"I mean there are things in the woods that cannot be explained." She stretched her shoulders back. "Now, tonight is the initiation ceremony. Despite your late arrival, there is time for you to clean up and make a good impression." She gave my tattered coat a stern once-over. "I suggest you use that time wisely."

That's it. No explanation?

She pried open a drawer under her desk and took out a scrap of paper. "This is your timetable. You will have tomorrow to settle in. Training commences the following morning. The two girls you are sharing an apartment with are both from noble families. I trust you will treat them with the respect they are entitled to."

I scanned the routine designed to dictate my new life.

0700	Reveille
0715 to 0800	Breakfast and morning routine
0810 to 0900	Cadet field training
0910 to 1000	Leadership and general psychology
1010 to 1100	Athletics
1110 to 1200	Nutrition and culinary science
1200 to 1300	Lunch

1310 to 1400	Field craft navigation and tactics
1410 to 1500	Stability and peacekeeping operations
1510 to 1600	Medical and first aid
1610 to 1700	Military and world history
1700 to 1800	Free/Study time
1800 to 1900	Dinner
1900 to 2200	Free/Study time
2200	Curfew/Lights out

"Nice and easy," I muttered under my breath.

"Do you have any questions?"

"Yes," I said, feeling bold. "Why did the council move me to this base?"

Macaslan's fingers stiffened. She drew herself up regally like a queen on her throne. "I'm afraid I don't understand what you're alluding to."

"There are plenty of military bases the council could have hidden me away in. Someone orchestrated this. Someone wants me at this base. Who?"

Or had I read this wrong?

"The general wants to know if it's been found."

What if my extraction from Gosheniene hadn't been the real goal here but an excuse for Jad to find whatever this *thing* was that his general sought? If that was the case, then my purpose at Tarahik was insignificant. Chances were they'd throw me back into Gosheniene or place me somewhere worse when they were done with me. I had to get the hell out of Tarahik.

Macaslan laughed, but I detected a hint of irritation in her voice. "I'm not privy to the council's motives."

Bullshit.

She looked over the report on her desk. "Freezing. That is your speciality?" Her glittering eyes awaited my answer.

I glared at her before speaking. "No. My powers have not... revealed themselves yet."

Her silence was not my desired effect, and I worried she knew I was lying. "Some casters are late bloomers with their magic," she said at last. "But never fear. Tarahik has a way of exposing the magic deep inside of us."

There was hidden meaning in her voice, but what she alluded to, I didn't know.

"Millie," she shouted. Even from this distance, I caught a whiff of cigarette stink from her mouth.

Millie poked her head in. "Yes."

"Please show this cadet to her room."

"Yes, ma'am." Millie tiptoed inside. She sank her nails deeper than necessary into my shoulder and led me to the exit.

I slapped the strange woman's hand away, my temper balanced on a fragile edge. I fixed Macaslan with a stare. "One more thing."

The commander's cheeks flushed with annoyance. "Yes."

"You've accepted me into Tarahik. Does that mean the hallucinations stop?"

Conjured or not, I couldn't face seeing Adaline again. Her wounded eyes, her sallow lips, her frozen, broken body—the images concocted in my mind, forming into one tumultuous wave of guilt. I hadn't killed her, but I hadn't saved her either.

She's gone. Buried and turned to dust. What I saw was the castle's twisted ruse.

But part of me was afraid that it was more than that. And if Adaline could return, what prevented the black-veined woman from returning too?

A muscle jumped at the side of Macaslan's mouth. "That depends on whether the hallucinations were caused by the castle... or your mind."

Fear sloshed inside me like acid. "Pardon?"

"You are dismissed, Miss Wayward. I have other business to attend to."

Millie grabbed my arm and gave me a spiteful glare. "You heard the commander. We're leaving."

I walked out the door, sensing Macaslan's eyes on me. But there was something else that followed too. Coldness crept into my bones—and it had nothing to do with the castle's freezing temperature.

CHAPTER NINE

S talked.

That was how I felt wandering the girls' dormitory, every corridor, corner, and stairway identical. Millie ambled ahead unfazed. But my paranoia was so intense, I wished my eyes would slip to the back of my head to see if anything pursued me. There was nothing there, of course, apart from walls adorned with gold leaf and corners filled with shadows. Millie's candelabrum barely filtered through the ominous dark. The candle she'd provided me flickered twice. I curled my hand around it, preventing the flame from blowing out.

Where is that breeze coming from?

I gasped from the shock of damp cold on my skin. Outside, wind whipped rain against the castle, like the storm had an agenda to rip the building apart stone by stone.

Perhaps someone forgot to shut a window farther down the hallway.

The rain-splattered windows shuddered in their frames. The walls seemed to constrict and groan with the changing pressure. It was as though the castle was… fighting back. Lightning brightened the hallway, and I jumped at the face that appeared at the window, scarcely avoiding banging into a marble statue—a gruesome gargoyle thing set carelessly as a trip hazard.

What the hell was that?

It was a face twisted with rage and anguish, skin pale and rotting, black blood dribbling from parted lips.

Millie stopped and stared. "Careful. You'll break something."

My heart somersaulted in my chest. "Careful? I thought the castle had stopped with the mind games?"

"It has."

"Bullshit. I just saw a face in the window. A horrible face."

"Mind your language." There was something wary in Millie's gaze as she peered around. "In places as old as Tarahik, you see ghosts in the windows and monsters in the shadows, but it's all in your head. Our imaginations create far worse games than reality ever could."

Knots of stress squeezed my back. "I saw a face."

"You saw your reflection."

My composure was on a knife's edge. "Thanks for the Zen wisdom. Forget it." My foot stumbled on the end of an oriental rug. "Why is there no electricity? This place would be easier to navigate if you could see where you're going."

Millie pursed her lips. "Thanks to continuous air raids on the power plant to the south, the electricity Tarahik receives is limited. It can't be spared from the base, which is in constant operation beneath the mountain. The only time the power is on in the castle is during the day. We're forced to live in darkness once the sun goes down." She kept her gaze fixed ahead. "Don't worry. You'll learn to live without it. Now, we need to keep moving."

My nails dug into my palms. "I'm sure the elite casters and humans in the Free Zones aren't living in darkness."

"No. I'm sure they're not." Millie clicked her tongue. "Humans must be protected. They come first. That's the way of the world."

That's the way they have the world, you mean.

We turned into another corridor that was whisper quiet. A blur of movement caught my eye. What I thought had been gold leaf was something else, patterns of roses and skulls entangled in vines. The image was spine-chillingly creepy. Water dripped down the walls, making the skulls appear as though they were crying.

Great. Now the rain is leaking through the building.

But a closer inspection showed it wasn't rainwater. It was condensation. And it dripped from the ceiling. Two fat splashes landed on my head, violently cold. My breathing became clouds of white. Coldness swept up my arms, forcing all the hairs to stand on end. The temperature had plunged drastically.

"Millie—" But the rest of my sentence stuck in my throat.

Millie was gone.

A crack, guttural and harsh, resonated ahead. I raised my candle a little higher. Something moved fast through the glow. Something pale.

No.

Fear paralysed my pulse. An icy sheet moved at a lazy speed across the ceiling. It drove down the walls, streaming across the floor and branching out in tendrils to trap me. I screamed loud enough to deafen dogs in the next town. The candle fell, snuffing out on impact.

I ran. The frigid air squeezed my throat, each breath a painful stab in my chest. The statue I'd nearly tripped on glistened like a hideous ice figurine. The gargoyle's gaping jaws made it look as though it were screaming. The ice gushed and rose behind me, intending to snare me in its embrace.

I swerved around a corner and slammed to a halt. The corridor ahead closed off to velvety dark. Adaline stood there. Her wet nightdress dripped fat puddles on the floor. Thick black blood pooled from her mouth. It had been her face I'd seen in the window. She pointed to the storm outside. Beyond the window, I could just make out the woods teeming with fog and rain. The trees bent in the wind, their branches clacking together. They reminded me of bony, skeletal fingers, ready to seize anything that wandered too close.

"Zaya." Adaline hovered toward me. Her voice was tender and childlike, but something in her expression was far from innocent. Her naked feet dragged on the floor, leaving watery stains on the carpet. She resembled a dog on a lead, mercilessly draggled and yanked by a petulant owner.

"Zaya." Her mouth widened into a yawning scream. "Get out."

The windows exploded in a high-pitched crash, sending jagged fragments across the carpet. I stumbled, my head striking the floor hard. Pain lanced behind my eyes, but I fought the dizziness and scooted away, not caring that glass cut my fingers and sliced my palms. Someone sobbed. It took a moment to register it was me.

The fast slap of footsteps came down the hall. A pair of hands grabbed me under the arms to plant me on my feet. "What are you doing down here? Why were you screaming?"

I spun around to find Colonel Harper. Worry and tension laced the fine creases on his brow. I couldn't meet his frightened eyes, afraid my face would betray me.

How am I going to explain the broken window and the damage?

Millie appeared from around the corner, face clouded with distrust. "What's going on? Why did you stray? My instructions were to follow me."

I didn't have a fallback answer. My gaze travelled back to the hallway. I felt hot and cold all at once. Adaline was gone. The windows were intact, the carpet dry. There wasn't even a hint of ice to suggest what had occurred.

This has been a mind game. Another hallucination.

But this time I didn't think it was caused by the castle.

Colonel Harper crossed his arms. His stern face indicated he was waiting for one thing—my answer.

The urge to throw up dallied in my throat. "I… I got lost."

"Lost?" Impatience flitted across his face. "And the screaming?"

"I got scared."

The excuse sounded lame to my own ears.

He scrutinised my face, studying every tiny detail. "And you thought crossing into an out-of-bounds section of the castle would help, did you?"

Huh?

At my blank expression, he grabbed a piece of black-and-yellow hazard tape from the floor, the kind used to close off crime scenes. He brought it close to my face to emphasise a point. "There are parts of this castle unsafe to travel. Under no circumstances are you to pass the cordoned-off sections."

I glanced behind me, failing to keep the dazed bewilderment out of my eyes. Now that Millie had returned with the candelabrum, my vision had adjusted. The hallway was a ruin of mouldy carpet, flaky plasterboard, and missing floor planks. My stomach shrivelled into the size of an acorn. I had no words to describe what this was. Had Adaline somehow manipulated the space around me, making me see something that hadn't been real? Had she brought me here to endanger me?

Colonel Harper cleared his throat. "Millie, go back to the commander and alert her of what's occurred. The binding spells in this hall will need to be re-enacted. No one must enter this passage. I'll take Miss Wayward to her apartment."

Millie scampered down the hall.

I sagged in defeat.

The colonel arched his eyebrows. "Come with me. Now."

He led me down several passages, the doors blank except for plaques with allotted numbers, eerily like cremation plots. We stopped at a door marked 362. Bad-tempered and brusque, the colonel knocked several times. "This is your room. Normally curfew is at ten, but due to the initiation ceremony this evening, you'll have till midnight to return to your apartment. Not a minute later. Understand?"

I nodded. He must have thought I was crazy. I was starting to think I *was* crazy. What was Adaline playing at? Apart from the black-veined woman, no ghost had done something as terrifying as this before. The floorboards in that place had been on the verge of collapse. I could have fallen straight through them. Had Adaline wanted to hurt me? Was she angry and vengeful because I hadn't saved her? Or was it because the black-veined woman had killed her, not me? Did Adaline want me dead?

The colonel watched me, perhaps trying to assess my mental state.

I stared at the floor, wishing I could sink into oblivion.

Sweet laughter erupted on the other side of the door, but there was nothing to suggest anyone hurried to answer. "Come on in," a voice called.

Colonel Harper pointed a strict finger at me. "Not a word of this."

He walked away, disappearing into the thick shadows.

I had never felt more lost or alone.

CHAPTER TEN

M y first thought was the colonel had made a mistake, because surely Macaslan had intended for me to sleep in the worst apartment in the castle. I walked around, examining every detail. I'd expected bunk beds and a communal bathroom—maybe a dungeon—but this matched an opulent hotel suite. Everything had been designed to be airy and light. The ceilings were lofty, the candlelit rooms warm and inviting. To my left was a living area with a white sofa, large hologram screen—switched off, obviously—and an oak bookcase, its shelves stacked with books on poetry, arts, and history. To my right was a stainless steel kitchen with a marble benchtop and modern necessities—kettle, gas cooktop, and microwave—styled to match the rest of the suite's classic decor. In the dining room, a magnificent chandelier was situated above a marble table, which was adjoined by a music room and grand piano. After two years of mining in a mountain and sleeping in a cell, this was luxury I didn't know how to contend with.

Something shuffled to my left. Two girls appeared in the kitchen. One was glamorous and petite, her wrists decked out with silver bangles. Straight away I pinned her for the type of girl who spent a larger sum of her father's money than his accountant did. She was about my height, with model looks and honey-blonde hair worn long behind her shoulders. Her black slacks and pink sweater showed off her curves, which were in the right places at the right angles. She stared at me with surprise, but her expression wasn't unkind.

The other girl looked like something you'd find at a rock concert—pale make-up, lips coated in black, dark hair blow-dried straight. Her black tights had holes in the knees, and her pleated miniskirt was held together with large safety pins. Her dark cat eyes observed me with an unimpressed frown.

I offered a thin smile but, remembering what Crawley had said about me smelling worse than the boys in the trenches, quickly lost it. Macaslan had said I was to share an apartment with two girls from noble families. But by *noble,* I'd imagined a well-respected family without title or fortune from the provinces. It was evident these girls were from the Free Zones—the sort of people who'd spit in my face if they knew where I was from. It seemed incredible that Macaslan would think pairing us was a good idea.

"Wonderful." The goth girl brushed her long fingernails through her stylish black bob. "We couldn't find a third roommate, and now we get lumbered with a stinking street orphan."

I assessed her white-painted clown face and wondered if the stud in her nose would leave a scar if I ripped it out.

The blonde girl nudged her roommate in the arm. "Don't be nasty, Lainie." Friendly lines crinkled around her eyes, but there was also the tiniest tweak of disappointment in them. "We don't have a problem with it, honestly," she told me. "I'm Talina Tessell. This is Lainie Binx."

Lainie wasn't as hospitable as her friend. She examined me from the top of my dishevelled head down to my new but scruffy boots, her intelligent eyes taking in the tattered fabric of my sleeve. "What happened to your coat? Did you have a fight with a chainsaw?"

I smiled. "What happened to your personality? Did you forget your meds?"

To my surprise, Lainie chuckled. She pulled out three glasses from a top cupboard and filled them with a dark liquid that looked extremely alcoholic. She passed me a glass and winked. "Enjoy it. From tomorrow night, drinking is strictly prohibited." She took a swig and made a sour face. "Shit, that burns." She guzzled another mouthful and boosted herself onto a kitchen stool, studying my appearance. "Seriously, you need a drink. What tricks did the castle play on you to make you look that shitty?"

"Lainie!" Talina opened her mouth and closed it again, mortified by her friend's behaviour.

Lainie grinned at her. "Relax. We're all roomies here."

I took a sip of the drink. It was strong and foul and just the way I remembered it back when I'd sneak alcohol into our dormitory at Brendlash. It tasted of immaturity and bad decisions.

Lainie gave me a lazy salute. "So, what's your name... your story... your disaster of a life?"

Talina dropped her head, blushing. "She means where are you from? Excuse Lainie. She wasn't bred for society."

"You're just jealous, skank."

"You're the skank."

Lainie shot her the finger.

They both erupted into laughter.

I watched the pair, their easy banter, their bright smiles. I used to be like that. Before Adaline. Before the black-veined woman. Before my life turned into a nightmare.

Talina stepped out of the kitchen to swat Lainie's arm playfully. She smiled at me, but it was tight around the edges. "So... where are you from?"

What the frig was my cover story again?

Everything was fragmented in my head. I couldn't relax. I couldn't focus. Adaline's screaming face was imprinted into my mind. My answer slipped out without any forethought. "Gosheniene."

Oh shit. Oh shit.

Talina's face lit up. "Oooh. That sounds exotic, like a seaside town."

I couldn't tell them the truth, so I chose to roll with it. "The orphanage there is one of the finest."

I directed this comment to Lainie.

She arched her eyebrow. "So fine they can't provide adequate clothing?"

Thankfully, I was saved from answering by Talina. She took my arm and led me into the lounge. "It's Zaya Wayward, right? The commander told us you were here on scholarship?"

I nodded. The right words were in my head, but my throat refused to voice them.

Talina offered a sympathetic smile. "Listen, the castle shakes us all up at first. It takes time, but you'll recover." Her eyes fell on my wound. "You're injured."

Before I could stop her, she pulled off my coat and unwrapped the bandage. Exposed to the air, the injury seeped and stung. A pink discharge that smelt strongly of overcooked meat oozed from the burn. Talina grimaced, but not in a disgusted way. More like she was trying to solve an impossible puzzle. "Cast-shooter, was it? I can probably do something with this, but I can't guarantee it won't leave a scar."

I sucked in a steadying breath. "Do something?"

She made an impatient sound in the back of her throat. "Sorry, I'm getting ahead of myself. I'm a healer. That's why I'm at Tarahik. I'm studying to be a nurse. Lainie is too, but she's a harmonist. She can calm people with her mind."

Lainie tipped her chin, obviously proud. "I can also make people experience nightmares if I desire it."

I didn't doubt her. On any other day, Lainie and I would probably get along, but this wasn't that time. Maybe it was her attitude that irked me. Maybe as a harmonist, she was deliberately channelling negative energy to test me. Whatever it was, I wanted to put a permanent black mark on those eyes. One punch from me and Lainie wouldn't have to bother with eyeshadow or mascara for several weeks.

Talina took my other arm and walked me to the sofa. "Sit."

I did as she instructed. She sat beside me, her hand hovering above my injured arm. She closed her eyes, inhaling deeply. For a long time, nothing happened.

I laughed, low in my throat. "Um… what are you doing?"

She slapped my knee. "Quiet. I need to concentrate."

Soft, calming warmth spread through my arm. It was a light tingling at first, like rain falling on my skin. Then it burned. The blistered flesh smoothed out in a way that reminded me of a ripple flattening on a lake, leaving nothing but a pink splotch of colour behind.

Talina opened her eyes. "Wow. That turned out better then I imagined. The bruising will disappear over the next few days."

I inspected my arm, amazed by the perfect, intact skin. Even the muscle felt stronger. "Thank you. But if you can already mend cast-shooter wounds, then why are you here? Shouldn't you be working in a hospital?"

Her eyes were bright and shone with amusement. "My homeschool teacher happened to be a healer and taught me to mend simple wounds. I'm gifted with healing, but still have much to learn."

Simple wounds.

If my injury was considered simple, then what the hell was happening out in the battlefield? I'd heard of casters losing limbs and being blown into small pieces by hex bombs but had thought they were stories fabricated by the council to frighten casters into submission. For nearly the past decade, I'd been sheltered in an orphanage that had refused to speak about the unsettling troubles in the provinces, then interned in a labour camp where no one dared to speak for fear of being punished. Whenever new prisoners had arrived, I'd pestered them for news on the provinces, but many had stared with empty eyes, their souls broken beyond repair.

What is Tarahik preparing me for out there?

Talina's happy smile deflated. "You still look... terribly unwell."

Lainie unwrapped a lollipop and stuck it in her mouth "It's the castle. It's got to her." She tilted her head at me. "You're pale, by the way."

I arched an eyebrow. "Jealous?"

The goth girl hissed like a scorched cat. "Oooh, she's feistier than she looks." She beamed at her roommate. "I like this one. I say we keep her."

Talina's cheeks coloured. "She's not a pet, Lainie."

"No, but she's still a stray."

I stood without realising it, my hands curled at my sides.

Perhaps wanting to defuse the tension fast, or sensing Lainie's jaw was about to meet my fist, Talina stood. "Let me show you to your room."

She looped her arm through mine and propelled me to the hallway. I was grateful the creepy little dead doll didn't follow us; I didn't have the mental capacity to deal with Lainie.

As we passed the first room, a sweet aroma of incense spilled forth. I cast a curious glance inside. The room was huge—probably ten times the size of my cell at Gosheniene. It didn't have a single bed either. It was a queen-size four-poster bed, dressed in puffy pink pillows and teddy bears. A cherry-coloured rug contrasted nicely with the grey carpet. Nestled beside the bedstead was a floor-length mirror where a collage of family photographs had been glue-tacked. On the other side, an array of moisturisers, perfumes, and make-up was assembled on a duchess of polished wood. It was enough to make anyone think they'd walked into an overly priced beauty parlour. I half expected a chihuahua to run out from under the bed.

The next room was abysmally bleak. Black walls. Black ceiling. Black carpet. On one wall hung a poster of the metal band The Scavenger's Daughter, a group of teen boys holding poses designed to look tough but alluring, their black hair spiked like bristles on a broom. Beneath the poster was a black-and-red chequered bed that frightfully resembled a coffin. A doll with pins in its eyes had been propped against the pillow.

Nice and charming.

"And here's yours." Talina led me into the third bedroom.

It contained a large bed covered in white satin sheets, the usual bedroom accessories—nightstand, dresser and mirror—and a decent-sized window. It was generic with no personality, but comfortable.

Talina smiled. "Do you like it?"

I didn't answer. The last time I'd had a room like this… well, my neighbour across the hall hadn't fared so well.

Talina's smile faltered at my silence. "Anyway, the initiation ceremony begins in less than an hour, so you'll want to look your best. Let me know if you need anything; otherwise, I'll leave you to it."

She slipped out the door, shutting it behind her.

Alone now, the lovely, cosy room seemed full of shadows.

Why hadn't I been friendlier? Talina had gone out of her way to be charitable.

And I could really do with a friend right now.

I groaned inwardly. Why had I messed things up so badly?

Outside, a blur of whispers travelled down the passage—the irritable, clipped sound of two people caught in an argument. I pressed my ear against the door.

"The other cadets aren't going to accept her. It's crazy the council brought her here."

"I don't care. She's nice."

"Nice? Did you see the look in her eyes? She was going to tear my throat out back there."

"Calm down, Lainie. Remember what the commander told us. She's been terribly mistreated at that orphanage."

"You don't really believe that crap, do you? That girl smells like a decade's worth of body odour. Orphanages do not deprive children of showering. She's lying, and so is Macaslan."

I slipped away.

This was wrong. I was wrong. And I wasn't meant to be here.

I crossed the room and wedged the window open. Down below, the bottom of the castle was lost in a swirl of mist. My plan had been to scale the roof and climb down, but Tarahik's elevation was higher than I'd anticipated. Any one of the slanted gables would make a foot in the wrong place fatal.

I was trapped.

The reality was, there was no escape from Tarahik.

CHAPTER ELEVEN

Priorities.

I needed to get them right. Running away was the plan, but I had to shower. Who knew when I'd get the next chance? Inside the en suite, different brands of body wash, soaps, and shampoos lined the vanity. A large mirror hung above the sink. Compared to Talina's flawless appearance, I looked like someone salvaged off a shipwreck. My hair hung limp. The skin beneath my eyes was black in half-moons, as though I'd had one too many punch-ups in a boxing ring. My lips had lost colour too. They were cracked and peeling at the edges.

There was no escaping the truth. I was scruffy, beaten, and homeless.

In the shower, I lathered myself with soap—something fruity—and let the water soothe away the aches and bruises on my body. I scrubbed vigorously at my skull, washing out the sweat and tangled hair, my nails clean for the first time in years. This was nothing like the communal showers at Gosheniene, where the water was cold and the usage timed. This was paradise.

Pity it can't last.

I tugged on a bathrobe and returned to my room. On impulse, I flung the wardrobe open. All the clothes were military and camo. There were a few dressier items, horrible and frilly and so not me, plus a fine collection of boots and heels.

Where would someone wear dresses and heels at a military base?

I didn't stop to think about who bought the items or how they'd guessed my size. I tossed the bathrobe aside and slipped into olive green camo pants, a khaki top, and a knee-length black jacket. Beside the bed was a field pack—the kind I'd seen the Haxsan Guard carry when they visited Gosheniene—large enough to hold sleeping gear, food, water, and weapons. I rummaged inside, found a flashlight, switchblade, goggles, two throwing knives, a compass, and—I couldn't deter a squeal of excitement—a cast-shooter. The weapon was unloaded, but I placed it in my holster belt anyway. If I ran into someone, I'd let them think I was armed and dangerous.

It's now or never.

Inching toward the door, I squeezed the handle and tiptoed out… walking straight into Talina.

"Hey, there. I've brought you hot chocolate and—" She did a quick assessment of my attire. "You do realise the initiation ceremony is a formal event, right? Wait. Are you going somewhere?"

Damn. Damn. Damn.

Lainie appeared beside her like a summoned spirit. The delight in her eyes reminded me of a satisfied cat that had cornered a mouse. "She's not violating the dress code, idiot. She's deserting."

"Deserting?" Talina's stricken gaze shifted back to me. "Why would you do that?"

I sucked in a steadying breath. "I don't belong here."

"Belong?' Lainie looked like she'd choked on a lemon peel. "Seriously? None of us belong here. Everyone at Tarahik is conscripted. No one gets out of serving the Haxsan Guard. We all have to do our bit for the war."

I walked back into the room and slouched on the bed. My heart pounded with the beat of failure.

But I don't believe in the war.

I'd seen casters sent to the firing squad because they refused to bow down to the council's philosophy. I'd heard casters screaming in their cells because they'd lost their children, children weeping because they'd lost their parents. The council wanted the ULD and its supporters destroyed at any cost. There was no limit to their brutality. Talina and Lainie wouldn't comprehend this.

They'd been brought up in the Free Zones, in a safe bubble where they never went without. Maybe, after a few months in the provinces, they'd see the ugly side of the world and understand, but for now, it was pointless to argue the issue with them.

Lainie fiddled with a stray thread that poked out from her black sleeve. "Listen, even if you did manage to get past the sentinels or Shadow's Wood, the celestial shield would obliterate you. That shield is not only designed to keep the enemy out but to prevent desertion too. There's no way out of Tarahik unless you're travelling by ship or aircraft. And if you're caught as a stowaway…." She made a graphic throat-cutting gesture.

Talina's eyes fell on my field pack. "You're infantry. Is that why you're running away? You can apply to be a nurse like us. We attend to the wounded at makeshift hospitals. We're not in battle."

My lips trembled. I tasted hot, bitter emotion in the back of my throat. "I'm not staying. Go to your ceremony and forget you saw this."

Talina squeezed her eyes shut. "We can't just forget it. If you make an escape attempt, they'll enact a truth serum on us and force the answer out. We'll be powerless against that potion. We'll tell them what we know."

Lainie inspected her black-painted fingernails. "And that's after they find your body splattered against the celestial shield like a fried egg." She walked in and dropped onto the bed beside me, tapping her ridiculously high platform boots on the carpet. "Listen. I like a kindred spirit. Rebellion is fun. But this is not something you can do without consequences. And in this case, the consequences equal death. This is your home now. You belong to Tarahik."

I turned away in defeat. I hated how sad and wistful they both appeared, like they'd already been overpowered by the castle and accepted it for what it was. But I couldn't. It wasn't the celestial shield that frightened me. Or Shadow's Wood. It was Tarahik. It was the castle's abysmal dark. It was the way the building groaned and shuddered like a hungry beast. It was the way that every nook and cranny seemed to hide a blur of movement I knew was not a trick of my eyes. Or how the stillness wasn't quite still but something growing louder and breathier in the shadows.

Talina handed me the hot chocolate. "You look like you could use some comfort."

My shoulders sagged. "I could use a punching bag, actually." The delicious scent of chocolate wafted up my nose as I took a drink. My taste buds surrendered, the chocolate tasting thick and sweet. I couldn't remember when I'd last indulged like this.

Talina eyed my combat garb with a critical once-over. "You can't wear that to the initiation ceremony. It's a formal event. You'll need to do something about your hair too."

A strange stirring rose in my stomach. "My hair?"

Lainie snorted. "Yeah. It's all uneven. Did you cut it with a hatchet?"

Talina intervened. "Ignore her. Lainie and I have to get ready, but I'll come back in twenty minutes and see how you're doing, okay?"

It didn't take a genius to work out the subtext. *I'll come back and make sure you're presentable.*

She snuck a peek at my wardrobe. Judging by the way she flinched, the clothes didn't meet her mark of approval. "So… we're good? You promise you're not going to try and run away?"

I crossed my fingers behind my back. "Promise."

She offered a stunning smile and headed toward the door.

I felt a gnawing need to apologise for my behaviour but settled on thanking her for the hot chocolate instead.

"No problem," she called behind her shoulder as she slipped down the hall. "But I didn't make it."

Lainie's smile was positively wicked. "I did."

The goth girl was still sitting uncomfortably close.

"You?" I checked the drink for signs of poison. Deciding it wasn't worth the risk, I placed the cup on the floor.

Lainie laughed, but it sounded wrong and—if I wasn't mistaken—excited. "I made it for you because… it helps, so I'd drink it if I were you."

"Helps?"

She darted a quick glance at the door, making sure Talina had disappeared. "Yes, with what I'm about to do."

Before I could comprehend her bizarre behaviour, she slapped her palm onto my forehead, hard. Blinding pain pierced my scalp, as though thousands of needles had perforated my head. I attempted to swat her hand away, but it was like trying to knock over a steel pole. "Hey, cut it out. What are you doing?"

There was something strange about Lainie's eyes that I couldn't process initially. They were large and grey and… glowing. Lainie didn't answer, just remained in that weird meditative state, her hand impossibly strong.

Panic crawled under my skin. I was swaying. Tilting. Falling.

"Don't be a bitch," I started to say, but my vision went fuzzy at the edges. My brain was lying in shards inside my skull, and someone was sifting through the pieces. The walls I'd built to seal my past came tumbling down.

Lainie was reading my mind.

"Get away from me." I shoved her off.

Lainie gasped, her dream faze over. She leapt away as though she'd been doused with cold water. For a moment, her pale make-up made her look as immobile as marble. "Wow. You are a seriously screwed-up person."

My breath was fast and erratic. "What?"

She smiled. "We should get along fine."

Sweat broke out above my upper lip. "That was an invasion of privacy."

She scrunched her nose, making a funny face. "I didn't read your mind, idiot. I'm a harmonist. I read emotions. Sometimes, I can see what causes those feelings, but they're never clear. Just disjointed images, really."

I failed to keep the anger in my voice under control. "I don't care. My feelings are mine. They're private. You had no right."

"Didn't I?" She tilted her head. "You came into our apartment moody and miserable. The commander would never let someone like you into the base, and yet here you are—and on the council's authority too. It doesn't add up."

"It's none of your business." I was terrified by how much she'd seen in that freaky vision of hers. Did she know everything? What would it cost to keep her quiet?

Lainie crossed her arms over her chest. "Actually, it is my business. We're sharing an apartment, and that means it's my right to look after Talina and myself… and to understand what we've been thrown into."

"You haven't been thrown into anything."

The prying, fixated glow in her eyes was full of mistrust. "Really? Who's Adaline?"

The question caught me off guard. I stared ahead, stubborn to the end. *Screw her.*

Lainie's voice sounded choked. "She's dead, right?"

I drew my hair to the side, creating a curtain between me and Lainie. "I don't want to talk about this."

"Listen to me. I know you saw Adaline this evening. The castle conjured her image to frighten you. You know Tarahik's tricks aren't real, right? They're hallucinations. It's a defence mechanism the castle employs to protect its inhabitants. It digs into your mind, finding your worst fear, and creates that illusion. Now that the commander has accepted you, the hallucinations will stop."

I stood and paced by the window. Outside, the sea was choppy, the white crests of the waves smashing together in a powerful surge. I wondered how many secrets the ocean kept beneath its surface. If the waves would ever lay them bare on the beach like Lainie had exposed mine. I wished I could be like the tide, drawing the secrets in, plunging them back into the depths where they belonged.

Lainie's wrong. It wasn't the castle. It was Adaline.

Lainie exhaled a long breath. I heard her soft footsteps on the carpet behind me. "Listen… when I delved into your emotions, I saw something else. You were in a cell. I couldn't see where exactly, but it looked like a prison. Did the council think you had something to do with Adaline's death?"

I willed myself not to erupt in a rage.

"Zaya?"

I turned from the window. "They pinned her murder on me, okay? What else do you want me to say?"

Lainie stepped back, blinking fast. I knew that under that white make-up, she was pale from shock. "But why? It's the thing you're afraid of seeing in your sleep that killed Adaline. I don't understand what that thing is, either."

Icy panic clenched my heart. The *thing* was undoubtedly the black-veined woman. If Lainie learnt a wraith was haunting my dreams, and she told the authorities, it would be the end of me. Necromancy was forbidden. As far as the world was concerned, it was a dangerous magic that had been purged long ago. No one could know that I possessed the power to see the dead.

Lainie smiled, but it was tight. "Listen, you have nothing to worry about with me. I didn't see anything. Not in the literal sense. I mainly sensed emotion. I felt your pain, your sorrow… your fear. And that's when everything cut off."

"Cut off?"

Her eyes turned dark with recollection. "Yeah. I think it was a barricade shielding your memories. I saw this place. It might have been a cave, but it was too dark to tell. In the centre was this crater. I didn't get too close, but I could tell it was deep… and damp… and cold. And it reeked. I've never smelt death before, but I knew that's what it was. There were screams coming from inside. A woman's awful, tortured cries. She was shouting a name."

A queasy flutter trembled in my stomach. I knew the best thing to do was deny any of this and pretend Lainie had mistaken a nightmare for reality, but my curiosity triumphed reason. "What name?"

"Yours. Whatever it was down there, it screamed your name repeatedly. I saw something move in the dark. I think it might have been a hand clawing at the mud and filth. Then everything went black. I was thrown from your mind."

I said nothing for a long moment. A shiver of premonition crept over my bones. The black-veined woman. It had to be her in the crater. I knew it but couldn't remember why. Or how?

Lainie gave an ironic snort. "Hey, relax. After all, it's not a real place. It's figurative. A space where you suppress memories you wish to forget. It's where you've put the face of the real murderer, this 'thing,'" she said with air quotes, "so you don't have to deal with it on a conscious level. I've seen it before. Not as dark as yours, but everyone has ghosts they'd rather forget."

I leaned on the wall for support, sick and hot. I was going to barf.

Lainie rubbed her hands over her arms, hesitant. "Listen, I didn't mean to upset you by reading your emotions. I just needed to know what Talina and I were dealing with. I won't tell a soul, not even Talina. I promise. It's totally natural for you to fear the person who killed Adaline, especially because they got away with the murder and you were blamed. But you're innocent. The council knows it. The commander knows it. That's why you're here. Tarahik is a second chance."

I kept my eyes on the window. The brisk wind picked up, the ocean soaring and treacherous. It sounded as though the waves were whispering and laughing.

Lainie tapped my shoulder. I hadn't even heard her approach. "You need to get ready for the ceremony. Drink the chocolate. It helps."

She offered me the drink. I cupped it in my hands, but the warmth had dwindled away.

Her retreating footsteps moved to the door. "I'll come back to check on you shortly."

The door shut behind her.

I took a mouthful. The sweetness was gone; the drink tasted cold and bland.

I wished I lived in a world where chocolate did help.

CHAPTER TWELVE

I used to be good with make-up. At the orphanage, girls would come to me for advice, seeking the best methods for high cheekbones, dramatic eyes, and the sexiest, sensual-looking lips. I was a master at making the simplest face appear elegant or striking. But that talent had died when I'd been sentenced to Gosheniene. The secret was *less is more*, but tonight my reservations got the better of me.

I boycotted make-up and deliberately kept my back to the mirror while I dressed, afraid to look at the ghastly image. The dress I slipped on was ankle length, white with black polka dots and puffy sleeves. It widened at the hips, making it look like I wore a ridiculously large hoop skirt. The neckline, with its frilly collar, didn't help either. It scratched worse than sandpaper.

Deep breath. Just get it over with.

I squinted into the full-length mirror, hoping to identify something positive in the reflection.

I resemble a woeful Little Bo Peep.

There was no colour in my cheeks. No hope in my eyes. My legs felt wobbly and heavy. I dropped onto the bed and buried my face in my hands.

Maybe I can fake an illness and get out of this absurd ceremony. I can flee the castle while Talina and Lainie are gone.

The click of a lock cut my thoughts off abruptly. The bedroom door knob twisted one way, then the other with a heavy metallic groan.

I don't remember locking it.

I glowered at the floor, reluctant to get on my feet. "Okay. Hang on a moment."

Lainie and Talina had said they'd check up on me, but I didn't think it would be this soon.

A lurching shudder shook the door. I stopped. An odd sensation tingled over my scalp—a sixth sense to be cautious. The knob twisted again, back and forth, each rattle more violent than the last, as though the person on the other side had difficulty opening it.

Person... or something else?

The air in my room turned chillier. The cold ripped through my lungs, each breath like an axe in my chest. A high-pitched crash that sounded deceptively like a bird had flown into glass cracked behind me. I spun around. The window's latch jiggled. The glass pane shook, as though invisible fists pounded it from the outside.

The blood in my veins turned to icy slush.

What the hell is going on?

I couldn't see anyone or anything at the window, but I knew something was close—and watching. A lump rose in my throat. Whatever it was had moved again. There was a shadow underneath my en suite door. It extended to the left and right as the thing inside my bathroom paced. A grating, scratchy sound clawed at the door. I held my breath, afraid to make a noise. This must have been what prey felt like when they were in plain sight of a predator.

Thump. Thump. Thump.

It pummelled the bedroom door.

It's... moving through the walls. It's moving like smoke around me, trying to find a way in.

I blinked hard twice, but the sounds didn't go away. Whatever this thing was, it was trying to access my room through any doorway or window it could find. The heavy thuds resonated through the walls. I pivoted in the direction of the noises. Every surface of my room sounded like it was being beaten with baseball bats.

This is a nightmare. It isn't real. It'll go away.

A lock clicked. The bedroom door inched open with a resounding creak. A sob broke from me, a hopeless, helpless noise I wasn't proud of. I grabbed the vase from the side table, bracing myself for a threat.

A shadowy figure emerged.

I brought the vase down.

"Whoa." Talina jumped back, her eyes large and wounded. "Were you going to hit me with that?"

I placed the vase back on the table, my breath caught in my throat. "No. I was…." *Crap. What's my excuse?* "I was getting water for the flowers. It needs replacing."

Her face scrunched into a grimace. "The flowers are fake."

"Um… really?"

Talina shook her head, blonde hair swinging loose around her delicate face. "Are you sure you're all right?"

I smiled, but my lips were like ice, stiff and cold and lacking credibility. "I'm sorry. I thought I heard something, but it was nothing."

The last thing I needed Talina to think was that she had a batty roommate, but given the circumstances, maybe that's what I was.

Her green eyes searched my face. "There's nothing to be afraid of in the castle, okay? If you hear noises in the apartment, it's me or Lainie."

And all the other dark, unexplainable shit that has a hankering for scaring me witless.

Talina raised her perfectly plucked eyebrows. She finally noticed what I wore. "Well, don't you look… interesting. Perhaps I should have made it clear before. This ceremony is more of a cocktail event."

"Cocktail?" I ruffled a frustrated hand through my hair. "Do I really have to go?"

"Yes. It's compulsory. You'll be punished if you don't attend."

"I'd rather take the punishment."

I'd also like to be a million miles away from this room.

Talina straightened her shoulders, her gaze intent. It was a look a mother would be proud of. "Come with me. We're going to fix this."

Talina's en suite turned out to be a big pink-and-white room with vintage accessories, floral wallpaper, and cream cladding. The bathtub was salmon coloured, the hand towels red to match the long-stemmed roses placed meticulously at every corner. The venetian mirror was a work of art, gilded and painted in bronze, large enough to reflect five people at a time. The entire bathroom was effortlessly chic—a style I could only dream of achieving.

Talina shoved me into a seat in front of the vanity. She held up a hand. "The dress has to go. The hair must change. The shoes need replacing. Make-up… it's needed. And your posture screams insecurity." A finger went up with each description.

My entire body felt leaden. "Gee, thanks. But can you blame me? This dress is hardly flattering."

And after what I'd experienced in my room, I didn't think I'd ever feel secure or happy again. My insides still spun in crazy flutters. It had to be a wraith trying to break in. That tight, creepy-crawly feeling over my skin, my clammy hands, the sensation I was being watched—that all happened in the presence of a wraith.

But which wraith? Adaline or the black-veined woman?

And why couldn't the ghost cross into my room?

Talina pulled my shoulders back and lifted my chin, forcing me to hold my head high in the mirror. "See? Already you look better. Confidence is everything. Now, the hair." She tugged a brush through my long tangled knots. "When did you last attend to it? It's too long, and it feels like straw. I think we should cut it just past your shoulder blades. That way, it's still long enough to style but doesn't overwhelm your slight frame."

She lined a set of brushes, compacts, rouge, and an eyelash curler along the marble vanity. The faintest trace of a smile appeared on her face. Being in her element lifted her spirits. I wished this makeover would lift my spirits too.

Talina slapped my shoulder. "No peeking. This is going to be a surprise." She spun my chair around, obstructing my view of the mirror. "I know exactly the style that will be perfect for your face. Trust me. You won't recognise yourself once I'm done." Grinning, she took up a pair of scissors and began snipping away.

I could only pray to providence that Talina knew what she was doing.

When she finished, my transformation rendered me speechless. She was right. The new length suited me. Using her healing abilities, Talina had made my hair healthy and nourished. Even the colour had changed. It was a darker, richer brown, the auburn more prominent. Now that my hair carried less weight, it curled loosely past my shoulder blades, framing my face with perfect balance. I looked like me again, before I'd been sentenced to Gosheniene.

"Beautiful," Talina whispered in my ear. She focused on my make-up, expertly applying the right shades in the right areas.

I examined my reflection in the mirror. I should have been crazy happy with the result, but I didn't have the energy to smile. Coincidences didn't just happen. Tarahik was bringing the ghosts to me. This castle had secrets; horrible, bitter, angry truths that hid in its walls, and now it had unleashed them to torment me.

Not one part of me felt comfortable, but I had to ask. "Do you know much about Tarahik?"

Talina powdered rouge onto my cheeks. "It's an old castle and teeming with history. The council have owned it for a while. I don't know who it originally belonged to. I think that part of Tarahik's history is lost."

"You haven't heard any… interesting stories about the place?"

She raised an indecisive shoulder. "Like what?'

"I don't know. Folk tales, perhaps. Or…."

"You mean ghost stories?" Talina gave a sullen shake of her head. "You know the council doesn't approve of that nonsense. And if you're caught talking about anything relating to that, you'll be locked away and punished. This is an old castle full of enchantments, that's all." She smiled weakly. "You don't really believe in that sort of thing, do you?"

I took in a shuddering breath. "No. Of course not."

"Good." Talina grabbed a curling wand. "Now, time for your hair."

A chill tiptoed down my skin. What had I nearly done? Even implying the supernatural could result in arrest. It had been dangerous and stupid to have brought Tarahik's history up for discussion. I needed to handle this on my own and not be tempted to seek help. Especially when I didn't know that person well.

"Do you do Lainie's make-up?" I asked, changing the subject.

Talina snorted. "No way. She does that to herself."

"She's very…." I pondered for the right word. "Intense."

Talina took a stray lock of my hair, twisted it around her finger, and let it fall in a curl past my ear. "She never used to be. Lainie was the sweetest person I knew, once."

"Really? What changed?"

She fiddled with the curling wand. "Her brother died."

"Died?" The word tasted heavy on my tongue "What happened to him?"

One thing my lack of memory was good for was that I was spared the loss of loved ones. I had no memory of my parents. I didn't know if I had siblings, aunts, uncles, cousins, or grandparents. If I did, and they were dead, that was a world of hurt I'd missed. Maybe I was the lucky one in that regard.

Talina put the curling wand down and wrapped both arms around her sides. "The council never said. Kylin was meant to be trained as a medic. It was what his parents wanted. But he wouldn't hear of it. He believed all caster men should fight for the Haxsan Guard and do their duty to protect humans from the ULD. He got what he wished for in the end. Kylin was deployed to Strizork, where the fighting was most intense. He died three days later. The authorities said it was a cast-shooter, but they insisted on a closed casket at the funeral, and that only happens when—" She inhaled deeply.

I patted her hand. "When the body is unrecognisable. I know."

Once, when Thessio had been absent from Gosheniene, his second in command had convinced the other wardens that a round of psychological warfare would do me a world of good. They'd achieved this by strapping me to an electric chair and zapping various levels of voltage through my body. My head had been pinned back, my eyes forced to witness terrible scenes of destruction and carnage. Holographic images of dissent rebels rounding up prisoners of war into lines for execution, and dark curses blasting battlefields like chemical explosives. There were other horrific displays, but those were the ones I remembered vividly. Each time the slideshow changed, the voltage peaked. If you wanted to re-educate somebody and make them hate your enemy, it worked best when the mind was tortured and the body in agony. Those scenes I witnessed scared me, but I knew what the wardens were trying to achieve. I would not let those images break me.

I shivered, trying to place those horrific war scenes back in the hole deep in my mind. I could imagine exactly what happened to Kylin. Closed casket indeed.

Talina's voice was raw and vulnerable. "Lainie was never the same after Kylin's death. Her attitude, her personality—it all changed."

"Do you know her family well?"

She nodded with a small sniffle. "Lainie and I went to school together in Accrington. That was before my father had me homeschooled. I used to holiday with the Binxs during Samhain because my parents were always working. Kylin would play the nastiest tricks on us, but it was all games in the end. I still miss him."

Lainie appeared in the doorway then, sucking on a lollipop. "Miss who?"

Talina jumped. "No one. I miss school. I was just telling Zaya all about Accrington."

"You? Miss school?" Lainie laughed, but it sounded dull and unamused. "You hated school. That's why your dad took you out of it."

I cast an uneasy glance at Talina, wondering how she'd cover up her lie. I had a hunch Accrington would have been as pretentious as its title sounded. Talina didn't strike me as hollow or conceited. Forced to mingle with stuck-up, egotistical bitches probably made Accrington High a living hell for her.

Talina's voice was too loud to be believable. "There are parts that I miss."

Lainie rolled her eyes. "That's a new revelation indeed. Anyway, look at what just arrived. Another gift from the commander." She lifted three handmade willow hoops that she'd had concealed behind her back. Each was woven into a web of different colours with matching beads and feathers.

Talina made a deflated sound in the back of her throat. "Seriously? Dreamcatchers? Is the commander afraid one of us is going to have a nightmare now?"

Dreamcatchers?

I knew very little about their magic, other than they worked like a spider's web. One would hang the dreamcatcher above them as they slept. At night, the web would ensnare nightmares, allowing the dreamer to sleep soundly. Creating a dreamcatcher was meant to be near on impossible. It took a very skilled and powerful caster to fashion one. Which begged the question: Why would Commander Macaslan waste her talents and time, when she was needed for far more important things?

A startling thought popped into my head.

She knows. The commander knows about my nightmares.

Why else would she have three dreamcatchers brought to our apartment?

Talina wrinkled her nose. "This is getting weird."

"Weird?" I tried to make light humour out of it, but in the mirror, my smile looked broken.

"Yeah, it's crazy. When Lainie and I returned from lunch yesterday afternoon, we found Commander Macaslan standing in the lounge room, performing magic. She said my father had called and asked for extra defensive spells in the bedrooms. The three of us are the only ones who can access our rooms at any time; otherwise, they're permanently locked. No one gets in. I mean… isn't that odd? And the other thing. I called my dad. He never asked the commander to perform any defensive curses."

Lainie passed me a crooked smile. "Maybe the commander doesn't want us bringing boys back to the apartment."

I laughed, but inside, my heart ticked like a bomb. A wraith had tried unsuccessfully to get into my room. If it weren't for Commander Macaslan's pre-emptive measures, it would have triumphed—and done who knew what? The knowledge clamped around my throat like an icy fist.

Lainie dropped the dreamcatchers on the vanity. "Anyway, how's your guinea pig doing?"

Talina spun me around, showing the full effect of her handiwork. My make-up looked natural and glowing, my skin creamy rather than pale. Wine red lipstick shaped the contours of my lips, providing them a fuller appearance. The coral pink shimmer on my eyelids gave my blue eyes more intensity. But I couldn't find joy in this. Not after learning that the commander knew more about my history than she'd let on.

She might even know more than I do.

Lainie made disgruntled sucking sounds on her lollipop. "The make-up is good. The hair is good. But what's with the dress? Are we going on a picnic?"

Talina flipped her the finger. "I'm working on it."

Laine's lips curved into a thin smile. "It's my turn to work some magic. I have a dress that's perfect for this emergency." She winked at me. "Come along, puppet."

I stood up, not really knowing where I was going or what I was doing. My mind was too centred on the commander.

She knows more than she's letting on.

Does Macaslan know about the wraiths?

Adaline?

The black-veined woman?

CHAPTER THIRTEEN

"Are you sure I have to wear this?" I struggled down the stairs in my new gown, terrified I'd trip.

Lainie's solution had been a black slitted cocktail dress with lace sleeves. It trailed behind me on the floor, flashing way more leg than was appropriate.

Her brows knitted together "You don't like the dress? Pity. I was going to let you keep it. It looks better on you than it ever did on me. It gives you the appearance of an *actual* figure."

I ignored the backhanded compliment. Putting an imprint of my fist in Lainie's face would be excellent for my morale, but I doubted it would respond well with the commander. And if I wasn't getting out of this castle anytime soon, then the commander's protection was priority. I had to talk to her. I had to learn what she knew.

We stepped out of the stairwell into an auditorium, my stomach doing a queasy tap dance, half nervous, half excited. The impressive auditorium had polished parquetry floors, mirror-clad arches fixed along the walls, and an incredible frieze of painted cherubs. But the crowning glory of the hall was the elaborate chandeliers, illuminated with tall white candles. It was evident by the size of the space that the auditorium had a variety of uses, but tonight it had been flamboyantly dressed for a ball. Couples danced in perfect time with the orchestra. The music carried through the entire hall in resonant harmony.

Lainie gave me a winning smile. "Sorry, ladies, but duty calls. I'll see you at dinner."

She made a beeline for the bar, deliberately swaying her curvy butt as she moved.

I wondered how much booze she'd had in the apartment and whether letting her go alone was a good idea.

Talina stubbornly looked away. "Let me introduce you to a few acquaintances."

I followed her around the great hall like a lost puppy. I didn't know where to stare. In this overly grand interior, with its illustrious guests and striking ornaments, I felt like a complete fraud. Packed with casters, the candlelit hall only got tighter, more claustrophobic as new guests arrived. I realised the appearance of wealth made people behave differently toward you. The women examined my fashionable gown and whispered among each other, trying to work out if a connection with me would benefit them. Men's eyes trailed after me, sizing up my *supposed* fortune. An electric awareness pulsed through my blood. I lacked the grace and poise these people valued. I might have looked the part, but the moment I opened my mouth, the masquerade would be over. And who were these people? There were young and old faces in the crowd, but none of them looked like cadets.

I held on tightly to Talina's wrist. "These people do not look like soldiers."

She gave me a pitiful pout. "Don't be silly. They're guests invited by the council. Men and women who live and hold positions of power in the Free Zones. There are cadets here too, though. See over there." She pointed to a young man who'd outdone himself with an immaculate black suit. "That's Fillian Ivanov. His father beside him is Count Ivanov. He is the third chief chancellor of the council—after the Seven Sovereigns, of course."

Fillian sipped his drink and looked bored. He lifted a silver spoon and used the back of it to examine his reflection, more preoccupied with his hair than the onslaught of ladies competing for his attention.

Count Ivanov talked among a group of wealthy courtiers, making grand gestures with his white-gloved hands. We were close enough to hear snippets of his conversation. "How saddened I was to hear about the recent devastation at Callithorne. Those poor men, ambushed by dissent rebels. It's such a pity.

Thank providence Fillian will never be put into a position like that. After serving the Haxsan Guard, he'll be working for me in the council."

His audience smiled and congratulated Fillian on his good fortune.

I kept my face very still, but a surge of anger pumped through my body. Count Ivanov had spoken of the deaths of Callithorne's troops like he'd lost a set of fine china. I examined the rest of the crowd. There were many young faces in the great hall that radiated superiority and confidence. They were wealthy cadets who would graduate and hold positions of power at Tarahik. Like Fillian, once their service to the Haxsan Guard was complete, they'd return to the Free Zones and be employed by the council. Their duties would probably entail them to conscript the next generation of unlucky casters.

I felt the urge to vomit.

Because this wasn't the real world. Initiated into a decade of military service was not glamourous, exciting, or something to be celebrated. These people had no idea what waited in the provinces. These people had no idea what was happening in the provinces, period.

I spotted the commander among a group of grandiose men and women. Commander Macaslan had ditched the lace blouse, wearing a deep emerald ballgown and matching gloves. She was as striking and standoffish as a queen, and everyone in her vicinity seemed to uphold her with reverence and respect.

"I'll be back in a moment. I need to speak to the commander." I headed toward the group.

Talina gripped my arm. "What do you think you're doing? You can't just waltz your way up to the commander. You can only speak to her by appointment."

"But her disciples are talking to her," I joked. "Look at them. I think they're about to bow down and pray for salvation."

Talina didn't smile. An invisible weight pressed on her shoulders. "You can't just... do things like that. You'll make a scene."

I crossed my arms. "Excuse me?"

Talina twisted the silver ring on her middle finger. "Do you see the boys and girls over there?"

I glanced in the direction of the far wall. A large group of boys and girls around my age loitered to the side. The girls' dresses were simple. The boys wore tuxes that were clearly hand-me-downs and half a century old. They stood together, awkward and lacking finesse. These were the casters without fortune or inheritance.

My kind of people.

The pawns on the chessboard.

The crowds parted around the group as though repelled by a celestial shield. So these cadets were good enough to attend Tarahik and potentially die in battle but not good enough to socialise with. A sick, acidic taste curled into my throat. I'd been thrown into a world where snobbery was valued above all.

Talina took up two champagne flutes from a passing waiter and placed one in my hand. "Those boys and girls are orphans. They're like you, brought here on scholarship." She squeezed my arm gently. "Everyone has a place at Tarahik. It's wise not to cross it. There will be a time to talk to the commander, but it's not tonight."

I gestured at my dress. "Then why did you help me? Why did you make me look presentable for this ceremony if you think I'm beneath you? If you think I'm one of them." I pointed to the orphans. "I suppose I should leave now so you don't have to associate with your inferior."

I had almost trusted Talina.

Stupid, stupid mistake.

She reeled back, fixing me with a hurt stare. "No. I don't see you as my inferior… or anyone, for that matter. I'm just trying to warn you of how it is. Not even I could walk up to the commander and speak to her. It's just… not how things are done."

I watched Macaslan on the other side of the room effortlessly claim command over everyone. Maybe talking to her tonight was a bad idea. There were ears and eyes everywhere. Someone would overhear. And chances were Macaslan wouldn't discuss any questions I had in such a public setting, especially about ghosts.

"I'm sorry," I said, and meant it.

"Sorry for what?" a bubbly voice asked.

Lainie appeared, batting her big eyelashes. Some of the drink sloshed out of her glass. I caught a whiff of alcohol as she leaned her arm on my shoulder, steadying her weight against me.

A flicker of embarrassment flashed across Talina's face. "How much have you had to drink, Lainie? That's a powerful potion. You don't want to get drunk on it."

Potion?

Lainie took up another glass from a passing waiter and guzzled the liquid down. "Just trying to enjoy myself. I'm certainly not going to get it from the conversation around here."

"You'd be wise to try and fit in. These are not the sort of people you want to upset."

Lainie waved her hand dismissively. "Like I give a damn if I offend them."

Talina stood rooted to the spot, her jaw twitching. "Your father will. The only reason people tolerate your behaviour, and the way you dress, is because of your family name… and because they feel sorry for what happened to Kyl—" She slapped a hand to her mouth, horrified by the near slip.

Lainie's teasing grin faded. I wondered if her eccentricities were an act of teenage rebellion or if something more disturbing brewed on a deeper level. I loved her skull earrings, her red-and-black lace dress, her dark make-up and chaotic hair. I had no problem with it, but I saw in the way others observed her that Lainie's style wasn't accepted. They might even think she was making a mockery of their customs.

Lainie slammed her empty glass on a table. "If Kylin's death taught me anything, it's that it's better to live the life you want than bow down to these conceited pricks. And you want to know something else?" She brought her face close to Talina's. "You're becoming more and more like them." She stalked over to the waiter for another drink.

Talina's beautiful face crumpled into despair. She glanced at me, swallowing hard. "I'm sorry for that. Lainie's a bit…." She dabbed her long pearl-coloured fingernails under her eyes.

I grabbed her arm and led her to a table where there was privacy. "Lainie's drunk. People don't act themselves when they're under the influence. Don't cry. You'll ruin your make-up."

Talina sucked in a shaky breath. "I hate it when Lainie gets like this. Because she's a harmonist, her emotions take over and she doesn't know when to stop. Honestly, I'm not like these people, but if you don't play to their rules…."

She didn't have to explain to me. I was harsh on her before, but Talina had been right when she said everyone had a place. I knew exactly where nonconforming led you.

I gave her a wan smile. "Lainie's grieving for her brother. It takes time. She didn't mean what she said."

"Talina," an overly saccharine voice called.

We turned to find a young woman in a backless ruby ballgown, the long train held off the floor by two women hired for the occasion. The girl's stunning blonde hair had been arranged in a pinned braid, curls cascading to brush the back of her shoulders. Silver stars had been clipped into the braid, glistening no matter what angle she turned her slim neck. She had the grace of a swan and the ability to finesse the hardest crowd. The entourage of men around her was evidence of that. She laughed sweetly, but there was a fire about her that threatened to burn you if you dared cross her path, visible by the way she examined me and my dress. Those silver-grey eyes were like molten metal.

Talina went stiff with surprise. "Countess. What an honour."

It was evident from the way Talina's lips curled into a smile of pure delight that she really did think this was an honour. And she curtsied. Yes, curtsied.

I snorted.

Up close, the countess had pouty lips I'd only seen on fashion starlets and perfect, unblemished skin. Her friends took up flanking positions around her, hangers-on that would never live up to the flawless good looks or supremacy of their queen bee. Every man and boy in the vicinity stared at the girls, rapt and open-mouthed.

The countess took Talina's hand and kissed both her cheeks. "How good it is to see you again, my dearest Talina. You're looking well." She flashed a set of pearl white teeth.

Talina's face glowed with happiness, her fight with Lainie forgotten as she delved into conversation with the countess.

"This is just like high school," a voice whispered into my ear.

Lainie had returned. She winked at me, her eyes glittering and ready for a challenge.

"Is that how you know the countess?" I asked. "From school?"

"Hell no. Indree's a few years older than us. Talina and I had the unfortunate pleasure of meeting the countess at social gatherings in Accrington. She's from a wealthy family—very influential in the Free Zones. Indree was conscripted as a nurse, but her father paid a large sum to the council to keep her out of harm's way. Rumour has it she's never treated a soldier for anything more than a common cold." Her eyes swept dangerously toward the countess. "Don't be fooled by her frivolity. She's a nasty piece of work."

I couldn't resist the urge to laugh. "I kind of figured that out already, thanks."

Actually, I knew exactly what type of girl the countess was—a backstabbing, lie-spreading devourer of souls. She could raise you to fame or destroy you. Every institution had one, and I was about to come face to face with Tarahik's.

Indree tapped Talina on the shoulder with her feather fan. "Aren't you going to introduce me to your lovely friend? She's all anyone is talking about."

Overcome by nervous giggles, Talina made the introduction. "Indree, this is Zaya Wayward. Zaya, this is Countess Indree Raminorf."

I forced myself to smile pleasantly and not set the countess's ridiculously large dress alight.

Indree's face was perfectly sweet. A slight curl on her upper lip was her only downfall. "It's a pleasure to meet you, Zaya. What a pretty dress you're wearing. Silk, is it? Don't sit down too long in that. Black silk sticks to your worst parts. It positively looks like seal blubber."

Her friends laughed around her.

Confidence flared inside me. "Are you talking from experience?"

Indree's eyebrows lifted into cold arches. My response was evidently not what she'd hoped. She brushed my question off with a wave of her feather fan. "I understand you're here on scholarship."

Holy casters! She's already had her minions out sniffing for information.

"You must be extremely accomplished," she continued. It was evident from her voice that this information was anything but agreeable to her. Her fake civility infuriated me. If someone jabbed a thermometer in my mouth, it would read a hundred degrees.

I plastered on an indifferent smile. "I am, thank you."

I knew how to play this game. She was sizing me up, seeing if I could be coerced into becoming one of her lackeys. She'd learn the hard way that I wouldn't be intimidated.

Talina was blissfully ignorant of the cool reception among us. She was like a puppy, eagerly trying to please the countess for a reward. "Zaya is looking to apply for a transfer from the infantry to nursing. Perhaps you could help her?"

Indree's eyes swept me up and down, as if I weren't up to the task. "Is that so?" It was a look that would have a normal girl's stomach spiralling down to her feet. "I'll be sure to put in a good word for you."

I beamed at her. "I'd be very grateful, but I'd rather achieve this on my own. In these troubling times, one must learn not to depend on others."

Indree's nose twitched, like she'd inhaled something nasty. "Of course."

Placing another kiss on Talina's cheek and ignoring Lainie entirely, the countess sashayed away.

Talina bounced on her heels. "Isn't she wonderful?"

I exhaled a scathing breath. "She's certainly something."

Something I don't want around when I have a loaded cast-shooter in my hand.

A large gong chimed, the deep succession ringing through the auditorium. People made their way toward the dining tables, which had been set with silver utensils and stunning flower arrangements.

Lainie took my hand. "I found our place cards before. We're over this way."

We found our table and hadn't been seated long when I felt eyes on the back of my head. The countess watched me from her troop of admirers at the next table. If looks could kill, I'd be carried out of the auditorium in a body bag.

CHAPTER FOURTEEN

Dinner was a surprise. Platters of grilled scallops, olives, soft cheeses, and exotic fruits were served, followed by a large banquet. Guests helped themselves to seconds and thirds. It bothered me that so much was wasted. At Gosheniene, we were fed the minimum tasteless gruel, which was never enough to leave you satisfied. There'd been nights where I'd gone to bed with pain in my stomach, as though the organ had shrivelled up in an endeavour not to eat itself. Prisoners had shared stories of bartering for simple things like eggs and meat in the provinces. The alternative was to steal. I put my knife and fork down, tasting raw emotion in my throat.

"Gotcha!" A tall lanky young man with a mop of messy blond hair dropped into the seat next to Lainie and dug his fingers playfully into her ribs.

She jumped like a jack-in-the-box. "Edric, you moron. You nearly made me spill my drink." She gazed at him with bright eyes. Forgetting formality—or just ignoring it—she pulled the stranger in for a long passionate kiss. Scratch that. It looked like two dogs sharing a scoop of ice cream. My nose scrunched in disgust. Was this Lainie's shameless way of giving the finger to the obnoxious, prissy cream of society? She'd already showed the telltale signs of being wasted: talking too loudly, laughing, stumbling. These were not the sort of people to make a scene in front of. A few of the guests at our table regarded her with abject horror, their forks frozen halfway to their mouths. Others glared with eyes so sharp, they looked capable of slicing glass. I squirmed in my seat. Lainie was already playing with fire, and kissing at the dinner table was like dousing those flames with gasoline.

Talina clicked her fingers at the love-struck couple. "Hello. People are trying to eat."

The pair ignored her.

Talina bit her lip in exasperation and passed me an apologetic look. "This is Edric Holloway. He was a year above Lainie and me at Accrington High. He's also Lainie's fiancé." She didn't sound like she approved of that last part. She took a carrot from her plate and tossed it at the pair. "Get a room."

Fiancé?

I knew people rushed into things and married young because of the war—but at nineteen and twenty? Lainie was still two years away from the legal age to wed. A lot could change in that time.

Edric pulled away with a dopey grin. "Wow."

Talina's eyes looked capable of shooting lightning. "Yeah. Wow. We've all lost our appetites. You two know better than to eat each other's faces at a public event."

Edric shot her the finger, but his smile was sweet and good humoured. His eyes found mine. "Hi. You must be the new roommate." He reached across the table and shook my hand.

"Hello." I couldn't prevent a stunned laugh. He had Lainie's black lipstick around his mouth.

Lainie wiped his lips with a napkin. Even with all that white goth make-up, her skin glowed. "Edric is in his second year of service to the Haxsan Guard as a trained fighter pilot." Her voice brimmed with pride and happiness. It was the first time I'd seen anything genuine about her.

The young man tipped his head in a modest bow. His shoulder-length hair curled under his jaw, wild and golden in the candlelight. He must have been going for that bohemian tortured artist look. Either that or he let his bed style it in the mornings. "I haven't seen any fighting yet, just been sent on rescue operations—flying in to aid people affected by the war, that sort of thing." A blush crept into his cheeks.

I warmed to Edric immediately because he was the opposite of everyone in the room. He'd ignored the dress code, or rather gone overboard with it, completing his look with chunky platform boots, a cowboy duster, a pair of aviation goggles around his neck, and a seriously large top hat that did a poor job hiding his unkempt hair. I'd never seen such a bizarre dress sense, but on him it worked. With his dorky grin and cheeky dimples, his presence could lift the darkest mood.

He's perfect for Lainie.

I hadn't known the pair for long, but there was no doubting the affection they had for each other when their eyes met. In any other circumstance, I would have said they were lucky. But we were living on the edge of a centuries-fought war and were soon to be thrown into the centre of its battle. I'd watched couples torn apart in Gosheniene. I'd witnessed men burying their dead wives in the camp's makeshift cemetery, seen women weeping over pictures of the men they'd lost in battle. I didn't envy them. And I didn't envy what Lainie and Edric faced. I'd decided long ago it was better to be alone in this world.

Lainie leaned in and kissed Edric on the cheek. "Where have you been? Dinner is nearly over."

Edric scratched at his eyebrow. "I've been with Captain Arden and his squadron," he admitted in a small voice.

"You what?" Lainie looked capable of spitting fire.

A weird, pent-up energy built inside me. Hearing Captain Arden's name had made the ground feel unsteady beneath my feet.

Please… please… do not let Edric and the captain be friends. I don't want to be in the company of that egotistic, condescending bastard.

Edric cast a furtive glance behind him. "Listen. I'm not supposed to say anything, but the three of you heard about the lycanthors outside the celestial shield, right?"

We nodded.

Talina's eyes went from concerned to alarmed. "Everyone knows. It's all anyone is talking about. Why? What's happened?"

Edric stiffened. "One of the lycanthors got through the shield."

"What?" I was too stunned to come up with any other response.

A note of incredulity crept into Talina's voice. "But that's not possible.

Nothing passes the celestial shield."

I recalled what Captain Arden had conveyed on the carrier-hornet. *The invisible boundary surrounds the base and keeps dissent rebels out. Any unauthorised entries are obliterated by magic."*

Was it possible someone had granted the creature access from the inside?

Lainie entwined her fingers with Edric's. "Are you being serious, Ed? This isn't one of your odd jokes, is it?"

He smiled, but his lips were tense. "I wouldn't joke about something like this, L. Captain Arden's worried. A lycanthor has never crossed a celestial shield before, but that's not the troubling part." He brought a glass of water to his mouth and guzzled it down. "No one knows how the creature did it."

Talina brushed a hand through her thick honey blonde waves; it seemed to be her go-to action whenever she was uneasy or nervous. "But they have the lycanthor in custody, right?"

The young fighter pilot shook his head, his expression hard but focused. "It got away. Captain Arden doesn't believe it was trying to hurt anyone.

Lainie's black lips were agape. "It's a lycanthor. What else could have been its motive?"

My skin prickled. "To create panic."

Three sets of eyes stared at me as though I'd manifested a second head.

I ignored their doubtful looks. "This wasn't about a lycanthor finding a pre-dinner snack. The creature was acting for the ULD. The goal was to show us we're not safe behind the shields."

Talina's face clouded with hesitance. "Maybe. But that's not really the ULD's style."

I gave a harsh laugh. "It's a war. The ULD depend on tactics, not style."

Lainie's fingers tightened around Edric's. In his presence, she seemed calmer and stronger. She was sobering up. "Is the shield still down?"

He traced his thumb along hers. "Colonel Harper reinstated the protective spells. Only part of the shield went down. I saw it with my own eyes. It was smashed, like someone had opened a doorway into the shield. There was ice everywhere. It was in the trees and the surrounding forest. The leaves on the ground were curled over and frozen. I'd never seen anything like it before. Not for this time of year anyway."

Ice.

A strange pressure built in my head. It couldn't be possible. But the evidence was indisputable.

She's followed me here. The black-veined woman.

Something sickly trickled down the back of my throat. The auditorium didn't appear so large or impressive now. The high ceilings and walls seemed to be closing in. My breathing felt constricted.

Panic. It was devouring me.

Is she here now? Somewhere on the grounds?

My eyes moved rapidly along the crowd, expecting to find a cold, dead face covered in veins among them.

My voice shook with terror. "I must talk to the commander. Now. It's urgent."

Talina's upper body went ramrod straight. "You can't talk to the commander, okay? We've been through this."

I flinched at how naïve she was in the face of this danger. "I wouldn't ask if it—"

A haunting, melancholic tune swept into the auditorium, the orchestra's percussions graceful but dark, the drums deep and shaking the air, as though a peel of thunder had echoed across the ceiling.

The conversation in the hall shut off in abrupt silence. The guests stood, turning as one to the front of the auditorium, where a large theatre curtain rolled back, not revealing a stage but a magnificent building of black rock that stood like an ancient monument, its tribune stand walled off by giant guardrails. Banners, tapestries, and flags with the council's Infinite Eye emblem fluttered from its towers. The facade was ornamented with statues of warlords thrusting their weapons as though battle were imminent. It was an impressive structure... and overbearing.

A lump stuck in my throat. The atmosphere in the room had changed. The crowd applauded and blew kisses to the Infinite Eye. Some even wolf-whistled. The fervour moved in a wave across the auditorium, everyone caught in mass hypnosis.

Talina nudged my elbow. "Zaya. Stand. Otherwise, they'll think you're saying something."

Edric and Lainie were on their feet, both zapped of energy, their faces beaten down. I stood, clapping with the crowd and not understanding why. A strange coldness gripped my chest. I must have looked like a toy monkey playing the cymbals, robotic and stilted.

I nudged closer to Talina. "What's going on?"

But there was no time for her to answer.

Commander Macaslan appeared behind the tribune stand. She looked more imposing now then she had in her office. Her wide gaze raked over the hall, a hawk peering over her dominion. The applause settled, the energy in the room now quiet with anticipation.

Macaslan tilted her head to the microphone. "Good evening. I'd like to cordially welcome our guests to the Tarahik initiation ceremony. Every year, young men and women from across the globe commence their training for the Haxsan Guard. To our young cadets, it is an honour to be selected for the Tarahik Military Base. No matter what your position, understand that at Tarahik you are expected to take responsibility, show obedience, comradeship, and an excellent level of physical strength. Above all, you are expected to attain results and make the council proud."

She didn't say what the repercussions would be for failure. I imagined it went beyond dungeons and lock-ups.

Her voice sliced through the silent tension. "Tonight, in front of our illustrious guests, family, and friends, our cadets will recite their oath of allegiance. This pledge is a contract that will bind them to their oath for the entirety of their service to the Haxsan Guard. As is customary, I would like you to kindly receive General Marcelo Kravis, who will conduct the initiation ceremony."

More applause spilled through the hall. General Kravis took to the stand. He was tall, his wild hair reaching past his shoulders and tinged with grey. He had a rectangular face with a pointed jaw, his Van Dyke beard doing little to hide the deep scar that ran past his nose and through his lips. I wondered if he'd been sliced by a blade at some point. Even from this distance, the scar had a raised, puckered quality about it. Large screens had been placed around the auditorium. A close-up revealed the general smiling to the crowd, but there was a lethal glimmer in his eyes. I suspected he had a temperament that could change faster than the wind. Disagree with him and he'd be the snake lying in wait, ready to strike.

General Kravis silenced the crowd with a wave. "Good evening. We are here, all of us, to achieve a common goal—the annihilation of the ULD."

A satisfied cheer broke through the assembly. My palms turned sweaty; my cheeks flushed. A fever had started among the horde.

General Kravis held out his hands, calming the audience. His voice was charming and in control, but there was a deceptive layer of cajoling underneath that no one seemed to identify. I wasn't imagining things. The more I studied Kravis's face on the screen, the less I trusted him.

His lips curled into a trace of a smile. "I am going to begin with a story. Until twenty years ago, it was a time of amity and goodwill, where all casters were united under the Infinite Eye, dedicated to protecting and serving humans. Back then, our common enemy was lycanthors, who hunted humans for sport. We have been at war with lycanthors for centuries. Out in the provinces, the Haxsan Guard was formed to defend the human population, to safeguard the Free Zones and destroy lycanthors. And for centuries, these laws were upheld without animosity. We were winning the war against lycanthors."

A stirring swept through the crowd, but no one disputed what was said. Talina gave me a cautious glance, most likely worried by my fisted hands. Sure, what General Kravis said was true, but it was mixed with half-truths. Lycanthors didn't choose to hunt humans for sport. Humans had been lycanthors' food source, just like fish were for bears and hares were for wolves. I found it cruel and wished it otherwise, but lycanthors weren't intentionally brutal. They were just another predator in the natural order.

Kravis released a slow breath. "Twenty years ago, everything changed. The uprising was led by a man who united ungrateful, seditious casters from the provinces. He believed that the age of humans was over. That nature chose for them to be extinct, and by keeping them alive, we were going against the natural order. He incited hatred toward humans living in the Free Zones. This caster was a visionary and an enthusiast and, in the end, a mass killer. You know this man as Morgomoth."

This time, the assembly burst into an uproar. It seemed incredible that these polished, pompous guests could suddenly turn into a livid, raging crowd.

Not much was known about Morgomoth. The council had seen to that. But from what I'd read in history texts back at Brendlash, Morgomoth had been the most depraved, cruel, and homicidal conqueror the world had known. He'd spoken of peace, of equality, but incited fascist ideals that resulted in years of war and carnage. I'd seen a photograph of him in one of those history books, taken when he was a young man, around the age I was now. He'd had innocent, boyish good looks back then—but the eyes were a startling grey, like flecks of steel. The colour reminded me of poison-tipped blades. A photo could capture many things, and it didn't take a genius to see the rage that pounded behind those eyes.

"Enjoying the festivities?" a voice whispered in my ear.

I spun around. Seeing Marek's face brought a sense of ease to my chest. "What are you doing here? I thought this was only for cadets... and guests." I let the caustic lilt in my voice let him know what I thought of that last part.

His lip twitched. "I'm a sergeant. I can go where I please. You didn't answer my question."

I surveyed the crowd. "I admit I'm not entirely sure what I'm listening to. Is this a ceremony or a rally?"

The sergeant inclined his head. "It's both."

Up on the tribune stand, the general urged everyone to settle down, his voice flowing like honey over the audience, slow and smooth. "Morgomoth believed lycanthors were put on this Earth to wipe out humans. This doctrine was endorsed by lycanthors. Together, along with Morgomoth's followers, they became known as the United League of Dissent. Their goal? To overthrow the council, open the borders of the Free Zones, and eradicate human existence. They brought a reign of terror to the world. Morgomoth may be gone— vanquished a decade ago—but his dissent rebels are still out there, upholding him as a martyr and fighting for his cause."

The audience watched, transfixed. No one disputed what was said. Apart from a few people who looked down at their feet, there was no remonstration.

On the screen, the general's eyes burned with cruel intensity. "That is why you are here, cadets. You need to be formidable, remorseless, unyielding if you want to stop the ULD and preserve our way of life. It is lycanthors that need to be exterminated from the Earth, not humans. And these rebel casters—the filth that call themselves dissent rebels—need to be taught to respect the council. They need to be punished for their alliance with the ULD. If they refuse, they will meet the same fate the lycanthors are dealt." His thin eyebrows knitted together. "The United League of Dissent despises us for everything we have built, for everything we have achieved. We must work together to preserve our beliefs and principles." He raised his hand in salute to the Infinite Eye. "Everyone for the Council. No one outside the Council. No one against the Council."

A unified, energetic roar burst through the auditorium.

Blood rushed to my head. I agreed the ULD had to be stopped, but this wasn't the way. I'd met dissent rebels in Gosheniene. They'd been casters struggling to survive in the provinces, forced to grow food they weren't entitled to eat, coerced into manufacturing goods they couldn't utilise, and conscripted into a cause they didn't believe in. Everything they worked for went to the Free Zones. There was no mystery why these people joined the ULD. The only thing they'd understood was that the ULD offered them a new way of life.

Marek caught my eye. His lips twisted into a sad smile. "You know, the Infinite Eye derived from the Eye of Providence, something our human ancestors looked up to and worshipped before the change."

I gazed around at the hungry, seething crowd. "I think it's lost its meaning over the centuries."

General Kravis tapped the microphone, rallying everyone's attention. He raised his left hand to his chest. "It's now time for our cadets to declare their loyalty to the Council of the Founding Sovereigns."

In unison, cadets around the room copied the general, hands pressed tight over their hearts. Mine beat fast beneath the fabric of my dress. Words appeared in a stanza on the screen above the tribune stand. Everyone spoke together.

"I swear this sacred pledge: I will be faithful and submit unconditional obedience to the Council of the Founding Sovereigns. I will uphold its principles and shall always be prepared to give my life for this oath. This is my pledge of allegiance to the Council of the Founding Sovereigns."

A searing pain erupted across my palm, as though someone had jabbed my hand with a red-hot poker. The Infinite Eye burned into my palm. It was a mark—a brand identifying ownership by the council. Next to me, Talina clutched her hand and blinked back tears. I knew her fear mirrored mine. Lainie bit her lip, refusing to look at her palm while Edric caressed it.

"Thank you," General Kravis said into the microphone. "That concludes the initiation ceremony. It is truly heartening to see the loyalty of our new recruits. I pray your tenacity and resilience will bring a swift demise to the crisis we face."

The crowd shrank, dispersing to the doors now designated as exits.

"What the hell?" I cried. The burn on my palm had left an unpleasant, tingling sensation on my skin, which grew worse the longer it was exposed to air. The edges of the symbol were blistered and black. I couldn't escape Tarahik now. I was bound by a magical contract.

"Welcome to the Haxsan Guard," Lainie said with bitter enthusiasm. She grabbed Edric's arm and propelled him toward the bar. "I need a drink."

I tried to wrap my exhausted brain around the idea that I was never getting out of here. I felt deceived, duped, tricked. I was so frazzled by what had occurred that it took me a moment to realise I was being watched. The sensation became so acute, I couldn't ignore it.

On the tribune stand, Captain Arden stared. I squirmed under the intensity of his gaze. A hot flush spread over my skin. I'd never cared about what others thought of me, but at that moment, his opinion mattered. It was as though—but I knew it to be impossible—he'd seen my defiance while the general had spoken.

A man in a grey suit with white-blond hair approached the young captain and whispered into his ear. My chest felt hollow. I didn't get a good luck at the newcomer, but somehow, I knew him. Memory pricked at my scalp, but the recollection remained buried deep.

I craned my neck and stood on tiptoes to get a better view, but the tribune stand was inundated with guests now, and I couldn't spot the pair. And yet I felt as though their eyes were still on me.

Talina cast a glance at the tribune stand. "Who are you looking at?"

Somehow, I remembered how to talk. "No one. At least, no one important."

I walked away, ignoring the sensation of eyes on the back of my head.

CHAPTER FIFTEEN

That night, my worst memory returned, tainting my dreams like a contagion.

Adaline had been dead for twenty-four hours. At least, she was found dead twenty-fours ago. I'd been incarcerated for twenty-two. The interrogation cell they'd held me in was a bleak, square room with grey bricks, grey floor, grey ceiling. Very unimaginative. An air conditioner circulated cool air, sending a ripple of goosebumps up my arms. My pyjamas seemed to cling to me like a chilly second skin, the trouser ends wet—a result from standing on the cold, frosted floor of the crime scene.

Strange that it hasn't dried after all these hours.

But there was nothing normal about room 216, or the wraith that had lurked in the shadows, smirking at Adaline's lifeless body. Not that I'd told the authorities about that last part. Whenever I thought about the black-veined woman, I questioned whether I'd truly woken. Surely I was asleep and this was a horrible nightmare.

I looked at the one-way glass window, certain someone monitored from the other side. I knew because I sensed their beady eyes on me.

Perhaps I should give them the finger for good measure.

I'd been questioned eight times in the space of a few hours. But now? Nothing.

Why have they left me alone? Why won't they tell me what's going on?

Every minute that passed added to my misery. I slumped in my chair, my body fragile and my head weak. There was plenty of room in the cell to pace, but I remained at the table, my stiff muscles protesting at the thought of physical activity. I was positive if I stood, my legs would flop like wilted flowers.

A buzzer broke the intense silence. My heart leapt with anticipation. The solid steel doors slid open, and a woman emerged. She was dressed in an expensive white suit, her blonde hair pulled back in an elegant braid, her make-up flawless. In her presence, the room filled with the wonderful scent of vanilla, but I knew by the way her lips pulled into a satisfied leer that she was anything but sweet. The *click, click, click* of her pointed heels made the headache in the back of my skull pound harder. I shut my eyes for a second, hoping the strain would go away.

She sat opposite me, her blue eyes bright and unblinking behind her metal-framed glasses. "Hello, Zaya. I've been sent here for a little chat."

She said "little chat" like we were about to be waited on with tea and biscuits.

I pressed my lips together to prevent my mounting anxiety from showing. Something was wrong. This woman looked… hungry. Her red lipstick made her lips monstrously large, as though she might gobble me up for dinner and use my bones for toothpicks.

She set her hands on the table and tapped her long manicured nails. "My name is Clarita Davies. Miss Davies to you. Thank you for your cooperation. I know this hasn't been easy."

I remained tight-lipped.

Miss Davies's fake smile grew larger. "Unfortunately, there are parts of your story that don't add up."

I fiddled with my wet sleeve. "There is a lot about this that doesn't add up."

She gave a hollow chuckle. "Indeed. To start with, forensics have confirmed that Adaline wasn't long dead when you entered her bedroom. Not even a minute. And then there is the door. You said it was open."

I nodded. "It was."

"Mr Colfringe was the hall monitor on duty. He went past room 216 five minutes before Adaline's death and confirmed the door was shut. Your bedroom door was closed too, and yet you stated that it was open when you woke."

My heart began thrumming in my ears. "It was. Someone must have opened it after Mr Colfringe left."

Someone being the black-veined woman.

Miss Davies arched her swanlike neck. "Mr Colfringe stated that when he found you standing over Adaline's body, the door was shut."

"Maybe... I don't know. But I didn't shut it."

"So if we were to examine the door handle, your fingerprints wouldn't be on it?"

"What does the door have to do with this?" The panic I'd worked hard to hide climbed to the surface.

"The door has everything to do with this. The tiny details are what solve crimes." Miss Davies leaned forward with a heavy sigh, but underneath I sensed she was brimming with excitement. "Zaya, it's time to come clean."

I tilted my head, questioning what she was referring to. She couldn't mean the black-veined woman... could she? Ghosts didn't exist in our world, or so the council had said. But I knew better. Did Miss Davies know better too?

She looked at me like I was on the highway to Crazyville, with no possible turn-off. "You killed Adaline White, didn't you?"

Blind panic seized me. I stood up, almost knocking over my chair. "I didn't. I told you what happened."

Mixed with some half-truths, but she didn't need to know that.

Miss Davies shook her head. "The council doesn't blame you for what happened, Zaya. When adolescent casters specialise in their powers for the first time... well, it can be an overwhelming experience. The magic takes over. Young casters are powerless to do anything when they're untrained." Her face morphed into an expression of tenderness and concern, but that was all it was—an expression. "We know you didn't intend to kill Adaline. Ice magic is an incredibly rare gift. If left untrained, it will not only be dangerous for others but you as well. Sadly, the girl's family doesn't see it that way. The Whites wish for the full force of the law to be brought upon you. The council are of another opinion."

Before I could utter a word, she cut me off. "Admit that you killed Adaline White by accident, and you serve four months in Denveitch Mental Asylum, where you will be properly taken care of and taught to control your magic."

The tension I'd been experiencing all day grew impossibly thick in my chest. "But I didn't kill her. I don't have magic. I never specialised."

Miss Davies took her glasses off and massaged the bridge of her nose. "There was no one else in the room. There was no sign of a break-in. You were the last person to enter room 216 before Adaline's death. Did the two of you have a fight?"

My heart sank. "It wasn't me."

Miss Davies inhaled a sharp breath. "Claiming that you haven't specialised won't help you. It won't give you a pass to the Free Zones. They will test your blood for magical properties, and when it returns positive, you will be in a far worse predicament than you are now." She scooted closer to the desk. "Admit that you killed Adaline White. The Denveitch Mental Asylum is the best possible outcome for you."

"I will not admit to something I didn't do."

The cutting glint in Miss Davies's eyes told me that was exactly what she wanted to hear. "Then I'm afraid you have sealed your fate. You will be transferred to Gosheniene Internment Camp."

A shudder of foreboding crept along my bones. "But… I didn't do it."

Miss Davies didn't respond. She moved to the door and pressed the buzzer. Two Haxsan Guard soldiers entered the room. There was nowhere to run. They chained my hands together and restrained my arms, using more force than was necessary.

Miss Davies shot me a triumphant look. "Crime cannot go unpunished. There is a carrier-hornet waiting to take you to Gosheniene."

I dug my heels into the ground, but my captors were too strong. They tugged me into the hall where Miss Davies waited, still smiling. After spending such long hours in the cold, florescent-lit cell, the passage was humid and dark. I felt as though I'd been pushed into an oven.

My head was in shock, my lips working without any control from me. "I didn't do it. I didn't do it."

Miss Davies's heels *clicked, clicked, clicked* in the shadows ahead.

I attempted to kick one of my guards in the shin. He responded by ramming his fist into my stomach. The pain blazed like an uncontained fire. I didn't say anything after that. The wind had been knocked out of me, my breathing slow and weak.

The guard tossed me over his shoulder like a sack of wheat. "Gosheniene is your home now, kid. No point complaining. There are plenty of innocent casters in that place. The council doesn't care that you're one of them."

Pain coursed through my body as though it were poison. My vision fluctuated in and out.

"Miss Davies," a voice demanded.

I lifted my head but struggled to make sense of the image before me. A man stood ahead of Miss Davies. He had silver-white hair and an immaculate tailored suit, but his face was lost in the shadows. His breathing sounded furious and heavy. "Where are you taking this girl?"

Miss Davies's voice was sweeter than honey. "To Gosheniene, of course. She has committed a crime and must be punished."

"The council didn't come to that decision. You did," the man argued. "This girl needs to be brought before a tribunal where the evidence can be properly assessed."

This time, Miss Davies sounded throaty and tense. "It has been assessed. Zaya is guilty. She goes to Gosheniene. Stop interfering with affairs that have nothing to do with you, Senator Kerr."

Miss Davies's heels started up again. My guards pursued her down the passage, each bump sending stabs of agony through my torso. I lifted my head to gaze at the man with silver-white hair.

Senator Kerr. Why is a senator here for me?

The darkness closed around him. My head drifted down. I collapsed in a pathetic heap on my captor's shoulder.

My eyes snapped open with a panicked flinch. Every part of me was alert, my body hot and sick as though a flaming coal had sunk in my gut.

Senator Kerr.

The man with the silver-white hair.

The man who had stood beside Captain Arden on the tribune stand.

I knew I'd seen him before.

I sat up, my chest and back slick with sweat. Outside, a pall of moonlight shone through the window, but still that sombre darkness crept into my room, playing tricks with my eyes. Even the wind started to sound like whispers, as though something was trying to beckon its way through the window.

I dropped my face into my hands.

Why had Senator Kerr tried to interfere with my sentencing? Did he know me? Did he know something about my life before the orphanage and my amnesia? Did he know about... the black-veined woman?

Who is Senator Kerr to me?

What is his connection to Captain Arden?

I slumped back onto my pillow, wishing my mind would wander off to a better place. A happy place. Or better still, to an empty, blank nothing. No more nightmares. No more pain. Just sleep.

Something bright and colourful caught my eye. Macaslan's dreamcatcher was on the side table.

It can't hurt to try.

I hung it above my bed, letting it dangle from the overhead light—which was useless to me thanks to the power being switched off.

Okay, Macaslan. Let's see if your spells really work.

I settled back into bed. My mysterious connection to the senator restlessly stirred in my mind for some minutes, but as my eyelids grew heavy, my mind slipped away into a deeper, darker place.

I didn't dream about Senator Kerr.

Or Miss Davies.

Or the black-veined woman.

It didn't bother me when something stronger than the wind rattled my bedroom window.

I was mercifully pulled into the dark.

CHAPTER SIXTEEN

I missed orientation. And lunch. And dinner. I'd slept nearly twenty hours straight. Talina and Lainie had joked that they thought I'd fallen into a coma when I finally emerged from my room. Perhaps I had. For the first time in two years, I'd slept without interruption. I felt strong, clear-headed, and energised. I spent the evening curled up on the sofa, listening to Talina's and Lainie's wild stories about Accrington High and their lives in the Free Zones. At lights out, we called it a night. I went to bed, comforted by the knowledge that the dreamcatcher would protect me.

I slept so well that in the morning, I had to run to first period. I slipped into the indoor firing range, hoping my late arrival wouldn't make a scene. Walking on eggshells was an understatement; I felt like I was tiptoeing across a field of unexploded bombs.

Colonel Harper's face settled into a sneer when he saw me. "Wayward! You're late."

The class eyed me with quick curiosity, enjoying my disgrace.

So much for sneaking in unobserved.

Harper fixed me with a cold stare. "Please enlighten us. What has been so pressing of your time?" Those blue eyes of his were like a mountain lake, pleasant to behold but flooding with danger underneath.

I was certain telling him I'd slept in wasn't going to cut it. Refusing to crack, I held my head high and strode across the firing range, taking my place among the other cadets. "I got lost, sir. But thank you for your concern."

"Concern?" He tilted his head at me.

Evidently, I'd ruined what was going to be a humiliating lecture.

Stupid man.

Did he honestly think he could shame me in front of the class? Me? Who'd been stripped of dignity so many times in the labour camp I'd lost count. I'd once been forced to surrender all my clothing, left out in the cold with nothing but a pathetic shift to cover my privates. That punishment had gone on for two days without food or warmth. Colonel Harper's strict address was nothing. Once you'd dealt with hunger and cold, there were very few things that could break you.

Colonel Harper projected his voice for us all to hear. "Now that we are all in attendance, class can begin." He steered his way through the cadets, his dark cloak waving behind him like the large wings of a bat. "From this lesson on, you will undertake exercises that will equip you for your deployment in the armed forces. I am not here to care for you, guide you, or counsel you. I'm here to train you for the Haxsan Guard. Today, you will learn target shooting. This is no easy feat, and I want you to listen attentively to the drill instructor I assign you to."

He pointed across the range. Six soldiers stood at the shooting gallery, two women and four men, each wearing a different colour armband. They were all in their forties except one. The last guy was young.

Holy frigging casters! How long has he been here?

Tall, stern, and stone-faced, Captain Arden looked like he'd been chiselled out of rock. He watched us cadets with impassive boredom, but when his eyes caught mine, a hint of irritation rose in his cheeks.

Harper leafed through the pages on his clipboard. "I have divided the class into groups of six. Each team will be recognised by a colour and assigned to a mentor. When I call your name, move to your Drill Instructor. Taza Allsworth… blue. Petric Baxter… red. Rebabius Clawson… yellow."

No second guesses whose name was last on the list.

"Zaya Wayward," Harper finally called after the class had been successfully allocated. The colonel peered from his clipboard, eyes still winter cold. The teams were evenly numbered, and it didn't take a genius to figure out which group I'd been assigned to. "Black."

With about as much enthusiasm as a prisoner walking to the gallows, I joined Jad's team. The captain didn't respond to me like he had the other cadets—he'd shaken each of their hands, but all I received was a silent nod. He led us to the shooting gallery where life-size plywood targets of men and women stood, each with different skin, hair, and eye colours. Their expressions ranged from scared to threatening to savage.

"We're beginning with stationary target practice," the captain explained. He directed us to the booths numbered from one to six. I was sent to the last one, the farthest from him. He began by outlining the safety instructions and training us in the use of different cast-shooters—handguns, revolvers, rifles. Some of the cadets bounced on the balls of their feet, eager to get started. Others looked as though they wanted to melt into the ground. The shooting gallery was spotless and sterile, with reinforced baffles along the walls. I assembled my cast-shooter and watched the cadets fire a few rounds. Some of them were good, just a few inches off the targets—which made me think mummy and daddy had paid for private target practice before—while others missed entirely, their bullets hitting the sloped walls. Jad observed each cadet and offered his expert opinion, making small adjustments to position and timing where needed.

When he reached my booth, his enthusiasm deflated like a balloon. "Okay, Frost Face. Let's see what you've got?"

My finger stiffened on the trigger. "Frost Face? What's that supposed to mean?"

"It means you're a hard person to get along with."

Huh. He had no idea.

I focused on the target, but something about its smiling face bothered me. This was meant to represent a real person, someone who was loved and important to a family. Perhaps the breadwinner? Or the nurturer? And I was expected to put a bullet in their head? My legs suddenly felt as stable as water.

"What are you waiting for?" The harshness in Jad's voice startled me.

Get it together, Zaya. This is just like those times when you threw rocks at cans. You never missed then. You won't miss now.

My plywood target was male, tall, with incredible dark curls. How convenient. I inhaled a breath, lined up the barrel of my cast-shooter with the target, and fired three consecutive rounds. My technique wasn't bad. I hit each solid black circle on the head, chest, and stomach. The boys in the class gave an appreciative whistle. Some of the girls clapped and yelled praise. Their dislike for me seemed to have faded from their faces.

Jad's black eyes were riveted on me. A sequence of emotions ran across his face—puzzlement, confusion—before finally settling on one I couldn't determine. Maybe showing off hadn't been such a smart idea.

"Keep practicing," he yelled to the class.

The cadets busied themselves with their weapons. Other than gunshots, a thick silence enveloped the room.

Jad pulled me aside, his gaze intense on mine. When he spoke, his tone bordered on spite. "Who taught you to shoot?"

I didn't know whether he dug his nails intentionally in my arm or if his hardened anger had made him lose focus.

I peered at him through my dark tangle of hair, my heart still stammering from the surprise of his malice. "No one. It was beginner's luck."

The corner of his mouth twitched. "I don't believe that for a second."

"Maybe I taught myself." I tugged my arm free, resisting the temptation to knee him where it would hurt.

He laughed without humour. "I don't believe that either. You shoot like a dissent rebel."

A shiver of apprehension crept through me. It had felt natural, easy, when I'd finally summoned the courage to shoot the target. Amnesia had wiped clear the first ten years of my life, but had this new-found talent been there all along—something trained and instilled in me, lying dormant until it was needed?

My parents are not dissent rebels. I know it in my heart.
But the heart doesn't always get things right.

The captain drew near, perhaps sensing my internal struggle. Feeling him so close made me catch my breath. I realised my frustration wasn't about target practice. It was about him. Why was he so awful to me? Why was he ready to believe what everyone else said about me rather than believe the truth?

Jad glanced over his shoulder, making sure our conversation wasn't overheard. His eyes snapped back to mine. "No one knows your true identity. I don't care where you're from or what your past was. As far as I'm concerned, you're here with the Haxsan Guard. But if the other officers at the base see something like that, they won't turn a blind eye like I have. They'll be suspicious."

"Suspicious of what?" I tipped my head to look him in the eye, which was difficult considering he was a foot taller than me. "So I shoot like a dissent rebel. It doesn't mean I'm one of them." The confidence in my voice faltered. I was losing my edge. "I have good aim from practise. I used to throw stones at cans in Gosheniene."

It sounded lame even to my own ears.

Jad kept his voice low and cryptic. "You don't know your own past. For all we know, you could be ULD. If General Kravis learns of your shooting skill, there will be no reasoning with him. He will remove you."

The panic inside me detonated. By "remove," Jad didn't mean I'd be shipped to another base or a labour camp. He meant permanently removed by lethal injection. There would be no trial, no evidence, just straight to execution. That was what happened to soldiers who were spies for the ULD. And if people saw me shoot like a dissent rebel, that was what they'd conjecture. Explanation and understanding didn't work in this world.

"Tone it down. Miss a few of the targets," Jad advised. "Don't stand out from the crowd."

The mounting tension in me erupted in volcanic proportion. "And what do you care if I'm removed?"

"I care about my orders, which are to monitor you."

"Monitor me?"

That didn't add up with what he'd conveyed on the flight to Tarahik.

His eyes darkened, seeming to realise he'd said too much.

"Who ordered you to monitor me?" I persevered. "Commander Macaslan? Senator Kerr?"

He flinched, a reaction I wasn't expecting. That last name had rattled him. His mouth hardened, his expression dangerous. "We're done here."

Before I could say anything, he walked away, shifting his focus to a poor girl who hadn't managed to hit anything but the back wall.

Commander Macaslan. Senator Kerr. Jad Arden. They were each hiding secrets. Secrets that involved me.

Why have I really been brought to Tarahik?

I was certain these three conspirators knew more about me than they were letting on. Perhaps something about my past? Maybe the ghosts?

I focused on the targets, doing a deliberately poor job of shooting any of them, eliminating the class's attention from me. But controlling my emotions was not a talent of mine. I needed to let off steam.

Making sure the captain wasn't watching, or anyone else for that matter, I arranged my cast-shooter into silencer mode and shot the target's stupid head off.

CHAPTER SEVENTEEN

When Colonel Harper assigned Jad as my drill instructor, it turned out it wasn't just for cadet field training but for all my physical classes. A situation neither of us was happy about. Jad was a tough love type of guy, and his presence in class was way too hard to ignore. It was clear everyone respected him and no one wanted to disappoint him. If you couldn't keep up, he left you behind. Over the weeks, he transferred many a distraught cadet to retraining platoons.

Sometimes the captain trained with us; other times he monitored from the sides with the other drill instructors. They'd scream at us, call us names, and emotionally break us down, but Jad was always strait-laced and silent, shouting orders only when necessary. I got the impression he never enjoyed the banter like his fellow officers did.

It was rare for the captain to be alone, but on the occasions when he was, I'd hassle him for information. Ever since he'd let slip that he'd been ordered to monitor me, I hadn't been able to rest. It pissed me off knowing I was being left out of the loop. My endless attempts to schedule an appointment with the commander went unanswered too. The suspense gnawed at me. Jad never failed to find a reason to avoid me when I questioned him, or worse, punish me with twenty laps around the oval for insolence. How exactly did a man monitor someone if he dodged that person like they carried the plague? What was going on here?

Over the weeks, the training intensified. Running and endurance marching, physical fitness assessments, weapons handling, hand-to-hand combat, and basic wilderness and urban survival became routine. In the evenings, I'd return to the apartment with bruises, bloody fingers, and blistered feet, my head suspended down a toilet bowl for an hour while I vomited from too much physical strain.

There wasn't a single night where I'd gone to bed without the dreamcatcher. I depended on it like a drug. I'd drift off into the blissful dark, certain that in my last moment of consciousness, something had tapped at the window or scratched at my bedroom door, but then the cool, dark waters of sleep submerged me fully, and I had no thoughts or cares. I was grateful for the extreme training. It meant I was too exhausted to see wraiths.

By the end of week six, I knew how to plot locations and measure distance on a map, navigate trackless terrain, and basic first aid. My stamina and strength increased. My muscles grew tougher, and my speed with cast-shooters became unparalleled. I enjoyed the jealousy this sparked among the cadets, and the anger that flashed in Jad's eyes whenever I triumphed.

Well, if you want me to tone things down, you'll have to man up and say something, won't you?

Often, I'd see the captain watch me with a mildly interested expression, other times it was with an intense, stomach tightening stare. When that happened, I smiled sweetly and fought harder, emboldened by my attitude. I had no idea what was going on in his head. There were times when he'd rebuke my behaviour for the class's amusement; other times, he'd shake his head and walk away.

One afternoon, during a ruthless athletics routine, a fierce electrical storm blanketed the sky, sending down a torrent of rain through the celestial shield and forcing class to be brought indoors. Our instructors decided it was an excellent opportunity to test our rope climbing skills. I was queued among the other cadets, waiting to take my turn, when the captain fell into step beside me.

"Frost Face." He forced a pleasant smile, but the low sound in his voice suggested this was anything but enjoyable.

I levelled a narrow look at him. "What?"

"Come with me."

I stared, my arms crossed. "Are you finally going to tell me why you've become my personal watchdog?"

A watchdog that runs away with his tail between his legs.

Irritation wrinkled the captain's forehead. "Come with me and you'll find out."

A mix of feelings flooded me. I crossed the gym, not bothering to keep up with his fast stride. The other cadets watched us, their curiosity so acute you could practically taste it in the air. At the back of the gym, we came to a heavy door that was permanently off limits to the cadets. I'd always wondered what was in there but hadn't the time or energy to find out.

Jad typed into the numeric keypad. "The colonel believes you're ready to take your training to the next level."

I froze. This hadn't been what I expected. "And what do you believe?"

The veins corded in his neck. "It doesn't matter what I think. I was overruled."

Ouch.

I returned a combative scowl, which he ignored.

The lock clicked, and Jad nudged the door open with his shoulder. "Just remember to tone it down. You don't want to catch the general's attention."

I crossed my arms. "Is that why you're training me in secret now?"

He didn't answer.

Inside was a large circular hall, the ceiling's steeple tapered to a point. The room was a cross between an armoury and a sports complex. Fencing pistes lined the polished floor. Swords, daggers, cast-shooters, maces, and crossbows hung on the metal walls. The place smelled of leather and rust. There were no windows, the room lit by artificial light. The vents in the ceiling circulated warm, stuffy air. This place hadn't been used in some time—judging by the grime on the floor, possibly years.

Dust tickled my throat. "When was this place last cleaned?"

Jad switched the air conditioner on. It didn't look like it had been maintained this past century. "This room is used to train advanced cadets only. We haven't had one of those for some time."

No shit.

The captain moved with purpose and strength around the weapons. He plucked an incredibly sharp sword from the wall and held it out for me to look at. The implement was smooth and highly reflective, almost mirror-like. Small inlaid chips of diamond glittered along the blade, as though the craftsman had decorated it to match the constellations in the sky.

Jad's fingers tightened on the hilt. "Do you know what this is for?"

A sharp feeling of amusement pressed me. "Cut and stab."

His mouth twisted into a barely there smile. "There's a bit more to it than that. This is an athame-sabre. It's made of black crystal from the Ta'Kazone region. See the runes." He ran his fingers over the blade's edge. At his touch, runes shimmered, infusing the space around us with a scarlet glow. I felt shrouded in an unearthly atmosphere, like I'd been teleported into the sun's rays. Jad dropped his hand and the sensation vanished.

I blinked back to reality. "What was that?"

"*That* was the weapon's power. Athame-sabres are enchanted with the four strongest elements of magic: earth, air, water, and fire. It takes an incredible amount of skill to summon its energies and use a blade like this."

I stood tall and gave him a look that was part incredulity, part annoyance. "Okay… history lesson aside, aren't blades outdated? They're no match for our modern-day cast-shooters."

That knowing smirk was back on his face. "And cast-shooters are no match for lycanthors. Those creatures are too fast and have incredible healing abilities. Unless the bullet is forged with silver and you can get a clean shot into the heart, nothing will stop them. Lycanthors can only be killed by weapons enhanced with magic."

He swung the athame-sabre in one agile motion. The runes shone a smoky red, burning brighter than fire. The blade would slash someone in one clean swipe. I wondered if Jad had ever killed a lycanthor with an athame-sabre before. Something about the way he practised with the blade told me he had, more than once. The hair on my scalp prickled.

A jaded edge hardened his face. "And of course, there's all manner of dangerous wildlife out there—stagmas, hellhounds, manticores, chimeras—"

"Okay, I get it. Point proven. Now when do I get to train with a blade?"

Because as much as I loved cast-shooters, athame-sabres could prove to be just as fun.

He regarded me with dark, evaluating eyes. "Now, unfortunately."

He passed me the blade. My fingers curled around the hilt. There was power in the weapon; it tingled against my skin, pulsating like an electrical current. A small stirring of strength welled up inside me. I felt tougher, more assured of my fighting abilities with the blade in my hand, as though its power was a tangible force flowing into every fibre of my body, making me unstoppable.

But there was one thing that bothered me. "Are there others like this?"

I'd never seen Thessio or the guards at Gosheniene with athame-sabres, which made me think they were rare. Come to think of it, I'd never seen an officer at Tarahik with a blade either.

Jad watched me with the sabre and exhaled a long, disapproving sigh. "Not all casters can handle athame-sabres. The magic is intoxicating and can be lethal in the wrong hands. Only the most skilled and disciplined casters are charged with using them."

His expression spoke legions of what he thought about training me with a blade. My muscles drew taut. Skill and discipline were something he evidently believed I lacked. It hurt more than it should have. I dropped my gaze, unable to bare the aversion in Jad's eyes, but it lasted only a second. Maybe it was the blade's magic planting the thought in my head, but I suddenly wanted to prove how worthy I was to use the weapon.

The captain took another blade from the wall—this one made of obsidian with strips of jade—and shrugged off his long jacket, his muscles annoyingly evident beneath the thin fabric of his shirt. He headed to a piste. For a tall guy, he moved with surprising grace. He turned to me with the same shrewd expression I'd first encountered at Gosheniene—the one that had made me want to slap him then and still did now.

"Now we practice," he instructed.

The runes on his weapon blazed alight, tainting the air with heat.

Never one to back down from a challenge, I joined him on the piste.

Over the next hour, Jad demonstrated several techniques—how to lunge, strike, and parry. He was certainly versed in the art of the sword, and it was no wonder the colonel wanted him to train me. The captain taught me to observe my opponent's behaviour, calculate my surroundings, and turn it to my advantage, things I never considered could help in a real fight.

"Dark urban environments are good for what?" he quizzed.

"Concealment." I dodged his weapon, barely missing the tip of his sword.

Jad feigned an attack from the right and lunged for my left shoulder instead. "Bright sunlight can benefit you how?"

I swerved out of the way. "At the right angle, it can blind your opponent."

The captain went in for a defensive strike. His blade hit mine with such accurate force, the colourful runes shattered. The sabre sailed out of my hand, landing with a heavy clang at the opposite side of the room.

The captain wiped his brow. "Good."

"Good?" I said through gritted teeth. "You nearly cut my hand off."

"I meant good—you're listening. Grab your sabre. That's enough practice for today."

"Today?"

"Yes. Colonel Harper wants these lessons to be frequent. Your next lesson is scheduled same time tomorrow." The sharp tone in his voice implied he wasn't looking forward to it.

My legs went weak, as though they'd suddenly disjointed at the hips. "You mean… I'm practising every day… with you?"

"I'm not happy about it either." He took up a towel and dried his face, his black hair sticking to his forehead in dark streaks. The room had been humid to begin with, but now it felt like we stood in an oven.

I caught a glance of myself in the mirror and wished I hadn't. My face was purple-red splotchy, my curls frizzed like I'd stuck a fork into a live power outlet. There'd been no point turning on that old dinosaur of an air conditioner; I was certain it had done nothing but circulate hot air.

We put the weapons away and sprawled on the floor, doing a few cool-down stretches.

"So athame-sabres are rare, right?" I sat up from my exercises, flinching at the amount of sweat I'd left on the floor.

Jad leaned his long tanned arms down to his feet and stretched his hamstrings. His fingers were covered in white scars and calloused from what was probably years of combat, but they were also lissom and slender. In another life, he would have made an excellent pianist. "Centuries ago, every Haxsan Guard soldier carried an athame-sabre. But it was apparent not everyone could be trusted with one, so the council had many of the blades destroyed. Something they now regret." There was a bitter underscore to his words.

"Why did they destroy them? Why not just take them away?"

"If you read the old history texts—which I doubt you ever will because humans burnt the majority of them—some blades were not only enchanted with the four elements but a darker and rarer power too."

"Like what?"

His eyes locked with mine. "There's all sort of untoward magic out there, and plenty of casters ready to use it. The one that sticks out to me the most was Larthalgule—an athame-sabre that's been lost for centuries."

"I've never heard of it."

"It was said Larthalgule was a blade for necromancers."

My pulse went all over the place. I laced my fingers together so he wouldn't see them tremble. "That's a banned subject. You shouldn't mention it."

A smile surfaced on his lips. "And there are consequences only if you get caught."

I couldn't believe how… laid-back he was being about this. My defences went up. This could have been a trick. And there was still that huge, unexplainable detail about why Jad was monitoring me, because as much as I hoped it was under Commander Macaslan's direction, any officer suspicious of my power could have ordered the captain to watch me too.

"It's a banned subject," I repeated, hoping to put an end to the conversation.

"What do you know of necromancy?" The question was direct and underscored with impatience. I couldn't be certain, but for a second I thought I saw something cold burn in the captain's eyes.

My heart stumbled. I queried the real motive behind this private training session. "I know only that it no longer exists."

He made a grunt of agreement. "According to the ancient texts, humans feared the power of necromancy. Necromancers were hunted down and destroyed under the council's orders. It's said the Larthalgule blade is the last remaining link to necromancy. The weapon was rumoured to raise the dead and bring eternal life."

The blood drained from my face. Even my vision blurred. "That is an interesting bedtime story, but I suggest you find a different fable to tell."

He laughed. "People aren't punished for telling stories."

My face pinched into something ugly. "I spent two years serving a sentence in Gosheniene. I assure you, people are punished." I stood and moved to the door. "Thanks for the session."

Jad followed, lagging a few paces behind me. "You should rest. Get some strength back. I'll give you a pass from your next class."

"I'm fine," I lied.

Something in the way he'd looked at me when he'd told me the story of necromancers had left me feeling transparent, as though he'd chiselled his way straight to my soul and dug out my secret. I feared he knew more about me than I wanted him to know. More than my dossier had revealed. But who was it for? The commander? Or someone else? And what was Jad doing reading forbidden texts anyway? Where did he even find one?

I increased my pace, realising being close to Captain Arden was like playing with fire.

CHAPTER EIGHTEEN

*N*ecromancers. *Ghost seers. Wraith whisperers.*

The words plagued me.

Rather than sleep that night, I took my anger out on the gym's punching bag. I needed to do something physically demanding, something that would exhaust and wipe my brain because so far, questions had spiralled through my head, preventing sleep. Not even the dreamcatcher could keep my worries at bay.

I set to my task with fierce zeal, my fury sparked by more than frustration. I was confused and scared about a magic ability not recognised by the modern world. The conversation with Jad had only reinforced how dangerous it was to see ghosts. I was lost and alone. There was no one I could talk to, not unless I wanted to be strapped in a straitjacket and tossed into the nearest firing line.

I'd made it halfway through my practice when Tusk Monahan, the base's superficial jock, strolled toward me. A collective intake of laughter from his friends alerted me something was amiss. The gym was surprisingly busy for this hour, lit by candlelight with nothing but the windows to offer a breeze, and most had been shut to prevent the flames blowing out. Colonel Harper was taking a private session over by the dumbbells, assessing his soldiers' fitness and documenting their progress on a clipboard. Tusk would never try anything in front of the colonel, so I wasn't too concerned when he approached the outskirts of my personal bubble. I mentally prepared myself for a challenge. But honestly, he'd have to be stupid to take me on, right?

Tusk had celebrity status among the cadets and enough bullshit to fill a septic tank. He was popular with the girls, idolised by the boys, and had smaller brain cells than a goldfish. He was tall and had so much gel in his peroxide-blond hair that it would ignite under a match. I'd heard girls refer to him as a Greek god. He would have been flawless except for a long scar that ran down his left arm. Tusk boasted he'd received it fishing off the coast of Karlinia when holidaying with friends—and that it was something to be proud of because all women loved a man with a good scar. Pity he didn't realise that excluded mental scars.

"Hey, Wayward." His eyes swept over my body in a way that made me want to punch his teeth out. "That's quite the workout you're doing."

Despite the sweat running past my nose, an icy sensation drifted over my skin. I was one of the few girls my age who didn't have body issues, but that didn't mean I appreciated being looked at like I worked on a street corner.

A dark stab of annoyance surged inside me. "What do you want, Tusk?"

Something about the way his mouth twisted into a sneer made me worry. "When I first saw you, I recognised you but didn't know from where. Well, now I remember." He crossed his arms in a ridiculous statement of machismo. "My father is a judge for the Council of Founding Sovereigns. He remembered your case. You murdered that girl at Brendlash Orphanage two years ago. My father investigated it. He says your scholarship is a ruse, that you're at Tarahik because you killed that girl on the council's orders, and this is your reward. You're not one of us, Wayward. You're from Gosheniene."

An entirely different chill took hold of me.

So now I'm an assassin too, another addition to my sin list.

I continued to hit the punching bag but with more force. "I'm not a killer."

"I have a proposition." His slitted eyes never wavered from mine. "There are cadets at this base I don't like. You teach them a lesson for me, and I won't get my parents to petition your removal from Tarahik. People don't want a filthy, murdering caster from the provinces at the base. And my parents have influence with the council. I can make your removal happen."

I couldn't help it. I laughed. "Blackmail? Seriously?"

He glared as though his eyes could shoot lasers through me. "I don't appreciate your tone, Wayward."

I spun toward him fiercely. "And I don't appreciate yours, so unless you want your nose to become a permanent fixture in your brain, I suggest you keep your lying mouth shut."

He didn't get the hint. He turned to his friends with a self-centred grin. "Hey, guys, I've news to share. Wayward here is from—"

Tusk never got to finish. I grabbed his arm and twisted it behind his back at an unnatural angle, forcing him onto his knees. Threatening physical violence was a definite no-no at Tarahik, but I wasn't good with rules—or impulse, for that matter. I kneed him in the nose, the bone crunching on impact. Tusk cussed and screamed. He sounded like a screeching bobcat.

"Wayward!" Colonel Harper marched toward me. "If you're going to break Mr Monahan's bones, do it on someone else's watch."

Harper was growing on me more every day.

Tusk's friends swept away from the scene like a wave at the beach. I would have gone in for round two and broken Tusk's jaw, but hands ripped me away.

Jad was in my face, his eyes lethal, the anger radiating off him. "Save that behaviour for the enemy."

Where the hell did he come from?

Outrage shot through me. "Tusk *is* my enemy."

I spun around to finish my work.

The captain wrenched me from the scene. His fingers pressed into my arm, but I knew from his calm breathing that he had his irritation under control. I'd hate to see what Captain Arden would be like in a real rampage. The force of his anger would hit harder than a hurricane, burn brighter than molten lava, cause more destruction than a magnitude nine quake.

I struggled to pull free. "Tusk is making up vicious lies about me."

My actions are justified, damn it.

Jad led me into a passage and away from prying eyes. "Whatever he says is his word against yours. Learn to take some control. Tusk Monahan is a coward and a wretch. He's weak, and he won't last long out in the field. You're stronger, smarter, and braver than most of the cadets on this base.

Soon, they'll start looking to you as a leader." His eyes sliced into mine with an intensity that left me breathless. "What you did in there is not good for morale. You need to ignore characters like Tusk Monahan and not beat them till they're bloody."

His reprimand sobered me. I wiped my eyes, unwilling to show emotion. "Tusk knows I'm from Gosheniene."

I could picture the backlash from this. It would be like a piranha feeding frenzy, me the poor fish in the centre.

Jad scoffed. "Do you really think Commander Macaslan would allow that?"

"I don't see why she'd have any reason to protect me. I was brought from Gosheniene because I have skills the base requires, nothing else. Or is there more to it?"

I crossed my arms, waiting for his response.

Uneasiness kindled in the hard lines on his face. He took a step away, seeming to realise his mistake.

"Why are you monitoring me?" I continued. "Who asked you to do it?"

Because how else would Jad have known I was in the gym and not tucked asleep in my bed?

The captain shook his head, but whether from exhaustion or disbelief, I wasn't sure. "I'm monitoring you because the commander doesn't know whether you can be trusted."

There it was. The truth. And it hurt.

Jad's gaze fell on my hands. "Go to the infirmary and get yourself cleaned up. Your fingers are bleeding."

I'd been so overcome with rage, I only now realised my knuckles were cut and stinging.

Jad gave me one last look of irritation and stormed away.

I didn't go to the infirmary like he'd instructed. Talina would mend the cuts fine on her own. But it was late, and when I returned to the apartment, I found her asleep.

It can wait till morning.

I wrapped gauze around my hands and jumped into bed. Sleep eluded me. Thoughts kept spinning through my mind.

The commander didn't trust me. Neither did Jad. But a new problem had arisen. Captain Arden had called me brave, strong, smart. I felt flushed and dizzy every time I thought on it.

CHAPTER NINETEEN

There was the usual Talina—the well-organised, sweet wallflower everyone knew and respected—and then there was the other Talina, a fretful, intense, temper tantrum queen. Behaviour kept exclusively for roommates. The moment I'd stepped into our apartment, I knew something was wrong.

She swung her legs off the couch and padded toward me. Tears streamed down her cheeks, ruining the make-up she'd painstakingly applied before dinner. "Why didn't you tell us the truth?"

Whoa. Okay?

I opened my mouth and closed it again. I felt like a naughty child in her cool, challenging gaze. "What's wrong?"

"What's wrong?" She sounded incredulous. "You lied."

Lied?

I was halfway to the kitchen but stopped, stunned. Everything had been fine at dinner. What had happened in half an hour to make things so… tense?

She sucked in a breath that might have been a sob. "Why didn't you tell us the truth about Gosheniene?"

She found out.

An awful thought struck me.

Tusk.

Had that egotistical jerk gone through with his threat?

But he couldn't have. For the past week, his nose had been plastered in a nasal splint. He couldn't breathe, let alone talk.

Lainie was seated on the couch, eyes riveted on the holographic screen. "Let it go, Talina. Now's not the time."

Alarm burned in my stomach like acid. "Now's not the time for what?"

My roommates exchanged a look, a long one. My fear escalated in response.

It was approaching nightfall. We had about ten minutes before the electricity was turned off till daybreak. The girls had already lit candles, the smoky scent thick on my tongue. I liked that they were prepared— there was nothing worse than being caught out in the dark—but tonight, the atmosphere was different. Normally the holographic screen would be switched off, but they'd left it on.

Talina pointed to the screen. "See for yourself."

On the screen, a news reporter, smart-looking but serious, stood huddled in a rain poncho. Dark clouds stretched across the sky, wind whipping her hair in a thousand directions. Hail pelted around her like ice bullets. Each time bursts of light lit the sky, thunder cracked. I recognised the building behind her—grey brick with metal wire bordering a large concrete wall. A scream seemed to echo in my head. It was summer, so why was Gosheniene shrouded in ice? Why was the labour camp half buried in snow?

The news reporter struggled to speak against the gale, and wind noise muffled the microphone. "Authorities... clueless... Gosheniene intern... attacked... deadly ice power. The work is similar... magic... destroyed... Idra and Jubris cities... earlier... the year."

The camera cut to a scene inside the camp, and the hairs on my arms stood on end. Prisoners were frozen in their cells, arms raised in a hopeless attempt to shield away the inevitable. Mine workers, their skin like white plastic, had their fingers curled solid on pickaxes and shovels. They looked like mannequins in a history museum, eyes glassy and vacant. Parts of the screen were blurred where the footage was too disturbing to be shown.

The camera returned to the reporter. This time she paced the front of the compound gate. "It's believed... no survivors, including... Haxsan Guard... on duty. We're going... cross now to—"

Talina reached for the remote and the screen went blank. An oppressive silence settled in the apartment, one I wasn't sure how to resolve.

"That was your home?" Talina's eyes were wide and disbelieving. "You told us Gosheniene was a seaside town."

Oh shit. She remembered that.

My frown deepened, my voice sharper than intended. "You assumed Gosheniene was a seaside town. I never lied. I just didn't correct you."

Tears threatened to prick my eyes. All those prisoners dead, reduced to ice figurines in their dank cells. No man, woman, or child was guilty in that labour camp. The only crime committed had been the refusal of the council's doctrine and a search for a better way of life. How could the world be so cruel?

"Were you ashamed?" The wildness had dimmed from Talina's eyes, but she still looked angry and humiliated, as though I'd deliberately played her for a fool. "Did you think we wouldn't talk to you if we knew you were from a labour camp?"

"Would you have?" I couldn't keep the venom from my voice.

When she didn't say anything, I took a page from Jad's book and stormed away to my room. I wanted to close my eyes and let the world drift away, forget what I'd seen and blank it all out, but instead I cried hopelessly into my hands. I threw myself onto the bed and cocooned myself in the blankets.

It took a long time for sweet darkness to drag me under.

The darkness didn't last.

A familiar dream sensation crept into my mind. I was in a forest surrounded by gnarled, twisted trees, their branches bearing over me. The earthly smell of the forest was replaced by a scent both sickly and ailing. The woods smelt… terminally ill? And cold. Snow pricked my skin. I felt as though I'd been dipped in a pool of liquid nitrogen, frozen to the bone.

A figure appeared through the dusky trees, coalescing into a familiar shape. My heart accelerated. Adaline stared at me, pale and fragile. The air seemed to shimmer around her, lit by phantom moonlight. She was worse now than she'd been in the dormitory. Her nightdress wrung wet from ice. White frost clung to her fingers, something I'd only seen happen on trees in winter.

"It waits in Essida." Her voice was lulling, hypnotic, like wind chimes carried off on a breeze.

But then her skin started to look darker and looser. Veins, thick and black, wrapped around her skin, as though thousands of bacterial worms strangled her from the inside. Her eyes changed shape. Her nose pointed outward. Her lips curled into a grisly smile. She was no longer Adaline. She had transformed into something else.

I was staring at the black-veined woman.

It was the soft shuffling sound of her feet that finally overpowered my horror. She hobbled, lurched, and then ran toward me, her movement robotic and stilted. The crusted-over cuts on her lips bled as her mouth widened into a scream. "Zaya."

I bolted upright, sensing something was terribly, terribly wrong, and not just in the dream. The temperature in my room had plummeted. I'd been so consumed by anger before I'd gone to bed that I'd forgotten to grab my torch. It wasn't on the bedside table where it usually was but stuck in the drawer, useless. I tried to feel my way for it, but the darkness was consuming.

Unease formed in the pit of my stomach. I sensed eyes on me. The intuition was so intense, nervous energy pounded my blood. I sat on the edge of my bed. A shiver of fear whipped up my spine as my vision adjusted to the dark. The dreamcatcher lay flush with my toes on the floor. It was ripped and damaged beyond repair. It looked as though it had met the claws of a sabre-toothed tiger.

The protective spell... it's gone.

That sensation I was being watched was real. There was a wraith present in the room. And that was when I saw it—a curtain of filmy white on the mirror.

Frost.

I slid off the bed. A sound like the soft tapping of a cat came from inside the glass. My room was so cold that flecks of snow dappled the floor, my breaths becoming clouds of white. Another tap, only this time it sounded like fingernails. My fear and curiosity worked together, an insurmountable pull that drew me closer. I glimpsed movement in the mirror. A pale, luminescent form emerged. It wasn't clear—more like an object viewed from underwater— but I saw enough to be afraid.

A boy. He was tall, his skin sunken beneath his eyes, his red-brown hair dappled in frost. He'd been dealt the same fate as Adaline. Frozen.

He touched the glass. Rickety letters appeared where his fingers met the condensation.

She hunts you.

The room grew darker. My heart rate increased.

My voice was whisper tense. "The black-veined woman?"

The ghost reared like a striking snake, a piercing scream breaking from his cavernous mouth. A resounding crack tore the mirror, the glass bursting outward. I flung my hands over my face, but it was too late. Shards pierced my skin. I tried to pull back, to get a clearer perspective on what had happened, but the wraith was gone.

"What the hell was that?" Lainie's voice drifted from the hallway. A moment later, she and Talina scrambled into my room. They were in their pyjamas, both sporting a serious case of bed hair. They looked at the glass scattered across the floor, eyes big and cheeks bloodless.

"What is that?" Talina's hands trembled at her sides. Her bare feet were blue around the edges. The cool temperature had receded, but an uncomfortable chill still lingered in the air.

I shifted my gaze. The glass had fallen into a pattern. No. Not a pattern—a word.

Melvina.

A shudder ran through me that did not come from the cold. I didn't recognise the name, and it was clear by Lainie's and Talina's blank expressions that they didn't either. One thing I'd learnt the hard way, though: some ghosts might have been harmless, but they didn't appear for no reason. This was a message.

The girls waited for an explanation. I chewed my lip and tried to think of a cover story, but my imagination failed.

Turned out I needn't have bothered thinking of an excuse, because the front door to our apartment burst open and a minute later, two soldiers swept into the room. They shoved Lainie and Talina aside. The girls shrieked and pressed against the wall like trapped animals.

"Zaya Wayward." The tallest of the pair pinned his black eyes on me. A pair of handcuffs jangled in his hand. "You need to come with us right now."

"What for?" I hadn't caused any problems of late, apart from breaking Tusk's nose—and honestly, I thought the drill instructors preferred he wasn't in class. It was a mystery why the guards were here—unless, of course, they knew about the ghost.

Panic compressed my skull. The wraith had just disappeared. It was too soon. And how could they detect something that wasn't meant to be real?

A vein popped on the soldier's forehead. "Resist and we'll take you by force."

I stared, unable to move. For the first time in my life, I didn't know what to do.

CHAPTER TWENTY

I went quietly. There wasn't much choice in the matter. Hard-faced and silent, the guards escorted me in their iron grips deep into the mountain. It was the first time I'd been in the underground base—a jumbled mess of gantry walkways, concrete floors, and corrugated iron. Access tunnels large enough to roll a tank through had walls covered in cables, blast valves, and steel pipes.

My pace must have slowed because the guards yanked me hard, leading me down a flight of worn, uneven stairs. On this level, soldiers moved in military precision from one compartment to another, solemn and unsmiling. I walked past with my head held high, but inside I'd fallen into a numb haze, each step heavier than the last. Down here the schedule was twenty-four hours, everyone alert and focused. I sensed eyes on me, judging, weighing, calculating. Their whispers made me think they knew *exactly* where I was being led.

Sweat broke out on my palms. Aside from gripping me like I had stuffing for bones, nothing could be gleaned from my guards.

A slimy taste crept into my mouth. "Where are you taking me?"

My captors remained staring ahead. I dubbed them Sneer-face and Pick-nose, because the former wore a permanent smirk only a mother would find endearing and the other had a fixation for picking his nose when he thought no one was looking. I made a mental note to wash my arm when this was over.

The pair marched me into a barely lit tunnel. The fluorescent lights flickered pale yellow, causing the passage ahead to be lost in ominous dark. It was a good thing I didn't have epilepsy. Interconnecting passages stretched to my left and right for what seemed like miles, and I was caught in that eerie awareness where I saw forever ahead but only a few feet at the same time.

I'm in a maze. I don't have the slightest chance of finding my way out.

A steel door waited at the end of the tunnel. I inhaled a shuddering breath. The closer we approached the intimidating slab of metal, the damper and colder the air grew. My skin tingled.

"Stand there," Sneer-face growled. He planted me in front of the door with more force than was necessary. His fingers moved across the numeric keypad too fast for me to detect the code. My heart pounded into my ribs.

Both men exchanged an amused glance and stepped behind me.

Why are they... closing in?

I could feel their hot breath on the back of my neck.

The question was on the tip of my tongue when the door groaned open to reveal... nothing.

It was pitch dark inside.

I shook my head, exasperated. "What is happening—"

Fists smacked my spine. I tumbled hands first onto a metal floor—at least, that was what it felt like, because the door closed and everything was swallowed by the dark.

No.

Nooooo.

The darkness was suffocating. I pummelled my fists on the door, but there was no answer on the other side. What was this place of eternal darkness? A punishment cell? A booby trap? A mass grave? A black hole to another dimension? The horrible possibilities were endless.

I ran my hands along the door that isolated me from the world, feeling for a handle I knew wasn't there. "Hey! You sons of bit—"

Blinding light showered me.

"Language, Miss Wayward."

The voice was strict and familiar.

I blinked back the burning dots that blurred my vision. The space around me slowly morphed into focus. I hadn't known what to expect, but it certainly wasn't a high-tech command room. Holographic maps showed places I'd never heard of, displaying troops' movement in various provinces. Computerised control panels beeped, blinked, and gave off an electric hum. Beside an oval table—probably where votes were cast on a course of action during wartime—stood Commander Macaslan. Her purple gown swept the floor, adding to her regal appearance, only tonight the heavy lines beneath her eyes made her pale face strained and fatigued. She too must have been summoned from her bed in the middle of the night.

Her grey eyes darkened into the colour of a storm. "Ladies never use profanities to express themselves."

I crossed my arms. "Ladies don't fight in the armed forces either. And they're not incarcerated in the middle of the night." My fear had dissolved, but in its place, anger surfaced. "What the hell is this?"

"I apologise for the theatrics." She didn't sound sorry at all. "This is one of the base's internal defence centres, safe from magic and prying ears… for now. The arrest was the only way we could sneak you in."

"We?" I gave my mysterious surroundings the evil eye.

Now that my vision had adjusted, the person leaning against the control panel was clearer too.

Son of a bitch.

Jad's obsidian eyes glinted with impatience, the tension in his shoulders more profound the longer he studied me. If I'd been an animal, the look would have made me bare my teeth, my hackles spiked. It was always one step ahead with the captain, followed by five steps backward.

If you don't like me, leave.

At the opposite end of the table, Colonel Harper sat beside a pompous-looking council minister. It took me a moment to register that the impeccably dressed men in the tailored suit was Senator Kerr. A ripple of suspense shot through me.

Darius Kerr was similar in age to the colonel, only his blond hair and trimmed beard were laced with silver. His suit was new and perfectly pressed, finished with matching cufflinks and a silk tie. The Infinite Eye was embroidered on his right lapel, proclaiming allegiance to the Council of Founding Sovereigns. A sudden sense of alarm clamped onto my throat when his eyes met mine. He smiled pleasantly, but I detected a layer of deceit under that flashy grin. Senator Kerr reminded me of a feral cat—playful one moment, but one wrong move and he'd cut you.

He's a politician. And not to be trusted.

Perhaps sensing the tension between us, Macaslan's lips squeezed tight, turning white. "Zaya, this is Senator Darius Kerr of the—"

"I know who he is," I snapped. I stared at him, the recesses of my memory stirring with painful recollection. "You were at my sentencing the evening I was taken to Gosheniene. Why?"

He stared at me beneath lowered brows, the crafty smile never leaving his face. "It's a pleasure to officially meet you too, Miss Wayward. And I was at that *excuse* for a sentence for the same reason that I am here now. I know what really killed Adaline White that night."

The paranoia I'd kept locked away exploded.

How could he know?

My mouth tasted dry and shrivelled. I couldn't breathe. My lungs juddered in spasms.

Normally, I was decent at keeping a close surveillance on my surroundings, but somehow Macaslan had crept up on me. She took my arm and steered me to the table, forcing me into a seat. That was probably just as well because my legs had about the same sturdiness as spaghetti.

This must be shock. Or is it relief… because finally someone knows the truth.

Everyone's eyes were on me. My body was cold and heavy, light and hot all at once.

How does the senator know? How could any of them know?

Darius fixed me with a piercing gaze. "The black-veined woman. That's what you call her, right?"

I didn't answer. The name had curdled my blood.

Macaslan settled into the chair next to mine. "We know of your ability, Zaya. While you are among us, necromancy is not something to be ashamed of… but I must urge you to keep it secret. This knowledge in the wrong hands will have terrible consequences."

Yeah. No shit.

Her mouth curved into a reluctant smile. Macaslan was graceful, aloof, and merciless. Seeing a flicker of empathy from her was sort of astonishing. "The black-veined woman has haunted your dreams for some time now. You must have questions?"

A pearl of sweat dropped down my neck. "Yeah. How do you know this? I never told a soul."

Cool, artificial air stirred the commander's loose curls. She was greyer than I remembered. "Senator Kerr and I have known about your necromancy for a long time. We are responsible for protecting you. That is why I placed defensive shields in your room and provided you with a dreamcatcher. On your arrival from Gosheniene, Captain Arden injected a tracker into your bloodstream. It monitored your magic and alerted me when you met a wraith. I have kept an eye on you for some weeks now. Captain Arden was chosen to be your mentor. He provides regular updates on your behaviour."

I looked at her with wide eyes. I must have appeared comically helpless.

What did she mean, *"We are responsible for protecting you?"*

Macaslan… Darius… Colonel Harper? They were in on this together? And Jad?

My internal temperature rose when our eyes locked. Hurt, anger, and betrayal dug into me, as though thousands of splinters had perforated my thick skin. So that was what the captain had been doing on the aircraft. When he'd healed my arm, he'd injected a tracker too.

Stupid. Stupid. Stupid.

I'd let my guard down.

Macaslan regained her poise, but there was seriousness in her grey eyes. "Adaline White's murder was not your first encounter with the black-veined woman. Your paths have crossed before. You were a child at the time." She hesitated, a look foreign to her. "Those memories were erased… we believe by the black-veined woman."

I pressed my lips together, afraid I'd scream.

My amnesia.

The black-veined woman had done this to me.

She was the reason why I couldn't remember anything. My parents. My childhood. She had done something to me, cheating me of the earliest years of my life.

Macaslan continued in a low, flat voice. "Two years ago, at the Brendlash Orphanage, she returned to finish her task. She mistook Adaline for you."

I stiffened. "She wants me dead?"

The commander nodded.

"But… why?" I squeezed my eyes shut, willing my fury to crawl back into its dark, subdued place, but it held its ground. That was when I realised Macaslan still hadn't told me what I most wished to know. "How do you know about this?"

And why are you protecting me?

Before the commander could answer, Darius stood and took command of the room. "We have made it our business to know every detail about you since you were a child, Zaya… because up until you turned eighteen, Macaslan and I were your legal guardians."

CHAPTER TWENTY-ONE

A strange fog hung in my head, one that refused to dissolve. This man in his flashy suit, wielding influence and power wherever he went, had been my legal guardian?

I looked at the commander for confirmation, expecting her to deny it. Her mouth was set in a grim line, but her eyes were honest. It was true. The pair had been my custodians. They were my protectors.

Darius fiddled with the coarse hairs of his beard. "I understand this comes as a shock."

"You think?" I had the sickening urge to laugh. "Who are you really? And no more lies. You don't just become legal guardians randomly."

I was hit with another startling revelation. For Darius and Macaslan to be my guardians, they had to be connected to my family somehow. Had they known my parents? Did they know what had happened to them?

The senator exchanged a terse glance with the commander. It was a look that said he would censor what I was about to be told.

I sent him a warning with my eyes. "Tell me everything… and don't leave anything out."

He expelled a reluctant sigh. "To explain everything, I will need to go back to the start. That will take time."

I sagged back in my chair. "I have time."

"Very well." Darius returned to his seat. He had the perfect nondescript look on his face, but I knew from the way he glanced at Macaslan that his mind was running on overdrive. "To begin, I have to tell you the story of a man who wanted to do the right thing but was caught in the path of two wrongs."

I squared my shoulders. "Go on."

"This man was a senior scientist for the Council of Founding Sovereigns… and a close friend of mine." He motioned toward Macaslan, a ghost of a smile stretching his lips as his eyes reflected fond memories. "The three of us attended school together. His name was Clarence Chauvelin. Thirteen years ago, Clarence was the head of the Human Research Program for the council. He was tasked with analysing human blood samples, bone density, and muscle strength to identify if the environment in the Free Zones was affecting the human body."

Lines of thought creased my brow. "Environment?"

"Nothing grows in the Free Zones. Everything is cultivated in the provinces. Water is purified in dams before it's released. Oxygen generators must be maintained for clean air to be vented and circulated. For humans, the Free Zones offer an unnatural, unfriendly… and potentially dangerous existence."

My lips moulded into a wicked smile. "Maybe they should take a hint. The world doesn't want them here anymore."

Darius clicked his tongue. "You don't mean that."

Didn't I?

Because of humans, casters were enslaved, treated as second-class citizens, and conscripted into a war against their own people—rebel casters who sought nothing but freedom and a better life. I'd seen atrocities committed from both sides in the war. I didn't know how to feel about it. My emotions were jumbled.

Shrewd wit sparkled in Darius's eyes. "Well, Miss Wayward, it appears the world does want humans in it after all… at least for the foreseeable future."

I shook my head, not following.

He sat back in his chair, clasping his hands firmly together. "Clarence discovered something in his experiments. He learnt that there are magical properties in human blood. It's dormant, but in each new generation of humans, the magic becomes more prevalent." His voice escalated with elation. "Do you not see it? Humans are evolving into casters. Clarence calculated that in another hundred and fifty years, the mutation will be complete. Humans will not exist. We'll all be casters."

I blinked, a million questions flying from my mind. "Why have I never heard this? Why has it never been made public? This could finish the war."

"It could *help* finish it," Darius corrected. "Being naive back then, Chauvelin believed the research could make a difference too, but the council disagreed. To speak plainly, they didn't want to hear it."

"Why?"

The senator's eyes shone as he looked directly at me. "Because powerful, influential casters who live in the Free Zones profit from the conflict."

"But the council is bankrupt. They're borrowing to fund the war."

"Yes… from powerful casters."

I stared at him for several heavy seconds. "But that's… wrong." I sounded like a little girl with no understanding of the world.

Darius's voice was tinged with bitterness. "Chauvelin realised he had to be smart if he wanted his research to account for something. The council immediately shut his department down. He thought he had no other alternative… so he took his research to Morgomoth."

A stab of horror sliced through me. There was so much I wanted to ask. So much I needed to say. But the words were stuck on my tongue.

Darius dipped his chin. "Some of the ULD's supporters were interested and hoped the research could make a difference. But Morgomoth believed it was further evidence that humans should be purged from the world sooner rather than later. A hundred and fifty years was too long to wait. Many of his supporters agreed with him. Morgomoth was an incredibly persuasive man… very efficient and practical in his means. But underneath his glossy exterior, he was domineering and hostile. He had no remorse for the things he did. Morgomoth strongly believed in the theory of evolution—that the extermination of humans was his right."

Darius's eyes betrayed a hint of emotion. "During Chauvelin's time with the ULD, he learnt that Morgomoth intended to find a weapon that had been lost for centuries. Larthalgule. It's a—"

"I know what it is." I spun my furious attention to Jad. Had the captain been intentionally throwing hints when we'd spoken in the gym? This entire situation started to feel like a set-up.

Jad's lips creased into a narrow line. He looked like he'd rather chew through wood than admit it to me.

I focused on the senator again. "It's an athame-sabre—a weapon rumoured to raise the dead and bring eternal life." My temper started to rise. "What would Morgomoth want with that?"

No one answered for a long time.

Commander Macaslan stirred in her chair. "Morgomoth was a necromancer. That's why the council feared him. Communicating with the dead is dangerous. Spirits are summoned for the purpose of divination, to foretell future events, or to gain the hidden truth. That's why necromancers have been hunted down in the past. As far as the council are concerned, necromancy died with Morgomoth's execution."

My head spun from the new information.

Well… this wasn't in the history books.

Senator Kerr's eyes drank me in. "Clarence never discovered what Morgomoth wanted with the blade, but my guess is it had something to do with annihilating humans. After Morgomoth was captured and vanquished, his lieutenant, Vulcan Stormouth, took control of the ULD. He intends to finish what Morgomoth started."

My chest swelled with uncertainty. "But he's not a necromancer… is he? He can't control the blade."

Darius stiffened. "That's why he needs you."

The full implication of his words struck home.

"Only a necromancer can control the blade."

No oxygen reached my lungs. It was as though the air had been sucked out of the room with a vacuum. "But… how does he even know about me?"

I was a nobody. An orphan. A prisoner. A servant of the Haxsan Guard.

Unless—

My heart flipped three hundred and sixty degrees. "The black-veined woman."

Pity flashed across the senator's face. "Her name is Melvina Raskovitch, one of Morgomoth's faithful servants. When Morgomoth was alive, he became obsessed with the idea of resurrecting an army of the dead. Something no necromancer had ever achieved in the past. Many of his loyal supporters offered themselves in sacrifice. Morgomoth was never able to revive their souls, save for one. Melvina Raskovitch. But she didn't come back the same. Her body continues to decompose. It's her soul that animates it. She is more monster than caster now."

She hunts you.

Melvina.

Now the meaning behind the wraith's words spoke with chilling clarity.

I tried to get my breathing under control, but my insides rioted. "So Melvina is after me because this... Vulcan guy, needs a necromancer to control the Larthalgule blade and finish what Morgomoth started?"

"And she nearly very well succeeded." Darius gritted his teeth. "After Morgomoth's death, Clarence told me that while he was with the ULD, there was a young girl among them. A child no more than ten who possessed necromancy... and who Melvina had taken a very strong interest in. Chauvelin did not tell me the full details of what occurred, only that he stole the child and took her to Brendlash Orphanage."

"Me." I bit back the strangled cry in my throat.

It was all starting to make terrible sense.

"Clarence found Macaslan and me and beseeched us for help. If something happened to him, we were to become your legal guardians. And by legal, I mean magical contract binding us to an oath. The council has no record of this arrangement. When the oath was sworn, Clarence informed us that your safety was paramount. You had to be kept hidden."

Macaslan shot me a pained look. "Chauvelin was found a week later. Frozen. Darius and I believed you were safe in the orphanage... and for many years, you were. Our plan had been that when you turned nineteen, you would be brought to Tarahik where I could keep an eye on you. You were simply meant to blend in. But those plans were destroyed on the night of that terrible storm, when the celestial shield that protected the orphanage failed. Melvina is a wraith animating a body. You were untrained in your magic and vulnerable, and she was able to get close to you."

Guilt seized me with an icy grip. "But she killed the wrong person."

Macaslan nodded.

"Hang on a moment." There was one thing that didn't add up. "If the black-veined… if Melvina and Vulcan need me to finish what Morgomoth started, why do they want me dead?"

Darius shifted in his chair. "Precisely what we have been trying to find out. For the two years that you were imprisoned in Gosheniene, I paid the head warden to look out for you. You were to be unharmed and kept secure. A few months ago, I arranged for you to be transferred to Tarahik."

So that was it. My sad, tragic story.

I turned to Macaslan. "Melvina knows I'm here, doesn't she? She broke the celestial shield the night I arrived at Tarahik. And what happened this evening? My dreamcatcher was destroyed. And the defensive spell in my room didn't do much defending, I might add."

She fixed her shiny eyes on me. "Only an incredibly powerful caster can break magic like that. You're right. Melvina knows you're here. Someone is talking to her… working for her." She sucked in a sharp breath. "We have a traitor among us."

CHAPTER TWENTY-TWO

Ringing filled my head.

A traitor.

Brilliant.

Not only did I have an animated corpse after me, but I had to keep an eye out for a spy too.

I irritably raked my fingers through my hair. "Do you have any idea who it could be? Any leads?"

Macaslan tapped the desk with a pale finger. "I have assigned that task to Colonel Harper. At this stage, we don't know how Melvina and the traitor are communicating."

Colonel Harper sat rigid in his chair, his arms crossed and his face malcontent. Judging from that expression, that was a no. There were no leads.

A wild thought danced in my head. "What if this person isn't communicating with Melvina? Maybe they're talking to Vulcan."

I didn't think I was grasping at straws here. Macaslan and Colonel Harper might have been looking at this from the wrong angle.

Darius was sitting still, but his eyes drifted wide. "That is possible. Vulcan's last known location was Idra and Jubris, and both those cities were destroyed in ice storms."

I shuffled my feet, uncomfortable. "Ice storms probably conjured by

Melvina," I pointed out. "And she's just devastated Gosheniene too." A lump, hard and sharp as a rock, grated my throat. I remembered the gruesome images of prisoners turned into ice figurines, hands stretched out, legs bent ready to run, unable to thwart the inevitable. My churning thoughts grew more chaotic. "Wait. If Vulcan and Melvina know I'm at Tarahik, why did they attack Gosheniene? Why did they attack Jubris and Idra?"

It made no sense.

Senator Kerr didn't answer right away but rubbed his chin instead, deep in concentration. I could almost see the troubled thoughts spinning in his eyes. "Before Clarence was killed, he stole something from the council. A map."

I raised my eyes at him. "A map? Leading to what?"

"We believe to the Larthalgule blade."

My body grew taut as a wire.

"No one knows where this map is," the senator continued. "Clarence hid it. Melvina has his notebook. Perhaps she was able to ascertain something from his scribbles. It's possible she believed the map was hidden in Idra, Jubris, or Gosheniene."

I exhaled a troubled sigh. "But it wasn't there."

And that was why Melvina had attacked those places. Out of spite.

My eyes snapped to Jad without any control from me. I recalled the conversation he'd had with Thessio the morning I'd been removed from Gosheniene.

"The general wants to know if it's been found."

I blinked back confusion, my voice levelled at the captain. "You were looking for the map at Gosheniene, weren't you? That's the real reason you volunteered."

Jad didn't deny it.

My pulse hammered with rage. "The general knows about this too?"

Next to me, Macaslan lowered her voice, as though she were afraid the walls were listening. "He is aware Melvina and Vulcan are searching for Larthalgule. Your part in this story is unknown to him."

I swallowed. If Kravis knew my identity, he'd kill me. I didn't know why, but my eyes locked with Jad's, hoping to find reassurance, but there was none.

His expression was dark and indifferent. Why was he even here?

More important, what was the Larthalgule blade? If Morgomoth wanted it, its power must surpass our modern-day cast-shooters, hex-bombs, and curse-grenades. It had to be something ancient and buried. For Melvina and Vulcan to continue searching for it, it had to be a force of destruction no presence on Earth had known.

Clarity struck.

"It waits in Essida," I blurted, my voice shrill.

There was a baffled pause.

"Excuse me?" Darius scanned the room, hoping someone might enlighten him.

I remembered Adaline's warning in the dream.

"It waits in Essida."

Adaline wasn't a crazy spectre haunting me out of revenge. She was trying to help me.

A hysterical note took hold of my voice. "It waits in Essida. Don't you get it? The map that leads to Larthalgule is in Essida." I explained what had occurred in the nightmare. My audience stared in disbelief, their brows furrowed as they pondered my words. "What's Essida? Where is it?" I persevered.

The muscles in Colonel Harper's neck strained. "It's an island city under dissent occupation. The rebels took control of Essida four months ago. The Haxsan Guard have not been able to force the ULD out. Thousands of civilians are trapped."

I stood too fast, my head swaying. "They're searching for the map. We should move quickly. I'd bet my life Vulcan is in Essida now. We need to find the weapon before either he or his forces do."

Macaslan yanked me back into my seat. "No one is going to Essida, especially you. You need to remain at this base where you're secure."

I bit back a nasty retort. My control balanced on a fine edge. "But if I go to Essida… with a team… Adaline will show me where the map is. We can bring it back here. The ULD won't have a chance of finding it."

"That is out of the question." Macaslan ran her fingers down her thin face. The shadows around her eyes reminded me of the hollow cavities in a skull. "No one is going to Essida. What you need to do is continue your training and keep a low profile. The last thing we need is for someone at Tarahik to grow suspicious of your necromancy. General Kravis cannot know what you are."

I pointed an accusing finger at Jad. "And what if *he* tells the general what I am?"

All my conflicted feelings about the captain boiled down to one thing. On a subconscious level, I didn't trust him. And now it had risen to the surface, exposed for the world to see. Jad did nothing but stare at me with a look that made my blood flow cold. The sting in his eyes hit like a slap.

Macaslan's nostrils flared. "I trust the captain. We all do. And so should you."

Before I could argue my case, she stood, proud and intimidating in her crumpled gown. "I will make sure you're not deployed on missions and kept secure at the base. The captain and the colonel will keep an eye on you."

I clutched the table hard. "Then what's the point of this meeting if we're doing nothing? Why did you tell me any of this?"

They'd dragged me in here in the middle of the night, told me I was hunted by a crazy half-wraith, half-corpse woman intent on using my necromancy to finish what her master had started, and that somewhere out there, a blade was key to annihilating human existence—and I was supposed to just sit here and do nothing. If Macaslan and Darius expected me to stay put—an obedient little girl they could manipulate—they had another think coming.

"The reason we brought you here was because we thought it was time you learnt the truth." The commander spoke with patience, like she was dealing with a slow-witted child. "You are old enough to deal with this now, but whether you have the emotional capacity to understand is still in question."

She silenced my protest with a flick of her hand. "We've led the Haxsan Guard and the Council of Founding Sovereigns to believe we're with the Infinite Eye, that our allegiance is with them and protecting humans, but our true intention is to overthrow the council. They've let casters starve in the provinces. They've thrown casters into labour camps and re-education programmes rather than stopping to think why these casters joined the ULD in the first place. If we want this war to end, then casters and humans must not look at each other as an enemy. And that will never happen with this council. We overthrow our leaders and elect casters and humans in a new government. Chauvelin believed that your magic could assist with that task. I hope he was right."

I tipped my head back and laughed. I liked what she was saying, but honestly, what world was she living in? "You expect us to do that—just the five of us?"

That would be like a goldfish taking on a shark.

A secret smile shaped her lips. "There are more than five of us, Miss Wayward."

Before I could ask what she meant, Darius's gold pocket watch sounded a small alarm. He checked the time and made a gesture that ended the formalities. "This meeting is finished. If we stay here any longer, we risk rousing suspicion, especially when this isn't being recorded."

"Recorded?" My eyes darted around the room, looking for hidden microphones.

Macaslan swiped a key card from the table and retreated toward the blast door. "This isn't a conference room, Zaya. It's a war room. Conversations are recorded and played back to a tribunal appointed by the council. Everything we do is monitored. If we go over time, that tribunal will want to know what was discussed." Her expression grew hard, deadly serious. "I will create new defensive spells in your room and will provide you with another dreamcatcher."

The door buzzed open and she slipped through. Colonel Harper trailed behind her like a private bodyguard. Jad, his eyes black and unforgiving, left without looking at me, which hurt more than it should have. I understood why he was angry at me, but surely he could see where I was coming from. He hadn't exactly been kind or trustworthy. I watched his retreating figure, wishing I could read his emotional temperature. He was hot or cold, never in between.

My eyelids drooped. I no longer had the brainpower to connect my shattered thoughts. I reflected fondly on my bed with its fluffy white pillows and soft sheets and let my feet lead me toward the door.

I hadn't made it two steps when I spotted Sneer-face and Pick-nose in the passage. "What the hell?"

Darius stepped beside me, his voice low in my ear. "I'm sorry, Zaya, but we have to continue punishment for appearance's sake." He raised his voice to the guards. "You can take her now. I think a night in a cell will make her think twice before committing any more misdemeanours."

I pinned the senator with a cruel glare, hoping he sensed my resentment right down to his bones. "You can't be serious?"

He observed me with dry amusement. "I never joke about anything serious. I imagine you should feel quite at home in a cell... only this one comes with a pillow."

Sneer-face and Pick-nose arrived and clamped the handcuffs onto my wrists.

Before they dragged me away, I turned to the senator. I was desperate to get something off my mind, something I'd been too ashamed to ask in front of everyone else because Darius's answer had the potential to bring me to tears, and I wasn't ready for others to see that.

"Did you know my parents?" I asked in a small voice, afraid of what his response might be.

He didn't look at me for a long time. At last, he focused on my guards. "Leave us. Wait in the passage till I call for you."

Sneer-face and Pick-nose cast suspicious looks my way but returned to the passage.

Darius shut his eyes briefly. "No, I didn't. It was Clarence who knew your parents, but he never mentioned who they were. He was silent on the matter whenever I asked. I'm sorry, Zaya, but after everything that happened, I can only assume your parents were dissent rebels... key players in the ULD's forces."

I stared in grim silence, numb inside. I'd been plagued by so many emotions tonight that I was too raw and exhausted to be upset. When Macaslan and Darius had explained my connection with Chauvelin, I couldn't deny it any longer. My parents had been rebels. They might have offered me up as bait to Vulcan and Melvina. Why else would Chauvelin have stolen me?

Sneer-face and Pick-nose returned. I let them lead me away without protest.

Zaya Wayward had lost her fight.

CHAPTER TWENTY-THREE

The plan wasn't that simple. Macaslan insisted I remain at Tarahik and do nothing rash. She and Darius would take care of locating the map. The logical part of my brain told me that was the smart thing to do—leave it to the adults. But the reckless part—the part that far outweighed reason—told me to take action. This left me with another dilemma: Where to start?

I grew antsier each day I didn't hear from Macaslan. There was no easy off button for my brain. Either the commander hadn't learnt anything yet, or she was deliberately keeping me out of the loop. Judging from the way Jad avoided me in the corridors, training rooms, and dining quarters, I was positive it was the latter. So much for keeping an eye on me. Everything was dependent on the map. If I wanted to know more about it and Essida, then I had to contact the one person willing to help me—and that meant removing my new dreamcatcher.

Dreams aren't real. Dreams can't hurt you. Adaline doesn't want revenge. She wants to help.

That was what I told myself the first night I hid the dreamcatcher in my dresser, stuffing it beneath a pair of trousers and shutting the drawer. The moment it was out of sight, the air in my room instantly chilled, the window clouding with frost. A thousand hesitations fluttered across my mind. Before I could change my decision, I slipped into bed, pulled the covers tight, and lost myself into the dark depths of sleep.

I don't recall how the dream began, only that I'd returned to that bleak, windswept ice land. But it wasn't Adaline I saw. Corpses in various states of decay loomed over me, their skin floppy and loose, like it would melt in a sickening splash. The threat in their oily eyes, the danger in their black cavernous mouths, made me question what had happened to make them so vengeful, to make them so full of hatred that they were hell-bent on ripping me apart.

And then the answer arrived. The black-vein woman coalesced from her blanket of fog. She reached for me with her skeletal hand, her lips pulling back into a monstrous scream.

Just when I thought she'd submerge me in her filth, I woke.

Reality swam back into focus. I was alone, sweating, and crying—wishing I hadn't risked such an inane task. But it didn't stop me trying to make a connection with Adaline. For a fortnight, I put myself through this agony. Adaline never appeared. I didn't blame her; if I were in her shoes, I'd stay the hell away too.

In the waking world, I was hopelessly lost and dejected, so when Colonel Harper announced one drizzly afternoon that my field craft navigation and tactics class would be rescheduled for later that evening, I wasn't disappointed.

At just past nine, I stepped out into the crisp night and started the steep ascent to Hillcrest Lawn, one of the few places where cadets could escape the demanding routine of base life, and where Professor Gemmell would teach tonight's class. The weather was still freakishly cold, the wind biting like teeth. Maybe it was the nightmare tension still playing tricks on my mind, or the night's cold energy heightening my senses, but I became acutely aware I wasn't alone. Somewhere in the foliage, a bird screeched, the kind it makes before swooping on prey. I shivered and hurried on.

At the top of Hillcrest Lawn was the old rotunda. Its broken columns, ripped-up pavers, and moss-covered stones reminded me of an ancient monument in an enchanted forest. All the cadets were huddled around the rotunda, wrapped in shawls and blankets. Tusk was among them. His nose had healed but had a permanent crook to it, which—on an absurd level—had made him more popular with the girls. He smiled when he saw me, a taunting spark in his eyes. I stubbornly stared ahead. If he threatened me in any way, I'd kick him where it frigging hurt. He'd never be able to contribute to the gene pool ever.

"Good evening, class."

Professor Gemmell, a friendly looking guy with orange hair and a zillion freckles, bounded into the rotunda, his smile wild and loopy. "It's good to see you all so bubbly on this fine summer night."

A few students gawped.

Professor Gemmell was an alchemist, a socially awkward genius among his peers, and a nutty teacher—the type of guy who lived in a one-bedroom apartment with twelve cats. Sporting flip-flops, tight tweed shorts, and a tie-dyed shirt, it obviously hadn't occurred to the professor that the weather was strange and that the mountain air was like stepping into a freezer. At least he wore a scarf.

He squeezed his hands together, leaning on the balls of his feet. "I'm guessing you're all keen to get started."

"Not really," a cadet shouted back.

The professor smiled and gave a thumbs up, not registering the comment. "Excellent, excellent. It's going to be a super fun class, a real treat. For the first time, things are about to get practical." He pointed to the sky and beamed. "Does anyone have any idea what tonight's lesson will involve?"

Apart from shivering, the class held perfectly still. Professor Gemmell often conducted unusual experiments. Maybe people feared he'd catapult them into the sky. Others exchanged glances, drawing on the same conclusion—the alchemist's light bulb upstairs had finally blown out.

He kept smiling, but it started to falter at the corners. "Come on, folks. This isn't hard."

Field craft navigation and tactics was an important class. Colonel Harper wouldn't have subjected us to the cold—or Professor Gemmell—if he didn't have a valid reason.

I craned my neck. The rotunda had no roof. The velvet sky overhead was bright thanks to the harvest moon. "The stars."

The science teacher fist pumped the air. "Yes. Excellent work, Zaya."

A few cadets had lost interest and chatted at the back of the class. Someone else yawned.

Professor Gemmell pointed a warning finger at the offenders. "Look alive, people." He circled the rotunda, flip-flops slapping. "Now I want everyone to imagine themselves in this scenario. You've survived a battle. Your friends are missing or perished, and you're alone in a harsh, unforgiving environment. Dissent rebels are drawing close. What do you do?"

"Get out," a boy said, his voice implying "duh."

"What exactly does this have to do with us freezing on a mountain?" another cadet cried.

The alchemist ignored the flippant remark. "Getting out is the obvious answer, yes. But how do you do that when your compass is damaged and you dare not speak into your radio for fear the enemy will hear you? Technology has failed you, folks. What do you do?"

The class exchanged glances.

I snorted. At this rate, my peers would be dead before they hit the ground. "You navigate your way out by using the stars."

The science teacher snapped his fingers. "Bingo. And that is where tonight's lesson begins. We're going to learn basic astronomy and how the stars can navigate your path. Astronomy is the most ancient of the sciences. Humans practiced it long before they developed the telescope and technology. Of course, the sky the ancients saw is vastly different from the sky we see tonight. Scientists have a theory that the cosmic shift in our solar system caused the cataclysmic changes to the Earth. The realignment of the planets resulted in the birth of new stars and constellations in our solar system. It's these constellations that help us identify true north. From there, we can determine west, south, and east. Let's get started."

The professor spent several minutes identifying constellations in the night. "That's Hecatina over there, the goddess of fertility." He pointed to a cluster of silver-white stars just visible through the mist. "Some astronomers refer to her as the naked deity. See how the stars make up the curved outline of her breasts."

"Boobs!" Tusk's eyes scoured the heavens. His grin was half sloppy, half sleazy. "So you're telling me when I need to locate true north, I have to find boobs in the sky?" His crass laughter filled the night.

I rolled my eyes. Once again, Tusk proved he had the brain aptitude of a Neanderthal.

A twitch developed in Professor Gemmell's eye. "Mr Monahan, if you can't say anything remotely intelligent, then please refrain from saying anything at all."

The Neanderthal blinked.

The professor turned his attention back to the stars. "Now, class, if you look just over there, you will see seven constellations perfectly aligned in a circle. Zorsk, Zarti, Zezsay, Zabel, Zariesa, and Zedlyn are the stars that make up the circle. The largest star at the top—and here you'll have to put your imagination into it—resembles a diamond. That star is the largest known in our solar system—minus the sun, of course—and points directly north."

"What's that star called?" A girl with a short pixie cut, one of the few who'd taken an interest in the class, stared quizzically into the night.

Professor Gemmell cracked a smile at me. "That's the Zaya star… otherwise known as the Hope Star."

I crossed my arms over my stomach, uncomfortable with everyone staring at me.

It's a clue into my past. A frigging star is a clue into my past.

Were my parents fascinated by the skies beyond our own? Maybe they were astronomers, or astrologers, or simply hopeless romantics. No. That wasn't right. My parents were dissent rebels and buried in the past. Zaya probably wasn't even my real name. Clarence Chauvelin had likely named me that when he'd stolen me from the United League of Dissent. Hope indeed. But hope for what?

Professor Gemmell tilted his head to peer at the constellations. "The earliest casters worshipped the seven gods you see in the stars. Zorsk was the keeper of peace; Zarti the god of wisdom; Zezsay, the goddess of love; Zabel, truth; Zariesa, health; and Zedlyn, god of strength—characteristics we admire and value." He directed our gazes to the large gemlike crystal at the top of the ring. "And finally, the brightest jewel in the sky, Zaya, goddess of hope." He gave me a sheepish grin. "For there is truly no greater or powerful emotion than hope. It brings optimism, faith, aspiration." He clapped his hands in a rush of elation. "Now, each of you grab a telescope and begin finding the constellations set on the class plan. No dawdling. This is important."

I shrank away from the class. Thinking about my parents had made my throat slippery and tight. I needed a moment to breathe. Alone.

"Are you all right?"

I jumped at the voice right at my shoulder.

Professor Gemmell's purple-rimmed glasses magnified his bright eyes. It was a disorientating sight in contrast to his skinny, lanky body.

I managed a small nod. "Just struggling to keep warm, sir. It's so cold for summer."

Thanks to a homicidal corpse cursing everything to a wintery death.

My lie slipped out easily, but the alchemist didn't look like he believed it.

Worry clouded his face, but there was something cryptic in his gaze too. "I've heard what people have said about you. Tusk spread it. But I can see the truth in a person's eyes. I read auras, you see. I know you are innocent of the crime you were punished for… and that you continue to suffer. It's difficult to overcome, but you will in time. Your name is well suited to you, Zaya. You will bring hope when it's needed."

I appreciated the kind words—really, I did—but there was no logic behind it.

And then something more alarming struck a nerve.

"Wait." I studied his face, scanning his large eyes for clues. "You know? About… me?"

"About your situation? Yes. Macaslan told me." His voice dipped lower. "You have my full support, Zaya. What I think you and Macaslan are doing is extremely brave. I'm proud to be involved."

"There are more than five of us, Miss Wayward."

That was what the commander had answered when I'd questioned the likelihood of us taking down the council. Here was one of those supporters in the flesh. How many people were in this secret collusion to destroy the council?

After a beat of silence, Professor Gemmell stared into the sky. The Milky Way was glowing a brilliant purple hue this evening. "Amazing, isn't it? You won't be able to see the Zaya star for much longer. Maybe another month or so, and then it will be gone."

My mind still lingered on the shocking discovery, slow to process what he said. "Sorry, what?"

The alchemist plastered on a smile. "I don't mean literally gone. There are twelve moons circling our planet, one prevalent each month. Next month the blood moon will occur. Its light will obliterate most stars from the sky. They'll still be there, of course. We just won't be able to see them. It will be an exciting time for us alchemists, but for others…."

I didn't like the sudden change in his tone.

"For others?" I prompted.

His bony shoulders slouched. "We haven't seen a blood moon in a decade. There's an old prophecy that has many casters afraid. It goes like this." He cleared his throat. "As the Moon travels between the Earth and the Sun, the Sun will become darkness, the Moon into blood, and on that great and terrible day, the blackest of magic will be reborn."

"That sounds ominous."

"I believe that is the point."

I scoffed. "It's foretelling a lunar eclipse, nothing else."

The alchemist looked at me like he hoped I was joking. "Eclipses are science, created by our human ancestors to theorise events they could never understand. It's inaccurate and nonsensical. What I'm talking about is magic. It's had many names in the past: fate, destiny, religion, science. Magic is the energy in this universe that holds everything together. Without it, nothing would exist. It's constantly evolving, mapping everything out."

I eyed him, sceptical. "So you believe in this prophecy? You really think the blood moon is prophetic?" A shiver jumped across my bones. Necromancy wasn't meant to exist in this age, but I was living proof that it did. There was no reason why prophecies couldn't exist either.

The professor shook his head. "The stars and the alignment of the planets provide clues to our future. I believe a blood moon foretells an event of significance, one that will impact us greatly."

"That something bad will happen?" I tucked my hair behind my ear.

"That dark magic will return," he corrected. "But that can be questioned too. Magic is neither good nor dark. It's up to the caster what they do with the power they possess. But not to worry." He bumped my shoulder playfully.

"Casters were afraid during the last blood moon and nothing happened. Unless you count Morgomoth's execution, of course. It's likely nothing will occur this time around. Now…." He steered me toward the rotunda. "Let's return to these misfits and do some work. I've got a test planned for tomorrow evening, and I'd like at least one person to pass."

He winked.

I couldn't catch his enthusiasm. Necromancy was considered dark magic. Could the prophecy relate to that somehow? It was a sobering thought.

Professor Gemmell looked me squarely in the eyes. "Chin up, Miss Wayward. There's no reason to look afraid. There's nothing to worry about, especially when it comes to your… ability."

But there was uncertainty in his eyes.

I wasn't sure who he was trying to convince—me or himself.

CHAPTER TWENTY-FOUR

It was late by the time class finished. I wandered back to the castle alone. None of the cadets passed for friendly, and Professor Gemmell had remained at the rotunda to document stars. A few flickering candlelights stayed on in the castle, just enough to guide me through the dark hills. It was weirdly deceptive seeing Tarahik this way. Anyone new to the area would have mistaken the lights for dotted towns in the distance, not the massive edifice it was.

A cold wave of air sidled up my neck, my nose filling with the sudden stench of damp earth. I turned toward the surrounding forest. It was too dark to see what hid among the trees in Shadow's Wood, but I had that creepy tingly feeling over my skin as though I were being watched.

I tugged my jacket tighter. There was a whisper in the air that couldn't possibly have been the wind. It sounded like...

"Zaya."

I jumped.

Something moved in the foliage, a blur of shadow darker than the immediate trees. Was it an illusion? A trick played by my tired eyes? Gusts of cold wind carried a foul, decaying odour to my nose, and I knew what lurked in the bushes was not alive. My feet took frantic steps away without any direction from me. Something pale and bloated hobbled among the trees, moving with an unnatural twitch. The creature's head twisted around, its eyes on me. They glowed like headlights, mucus coloured and opaque.

"Zzzzaaaayyyyaaaa!"

The muffled scream pierced my skull.

I tore downhill.

Screw this. To hell with bravery.

Leaves crunched under my feet, long grass threatening to trip me. I was too preoccupied by what was behind me to take notice of what lay ahead. My foot came down on something hard, my ankle twisting. A gasp tore from my throat as I face-planted onto the moist ground. A girl lay crumpled on the grass beside me, legs drawn to her chest in a foetal position. It was the girl from class with the pixie cut. I think her name was Lunette. She groaned, holding her stomach with both hands. Her eyes rolled back lazily in her head.

Was she sick? Had someone hurt her?

I shook her arm, my voice urgent and concerned. "Hey… hey, wake up. We need to move. There's something in the—"

She sat upright, faster than was possible. Her hands closed around my wrists, her strength unparalleled. "Did you see it? In the woods?"

The hair prickled on my arms.

Lunette wasn't hurt. She looked… possessed.

She studied me—or at least I thought she did because her eyes swivelled in different directions. "I know you saw it. They surround you… always three, soon to be five. She's waiting, always watching. She wants the missing pair."

Recognition punched me in the gut. Back at Gosheniene, I'd been forced to attend a class where we had to identify evidence of voodoo. I'd seen horrible pictures of casters with their mouths sewn shut, criss-crossed with black stitches, and their eyes rolled in their sockets. Mrs Heartlace had said the men and women were clairvoyants—casters who had visions of the future. Because they were not allowed to speak of what they saw, the council demanded their mouths be permanently closed. Seeing those photographs had left me feeling sick and disoriented, like the way I felt now, because Lunette wasn't possessed. She was a clairvoyant. And she was having a vision about ghosts.

"She wants the missing pair"?

What does that mean?

And by "she," did Lunette mean….

My stomach swirled. I shot a terrified look at her. "What is the black-veined woman after? What's the missing pair?"

It was the wrong thing to say. Lunette's face went deathly pale in the white moonlight. I tried to wriggle my wrists free, but her grip was like a pair of iron clamps. She was desperately frightened of the prophecy polluting her mind. If she was seeing who I suspected, she had every reason to be afraid.

Sweat trickled down her apple-shaped face. "She claimed three. Now she needs the final two." Her eyes settled on mine, her expression that of someone older than her years, someone who'd witnessed terrible things. "Don't you get it? It's us. We're the missing pair."

A blanket of fear wrapped around me. "Tell me—"

A cry tore from Lunette as she jolted forward like she'd literally been thrown out of her vision. My wrists released, I crawled away a few paces, my heart pounding so loudly it must have echoed across the entire lawn. Slowly, colour returned to Lunette's face, her breathing calm.

Now that she'd returned to reality, she scanned her surroundings. Her chocolate brown eyes found mine. She studied me for several seconds, then burst into tears. "Please don't tell anyone of this," she sobbed. "If people learn of my visions, they'll lock me away."

My fear gave way to momentary sadness. "I won't tell a soul. I promise. But I need to know what the black-veined—"

"No." She leapt to her feet. "Don't say her name. I must go. I can't stay here anymore. Tarahik isn't safe. Not for me. Not for you. You have to leave."

She ran downhill, kicking dew and grass into the air. I didn't bother pursuing her. My chest heaved too heavily from violent spasms.

"They surround you… always three, soon to be five. She's waiting, always watching. She wants the missing pair."

I scrambled to my feet. I had to find Commander Macaslan.

CHAPTER TWENTY-FIVE

The elevator descended fifty, sixty-plus levels, deeper than I knew the base went, and opened to a long corridor lined with metallic doors. A headache pounded behind my eyes, but I marched ahead with one goal in mind—find Macaslan. She had to know about Lunette's vision.

I was halfway down the corridor when I registered something wasn't right. Some of the doors were ajar, as though someone had forgotten to close them in their haste. I snuck a peek inside. For a moment, reality didn't match what I witnessed. A large assembly of casters was gathered around holographic projectors, their eyes glinting in the artificial light. Tears. They were crying. A young woman had her hands cupped over her mouth, strain evident on her creased brow. I checked the scrap of paper the head office had provided me minutes ago, detailing the level and room number the commander could be found in.

Level sixty-two, room seventeen.

There'd been no mistake. I was on the right level. And the head office would never have sent me down here if the base was in the middle of a crisis. So why was there a tense charge in the air, like lightning was about to strike?

A few gasps rippled through the briefing rooms. I stood on tiptoes, peering over the sea of heads. War footage was aired. Buildings were ablaze and toppling into charred heaps, the jagged debris pointing out like crooked teeth in the smoke. Roads were blocked by blackened rubble. Even if I knew where this city was, I doubted I'd recognise if after such destruction. The speakers shuddered as sirens blasted on screen, the fear-inducing noise throwing the city inhabitants in a frenzy.

A wave of emotion swept through me. In training, the instructors told us to be vigilant in a crisis. They'd trained us with a plan, how to rescue, how to combat, how to strike the enemy down. But they'd never taught us how to witness atrocity and be powerless to do anything. The horror of seeing the devastation, mingled with the guilty relief that it wasn't me feeling the bloom of fire on my skin or the taste of ash in my mouth—well, that was the part that ate away at me.

Not everyone in the briefing rooms was focused on the screens. Some casters were seated at control panels, typing promptly into tablets, probably sending coded messages and instructions to the Haxsan Guard on scene. Was Jad one of them? Was he inside that burning city right now?

"Hey! You there!" An officer emerged from one of the briefing rooms.

Before I could process my confusion, the man was in my face. He must have hit the gym five times a day because his arms were bigger than my legs. "You can't be here, kid. All floors below level fifty are restricted. You need to turn around and leave." He tilted his chin toward the elevator, hinting for me to get a move on.

I stood rigid, torn between wanting to retreat immediately and finding Macaslan. "I need to speak to the commander. It's urgent."

The man narrowed a look at me.

Oh, come on. Could one thing please go right?

I rummaged my brain for an excuse. "Head office sent me."

It was kind of true.

The officer gave an exaggerated snort. "Nice try. Head office didn't radio ahead, so whatever it is you're after from the commander, it will have to wait." He unhooked his radio, spittle flying from his mouth. "Clarzo, I thought you'd limited the use of that lift. There's a girl down here."

A static, crackly voice shouted something back impolite.

A flush of anger crept in my cheeks. "Sorry, but I don't have time to wait." I ducked past him, hurrying down the passage, searching the briefing rooms for the commander. But the officer was just as fast. He snared my arm and dragged me back toward the elevator like I was a doll with plastic for bones. I tried wriggling out of his hold, but it was like fighting a concrete wall.

He grunted. "Listen, girl, we've got a situation here. The commander is with General Kravis and Colonel Harper in the control centre. Even if you did *happen* to bypass me, security will never let you through."

Sparks of fury ignited a fire inside me. "What is happening? What was that city burning to the ground?"

The officer exhaled sharply. Punching the button at the elevator, he shoved me inside, barricading any chance I had of getting out. "Next time you come down here, I won't be so nice. Got it?"

My lips shaped into a defiant smirk. "If Clarzo does his job, there won't be a next time, will there?"

Blood rushed to his face. Clearly Clarzo didn't inspire confidence around here.

The doors sealed, the pop of suction emphasising one point.

I've failed.

The elevator climbed the metal shaft, only it didn't go all the way. It clanked to a stop at level sixty. A boy entered. He hummed a tune in time to the music that blasted out of his headphones, his fingers rhythmically playing the air guitar.

I recognised his dirty blond hair, grey duster, and aviation goggles. "Edric?"

Edric swivelled around. I was surprised he'd heard me. I was also surprised he hadn't shattered his eardrums from the music.

His face split into a grin. "Zaya, my man... I mean lady." He dropped the headphones around his neck and slapped me a high five. "So, you got selected for the mission too, huh?"

I stared, the gears in my brain spinning.

Mission?

Edric pressed the button for the forty-third floor. "I can't wait to fly and shoot some dissent rebels down. It's gonna be brutal out there." He bounced eagerly on the balls of his feet, reminding me of a kid on too much sugar. "I hope we get to Essida in time, save what's left of it, at least."

My heart beat in crazy rhythm. "Essida?"

He raised his eyes at me. "Yeah… you know… the city that's under attack."

I opened my mouth, then shut it again.

In my mind, I summoned a diagram of Tarahik and mentally scanned the base. Tarahik's hangars, along with fuel and the armoury, were located from levels forty to fifty. Edric had proved he was a capable pilot. If he was heading to the forty-third floor, then the base was sending out fire-crusaders… to an already burning city.

From the footage I'd witnessed, Essida needed medics like Lainie and Talina on scene, not a unit of fighter jets. Essida was under dissent occupation. Did that mean the ULD had the map and were burning the city to the ground… or was this General Kravis's work? Destroy the city and the map would be lost forever. It was a malicious plan, and a strategy I didn't doubt the general would lower himself to.

Edric's gaze settled on mine. "Everything all right? You look… frazzled."

"I missed some of the brief." I tried to keep my tone neutral, but the hysteria in my voice rolled thick into the air.

"Dozed off, hey?" He elbowed me in the ribs. "It's good to have you on board, Zaya. You're the best shooter I've seen. You'll be with Captain Arden and his squadron, I suppose?"

My pulse edged up a beat. "Uh… yep."

Edric rattled on about the brief, but I blanked him out. My irritation climbed. Macaslan, Colonel Harper, Senator Kerr, and Jad had deliberately left me out of this. It stung because they knew how important Essida was to me. I was the sole reason they even knew about the map being in the city in the first place.

Ungrateful jerks.

Fine. They didn't want me on the mission. I got it. But they couldn't prevent me from going to Essida. I'd played their game long enough. It was time to take matters into my own hands.

"It waits in Essida."

I was confident that once I arrived at the city, Adaline would show me the way to the map. But I wouldn't stop there. Macaslan had told me necromancers in the past summoned spirits to gain hidden meaning and inner truth. Well, if that was what it took, I'd call Adaline and find out exactly what the black-veined woman was planning with the Larthalgule blade—and how Lunette and I were involved.

"Hey, Zaya?" Edric's eyebrows bunched together. "Shouldn't you be getting out here? Your squadron are leaving from this runway."

I was so consumed by thought, I hadn't realised the elevator had stopped and the doors were open.

Edric, blessedly still for a change, watched me.

I pulled on an unflustered face. "Damn nerves. Got the better of me for a moment."

I stepped casually into the hangar, but inside I was convulsing in terror. Hot air caused my skin to break out in sweat, the stench of fuel, fumes, and metal permeating everything. Even the ventilation shafts seemed clogged with it. Soldiers suited up in heavy protective gear prepped carrier-hornets and fire-crusaders; others talked strategy in small groups. I'd seen this before in training. They'd called them practise scrambles. But this was the real deal. I knew because of the tension in the air. If tension was like electricity, this was high voltage.

I weighed my options.

Jad was in charge, and the captain wasn't the type of guy who did things on a whim. He was leading an important mission and would know the number of soldiers taking part. The people down here were meant to be here. An impostor would quickly be discovered.

Stay calm. Stay calm. But think fast.

I ducked behind a stack of crates to pull my head together. Somehow, I needed to sneak onto a carrier-hornet without being seen. I searched the crates. They were full of tactical gear, radios, food, and blankets, but nothing that could help my predicament.

"What's this?"

I jumped at the voice over my shoulder.

The soldier had her cast-shooter expertly aimed on me, her eyes narrowed in suspicion. "You don't have permission to be here, girl. Explain."

I tried on a helpless face. "I'm lost... and when I saw all this, I got scared."

The woman was young. My guess was only a few years in the armed forces. And she was roughly the same size as me. Dressed in uniform, she had the black helmet wedged between her hip and arm. A quick glance past the crates showed me soldiers were boarding the carrier-hornets. She must have been on her way to join them when she'd spotted me lurking.

The impatient look on her face shifted. My puppy-dog eyes had done the trick. She sighed, moving her cast-shooter away. "I'll take you back to the castle. Just promise you won't come down here again or—ahh!"

In the split second she'd taken her eyes off me, I struck. She cried a short, gurgling scream—not loud enough for anyone to hear, thanks to my hand closing around her mouth— and dropped the cast-shooter. The helmet fell next.

Come on… pass out… pass out….

The vessels in her neck strained. Her eyes bulged so wide, I was afraid they'd pop out of their sockets. She gave me one last pleading look—which I really could have done without—before she went limp in my arms.

"Sorry," I whispered as I set her down, because really, what else was there to say?

Adrenaline shook my hands as I stripped her uniform. Thank providence she had clothes on underneath, because once the jets left the base, damp mountain air would sink into the hangar and the temperature would drop. I stole a blanket from a crate and wrapped it around her. Maybe she'd forgive me if she stayed warm.

I slipped into the uniform. It was loose at the hips and too big in the chest, but seriously, who'd have time to notice? I hurried across the hangar, keeping the visor down on my helmet. Bursts of instruction from the communication centre flowed through my earpiece, updating new information and coordinates. I memorised everything. Once I separated from the squadron, I'd have to survive on my own wits.

It was a tight squeeze inside the carrier-hornet. Most of the soldiers were quiet, too focused on their task ahead to talk. I understood their sobriety. They were like ants in a huge colony, working as a unit. Essida was their nest, the place they had to defend—or destroy, depending on who had coordinated the first attack. If one soldier fell, they'd be replaced. So why bother getting to know anyone? It was tragic, but when the time came, it meant slipping away would be easier.

A few soldiers had their helmets on, but I was the only one with the visor down. I hoped it didn't make me suspicious—which led to my next problem.

Jad.

I froze, not from the shock of seeing him but because he was close. His dark hair stood out to me like a beacon, those black eyes radiating stamina and resolve. People nodded gravely at him as he passed. When he drew near, panic unravelled in my stomach. If anyone could put an end to my plan, it was Captain Arden.

Frightened by his proximity, I turned away, not breathing till he climbed the metal ladder and disappeared into the cockpit.

Too close, Zaya. Too close.

I peered down at my gloved hands. They were trembling.

Calm down. Calm down.

A sonorous ring ran through the craft, warning of the upcoming take-off. The carrier-hornet started taxiing down the runway. The engines rumbled fiercely, the choppy *thump, thump, thump* of the rotor blades sending fierce vibrations through the hornet. My ears popped as the plane lifted.

At first the sky was clear, the mountains majestic, the trees a sea of green below. But once we climbed to higher elevation, everything changed. Dark, impenetrable clouds wrapped around the hornet. Wisps of snow swirled from window to window, materialising into fist-size pieces the farther we ascended. My confidence lapsed. We were flying into an ice storm.

CHAPTER TWENTY-SIX

The storm wasn't violent, according to the information in my earpiece, but wind buffeted the plane, throwing us into heavy turbulence, and freezing rain streamed down the windows to thicken into slush. Every arduous hour farther into the storm saw my stomach cartwheeling up to my throat. The soldiers remained silent, heads bowed and eyes closed, as though dreaming of being anywhere but here. It wasn't till the sky filled with burning light and we smelt smoke in the air that their expressions radiated into full-blown anger, their hands tense on their weapons. A cold, sick dread spilled into my gut.

Most of these soldiers might not come back.

Reinforcing my fear, one man kissed the steel locket that dangled from his neck—a silent farewell to the family photographed inside perhaps?

Outside, the clouds parted to reveal an island dotted by fires. Essida would have been a beautiful city once. Built in the mountain, I imagined it a place perfect for holiday makers to breathe in the sea air. Now it resembled a burning wasteland, its narrow, shadowy streets wrapped by thick smog. Plumes of smoke billowed from the settlement like rising mushroom clouds. Wild and unstoppable fires crackled with energy, ready to consume the island in a blazing embrace.

The hornet dipped, the pressure in my head increasing with the fast change in altitude. Jad clambered down the ladder in strict captain mode. His face was stern and his shoulders were broad, making him invincible and godlike. He addressed the soldiers, a war speech meant to inspire his men. I didn't tune in till he explained the mission.

The captain's eyes lit in battle-serious fervour. "Every road, runway, and path into Essida that hasn't been destroyed by firebombs is now overlooked by dissent rebels. It means any feasible way into the city is off limits. The plan is to land at the beach a quarter mile out from the mountain. From there, we'll track through the forest till we get to Nyagor. It's a cliff face roughly three hundred feet high. We'll be climbing with nothing but netting and rope. At the top is where the Haxsan Guard has made camp. There, you'll join the other assault troops under Colonel Sparus's command… and take back Essida."

Cheers, hoots, and cries rang through the cabin. Soldiers brandished their weapons. I guess in a strange way it made them feel alive.

Jad didn't join the short burst of zeal. His stony gaze weighed his soldiers, the harsh light painting his face in stark shadows. Back in the hangar, it had been too dark to differentiate between the uniforms, but now with the island's fires casting hellish light into the hornet, I realised Jad's attire was different. He was still dressed in black—black cargo pants, black windbreaker, black utility shirt—but it seemed odd that he'd separated himself from the rest of us. And why were the troops leaving his command once they arrived at the camp? Jad's face revealed only intense concentration, but there was something else happening behind his eyes. Something deeper was going on inside the captain's head.

The plane's thrusters rumbled, the deck plating rattling as we made a rocky, spiral descent onto the beach. Immediately, the disembarking ramp lowered. The troops followed Captain Arden onto the sand. In Gosheniene, prisoners had reminisced about the tantalising taste and smell of the beach—of sunlight and cool ocean breezes, and the warm sensation of sand between your toes. But this was nothing like those whispered memories. The wind reeked of smoke, not sea salt. Fine layers of sleet and ash blanketed the sand. Even the sea appeared dangerous, the waves smashing the rocky coastline with hurricane force. It seemed incredible that a place could burn and snow at the same time. But nothing about this was normal. The ice storm spanned miles, passing even Tarahik's borders. There was magic at work here. Dark magic.

The black-veined woman is close.

Airlifters thundered above, dropping in troops and crates of medical supplies. A crew of field medics started a makeshift hospital by the trees. They attended to the wounded brought in on stretchers, carts, or wheelbarrows—basically anything that could be used to transport the injured. A violent tremble passed through me. I'd expected to be confronted by burnt buildings, shattered dreams, and destroyed livelihoods. I'd forgotten about the broken bodies.

Through the onslaught of snow and teeming embers, I recognised two of the medical non-combatants. Lainie's black bob surrounded her face in a dark cloud, no longer sleek but mussed from wind and sweat. She inserted a syringe into a screaming man's arm. His leg looked like it had been pulverised by a meat grinder. Talina stood by the shoreline next to an air ambulance—a wide-body aircraft with a surgical hospital inside—and directed soldiers who carried the wounded slung over their backs. Even from this distance, her fatigue was easy to spot. Her shoulders were stiff, and her face was etched in panic. I wished I could go to her, but I had to focus on my task.

Jad shouted a command. The troops trudged at a brisk pace into the trees. The ground was soggy from the snow, and the wind blew hot ash onto our visors. Grass, weeds, and hidden rock fragments threatened to trip even the hardiest foot. I dropped my pace when a jagged rock formation appeared through the dense forest, standing like some massive monument to nature. Nyagor. I was grateful I wasn't climbing that monster of a cliff face.

Certain no eyes were on me, I darted behind a tree and waited till the troops vanished in the vast maze of forest. Hot gusts from the fires left me sweating and frustrated, my fingers so tight they were locked on my cast-shooter. Incredibly, the snow wasn't melting—more proof there was nothing normal about the ice storm. A flash of doubt robbed my concentration.

What if Adaline doesn't appear?

Macaslan had warned me to stay clear of the black-veined woman, and I'd literally stepped out into her hunting ground.

I shook my reservations away.

Keep hidden. Don't lose focus. This plan will work.

From my hideout, I watched the troops disappear into the haze. I skidded down a slope of thick-rooted trees, trusting that Adaline would appear and show me another path into Essida, one where I didn't have to climb the mountain range. But when the ground finally evened out, I stood alone in the snow and ash, pummelled by howling winds.

Come on. Where are you? Where are you?

Nothing.

No ghostly manifestations. No eerie creaks in the forest. No chilling voices.

No Adaline.

I'm alone.

Light danced spottily in the trees ahead. Too late, I registered the horrible truth.

Fire.

Flames surged up the trees, leaving the trunks behind in blackened poles. Sparks rained, igniting leaves and twigs. I couldn't believe how fast the fire rushed from one branch to the next, consuming everything in its inferno. I dropped to my hands and knees and army-crawled back up the slope. My chest was tight from exertion, my muscles screaming. The smoke was so thick, my head became a disorientated mess—which was why it took so long to recognise the dark form nestled in the shadows.

The shock of seeing him caused my foot to slip out beneath me. He sprang. There was no time to put up my defences. The stranger lifted me off the ground, my feet bicycling through the air. I kicked and thrashed, but the man was too strong and easily backed me into a tree. He tore my helmet off. Burning winds stung my eyes and clogged my nose.

Jad's eyes simmered with rage. "You never listen, do you?"

The ferocity in his voice startled me. "Let go."

The captain's fingers bit into my arm. "Do you know how much danger you've put yourself in by being here?"

My scalp prickled. I should have been grateful I was no longer alone, but I wasn't exactly in a rational state of mind. I slapped his arm away. "I have every right to be here. I need to find that map."

The hateful look on his face made me squirm. "There was a plan in place, but now thanks to you, I'm going to have to re-evaluate." He rubbed his hands across his eyes. Perhaps I was imagining things, but when his gaze wandered back to the fire, the blaze seemed to contain itself, like it hit an invisible firewall. But that couldn't be possible, could it?

The captain closed our proximity. "You could have ruined everything," he continued in that lethal tone. "The way back to the beach is obstructed by fire. You'll have to come with me."

He didn't sound pleased about it.

"I'm not joining your rescue mission. I'm here for the map." I crossed my arms and cemented my feet in the snow, which fast became covered in soot.

He shook his head, glaring at the ground. "I'm not on a rescue mission. I have my own operation. Now take that uniform off. Where we're going, it will get you killed."

I unzipped my black jumpsuit and threw it at his feet. "How the hell did you find me?"

The look he shot me was half smile, half sneer. "I'm familiar with all my soldiers. I recognise an impostor when I see one. I watched you leave the squadron and doubled back." He examined the tar black clouds overhead. The mountain no longer looked like a mountain but a volcano, shooting fire and black smoke into the sky. "Come on. We're running out of time."

Reluctantly, I followed him up the slope to a road that snaked its way around the mountain edge.

I kept my head down, keeping close behind him to shield myself from the hot winds. "What is your mission?"

The captain passed me one of his trademark you're-a-real-pain-in-my-arse kind of looks. "I was sent here to meet a contact, a spy placed high in the ULD's ranks. This man works for Senator Kerr. He has information about the map."

I closed my eyes for a moment, feeling incredibly stupid. Macaslan had worked out a plan after all.

The captain took out two red armbands from his windbreaker and wrapped one below my shoulder. The other he tied around his bicep. The

ULD's insignia was patched on both—a circle with a dissent swastika in the centre, held by an eagle and griffin.

My stomach squeezed in revulsion. "I'm not wearing this."

I would have torn the armband off and stomped it into the ground, but Jad caught my wrist.

His voice was authoritative and stern. "These are our only safeguards in Essida. We'll be posing as civilians who have sided with the rebels. It's our only way in and out of the city. Think about it."

I did and knew he was right. Slipping into Essida on my own was fast becoming a joke. I'd been ill-prepared and hadn't thought it through.

I touched the armband. It was rough and bristly beneath my fingers. And was that a spot of blood above the insignia?

I swallowed. "How did you get these?"

The captain clicked the safety off his cast-shooter and didn't look at me. "You don't want to know."

Without another word, he headed into the snowy, fire-lit forest. My resolve weakened. No matter what decision I made tonight, it would lead to inevitable danger.

CHAPTER TWENTY-SEVEN

We reached Essida from a cave—an ancient escape route that narrowed into a steep track through the mountain—and climbed from a manhole into the town square. My first inclination was to cover my nose and block the cooked, meaty stench carried by the wind. I stopped midstep, my jaw agape. Flames fanned out across bombed-out buildings. The cobble roads were lined with sulphur and ash. Except for the crackling flames and the sound of machine guns fired in the distance, the market square was silent. And empty.

I rubbed my arms, spooked by how vacant the streets were. "Where is everyone?"

Jad examined the burnt-out market square, his eyes blazing like the athame-sabre in his hand. "They're either long gone… or dead." There was no life in his voice, no emotion, just cold hard fact.

Something sticky built in the back of my throat. I snuck a glance at his cool, calculating expression. How could he be so impervious to what surrounded us? The flames cast terrible shadows across his face, his lean, muscled body moving with purpose through the square. He looked like an avenging angel sent to wreak havoc on the Earth.

I sniffled, wiping my nose on the back of my hand. "Did the ULD do this?"

Surely only they could be to blame for Essida's destruction? But the more the hungry inferno shot sparks like New Year's fireworks, the more I realised only advanced weapons could be responsible—weapons the Haxsan Guard possessed.

Jad marched on, never slowing his stride. "General Kravis ordered the attack. Macaslan organised the rescue mission."

I froze, glaring at the back of his head. "Why would Kravis do this?"

The captain spun around, flushed and feverish-looking, his eyes intense on mine. "Because the ULD believed someone in this city had the map. Vulcan Stormouth offered a reward in exchange for it. Kravis made sure no one would be tempted to take the offer."

"By destroying the city?" I tossed back a disbelieving laugh.

The heated glare in Jad's gaze softened. I knew no matter how hard he tried to hide it, he didn't agree with the general's method either. His fingers locked tighter on his weapon, the muscles in his neck straining. "Take a breath and pull yourself together, Zaya. I need you calm. My contact's meeting point is not far from here. We get in and out. Understand?"

A dry burn formed in the back of my throat. "Fine."

Because what other choice was there? I wasn't even supposed to be here. My plan had fallen flat on its face. Jad was my ticket out of Essida. I was at his mercy now.

The captain led me into the maze of debris, sifting through the ash with his boot and kicking rubble aside. Something rolled out to land face up at my feet. Horror clouded my brain. It was a blackened skull.

Strange, powerful grief erupted in my chest.

That meaty, barbequed stench is… people.

Vertigo closed in, my legs weightless.

I didn't hear Jad approach, but his voice was suddenly there, low and deliberate in my ear. "Don't look at it. Keep your eyes focused on me and don't stare at the ground."

I shivered, unnerved by the conviction in his tone. How many charred bodies lingered around us?

Jad swung his athame-sabre, hacking a path through the burnt wreckage, the blade's power melting the crumbled slabs, twisted metal, and broken glass like they were made of butter. My feet drifted after him, one unbalanced step after another.

Kravis did this. Kravis killed these people. Kravis is responsible.

A wild, overwrought rage bubbled inside. But the time to mourn would have to come later. Jad was right. I had to keep my cool; otherwise anger would make me do something regrettable.

We took the back roads into an industrial estate, weaving our way between lofty warehouses and crooked buildings, and came out to a road blocked by burning vehicles and damaged tram cars. The buildings were reduced to skeletal frames, the footpaths blackened to burnt rubble. Even the road had lifted in places, pipes broken and gushing water.

I blinked over and over, my world spinning out of orbit. Crowds converged in crying mobs, pulling survivors from the destruction. Others had made up their minds to flee. The dead were piled under blood-soaked sheets. Sometimes, the cloth failed to hide a body part, the skin burnt and split, already enveloped by flies. I threw a hand over my mouth. The flies' incessant buzzing, the uncontrollable screams, and the roar of the flames sounded like a symphony recorded straight from hell.

Jad took my elbow and steered me through the crowd. "I told you not to look."

I slapped his hand away. "What do you suggest I do? Walk with my eyes closed?"

Not even a blindfold could save me from this. The smell of burnt flesh hung in the air like a poisonous fog. Fumes deprived my lungs of oxygen. Witnessing this devastation had caused a part of my soul to shatter, broken forever.

Jad wrapped his hand firmly around mine. "Keep your attention focused ahead and nothing else. We can't help these people, Zaya."

The sensation of his fingers locked with mine shocked me. Perhaps if I was thinking straight, I'd have the decency to pull away, but my willpower had vanished. And some intrinsic part of me didn't want to let go. Jad was probably making sure I didn't wander off and do something stupid, but for me, holding his hand was an affirmation that I wasn't facing this horror alone. That I had him. That he understood, even if he wasn't being entirely civil about it.

He wrenched me away from the pandemonium. It hadn't escaped my notice that the captain checked over his shoulder several times, his upper body rigid. I sensed fury radiating off him and was suddenly unsure of what, or who, to be afraid of—Jad or what he'd seen. I cast a glance over my shoulder, squinting through the smoke. Bright flames danced along the road, casting everyone in silhouette, but nothing else stood out.

I squeezed his hand. "Judging by how tense you are, I'd say we're being followed."

His silence confirmed my fear.

When no one was watching, Jad ushered me into a narrow cobblestoned alley lined with lopsided brick buildings. The windows were barred. Old newspaper clippings littered the ground. At the end of the lane, the harbour was a placid, depthless black, a forest of ships bobbing gently in the current, mocking us with their serenity. His grip went slack, his hand falling away from mine. He peered up and down the empty alley, examining the shadows.

I cleared my throat, but my voice came out high and desperate. "Is someone after us?"

Jad moved his hands along the wall, tapping the bricks with his knuckles, surveying the grouting.

This was strange behaviour indeed, and not warranted if we were about to be seized upon.

"Jad?"

"Yes, I heard you."

His damp black hair fell forward as he moved his fingers along the bricks. Something unimaginable happened at his touch. The bricks' surface rippled like waves across water, Jad's hand sliding into the building beyond. A secret entry. The magic was beautiful, ebbing and flowing, reminding me of the colour pigments found in oil. In a daydream, I leaned forward to touch the magic for myself.

Jad grabbed my wrist with an unbreakable grip. "Don't. It's a glamour and not to be meddled with. My contact is in there, but we don't know what else is too. Let me go first. After five minutes, if I don't come out, you need to leave."

Pure panic shot through me. "Leave?"

Without... you?

Jad took out a polished metal cylinder from his windbreaker. He closed my fingers around it, pressing my thumb onto the canister's small pad. A kaleidoscope of blue light blazed out of the metal cylinder, encasing the alley in a shimmering glow, like the entire place had been transported under the sea.

His eyes pinned me in place. "Only the person holding this rune-cast is protected by the light. The light casts you invisible. If I don't come back, you need to return to the beach and get into an air ambulance. Do you remember the way?"

I blinked in astonishment.

Leave him?

"Do you remember the way?" he repeated with more force.

I shook off my confusion. "Yes, but... why?"

My heart raced. What was the meaning behind this?

Jad sounded breathless. "Because you're more important than me, and you need to get back to the base." His gaze returned to the rune-cast. "This will make you invisible, but it won't protect you from the elements. Be careful."

He tore his hands away from mine. The sudden loss felt as though I'd been thrown out into a remote, empty abyss. Jad reached for the cast-shooter at his belt, inhaled a breath, and immersed himself in the glamour.

Shameful, aching guilt swept through me at the idea that I was somehow more important than him. I thought about the sacrifice Jad was making, instant warmth spreading into my cheeks, the blood hot in my face. No one had cared for my well-being before—at least, they'd never shown it, just worked on it in the background without my knowledge, like Macaslan and Darius had. But this kindness seemed out of character for Jad. And the way I responded to it was out of character for me. My hand still tingled where his fingers had made contact.

Oh no.

Oh. No.

The last thing I needed was to be crushing on my mentor. I'd been sweating all night, but now I was sweating for an entirely different reason. No. There had to be another cause for my confused feelings. But when I searched for an answer, none came—save for one I wished to deny. The troubling fact was that my feelings for Jad had been creeping up on me for weeks, and now they were in my face, demanding my attention.

This can't be happening.

I sat huddled against a dumpster, each second like a ticking time bomb in my heart. An awkward shadow slid across the ground. I peered up to see only Jad's hand protruding from the glamour, signalling the all-clear. I shot to my feet, a shiver of apprehension dancing up my spine. Slipping my hand into his, I stepped into the glamour, aware there was more than one danger I was encountering tonight.

CHAPTER TWENTY-EIGHT

I entered what was unmistakably a church. Stained-glass windows threw squares of colour across the nave. Angel effigies stared down from a dome ceiling, their eyes freakishly real. Magic had replaced religions long ago, but some casters still found comfort in the old sanctuaries, mainly as refuges for the homeless. This church was no different. Blankets had been strewn across the pews, pillows propped in the corners. Empty food tins littered the dusty floor. There was no altar cross. Anything valuable had been stolen long ago.

I let go of the small pad on the rune-cast. The light that had been my only comfort vanished, leaving me visible and exposed. I hoped my expression was clear of the confused, messy emotions I'd experienced in the alley, but judging by the way Jad watched me, my face was transparent.

I offered him the rune-cast. "Thanks."

He shook his head. "Keep it. It's yours."

The flame light through the windows outlined the perfect symmetry of his face, making him appear breathtakingly handsome.

My troubled feelings spiralled back. "Um… sure. Thanks… again, for the… ah, rune-cast."

What is wrong with me? I sound like a lovesick schoolgirl.

Jad's mouth hinted at a sly smile. "Are you okay?"

"Yep. I'm fine. Never been better."

Get a grip, girl. Get a grip.

He stared down at me, his raised eyebrows showing he was unsure of what to make of my abrupt change in attitude. "I think you might be in shock."

I met his eyes but didn't answer.

You have no idea.

I hoped to defuse the tension inside me by focusing on the church. This place could give Tarahik a run for its money on creepiness. The tapered ceiling disappeared into darkness, but I swore strange faces peered out, white and marble-like with broken, eroded cheeks. I jumped at the rustle of commotion above, imagining a winged beast about to claw me off the ground like a mouse, but it was only a pigeon flailing its feathers, annoyed at being disturbed. Now that my eyes had adjusted, what I thought had been dark, empty spaces in the stone walls were crypts filled with dusty coffins, the stillness so intense, it made me think skeletons might jump out at any moment.

A heavy feeling of doubt pressed upon me. "Your contact is here?"

The place didn't scream security and protection to me. It spoke of loneliness, destitution, abandonment. Even the air reeked of soiled linen and blocked drainage.

Jad rubbed his jaw. Hair fell over his face, hiding his expression, but I sensed what he was thinking by the disdain in his voice. "We're late, and my contact is long gone." He kicked an ornately carved cross, knocking it to the ground. It splintered into thousands of tiny fragments.

I hated seeing the spasm of failure cross his face. "Maybe he never came," I suggested. "He might have got caught in the bombings, or in the...." I trailed off, deciding it was both in our best interest not to think about the horrible possibilities that could have befallen Jad's contact. The captain was angry enough as it was.

Jad squinted at something ahead. He trod carefully through the pews, his feet disturbing the dust. "No. He was here. See the footprints?"

Footprints?

A barrage of questions popped in my mind. Jad was right. A second pair of shoe markings made a path to the altar. But there was something off about the footprints. They didn't seem genuine, almost as though they'd been deliberately made in a hurry—or as a diversion.

A soft noise broke the silence behind me, like fabric moving, or a stir in the breeze, or…

"Who is she?"

I spun around, scooting back a step.

A man stepped out from the confessional booth. His eyes centred on me with a mistrustful glare, sending a chill of dread through my veins. There was something off about him. His black-and-grey dissent uniform was too large on his scrawny body, tattered and singed from fires. His shaved scalp was so dry and dirty, it looked as though he showered in mud. He was young, somewhere in his thirties maybe, but the shadows that drowned his eyes made him look older. It took a moment to comprehend that the object he pulled from the waistband of his trousers was a cast-shooter—aimed solely at me. Whatever composure I'd regained hovered away, completely out of reach.

Total shock and surprise crossed Jad's face. He raised his hands in a placating gesture. "Tejor, she's with me. Put it down."

Great. Darius's infiltrator is an unstable, gun-toting vagabond.

Tejor's face went white, his eyes wide and wild. "I was told there'd only be you, Jad." The cast-shooter teetered in his hand. He smelt like a man who'd broken out into a serious sweat.

Jad regained his breath, keeping his voice level. "There was a change of plan. You can trust her."

The spy let out a bitter chuckle. "You can't trust anyone. Not anymore. You taught me that, Jad. Don't forget, I listened to your lessons."

"Then listen to me now. Lower the gun. She's not a threat."

A slimy, bitter taste crawled into my mouth. I'd been faced with cast-shooters before. The prison guards at Gosheniene had pulled them on me all the time, but they'd done it to frighten me into compliance. Tejor was a spy and unhinged by the atrocities he'd witnessed, which made him dangerous. My hand reached instinctively for the cast-shooter in my holster. Tejor was our contact, our only source for information, but if it came down to it, I'd shoot him.

Jad inched forward. "You kill her and you'll have to deal with Darius's wrath. That's not something you want to experience, trust me."

His words caught Tejor's attention. The man broke down and sobbed, a hopeless, desperate sound. If I wasn't so afraid, I might have felt sorry for him.

The threat over, Jad's eyes took on a hard edge. "Drop the gun and kick it over."

Tejor collapsed into an awkward heap against the communion rail but slid the cast-shooter across the floor. The captain knelt and secured it in his windbreaker.

Jad's voice was a low, harsh whisper in the church. "You have information we need."

It wasn't a request.

Tejor shrank back in alarm. "Not here. I'll tell you once we leave… once we're safe on a carrier-hornet."

I drew several sharp breaths, bracing myself for the fallout, because the severity in Jad's expression told me that wasn't an option.

The captain shook his head. "You're not coming with us."

Tejor moaned, driving his palms into his bloodshot eyes. "I can't stay with the ULD any longer. I can't pretend anymore. You don't know what it's like… the things I've had to do to keep up the charade. I've had enough."

Jad's mouth turned hard with disgust. "You owe Senator Kerr a debt. Now he needs you with the ULD and reporting from the inside."

Spittle flew from Tejor's mouth "Then tell Senator Kerr to send someone else."

The spy's vulnerability sent a wave of despair through me. What had he endured with the ULD? I'd heard reports that casters held prisoner under dissent occupation were forced to join the cause, and if they refused, they were hung and burned along the border of a Free Zone—a demonstration to the council and humans alike that the ULD's philosophy was the right one and the only one, and anyone who believed otherwise would be destroyed. Did Tejor have to commit to barbarism like that? The hairs on my scalp prickled. Maybe it was time for Tejor to come home. He needed help.

Jad opened his mouth to argue, but something in his eyes shifted, defusing whatever thought had crossed his mind. "All right, you can come with us."

Tejor blinked.

I blinked.

What is going on?

CAS E CROWE 197

Jad's voice was grave but determined. "First, tell us what you know. This place is secure. On the hornet, I can't guarantee everyone is on our side."

My throat went dry. The captain meant spies.

Tejor wiped his arm across his sweaty forehead. His eyes glimmered feverishly. "Melvina Raskovitch is here for the map. She destroyed Jubris and Idra and that internment camp in search for it, but now she knows it's definitely in Essida."

Jad stared, his face etched with worry. "Does the map lead to the Larthalgule blade?"

Tejor shrugged. "No one knows for certain. It's top secret. Melvina Raskovitch... she's aware of more than she lets on. It's almost like she and Vulcan Stormouth are psychically linked. That's how they're communicating."

"Telepathic communication." Jad bowed his head and shut his eyes, as though this entire conversation was giving him a headache.

My vision spun. A deep buzzing rose to a crescendo in my head. I'd heard Melvina's voice in my mind. She'd haunted me by accessing my dreams. Was I psychically linked to her?

Tejor drew back, his spine stiff. "I do know that Melvina and Vulcan are up to something that has to do with the approaching blood moon. Melvina murdered an illusionist and a trickster some years ago, and more recently, she killed a telepath in an orphanage. Word is she needed their magic... something to do with a sacrifice. I've heard talk from ULD officers that Melvina is searching for a clairvoyant." He swallowed. "And a necromancer."

My entire body hummed with terror.

"They surround you... always three, soon to be five. She's waiting, always watching. She wants the missing pair."

Illusionist. Trickster. Telepath. Clairvoyant. Necromancer.

Melvina had three out of the five.

But why?

Tejor wrung his fingers against his filthy scalp. "Melvina is five steps ahead of you, Jad. She knows that Darius Kerr and Commander Macaslan are finishing what Clarence Chauvelin started. She's learnt the identities of the clairvoyant and the necromancer... and she's aware that both girls are secure in the Tarahik Military Base. There are defensive spells shielding both girls. But it's only a matter of time till Melvina finds them."

A trickle of sweat ran down my spine, my curls pasted to the back of my neck.

Lunette.

She was planning to leave the base. Tonight.

But she couldn't, right? The celestial shields would prevent it. But if Melvina knew Lunette was a clairvoyant, then the traitor did too, and that gave me more reason for concern. Lunette was in a fragile place right now. She'd put her trust in anyone who told her they could get her out of the base. And that was just how a traitor worked, with lies and deception.

Dread gripped me. I had to warn Lunette somehow.

Jad's mouth turned grim. He kept his attention focused on Tejor. "What is the sacrifice for?"

Tejor's eyes darted frantically from me to Jad. "I don't know. I've told you everything I'm privy to. Now we must leave. Once Melvina finds that map, she'll destroy this place."

Jad's gaze remained cool and confident, but his fingers delved secretly around his holster, touching his cast-shooter. "We're leaving, Tejor. You're staying here. Find out what the sacrifice is for and report back."

Tejor flinched like he'd been slapped. A series of emotions played over his face—confusion, doubt, alarm—before finally settling on maddening rage. "No. You told me I could come with you."

The captain shook his head. "You have to remain with the ULD and gather more information. If you come with us and the rebels see, we risk the mission. And there's no room for you on the hornet. We have to take as many of the injured as we can to Tarahik so they can get proper medical treatment."

A hysterical laugh burst from the spy. "No room on the hornet?"

Something cruel flickered in his eyes. There wasn't time to shout a warning, because in one convulsive moment, Tejor pulled out a sleek black metal object from his uniform. My body pulsed with shock. He had another cast-shooter. Tejor wasn't the fool I'd believed him to be. He'd come prepared. He waved the gun at Jad before swerving the barrel toward me. "I guess I'll have to take her place, then."

Gunfire exploded in my ears, a disjointed boom that split the silent church. I looked down, expecting to see a hole ripped inside me and to be consumed by excruciating pain, but there was nothing. Instead, Tejor sagged to the ground. His chest was a punctured mess of sprayed tissue and blood, his eyes locked in a final expression of horror. Next to me, smoke wafted out of Jad's cast-shooter. Everything had happened so fast, I hadn't seen him take the weapon out.

The captain crouched over Tejor's body, feeling for a pulse. "Dead."

No shit.

There was so much blood, I was afraid I'd be sick if I looked at it any longer. "Why didn't you shoot him in the leg or something?"

Jad looked at me with an expression that said he hoped I wasn't serious. "That wouldn't have stopped him from shooting you. I can guarantee as soon as we turned our backs, Tejor would have shot us both dead. His mind was too far gone. If we'd let him come with us, he would have cracked and given us away."

The captain searched Tejor's pockets, snatching several knives for his collection. He moved toward me. "Put on the rune-cast. If Melvina is in this city, I'd rather she not see you."

It took me a moment to comprehend what he was saying.

Melvina.

The black-veined woman is near.

I switched the rune-cast on, the instrument immediately enveloping us in its bright sapphire light. Jad led me out of the church, giving my hand a gentle squeeze for courage. It was the only thing that soothed the panic in my chest.

CHAPTER TWENTY-NINE

I don't know how long I walked with Jad holding my hand, urging me forward. The light in our rune-cast burned out like a flame diminished by a sea breeze. The magic needed charging. Without its protection, Jad insisted we keep to the backstreets, which turned out to be an intricate network of twisting laneways through the derelict slums. Whoever had designed the area hadn't wanted to waste space, because the buildings were tightly crammed together, giving the impression of walls closing in—or maybe that was my fragile mind playing games with me.

I blinked, the ground feeling unsteady beneath my feet.

I squeezed Jad's hand, surprised by the unexpected taste in my mouth. "I think I'm going to be sick."

My legs buckled, the sidewalk rising toward me.

Jad caught my waist and propped me against the wall. "Tilt your head back and breathe."

I wondered how often he caught fainting girls because he seemed to know exactly what to do. Firelight painted his face in alternating shades of red and gold, his attitude amazingly calm after what we'd endured. Me? I wiped my eyes and tried to focus, but the image of Tejor's lifeless body kept chiselling at my skull. There'd been so much blood, more than I thought possible. I peered down at my trembling hands. A choked sound worked its way from my throat. There were wet, crimson dots splattered on my skin.

I'm wearing pieces of Tejor.

"Close your eyes," Jad instructed. "Breathe deeply."

Breathe?

Was he serious?

The air was polluted with the stench of charred metal and melted plastics. Breathing wasn't helping.

My eyelids slipped lower and lower. Jad's arms wrapped around me, the only thing keeping me together. Normally I'd detest weakness like this, but my brain was slow. Without thinking, I buried my face into his shoulder, relishing his embrace. After so much death, I needed to feel alive. Up close, Jad smelled of leather, metal, and mint. I felt the rise and fall of his chest, my own heart stuttering in response. Jad lifted my chin and stroked my hair soothingly from my face. His eyes were so dark, tiny images of me reflected from the pupils. His finger laced around one of my unruly curls. Then, seeming to realise what he was doing, he pulled away. The muscles in his throat tensed, and he wouldn't look at me. The warmth I'd experienced subsided like the tide drawn back, leaving me cold and humiliated, which was only made worse by the stiff, uncertain way he avoided me.

"You're in shock." His voice didn't sound steady anymore. He took a small canteen out from the pocket of his windbreaker. "Here, drink this. It's asith potion. It'll help."

Whatever solace I'd found in him disappeared. What had I been thinking? In my weakened state, I'd allowed myself to get close again. Jad was examining everything in our vicinity but me. A heavy ache pressed down on my shoulders. Was he really that ashamed of me?

Am I really that terrible to him?

Determined to prove to him—and myself—that it didn't matter, I tossed my head back and snatched the canteen, taking several unpleasant swigs. It burned like liquid fire down my throat.

The captain did the right thing, idiot. He saved us both from making a seriously huge mistake.

So why did I feel like I'd been caught hook, line, and sinker, a small creature left to flap and die on the shore?

The lines around Jad's mouth hardened, and I knew he didn't approve of my haughtiness. "Don't drink it too fast. It's a powerful potion." He scanned the alley ahead. "Let's keep moving."

Powerful was one word for the drink. My insides tingled, a flourishing, energised heat exploding through every fibre of me. Vitality drove new strength in my mind. I swallowed several greedier sips, embracing how the potion numbed every ache inside.

Jad let out an evasive sigh. "I'm not kidding. That potion can have serious side effects."

I jerked my chin toward the road, my expression cool and sure. "Let's just get out of this city, okay."

Adaline hadn't arrived to help me. There was no point being here. And I had to get back to Tarahik and make sure Lunette was safe.

The captain shook his head and walked away. I followed at a safe distance behind him, sneaking mouthfuls of the potion. The road wasn't labelled well—or maybe it had been once, before the fires—but I knew just by the upturned garbage bins and litter clogging the gutters that this place was a shithole even before the bomb drops. The sidewalk was cracked and dotted with potholes, the rows of terraced buildings obscured by ash, their black windows staring out like haunted eyes.

Jad kept his attention on the fires. It hadn't escaped my notice that the longer he stared at the blazes, the more they seemed to detach from everything we approached, as if we were somehow shielded by a hidden force.

I fixed a glare onto the back of the captain's head, hoping he could feel it burn right through to his skull. "What's your magic type?"

He quickened his pace. "That's my business. Not yours."

"It's odd how the fires keep their distance from us... almost like they're under someone's control." I darted around to face him, scurrying backward when he didn't slow his pace. "You're a fire wielder, aren't you? You can manipulate flames?"

His eyes turned cold with darkness. "My magic is just that—*my* magic." He strode swiftly ahead.

I took another swig from the canteen, my confidence fuelled by the potion. "What are you angry about, Captain?"

Because seriously, I wanted to know. Humans and casters were fearful of fire wielders, but somehow, I didn't think Jad's hostility was caused by me discovering his magic.

He was angry at me, period.

I'd come to Essida and interrupted everything, Tejor was dead, and Jad had lost his last chance of finding the map. Because of me, Macaslan and Darius would never learn what Melvina and Vulcan Stormouth were planning with the Larthalgule blade. Because of me, Jad had failed his mission. And there would be consequences.

This is all my fault. No wonder Jad can't stand to look at me.

I dropped back a few steps, crestfallen.

Why couldn't Adaline have appeared and made this trip to Essida worthwhile? Why do ghosts have to work in mysterious ways?

The captain continued down the road at a rapid pace, unaware I wasn't following. The potion was no longer holding influence, my vigour sinking like quicksand. Something cold pinched my shoulder. I spun around. Nothing. Only shadows and the endless gaps of black down the narrow laneways.

Great. Now I'm feeling things.

But there was a disparity in the air, a cooling of temperature that wasn't natural. Across the street, a hanging sign creaked on its hinges. The shopfront was a bookstore that had seen better days, the wood rotten, the glass smudged by cobwebs and dust. The longer I stared at the broken building, the more I couldn't comprehend what my eyes witnessed. A luminescent fog curled out from underneath the door. It grew thicker, gliding effortlessly over the road toward me. I blinked hard. The fog changed, manifesting into a ghostly presence. Adaline. Her skin was translucent and frozen, the dark pools beneath her eyes wild and wet.

She pointed to the bookstore. Her voice was a fierce whisper in my head.

"Inside is the answer you seek."

CHAPTER THIRTY

I broke into an automatic jog, clambering up the bookstore's rickety porch steps. Adaline's insubstantial form flickered beside me—a beacon directing the way—and then she was gone. Judging from the peeling paint and rotten floorboards, the shop had been abandoned long before the ULD occupation. The door's window was smashed. Gently, I laid my palm on the windowpane and located the latch on the other side. But I wasn't gentle enough. Pain sliced my palm. I choked back a gasp. A small glass shard was wedged in the thick of my flesh. I tore it out and swore, my blood trickling thick and fast.

Stupid piece of—

"How is it you can shoot a moving target from fifty yards away but still be the clumsiest person I've met?"

I spun around.

Jad had his cast-shooter raised at the shadows, his finger poised on the trigger. I'd never even heard him approach. He studied me with vigilant eyes. "What are you doing?"

I had to fight the urge not to grit my teeth. "I'm doing what I came here to do. I'm following Adaline."

The tension rose in his shoulders. His gaze moved to the door, as though he expected to see Adaline himself. "Let me go first."

"No time for chivalry, Captain."

Besides, we're in my element now.

I wandered inside.

Eerie ripples of flame light filtered through the windows, sending shadows across most of the bookstore. Jad followed close behind. He switched on the short-range flashlight mounted on his weapon. The light bled into the dark air, offering brief glimpses of objects. Whoever owned the place had been a serious hoarder of antiquities. Bookshelves were filled with volumes, so heavy the floorboards warped under their weight. Gas lamps, teapots, and portraits were swathed in cobwebs, and lost tech gadgets from the human age—which must have been worth a fortune—had been left on shelves to collect dust. Something moved above me in the hazy darkness. A ruined chandelier hung like a shrivelled spider from the ceiling, teetering off balance. This graveyard of a building was crumbling away, our footsteps sending creaks through the floor, which in turn travelled up the walls to the ceiling. I stepped out of the chandelier's path, afraid it would collapse.

"Be careful where you tread," I warned.

This place was a trap of loose floorboards and holes.

I wound carefully among the shelves, examining the aging scrolls and grimoires bound in black leather, arranged in alphabetical order by subject. There were spells to exterminate humans, moon magic for demon summoning, and hexes to manipulate victims.

Jad picked up *Lunar Magic for Demon Mustering* and snorted. "They still call the creatures of the deep 'demons.' That's medieval of them, don't you think?"

I shrugged. I'd never met the underground monsters that resided at the Earth's core, and I had no interest in doing so. I didn't care what they were called.

Jad shoved the book back. "Is the map here?" His voice was barely a whisper, but in the dark, it sounded much louder.

"I don't know. I guess we just wait until Adaline reappears and—aah!"

A book tumbled from the top shelf, smacking me above the eye. It bounced onto the floor, sending up a wave of dust.

"Look inside."

This time, Adaline's voice boomed in my ears, like I had my own personal foghorn in my head.

I took up the book. It was tattered and falling apart at the spine, undoubtedly held together with magic. There was no title or blurb. Inside, pages edged in gold were filled with hieroglyphics written in coppery ink.

Jad leaned forward. "What is that? I don't recognise the language."

"And you think I do?"

"I thought your ghost would have given you a clue." There was something wicked in the way he said it, like he believed this situation was a bad joke.

I regarded him with a jaded edge. "My ghost does help. See."

Halfway through the book, the pages went hollow. A parchment was hidden in a compartment inside. It was water stained and torn on the edges, but otherwise in good condition. My spine tingled.

Please be the map. Please be the map. I need to prove that this is all worthwhile.

I unfolded it and soothed out the creases.

I stared, unsure what to make of the empty piece of parchment.

Jad's eyes darted to mine, his mouth curling into the beginning of a taunting smile. "Well, that was disappointing." He headed back toward the door.

My feet remained firm on the floorboards.

Why did Adaline lead me to this? There must be more to it.

I flipped the parchment around, wondering if there was something on the other side I'd missed. A drop of blood from my cut palm dripped onto it, but rather than soaking into the parchment, it expanded, working into a series of interlaced markings and lines.

A fresh breath of optimism poured into my lungs. "It's a blood map. Jad. Look. It's a blood map."

In the corner of my eye, I saw his retreating figure rush back. He snatched the map and surveyed the points of reference. The surge of satisfaction I experienced on seeing his surprised face nearly lifted me off the ground.

"This is in a language I've never seen," he admitted. "We need to get this back to base and let a palaeographer look at it. We can then identify the topography and work out where the Larthalgule blade is."

I drew in a relieved breath. Finally, we were on to something.

Loud static cut through the dark, almost like someone had powered on an electric razor. The captain took out a small transceiver from his windbreaker. "Marek, I'm here. What's happening out there?"

Of course the captain would have a way of communicating with the Haxsan Guard, or in this case, keeping an extra pair of eyes out for trouble.

Marek's response was crackly on the other end. "Jad... incoming... leave immediately."

Jad waved the transceiver in the air, searching for a stronger signal. Essida was high in the mountain. Until we reached lower elevation, I didn't think there'd be a chance he'd find it.

The sergeant's voice sounded thin and distant on the other end. "General Kravis... pulled... Haxsan... from... the city. He's ordered... fire-crusaders... strike. There... incoming bombers... head back to... beach."

The transmission was broken and distorted, but the message was clear. Inner turmoil took over my heart. Kravis's had wanted to win Essida back and drive the rebels out. But now that he couldn't, he preferred the city to be in no one's hands than in the hands of the enemy. He was no better than the people who'd invaded Essida in the first place.

Jad brought the radio to his mouth. "How long?"

Marek's voice dipped in and out. "Three minutes. There's something... else. Intelligence hacked... ULD's radio frequencies. Trajan Stormouth... spotted in the city."

Jad nearly dropped the radio.

The terrified look in his eyes sent cold razors along my skin. "Who's Trajan Stormouth?"

Was he related to Vulcan somehow?

Jad shook off his daze and moved to the door. "It's a mistake. Trajan Stormouth is dead."

I ran after him. "How do you know?"

Because the ULD didn't get things wrong. If they spotted Trajan Stormouth in the city, whoever that was, then it was him and none other.

Jad paused to glance back at me. "I know because I killed him. The murder of Vulcan's son put a target on my back." He pointed at the map. "Put that away. We need to leave. Now."

A strange sensation took hold of my chest. Jad's face had lost colour, his hands stiff. I'd never seen him look so angry or afraid. I folded the map and placed it in my back pocket. A knot of fear swelled in my stomach.

We must get out of this city. Then it's over. We're safe.

We clambered into the forsaken street…

And straight into an ambush.

CHAPTER THIRTY-ONE

Four masked rebels armed with cast-shooters barricaded our path. Two more stood close to me by the door, wielding serrated-tooth blades, the kind you'd find in an abattoir. We were desperately outnumbered and out-weaponed. How the rebels found out about us was unclear. We still wore dissent armbands, which meant someone had tipped them off—someone high in the Haxsan Guard ranks who knew about Jad's mission. Our mysterious traitor.

The leader of these trigger-happy dissidents stepped forward. The ground was dry as bone, his heavy boots crunching small debris into dust. I had an image of my own skull flattened to crumbs beneath those boots but shook the illusion off. Jad hadn't buckled in defeat, and I sure as hell wasn't about to either.

The leader raised his cast-shooter at Jad. "Captain Arden. We've been looking for you a long time." His mask must have been equipped with a voice modifier because his tone was metallic and anonymous. Something about it was mocking too, like he found Jad's title amusing. "On your knees, Haxsan scum."

Jad glared—a stare reserved for people he wanted to pummel into meatloaf—but stood his ground. The tension grew thick around us, a raw, negative energy building up like an electrical storm.

The rebel slammed the barrel into Jad's chest. "I said on your knees."

Pain flashed across the captain's face, but he stubbornly remained on his feet. A dangerous glint lit in his eyes that wouldn't win us any favours.

And that was when things went bad.

Sirens blared unpleasantly close. I'd experienced three practice drills at Tarahik—black alert (attack imminent), red alert (attack likely), green alert (all clear)—each with a unique ring for identification. But none of those rehearsed exercises could have prepared me for the terror-provoking, high-pitched wail that split my head now. A formation of fire-crusaders extended across the sky, more than I could count. Their hot exhausts sent out a crackling roar that sliced the night in half. The noise was as much felt as heard, the vibratory pressure hammering my chest like it was trying to pulverise my heart. The clouds lit in a beautiful display of orange and red bursts. And then the bombs dropped. Buildings ruptured in fountains of fire, shooting out twisted chunks of shrapnel like missiles. Monstrous dust clouds surged through the streets.

Our captors stumbled around in surprise, weapons lowered. It was the diversion Jad needed. He lunged at the leader, tossing him to the ground with deadly force. Several fractures split the man's mask. He didn't move again. The other dissent rebels gained their senses and swarmed Jad. He ducked their hammering punches and swinging fists. They grappled, shoved, and slammed into each other, a mess of arms, legs, and grunting.

Somehow through the madness of their fight, Jad managed to fix his eyes on me. "Get to the beach. Now!"

My spinning mind formulated one coherent thought.

Run.

And then I was blown off my feet, the pavement rippling beneath me as another round of bombings detonated. I was uncertain where I landed. Thick smoke made it impossible to get a clear view of anything. Gulping air, I tried to get back onto my feet, but my legs trembled and refused to move.

Am I injured?

No. I didn't think so.

Ahead, a form materialised through the smog.

Jad.

The captain fought his way through the black smoulder and pulled me onto my feet, searching for injuries. "Are you all right?"

"I'm fine," I lied, relieved to see he was okay. The same couldn't be said for the rebels. They'd been hit by a shower of flames, their bodies unrecognisable among the filth. I stepped back, hoping to lean against the wall for support, but it was no longer there. The bookstore was gone. The street was gone. We were standing in a graveyard of ruins.

Jad took my hand and hurried me through the debris. His face was covered in cuts and scrapes, his thick hair lined with ash. Judging from my own stinging cheeks, I hadn't fared much better.

Heat torched my throat, my voice hoarse. "How are we going to get back to the beach? Nothing looks the same."

Jad pitched sideways, avoiding a burning pothole the size of a small crater. "My compass. The beach is north of here."

We ran in a crouch to the nearest populated street. Crowds scrambled in multiple directions, my ears ringing from their panicked screams. The bombs never stopped. Bricks and burning metal rained down. Parts of the pavement exploded in molten crags. My hope deflated.

We're going to be leaving Essida in body bags. That's if there's anything left of us to find.

Jad stopped suddenly, and I nearly barrelled into him. His eyes frantically swept the sky. "Can you hear that?"

I didn't think it was possible to hear anything above the boom of explosions or the screaming cacophony. But then the faintest sound, like a sheet flapping in the wind, or the tide coming in, broke through the rumble. It grew louder, raising the short hairs along the nape of my neck. Something large swept through the smoke ahead. It had to have been forty feet in length. I had an awful feeling the real horror was just about to begin.

Jad's cry caught the attention of onlookers. "Stagma."

He dove, knocking me like a bowling pin to the ground with him. A few people around us weren't so lucky. They were flung backward in the surge of hot air, slamming into the side of buildings and careening onto fallen powerlines. The thing that swooped over us was just a blur at first, something large that blended with the flames. Then I saw a flash of ruddy scales and a red slitted eye, burning as brightly as a flare light. Its barbed wings thumped shock waves into the street. The creature extended it massive jaws and bellowed a torrent of fire into the night.

I'd never seen a stagma before. During the human age, the creatures had hibernated beneath ground, but once the Earth's lithosphere changed and the tectonic plates shifted, they'd been reborn into the world. Now they were captured and sold on the black market to the ULD, trained as weapons in the sky.

The stagma dipped in and out of the clouds, magnificent and dangerous. Another stagma joined it, their enormous wings gliding fluidly across the night. They were met by another... and another, until hundreds of the creatures soared across the city skyline, spurting fire. They clipped fighter jets, their large talons tearing the aircrafts into metal chunks, letting them fall like projectiles into the streets.

Jad and I tore down the sidewalk into a maze of back alleyways and low buildings. A stitch grew under my ribs, my legs protesting fiercely. I couldn't keep up. Jad whipped around a corner at the same time a blast erupted in the building beside me. I swallowed a scream, or maybe the force of the explosion threw it back into my throat. Heat-blasted air propelled me backward, pieces of roofing narrowly missing my body as I landed in an ungainly heap on the ground. There were flames and smoke everywhere, the alley sealed by rubble.

Jad?

Had he escaped?

Was he lying on the other side injured?

Or worse—dead?

Rolling into a foetal position felt like the best option at that moment, but I refused to let despair win. I climbed onto my feet and moved jerkily back the way I'd come. Only I didn't know where that was. The narrow laneways weren't recognisable, and every turn I made led to a dead end.

Exhausted, I slumped against a wall and angrily blinked away tears. Vertigo closed in, my world threatening to slam around me.

Only one thing struck clear.

The cold, guttural voice that called my name.

"Zzzzaaaayyyyaaaa."

My fingers instantly sought the cast-shooter at my side. "Who's there?"

In answer, pricks of snow swirled against my cheeks. The temperature changed drastically, going from scorching heat to a wintery gale. I pressed the back of my hand against my mouth, trying to quieten my frightened, gasping breaths, because I recognised that voice. I knew that cold, deserted feeling. Thin sheets of ice crept along the cobble path, making everything look like it had been transported to the Arctic. This wasn't the work of a wraith. This was the work of the worst kind of evil. The black-veined woman.

An intangible energy grappled my legs. Before I could comprehend what happened, I was propelled down the alley like a speed skater, the breath knocked out of me. The mysterious force threw me into a courtyard, the kind of place where children met to play hopscotch after school, only now it looked like it had been submerged in a frozen lake. The black-veined woman waited in the centre. Her skin was chalky and whiter than snow—the face of death. Long strands of black hair were held off her face by ice needles entwined in a shockingly sharp crown on the top of her head. When she smiled, her teeth ended like ice blades.

A cold ripple of despair worked its way inside me. "Melvina."

"Melvina," the woman cooed back in a childish, sing-song voice. Unguarded fury clouded her dark eyes. "You should have listened to your commander and stayed in Tarahik. Hand me the map. I know you have it."

"I don't know anything about a map," I lied.

The map was still tucked in my back pocket, and unless I took it out and waved it like a white flag, she wasn't going to get it.

Her cruel eyes cut into mine. "I felt its magic come alive once your blood made contact, idiot girl. The map can only be read by the dead, or in your case, a necromancer. Now hand it over, or I'll be forced to do something drastic." Her smile curled, spiteful and vicious.

On cue, two dissent rebels emerged from an adjoining alley. They dragged a man who looked like he'd been beaten with a truncheon. His face was flushed in raw, pink spots where the skin hadn't yet darkened into bruises.

Horror and shock rattled me. "Jad."

Blood trickled down his face from a cut under his hairline. His left eyebrow had swollen into a lump, and his upper lip was split and bleeding.

Even though pain must have racked his body, he managed to turn his head toward me. I sensed a swelling in my chest. I had to get him out of here.

One of the captors kicked the captain's leg, forcing Jad onto his knees. He turned to Melvina. "We found this one snooping, pretending to be one of us. He's been working with the girl. We've seen them together."

He tossed the captain's armband onto the ground and spat on it.

Melvina studied Jad the way a cat did before it toyed with a mouse. Her rotting features looked green in the weird interplay of colours brought on by the raging fires and stagnant ice. "Captain Arden, isn't it?" She made a noise that might have been a snarl. "Vulcan Stormouth is very interested in you. I believe he's placed a large sum on your head."

Jad shot her a sneer of disdain.

Melvina turned to me, something wicked dancing across her expression. "Unless you want your captain to be blown into pieces, I suggest you hand over the map."

The rebels levelled their cast-shooters at Jad to emphasise her point. A red glow flared in the barrels. All they had to do was pull the trigger and he would become a messy exhibit of blood and flesh on the ground.

A tap dance of guilt jumped in my stomach. I fought to conceal the stress from my face as I tugged the map from my back pocket and held my cast-shooter against it. "You want the map, then hand the captain over first. Otherwise, I set it alight."

Jad struggled against his captors, the panic in his eyes signalling that was a bad idea. I didn't care.

A slow, scheming smile twisted Melvina's features.

Come on. Do it. Take the bait.

My hope started to untether. She wasn't falling for it.

I tipped my chin in an expression of bravado. "I'm serious."

My finger twitched, not quite touching the trigger but close enough that it made a muscle in her jaw jump.

She waved her hand and that same invisible force I'd experienced in the alley ripped the map from my fingers, sending it floating straight into her thin ones.

She'd taken the bait.

I swung my cast-shooter onto the rebels. Cold sweat slicked my palms, but at this range, even with an awkward grip, they'd be hard to miss. I fired one disjointed burst after another into their shoulders and knees. Jad dove for cover, rolling to the safety of the shadows.

I swivelled my weapon back onto Melvina. Her triumphant smirk turned to outrage. I blasted her, a clean shot straight through the chest. The impact threw her backward. Black liquid pooled below her mangled body. It smelt rotten, like dirty river water and fish.

Jad gathered the rebel's cast-shooters and slid them in his coat. "That was stupid. Don't take another risk like that again."

I glared. "Then don't get captured again."

Before he could rebuke me, I darted across the courtyard to where the map lay, stuck in the sticky mess that had been Melvina. Parts of her body sagged and dripped like ice cream on a warm day. My fingers curled around the parchment...

And her eyes slit open.

Her hand closed around my wrist, sending icy tendrils across my skin. I screamed. The lower half of my arm felt like it had been submerged in acid.

A mirthless laugh tore from Melvina's throat. "Stupid girl. Cast-shooters cannot kill me." She rose to sitting, her ripped chest flapping grotesquely in the wind. "The map is mine. And so are you."

A rush of scorching heat swept past me. A wall of flame hit Melvina, trapping her in a fiery enclosure. She thrashed and kicked, but the flames simply transferred from her legs to her upper body. An ear-splitting shriek tore from her throat.

I scrambled backward, making sure the map was safe from the fire. Jad stood at the opposite side of the courtyard, a fireball blazing in his hand. He didn't seem to have a problem using his powers now. His eyes shone against the blinding light, making him appear otherworldly and demonic. He hurled it. The second round of flames landed with a deafening roar on Melvina, eliciting more screams.

I didn't stop to think about what I was doing. If the map didn't exist, the ULD would never find the Larthalgule blade. It was the best option Jad and I had.

I faced Melvina. "You want the map? Here it is. It's all yours."

I tossed it into the flames.

Her scream of anguish threatened to rupture my ears.

Jad grabbed the back of my coat. "The flames will wound her, but they won't kill. We don't have long."

We darted into the alley. I swallowed the hot waves of air that danced at the back of my throat. I couldn't help but look back. Melvina met my eyes through the flames. They brimmed with murderous intent. Her skin had changed, now slimy green like an avocado left too long to ripen.

Black veins snaked up her neck. "I'll find you, little necromancer."

The flames exploded.

I turned and ran.

CHAPTER THIRTY-TWO

The forest had changed drastically. Trees were reduced to burnt trunks, their blackened bark falling into ash beds on the ground. The wildfires were out, but in a twisted, vicious cycle, wind and swirling snow now buffeted us from every direction, the air so cold I could see my breath in front of me. Somewhere out there, Melvina had recovered, her power transforming the island to winter. I peered up to the darkening sky, shrouded in storm clouds so thick that within minutes, heavy snow surrounded us.

Jad and I plodded through the white landscape. Slush seeped into my clothes, causing my body to tremble so badly my teeth smacked together. We were joined by survivors who'd escaped the city, their hands stuffed under their armpits for warmth. They banded together, a gathering of refugees that trudged through the forest, lost and searching for the next chapter in their lives. They'd probably heard the Haxsan Guard had a makeshift hospital with air ambulances at the beach, but there were so many desperate, traumatised people, it wasn't possible to help them all.

Jad didn't talk to me. He was either too angry about the map or struggling too much from the cold to bother discussing what I'd done. He rubbed his hands together, trying to keep himself warm and alert.

My own eyelids drooped, the ends of my fingers stiff enough to crack. In that half-conscious moment, white noise stabbed at my ears. I ignored it,

taking it for a side effect of the cold. But then it started to sound more like...
a voice. Cruel, lethal... brimming with hatred.

"Did you think I was dead, little necromancer? I am here. I am alive. You
cannot run from me. You are trapped."

Icy panic shimmied up my spine. I had watched Melvina explode in
a fiery burst of ichor, blood, and guts, yet here she was taunting me, our
minds tuned to the same frequency. I spun around, half expecting to find her
lurking behind a tree, waiting to pounce, but there was nothing besides frosty
shadows and forest.

Jad turned, startled by something I'd failed to see. His gaze wandered
beyond the trees to the mountain, quizzical and intent. "Do you see that?"

I squinted through the haze. Low-lying clouds churned around the snow-
capped peaks, hungry for destruction. Several fast, white-hot flashes split
the sky, forking down the mountainside in consecutive hits. I knew from
geography class at the orphanage that mountainsides were naturally unstable.
The deep, ominous crash of thunder didn't help. The piercing clap ricocheted
across the ranges, unsettling snow and ice. My mouth closed around the
horror climbing up my throat, preventing it from rising into a full-blown
scream. The mountain began to collapse under its own weight. The avalanche
picked up boulders and snapped trees like toothpicks, a roiling storm of snow
and wind expanding out in all directions.

Jad grabbed my hand, forcing me into a sprint. "Run. Run now."

We dodged blindly through the trees, the ground bucking and lurching
beneath us. The entire island was rumbling like a ship on a savage sea. I risked
a look behind my shoulder and wished I hadn't. Essida was buried in a white
tomb. I imagined people scrambling like trapped animals in the streets only
to discover exits packed by snow, their bodies cemented and forever preserved
in a frozen cast. Maybe in a thousand years, casters would return to this
location to excavate Essida and try to piece together its tragic past.

The city was gone.

We were next.

A stampede began for the beach. One scream was horrible to hear, but
when thousands of cries, sobs, and shouts of terror surrounded us, it fuelled
nothing but my own instinct to survive. The ground broke in massive fissures,

swallowing trees and people. It wasn't choosy. Behind us, the forest was lost in a speeding blur of white.

We broke onto the beach, struggling to find traction on the thick sand. The captain stilled for a moment, his jaw firmed up in surprise. Half the fleet was in the air, their heavy spotlights sending blinding shafts of colour across the shore, rotor blades spinning mini-snowstorms. Only a few lighter aircraft and four air ambulances remained near the water's edge, inundated by survivors. We tore toward it. Soldiers blocked the entrance, firing cast-shooters into the air to frighten away the crowd. There simply was not enough room to take any more survivors. Jad forced his way through the panicked mob, clasping my hand so tight I thought it would dislocate at the wrist. The crowd jolted, shoved, and heaved. If I got off this island, my entire body would be one large bruise.

A soldier recognised Jad as a commanding officer and let us through. We sprinted up the ramp into the air ambulance. My insides squeezed in revulsion. The wounded lay in stretchers and were hooked to ventilators. Others stared blankly while they bled through their bandages. Interspersed among the equipment where space could be found, survivors moaned in pain and sobbed into their hands. There were shouts to "Leave now" and screams to "Get a move on."

Jad's radio crackled with static. Marek's voice croaked through the transceiver. "Jad? Jad?"

The captain brought the radio to his mouth. "Marek, where are you?"

"In the air. Colonel Sparus is dead. You're in command. Jad, the ocean is icing over. You need to get the last of the fleet off the beach. If you don't leave now, the fuel will freeze."

I whirled around. Never mind the fuel. If we didn't leave now, we'd be swallowed by the avalanche.

Jad ran frantically toward the cockpit. The crowd parted for him, seeming to realise he was someone of importance. No one could fly this aircraft like Jad. We needed him to get us out of here.

I stepped to the side out of the way. My legs were stiff like wooden posts now, and when I wiped at my hairline, my fingers came back smeared with blood. A sob hung in my throat. I hated abandoning people on the beach, but Melvina had sealed their fate. We had no option but to leave them to it.

The rotor blades spun into motion, the engine sending vibrations through the floor. The ramp hadn't closed when we lifted off the beach. From the air, I could see down to the shore. People ran into the water, preferring to drown in the treacherous waves than be buried in snow. I think they may have been shouting for us to come back, but their cries were lost against the roaring wind and heavy rotor blades. Others huddled together, waiting to die in each other's embrace. Some even scrambled in desperate bids to find higher ground, kind of like ants before a downpour. But it was too late. The avalanche plunged forth, a tsunami of snow, burying everything and everyone.

Please forgive us. Forgive me.

The ramp finally closed.

I dropped to my knees, succumbing to the enormity of emotions.

CHAPTER THIRTY-THREE

I drifted in and out of consciousness. Light flickered at the edge of my vision, the specks growing brighter. Slowly, realisation surfaced.

I'd escaped Essida.

I was in an air ambulance.

I was safe.

Bit by bit, my sterile surroundings settled into focus. Patients were hooked up to tubes and plugged into machines that beeped in heavy rhythm with their hearts. Somewhere, a ventilator pumped oxygen into someone's lungs.

I hauled myself up to sitting, surprised when a sharp, scratchy pain on my wrist restrained me from standing. I was on a stretcher—and handcuffed. A catheter protruded from my other arm, attached to an IV drip that injected blue liquid into my veins. Someone had cleaned and bandaged my cuts. I turned my arm over, staring at the peeling black skin.

I'm burnt?

My eyes had to be deceiving me.

"You're awake." Talina's face morphed into shape by my side. Her complexion was washed out, her blonde hair a mess of sweaty tangles.

I licked my parched lips. The panic in my mouth tasted acidic. "What happened to my arm?"

"Your arm has been burnt, but it's okay. The potion you're receiving will heal it in a few hours. You won't even see a scar." Talina offered a short, woeful attempt at a smile. Her eyes were red and watery. I wondered if she needed to lie down too.

She shone a penlight into my eyes. "You passed out some hours ago. I just need to ask you a few routine questions. What is your name?"

I squinted, my eyes sensitive after waking from what felt like an eternity of darkness. "Can you turn that off?"

"Your name?"

"Are you frigging kidding me? You know who I am."

"Yes, but I need you to say it."

"Why am I handcuffed?"

Talina cast me an uncertain look. "We'll get to that later. What is your name?"

"It's Zaya."

"And your occupation?'

"This is stupid. I'm a cadet."

"And the last thing you remember?"

I lifted my eyes to the ceiling, hating the images that revolved around my head. "I remember watching thousands of people die. Cheerful, I know."

Talina stilled for a moment. She flicked the penlight into my opposite eye.

I swatted it out of her hand. "I swear, if you shine that thing at me one more time, I'll shove it so far up your nose, they'll need pliers to detach it from your pulped brain."

Her shoulder's visibly relaxed. "Oh good. You're still you. I was worried you had a head injury." She pocketed the pen. "You've had a double dosage of asith potion, which is why you're drowsy. I just injected you with an analgesic spell for the pain too. That drug should kick in any minute now. Otherwise, how are you feeling?"

I scowled. "I'd feel much better if there was no turbulence on this damn plane."

And if I hadn't been burned.

Or nearly buried in an avalanche.

I tugged on my handcuff. "Want to explain why I'm chained up?"

Talina rubbed the balls of her hands into her eyes. I immediately braced myself for bad news. "Captain Arden insisted you remain shackled for the flight. I don't know why. I guess you must be in trouble."

"Oh, you really think so?"

She gave me a dry look. "Just try to relax."

"Relax?" I pointed to my restraint. "Again, I'm handcuffed. What did Captain Arden say?"

A flash of doubt crossed her face. "Nothing. He said I was to remain with you and clean you up for your hearing."

"Hearing?"

"Or maybe it was a trial. I can't remember which."

An oily slither of dread curdled in my gut. "But I haven't done anything wrong." The words fell flat in my mouth. It wasn't entirely true. I'd apprehended a soldier, seized her cast-shooter, been a stowaway on a carrier-hornet, and destroyed the map everyone was searching for. But it had all been for a noble cause. It hadn't been criminal. Not in the end. A hearing meant a council would vote on whether there was enough evidence to send me to trial. A trial meant persecution. Persecution resulted in punishment. Punishment meant I'd be returned to an internment camp.

Stay calm, Zaya. Don't let yourself be vulnerable to fear.

I was confident under the Haxsan Criminal Justice Scheme that to place someone under arrest, the person had to be conscious when you read them their rights, which hadn't happened. That meant Jad's arrest was unlawful. I knew because I'd looked up the scheme for a little light reading—and because I wound up in trouble so often, I needed to understand the legal loopholes. If I could prove what I'd done had been for the greater good, then no further legal proceedings would follow. Jad was angry and hadn't acted rationally. All of this was a mistake. He'd realise that and set things right.

Talina rubbed the back of her neck. "I'm sorry, Zaya, but I'm powerless to do anything. At least you're looking better."

I glared. My clothes were damp from sweat, my hair blackened from ash. A dirty wet dishcloth would have looked more attractive than me.

Talina shifted her weight and hugged her middle like she might be sick.

My anger took a back seat. My priority was going to have to wait. "How are you holding up?"

A tear streaked past her cheek. "I had to leave them behind. All those people I tried to save… in the end, I had to choose who could go in an air ambulance and who had to remain. I left them to die."

The way her face fell made me shiver. "You didn't have a choice. You followed orders. It isn't your fault."

"It doesn't matter who's at fault. What I did doesn't make it right."

I had no answer for that. I guess in some way, we were all guilty.

The muscles in my body strained, realisation dawning on me. "Where's Lainie?"

If she wasn't here working with Talina, then….

My expression must have given away my fear because Talina took my hand. "Lainie's okay. There's an ICU on the plane. She's there attending to patients. I haven't seen her since we've been in the air."

My anxiety eased. Of course doctors would want Lainie at the ICU. Her powers would be keeping everyone calm and focused. She'd be a vital asset.

Talina dragged her eyes to the window. Daylight popped out from behind sunlit clouds, the top of forest trees visible in the golden rays.

I shielded my eyes from the peaceful band of colour rising on the horizon. It seemed incredible that nature could still be beautiful after such a terrible atrocity.

Rapid changes in air pressure caused my ears to pop. "Are we landing?"

Talina nodded. "The wounded will disembark first, so we'll be on the plane for a while yet. I'm to remain with you until you're handed over to the guards."

A spasm of fear shot through my legs.

She leant forward to peer out the window. "We're nearly at Tarahik. I can see our landing pad. Remember what I said. Try and relax."

I sank back into the stretcher.

Try and relax. Sure.

CHAPTER THIRTY-FOUR

It wasn't a coincidence that when I stepped off the plane into the hangar, Sneer-face and Pick-nose were waiting to greet me—which meant they were quick to shackle my hands and take me into custody. Commander Macaslan was among them, looking as though she wanted to spear me with her eyes.

My shoulders sagged in her presence. "I can explain—"

"I don't want to hear it," she snapped.

Her anger caught the attention of onlookers, and believe me, there were plenty. She took my arm and steered me away from the crowd. The hangar was unrecognisable. The infirmary must have been overrun with cases because every corner, space, and niche of the shelter had been converted into a sloppy makeshift hospital. Medics ferried the wounded on cots and stretchers, trying to find a space on the crowded floor where a doctor could attend to them. The stench of burnt flesh, festering wounds, and soiled linen saturated the air, the heat making it feel as though it were clogging my pores. Bile rose in my throat. The idea that injured, dying casters lay here lost and unknown tormented me. I didn't focus on the bodies shrouded in white sheets. The pain would rip my heart in two.

My resolve faltered under Macaslan's strict gaze. "Can we please do this somewhere else?"

Those cold grey eyes gleamed like blades. "No, we cannot. Thanks to you, I don't have time to be somewhere else. Captain Arden radioed ahead. I know what you've done. Destroying the map? It will be a miracle if Senator Kerr can convince the council to acquit you of these charges. His influence extends only so far."

"Charges?" I shook my head, confused. "But I haven't been charged with anything. None of this is fair—"

"Fair?" Her nostrils flared. "Sneaking onto an aircraft bound for a dissent-occupied city hasn't put you in a favourable light, Zaya. General Kravis is aware someone in the base is talking to the ULD. He's convinced you're that traitor."

Her temperament was like a lash across the skin, hot and burning.

"You know I'm not," I whispered. "I went to Essida and destroyed the map because it was the right thing to do. The ULD can't get their hands on it. And neither can General Kravis. You know he wants it."

She raised her slender neck and glared at the ceiling but didn't deny it. "What you did jeopardised the captain's mission. That map was our only chance of finding Larthalgule."

I blinked, stunned by her admission. "Larthalgule needs to remain hidden."

She flashed me a deadly scowl. "What do you think we're trying to do? We intend to destroy the blade, not put it in a museum for everyone to see."

I folded my arms, every part of me trembling with fury. "And do you trust the people at Tarahik with a weapon like that? Because I don't. No one should have control over something that powerful, especially when no one understands the blade's sorcery."

"It's a necromancer's blade. Only a necromancer can control it. We wanted you to destroy it. That was the entire point behind Captain Arden's mission. Find the map. Find the blade. Vanquish Larthalgule."

I pressed my lips together and inhaled through my nose, trying to suppress my mounting anger. "And what if I couldn't do it? We don't know what kind of magic is involved in vanquishing an athame-sabre.'"

The commander closed her eyes briefly. "I understand your logic in destroying the map, Zaya. I really do. But you should have left this to Darius and me. Until Senator Kerr can clear your name—*if* he can clear your name—Captain Arden and I have no choice but to follow procedure." She turned to the guards. "Take her down to the detention centre."

A swarm of butterflies scattered in my stomach. The detention centre was in the lower levels of the base, where central heating ended and the cold, dank air of the mountain set in. War crimes, desertion, and cowardice were the felonies most soldiers were imprisoned for in the cells.

Sneer-face and Pick-nose took each of my arms and marched me through the hangar.

"Wait." I craned my neck over my shoulder, desperate for the commander to hear me. "Lunette Collins. She's part of this plan. Me and her. And she's in trouble."

I was afraid of being too cryptic, but Macaslan stilled, a flicker of hesitance crossing her face. She recovered, her expression blank as she offered a non-committal shrug. "Don't pin the blame on others, Miss Wayward. You're in enough trouble as it is."

She spun around, her stride quicker than it had been previously.

Sneer-face tugged on my arm, yanking me close to his face. "Your reflective starts in ten minutes."

I cringed at his foul breath. "My what?"

"Reflective. It's the time given to you before your hearing, which is scheduled for two o'clock."

Pick-nose chimed in. "You'll be incarcerated in a pitch-black cell where you won't be able to make sense of the seconds, minutes, or hours."

I fought to make sense of what he was saying. And then it clicked. Sensory deprivation was a favourite game with the Haxsan Guard. First, the silence would be all-encompassing in the cell. I'd have nothing to do but stare ahead and be consumed by thoughts. It would be impossible to stimulate myself. I'd doze on and off out of boredom. I'd lose track of time. Grow increasingly paranoid and start pacing like a caged animal. My mental alertness would slow down. Hallucinations would kick in. I'd start to believe I was floating in the farthest vacuum of space—as was their intention. Extracting information or eliciting a confession at a hearing worked best when the mind was frazzled.

Sneer-face chuckled. "It's either reflective or the beasts. I'd prefer the former if it were me."

I stared, fixated on what he'd revealed. "Beasts? What beasts?"

The pair laughed.

"I need a moment with the prisoner" a voice interrupted.

I turned to find Jad standing behind us. He'd cleaned himself up and changed into his regular Haxsan Guard attire. Someone had bandaged the cuts on his face. Annoyingly, the bruises that remained on his tanned skin provided him with a bad boy charm. Every nurse in the vicinity must have caught their breath healing him.

The guards hesitated at first but, realising this was a direct order, scooted away, quickly absorbed in the crowd.

I lifted my shackled hands. "Want to explain this? I thought we'd really bonded back in Essida."

The captain's eyebrows set into a stubborn line. "You brought this on yourself, Zaya."

Macaslan had planted a seed of anger inside me. Now in Jad's company, that anger grew into full bloom. "This could have been avoided if you hadn't radioed ahead. You know why I destroyed the map."

He rubbed a hand across his eyes. "I didn't rat you out. I learnt on the air ambulance that Intelligence was listening in through my radio. They didn't hear everything, but they heard enough. In the end, I had to follow General Kravis's orders and detain you."

Choked fury worked its way into my voice. "General Kravis knows?"

"He knows you destroyed the map."

"And does he know about... me? That I'm a... necromancer, I mean."

Jad shifted uneasily, hesitating for a fraction of a second. "I don't believe so."

My tone turned desperate. "Don't believe so or you know so?"

He cupped a hand at the back of his neck. "Listen, I'm going to do what I can to get you out of the hearing, but it will take time—"

"Jad. Jad. Over here." A petite nurse in a white ward dress skirted through the crowd, waving at the captain. She was young and incredibly pretty, with platinum blonde hair that fell past her shoulders in perfect curls. A warm, creamy complexion complemented her rosy cheeks. Tall and lissom, she moved with graceful confidence. I recognised her and wished I could spit venom. Indree Raminorf.

What the hell is the countess doing here?

Indree never worked if she could avoid it, preferring to groom herself somewhere with a manicure.

She propped her arms around Jad's neck, curling her fingers into his hair, her slim figure pressing against him in an inappropriate way.

Wow. Boundaries, lady.

Her lips shifted into a seductive smile. "I've been so worried. I was frightened you wouldn't come back."

And then she planted her lips on the captain's in a long, sultry kiss.

For a moment, I couldn't form a coherent thought. It was like the sides of my brain had been fastened together with a drilling machine. Jad stilled, seemingly taken aback. At any point, he could have broken the kiss off, but he didn't. This wasn't just some crazed woman throwing herself at him in hope of winning his favour. Jad kept his personal life private. I just hadn't realised he'd kept Indree private too. They were together. The evidence was indisputable.

Indree finally pulled away with a gruesome sucking sound. Her eyes fell on me, lingering on my shackled hands. She turned to Jad with a jaded pout. "This is the girl who put you in danger? She should be locked away." She surveyed me from head to foot. "Ugly little thing, isn't she?" she spoke into Jad's ear, loud enough for me to hear.

A silent scream echoed in my head.

She doesn't even recognise me.

I wanted to break every bone in Indree's ugly body, rip out that dishwater blonde hair at the roots, and smack her sallow face into the hard stone of the hangar.

The captain's black eyes settled on mine. He looked... lost.

The guards appeared. Sneer-face took my arm and swatted me on the back. "Wayward, we're on a tight schedule. Move."

Numb, I let them lead me away from the humiliating scene. I would have preferred staring down the barrel of a gun than witness that disgusting locking of lips. I needed to blank my mind, focus on something else, because the image of Jad and Indree entwined together would burn into my memory forever if I didn't.

Bad timing that I was being sent to reflective.

CHAPTER THIRTY-FIVE

I wasn't in the mood to reflect. What I really wanted to do was punch something—like my guards. Sneer-face and Pick-nose swept me out of the elevator into a lengthy torch-lit passage flanked by rows of solitary confinement cells. The detention centre lived up to its name. The doors were sealed shut with iron bolts, the food tray slots etched with barbed wire. That seemed overkill to me. I didn't think anyone was skinny enough to get through a food tray slot, but I suppose if you starved someone enough, anything was possible.

A flutter of fear worked its way from my gut, pounding against my ribs. Behind those doors was profound darkness where the air, shadows, and silence were an oppressive weight. I imagined it was like being locked in a coffin or falling into the deepest subterranean void. Monitors displayed footage recorded from night vision cameras inside the cells. Most of the prisoners lay curled in foetal positions on metal cots; others were strewn on the floor. I didn't think it was from despair or lack of motivation. These guys had been chemically induced to a conscious-zombie state.

Sneer-face turned his gaze from the screens. In the fragile light, his smattering of freckles was the only thing that gave colour to his youthful face. "Glad you're the one being locked away and not me." The confidence in his tone sounded forced.

My mouth split into a grin. "Would you like me to hold your hand?"

A flush crept into his cheeks. "Keep moving, traitor scum."

He gave my shoulder a hard punch, adding another bruise to my collection.

We continued down the derelict passage, our pace slower, caution in every footstep. This deep in the mountain, water had seeped into the bedrock. It trickled from the gnarled tree roots that wrapped the ceiling, the continuous *drip, drip, drip* ominous in the dark. Even the walls were clammy with cold moisture.

"Do you hear that?" Pick-nose stopped midstride. He flashed an anxious glance at his pal. "I think there's something in here."

Sneer-face shook his head wildly. "It's water. Nothing to worry about."

"No. Listen. That isn't water. It's something else. It's—" He slapped a hand to his mouth. "There! Did you hear it?"

"All I hear is you moaning like a sissy."

"I'm telling you there's something in here."

I listened with bated breath. "Perhaps it's the beasts."

"Shut up," they both shouted in unison.

Pick-nose was right. The sound was faint at first but grew higher and sharper, like someone struggling to breathe and sucking in long, choppy pants. We'd taken a few more steps when the sound split the air again, louder this time. My captors responded by gripping my arms so tight I feared they'd rip me at the spine. The scratchy, choky gasps seemed to go on and on, worse than nails down a chalkboard or the squealing brakes on a bicycle. Goosebumps jumped across my skin.

A red light blinked on the monitors. The hoarse breathing was coming from a set of speakers built in the doors.

My chest cinched into a knot. "It's the prisoners. They're struggling to breathe in their cells."

My body vibrated with shock. A restrictive air spell must have been pumped through the ventilation system—a timed, invisible barrier that wedged itself in the nostrils and mouth. I imagined it was like being submerged in water for minutes on end, heart pulsing in your ears, lungs burning, the absence of oxygen blindingly painful in your head. The spell would have provided access to one lungful of air before it repeated its torture all over again. I stared open-mouthed, my mind grappling with this level of cruelty.

Pick-nose shook his head, his eyes glued on something the rest of us hadn't yet registered. There was a splash ahead—a footstep in a puddle, perhaps? A shape detached from the dark. Two women adorned in white ankle-length dresses emerged. They were an odd pair, one tall and bony, the other short and doughy around the middle. But that wasn't what was so off-putting about them. They had a wilting quality to their skin, which was sickly pale and far whiter than any corpse. Their eyes didn't sparkle with life or energy either but rather were lacklustre and glassy.

The plumpest of the pair sauntered forward. "Good evening, Miss Wayward. We've been looking forward to receiving you." A satisfied, self-indulgent smile shaped her lips, her voice low and guttural. "You have been brought here to reflect. Prisoners only learn to repent when they are stripped of essentials. You can take away food, water, shelter, but they can survive without those for hours. What they are dependent on every second is air. Rob them of breath and they languish in their cells, conscious, restless, disturbed. Only then will they reflect. Only then will they seek penance for their sins."

It would also send them into a permanent state of madness, but that obviously wasn't a concern for her, or the Haxsan Guard. I glared, not even trying to conceal my scepticism.

The woman's flabby cheeks drooped when she smiled, reminding me of melting candle wax. There was a smell about her I couldn't identify—metallic and vinegar-like. It made my head woozy. "My name is Argie Narkiss. I am the psychiatric warden down here. This is my assistant, Miss Grever."

Miss Grever was tall, scarecrow-like, and a hundred times creepier than Miss Narkiss. The assistant rolled out a restraining chair with a huge wicked needle attached to it. A collection of scalpels and surgical scissors was built into the armrests, the sort of thing you should only find in an operating theatre. She tilted her head and examined me the same way a dog salivated over a bone.

Miss Narkiss moved closer, a robotic, reanimated structure to her actions. "Despite what you may have heard, this is not a place for punishment. This is a place for you to reflect on your misdeed, renounce your mistake, and, above all, seek atonement."

I swallowed hard. "Yeah, you've said that already. What's the needle for?"

One of the many rules I learnt in Gosheniene: if the wardens continued to lead you into a false sense of security, they were lying.

I started to back away, but the guards detained me, their fingers tight with anticipation. In the women's presence, Pick-nose perspired heavily, long pearls of sweat dripping down his nose, glinting like raindrops in the orange haze of torchlight. It did nothing to appease my own mounting anxiety.

Miss Narkiss bared her teeth when she smiled. "That's to get you comfortable and begin the healing process, dear." Her eyes darted to my captors. "Boys, bring her forward."

The guards did look like boys too. Silly and frightened, they dragged me toward the chair. I pressed my feet into the floor. Stones ground into the soles of my boots, grating against the wet rock.

I struggled in their fierce grip. "What if I don't repent? I can be very stubborn."

I wasn't going to seek forgiveness for something that wasn't wrong, nor did I have any intention of wasting away in a cell.

Miss Narkiss ran a tongue along her lips. "The Tarahik Military Base has no use for disobedient soldiers... which is just as well for us. It means we don't have to hunt for dinner."

Horror scraped deep into my bones, because now I identified the smell that lingered around her—rotting meat. It was painfully transparent. There were still bits of tissue wedged between her teeth from her last meal.

She reached for my arm. The needle poked out from her clenched fingers, which resembled meaty sausages. "Now this won't hurt a bit, I promise."

I did the first thing that came to mind—kicked my booted toe into Pick-nose's knee. His arms shot out in reflex to prevent a fall, exposing his middle. I thrust my boot into his stomach, amazed by my own strength when the impact propelled him backward. His head struck the wall with a sickening crunch. If it weren't for his shallow moans, he would have looked at peace in a coffin.

My surprise attack caused Sneer-face to topple too. His feverish eyes flashed dangerously as he sprang at me with a war cry. I couldn't dodge his wild, jerking hands. He grabbed a fistful of my hair and slammed me into the wall. It hurt like hell, but I was closer to the torches now. Before Sneer-face could deliver his next blow, I seized one from a bracket and swung. There was a wet thump as the torch made contact with his head, followed by a resounding "Oomph." He collapsed on the ground, his eyes rolling back to whites.

The women had fled into the dark. The atmosphere in the dingy tunnel changed drastically in their absence. The prisoners' suffocating gasps for air had stopped. No water dripped or streaked down the walls. Everything was silent, as though all life had been sucked away.

I didn't want to remain a moment longer in this spooky place. I dropped to my knees and searched Sneer-face's pockets. A silver key fell to the floor, but my trembling fingers had trouble clasping it. I had to mentally force myself to stop shaking to unlock my restraints. They fell in a mangled heap on the ground, my wrists swollen and sore. I got onto my feet and set off down the tunnel in a swift pace toward the elevator.

There was a wet, slithering sound in the dark. "I don't think so, Miss Wayward."

Miss Narkiss emerged from the shadows, but she'd changed. Her skin was no longer pasty and flaccid but green and scaly like an alligator. At her hips, her lower half had formed into a serpent's tail, where multiple legs branched off the sides—something caught between a millipede and a jellyfish.

Terror crawled over my skin, setting every nerve ablaze. Thousands of years ago, cross-species transformation was used as punishment on casters. The victims had never recovered. They'd isolated themselves deep in the mountains, where it was rumoured they'd bred. I was seeing first-hand the monstrous depravity caused by our ancestors.

Miss Narkiss's insect-like legs bunched together, rearing her reptilian body to the ceiling. She opened her jaws, dislocating them so she could swallow me whole. Her hot breath reeked of uncooked meat. I staggered backward, my shoulder knocking a torch from its bracket, both it and I falling to the ground, the flame burning out on impact. I rolled to the side as her snapping jaws came down.

"Where are you? Where are you?" Miss Narkiss slithered from wall to wall, the quick pitter-patter of her feet making my heart pound that much harder against my chest. The slimy weight of her tail lashed the air. I crawled toward Sneer-face. It was a good thing he was unconscious, because he would have wet his pants in the face of this danger. I took the cast-shooter from his holster and clicked the safety off.

"There! There she is." Miss Grever materialised from the dark. Her scales were large rigid plates, brown and hard in texture like a pangolin. "Let's eat her. I'll have the upper half. I know how you like the legs, Argie. Kravis won't mind. He'll be happy to know she's gone."

Kravis.

That son of a bitch had never intended for my case to go to a hearing. He'd wanted me out of the picture.

The two women sailed toward me. I aimed the cast-shooter and fired. A white bolt of lightning surged from the weapon. It hit Miss Narkiss, snaking up her body in a blazing fork of silver brightness. High screeching cries tore out of her throat, every muscle, limb, and joint spasming. She sprawled on the ground, body shrivelling like a dead spider, multiple legs clumped together. Her black eyes stared unblinking at the ceiling.

"Nooooo!" Miss Grever sprang for me with a piercing scream. She dodged the gunshots, too fast for my bullets to hit her. I estimated the time it would take her to reach me and fired three consecutive shots into the ceiling. It exploded in a colossal crash. Bedrock rained down, burying Miss Grever in a wave of rubble. I didn't wait for the dust to clear to see if she'd been squished into a pancake, just hurtled down the passage. It was longer than I remembered, because the elevator looked distant, like a doorway in a nightmare that seemed to drift farther away.

A thin scream resonated behind me. Miss Grever had crawled her way out of the rubble. She was coming after me.

I scampered inside the elevator and punched the button.

Come on. Close. Close.

Miss Grever's scaly reptile-like body was nearly at the doors. She extended her jaws, the meaty stench of her breath filling my nostrils. I leapt out of the way as her forked tongue slithered inside, leaving a puddle of drool in its wake. The elevator gave a vibratory judder. The doors slid closed, chopping the tongue in a clean cut. It dropped to the floor, twitching like an insect's tail at my feet.

Yelling in disgust, I staggered away and punched the button for the hanger. But something wasn't right. The rattle of pulleys grinding against cables stopped. Above, the fluorescent light flickered. Everything went utterly still...

And then the elevator dropped.

CHAPTER THIRTY-SIX

I was too shocked to scream. The elevator plummeted down the shaft like the weighted blade of a guillotine, the floor seeming to rush at me. My organs jammed into my throat, my gut curdling with burning nausea. It was amazing how seconds felt like hours when you had no idea how long you'd been falling. This was an eternity. I didn't know what was worse, bracing for the impact or not knowing when it was about to strike.

A muffled *boom* rang below the floor, the brakes grounding the lift to a sudden halt. My shoulder hit the galvanised floor hard, my courage fleeing. The platform groaned and creaked. The lights flickered, then shut out. Everything went dark.

I didn't dare move. Crying for help wasn't an option. I was far below the detention centre, deep in the mountain. No one would hear me. I had an image of my body left down here for weeks, the lack of ventilation building the pressure up like a slow cooker, depriving my corpse of hydration. My skin and organs would reduce to a chunky gunk. Bodily gases would cause parts of me to explode.

I curled into a ball of despair, my hands tingling in apprehension.

What am I going to do?

A rush of cool air danced across my cheek. That was odd. There shouldn't have been a breeze in a sealed environment like this, especially when that breeze had eerily felt like… fingers.

I bolted upright, struck by how ominous Adaline was sitting by my side, a skeleton stitched together by frozen tendons, wet sinew, and rubbery tissue. Gory threads of flesh drooped off her bones, collapsing into fat puddles on the floor. I gave a hoarse cry and scooted back. That was one scare I really could have done without.

Panic compressed my chest. "Did you do this to the elevator?"

Adaline nodded.

"Why?"

Her voice echoed chillingly in my head, childlike and forlorn. *"I have something to show you."*

Then she vanished.

A mysterious jolt shook the elevator. The doors opened with a sharp, tinny whine, a ribbon of light slicing through the lift. Beyond the elevator was an underground cavern. Ridged with treacherous rocks, the walls had to be hundreds of metres high, tall enough to hold a skyscraper. Natural light— though I didn't know how it reached this deep in the mountain—spilled from massive dolines in the ceiling. It filtered onto rows of mirrored slabs that protruded from a large lake, giving the impression of a watery graveyard.

Nothing beyond the detention centre was meant to exist in the mountain. So, what was this place?

Gingerly, I followed the granite steps down to the ghostly cavern, my footsteps soundless on the sodden rock. When I glanced over my shoulder, the elevator was gone; there was nothing there but a solid cave wall covered in green sea moss. I swallowed back the fear on the tip of my tongue.

I sensed Adaline's presence beside me, her wispy fingers gently stroking my cheek. *"This way."*

I delved deeper into the cavern. Salt spray caressed my face, but other than an impressive waterfall cascading onto the rocks, nothing moved. Oddly, the waterfall didn't make a sound either. Nothing about the cavern felt real, more like a dream or a place that lay outside of existence, not defined by natural science.

At the edge, I dipped my booted toe into the lake. The water didn't ripple.

"Over here." Adaline began to take shape amongst the slabs, her lower half

submerged. She resembled a monstrous dead mermaid.

I waded through the water, unnerved at how stagnant it remained. At least it was only waist deep. I carefully wound my way through the lengthy passages, the mirrored slabs towering over me like sentinels. The farther I trekked, the taller they became, my image mirrored thousands of times in a twisted optical illusion, making it impossible to maintain a sense of direction. All I had was Adaline to guide me, glowing like a will-o'-the-wisp through the water.

"Wait up." I was met with resistance, rocks and mud sliding out beneath me. I had just made the conscious decision to turn back when the atmosphere changed, the air thick and charged. Fiery smears appeared in the mirrors. They were distant at first, mottled, then, like a camera lens, sharpened into focus.

Names.

Thousands. Millions. More than anyone could possibly count came alive in the mirrors. They lit the cavern in a pale tint of orange, the colour of sunset before it descended into night. Overwhelming sadness crept over me. These slabs were graveyard markers, paying tribute to the fallen in this never-ending war. What I stood in was a reflecting pool to grieve and heal. There were no birth or death dates with the names, probably because the bodies had never been found. The polished glass was the only reminder they'd existed. It was sombre and dismal, and it irritated me that this place was deep in the mountain and not on the surface where the fallen deserved to be honoured.

"Zaya."

I whirled around to find Adaline beside me. She was fading, the sharp curves and contours of her figure erased away like an ill-attempted sketch. She pointed to the end of the passage and gave me a small tragic smile.

Then she was gone.

Following her direction, I plodded heavily past the slabs and come out to the centre of the lake. The distant banks were lost in velvety black, the water deeper and darker. Judging by the damp surfaces and briny ocean scent, the cavern was submerged at high tide, which only added to that gnawing sense of danger in my gut. How long did I have until the tide swept in?

Why did you bring me here, Adaline?

But more importantly, how the hell was I going to get out?

I squinted. In the centre of the lake was a small island of rock.

"Swim," Adaline's voice instructed.

"No way."

The blood in my ears pounded loudly. I was not about to throw myself into a large expanse of water where anything could lurk.

"Swim." Adaline's tone was a strict command. *"The island is your only way out of here."*

Inhaling a shuddering breath, I moved deeper into the lake. Piercing cold stabbed my body as I submerged fully into the water, my head slicing in and out of the surface like a bobbing apple. I forced my arms and legs into a breast stroke and swam toward the island, my clothes billowing around me. The water was so dark I couldn't see a hint of rock or marine life, but my head played tricks regardless, picturing thousands of bloated corpses hidden in the depths, their waterlogged bodies coming to devour me in a piranha feeding frenzy, the surface bubbling in sick red splashes.

My hand hit rock. Trembling, I hauled myself onto the island, the once serrated edges worn to a smooth, slippery texture like glass. The island was no larger than the elevator had been, barren except for a single light that glowed brightly on top of a stone plinth. No, not a light. A grimoire, burning bright and shrouded in magic. At the exact moment my fingers made contact with the book, it burst alive, pages blazing white and fanning. It froze on a single page. Black liquid seeped out like oil, forming into a gruesome animated display.

A young man asleep in his bed materialised on the page. I recognised him as the ghost in my bedroom mirror, only in this image he was alive, his red hair a mess around his face as he slept. I felt ill watching him, as though I were intruding on a private moment. A shadow crossed his face. Long fleshless fingers reached down for his sleeping body. I screamed as the black-veined woman thrust her fist into his chest, closing her fingers around his heart. The boy woke, eyes wide and staring, his face splattered with his own blood.

The image dissolved. In its place, another scene emerged. A young thief, barely past his teens, rummaged through wreckage on his hands and knees, too preoccupied in pilfering coins to take notice of the hunched shape appearing from the thick shadows of the alley. The black-veined woman twisted his neck like a bottle top, opening a large wound in his throat. Blood spilled onto the cobbled ground.

I flinched and looked away from the grisly scene. I knew the right thing to do was close the book and walk away, but a palpable force kept me as immobile as a statue, forcing me to witness these horrible murders. I couldn't shut my eyes. Whatever this was, it wanted me to see.

The scene changed.

No. No, no, no. Please don't make me watch this.

I was staring at myself, the usual brightness in my eyes made dull from tears. My seventeen-year-old self was screaming and bawling. Next to me, Adaline's bloated, frozen corpse was lying on the bed, the wounds in her wrists still bleeding. The black-veined woman was standing by the corner. She hovered toward me like she was on an invisible conveyor belt, her toxic laughter seeping into my ears, poisoning any coherent thought.

"I don't want to watch this," I screamed to the cavern.

And that was when my world exploded. A rush of pain ripped through my skull, like someone had rammed a tyre iron through my head. I fell to my knees. The grimoire's light was swimming through me, ebbing in and out. Heat surged up my arms and through my legs. The agony that tortured my body built to a crescendo.

And then... nothing.

I sensed I was still physically present but disconnected from my body, my mind struggling to comprehend this out-of-body experience. The lake and cavern were gone. I was standing on a steep cliff face that overlooked a gorge. Sea spray rained onto my skin. The ocean waves churned into the estuary below, the sky eclipsed by clouds.

My lips quivered. The cliff ended in a sheer drop; one misstep and I'd be lost to the dark sea below. Rain started to whip into eddies around me. I narrowed my eyes, straining to see. A concrete arch dam, at least a thousand feet in height and length, stood impressively in the gorge. It held back the ocean surge and kept the freshwater reservoir protected on the opposite side. Gates and turbines were installed at regular intervals above the spillway. A bridge ran the length of the arch wall. In the wild weather, its fence looked flimsy and unsafe.

Why am I here?

I searched my surroundings, but the landscape was empty. I was alone. Lightning zigzagged across the sky, illuminating the dam's impressive structure. From the bridge rose a large tower, its upper platform topped with a glass rotunda. Someone stood at the observation deck. Even from this distance, I sensed their eyes appraise me from head to foot, pinning me like a moth to a board.

"Zaya, I see you. I know what you are."

The voice was deep and lethal, like the crumbling of rock and earth.

"Join me."

Every syllable was painful in my skull, as though acid was eating away at my brain.

"Join me. Join me. Join me."

"Enough," I cried.

For a space of a heartbeat, everything went black.

I opened my eyes to a new environment. Forest trees soared into the sky, their gnarled roots buried firmly in the ground. Snow fell, torrents of it, the branches a white blur overhead. Morning sunlight filtered through the leaves. Without it, the forest would have been pitch black.

Stay calm. This isn't real. This is a trick of the grimoire.

The air smelt of damp earth and rotten leaves. Precipitation had iced over the ground, making it difficult to walk. It took a moment to register that someone stood among the trees. Her hair was black and short, blue eyes cutting straight into mine.

Lunette. What is she doing in my vision?

Fear fluttered in my veins. Something wasn't right. Lunette was propped against the tree, her skin resembling glass. I took a few cautious steps forward. No, not glass—ice! She'd been painted in frost. White crystals streaked her hair. Her throat was packed with snow, crammed so deep it had frozen her windpipe. A gash had been ripped through her torso.

My hands shook as I raked them through my hair. This wasn't a dream. Or a vision. It was real.

A twig snapped behind me, a hand closing over my mouth. I wrestled in the arms of my assailant, but they were so strong it was like fighting a steel beam.

"Be quiet... and for providence's sake, stop moving." His voice was a sharp whisper in my ear.

Whoever held me let go. I whirled around.

Colonel Harper stared at me, the strands of his dark hair a halo around his face. He'd been out in the woods for some time, his clothes flecked with snow, his trousers damp to his knees. "What are you doing out here? You're not supposed to be in Shadow's Wood."

"Sir... I...." But how was I meant to explain any of this when I didn't understand it myself? I turned my gaze back to Lunette. "She's dead. She's dead." My voice bubbled toward hysteria.

A shadow of worry appeared under the colonel's eyes. "We need to get back to the base immediately. Do you understand? Melvina is on the grounds. She must have followed you from Essida."

His words ran thick and slow through me.

I failed. I didn't get the warning to Macaslan in time. Lunette is dead because of me.

"Zaya, we need to leave now." Colonel Harper started in the direction of the base, his strides frantic. "Don't you understand? Someone opened the celestial shield. There are dissent rebels in the woods."

I made an effort to run after him, but my legs were as sturdy as water.

And then the shadows appeared. Everywhere I looked, ghosts hobbled toward me, their pale hands outstretched. Melvina's victims. The black-veined woman had done horrible things to them. Some of them were missing limbs or part of their faces; others had icy holes burnt into their flesh. They cried for help, their voices deep and unearthly. Wherever I looked, I was met with empty, lifeless eyes.

"Go away! Go away! Leave me alone." I tried to swat them away, but my hands went straight through their fleshless bodies.

More faces appeared, solemn and pained. The two boys I'd watched Melvina murder stood silently at my side, their faces sad. Black dots stretched across my vision. The last thing I remembered was the stench of death before I collapsed into the dark.

CHAPTER THIRTY-SEVEN

"I'm worried about her. She's been out of it for days now. And she's really pale."

"She's always pale."

"You know what I mean… sick pale."

"She's had ten shots of asith potion, Talina. She probably won't wake up for another week… if at all."

"Stop it, Marek. You shouldn't say things like that in an infirmary. It's bad luck. I have faith she'll recover."

"Even if she does wake up, she could be permanently damaged."

Silence.

Permanently damaged?

Hot rage simmered down my throat.

Who the hell was referring to me as broken goods? I fought to peel my eyes open, but my lids stuck together as though sealed with glue. I rubbed the sleep out of them and blinked for the first time in days. I was tucked into a linen-sheeted bed with metal side rails. A row of similar beds stretched out on either side of me, occupied by sick and wounded soldiers. Some of the patients were wrapped in heavy bandages caked with dry blood; others were so badly disfigured I couldn't tell whether they were male or female. Medicinal alcohol was heavy in the air, but it couldn't disguise the scent of blood, soiled linen, and blistered flesh.

I wished I'd remained unconscious. Every part of me ached, like I'd been torn apart and set back together with a soldering iron. I had vague impressions of two people moving in and out of focus. One of their faces lifted into a familiar smile.

"You're awake." Talina flung out of her chair and enveloped me in a hug. Her embrace crushed my ribs. "We've been so worried. You're in the recovery ward."

"Yeah, I figured that." My throat was parched, my voice lazy and slow. "How long have I been…?"

"Unconscious. Nearly two weeks."

"Two weeks!" I bolted upright, which made the hospital ward spin dangerously. "But my hearing was scheduled—"

"It's okay." Talina gently pushed me back onto the pillow. "You've been acquitted. I know you're not the biggest fan of Commander Macaslan, but you're in her debt now. Despite the odds, she somehow managed to clear your name."

Meaning Darius had worked his magic, literally.

The relief this news brought to me was short-lived. Standing at the end of the bed was Marek, the sternness on his face causing my nerves to fluctuate. His skin was black under his eyes, a few small cuts visible on his face. He kept peering at the door, his hands clutched into fists at his sides, as though he expected a threat to walk in at any moment.

My spine stiffened. "What's going on?"

He didn't answer.

Talina gave my hand a gentle squeeze. "You collapsed in Shadow's Wood. Colonel Harper brought you in. Macaslan was furious. Neither of them would give me information about what happened to you in the woods. I'm the only one allowed to administer your potions. Apparently no one can be trusted with that task but me, whatever that means. Marek has been watching you every day since you were brought in. There's a guard stationed here night and day. It's all been very strange." Talina dragged her fingers down her face. She looked like she hadn't slept in days.

I stared at Marek with growing anxiety. "I'm under surveillance?"

I didn't think it was because I was a prisoner. Macaslan and Colonel Harper were doing everything in their power to keep someone away from me—someone who knew what I was and wanted me dead.

General Kravis.

My pulse hammered in my ears. Why had I been in Shadow's Wood? I closed my eyes, trying to recall that disorientating night. I remembered being taken down to the detention centre and fleeing Miss Narkiss and Miss Grever, but after that, everything was a blur.

I swallowed, my throat tense. "What happened to me?"

Neither Talina nor Marek responded. They looked as though they wanted to know the answer themselves.

Two orderlies in blue scrubs appeared. A young man in the opposite bed must have died sometime in the night, his fingers clutching the blanket as if he'd been trying to huddle underneath it. I watched in fascination as the orderlies effortlessly plucked the corpse off the bed and tossed him onto a trolley. They did a poor job of covering him with a white sheet. His limp neck had twisted around, his glassy eyes staring at me.

Are his lips... moving?

"*Lunette, Lunette, Lunette,*" the corpse's phantom voice whispered.

I turned away, the gruesome clarity surfacing as though my mind had fallen from a black hole and back into this dimension.

The cavern... Adaline... the disjointed images from the grimoire... the ghosts writhing in agony in Shadow's Wood... Lunette.

Lunette!

She was dead, killed by Melvina.

It all came back with horrible transparency.

Talina flattened a hand on the bed for support. "Zaya, what's wrong? Do you remember something?"

I clutched my blanket as though it were a lifeline, just like the young soldier had before his death. The similarity sent a cold ache through my bones. "Did they get Melvina? The dissent rebels in the woods? Did they get them?"

They have to be under lock and key, surely?

Talina's fine-boned face shifted into alarm. "Dissent rebels? In Shadow's

Wood?"

My skin went damp along my lower back. I told her what had happened the night I'd found Lunette's frozen corpse—eliminating the cavern and the ghosts from my tale, of course.

"What do you mean, a body was found in the woods?" She exchanged a terrified glance with Marek.

He dipped his head, his expression shifting into pity. He must have thought I was delusional. "There's been no report that the celestial shield was opened, Zaya. Dissent rebels didn't enter Tarahik. If a body was found in the woods, it's news to me. Are you sure you weren't dreaming?"

The blood rushed from my face. Macaslan, Harper, Darius—maybe Jad—they'd covered it up, making a smokescreen out of Lunette's death. Goosebumps popped out over my arms. If they had concealed Lunette's death, then that meant Melvina and the rebels had fled.

Talina pressed her lips together. "You had a head injury in Essida, and you've suffered severely. All of this is some sort of post-traumatic reaction. It was just a dream." She squeezed my hand again, a maternal gesture meant to assure me my coma-induced nightmare was simply that—a nightmare.

"Just a dream," I repeated dumbly, feeling eternally alone.

Talina plastered on a smile, but it teetered at the corners. "What you need is rest. My shift ends in a minute. Normally I used to sit by your side and hope you'd wake, but this time I promised Lainie I'd go with her to check on Edric."

I gaped. "What happened to Edric?"

When she didn't answer straight away, I tossed the sheets aside, but Marek was quick to restrain me. It was just as well. Yellow dots burst before my eyes, vertigo closing in.

Talina drew closer, regulating her volume so she didn't wake the other patients. "Edric's not doing so well. Physically he's fine… but he's in the psychiatric ward. He's troubled. Lainie's not coping with it."

A tight swelling enveloped my chest. "You mean he feels guilty about murdering civilians in Essida?"

I had wondered if Edric was one of the fighter pilots bombing the city. This confirmed it. I didn't blame him. He'd been following General Kravis's orders, but I could understand the self-destruction he now faced. Every time I'd hurt someone in Gosheniene to save my own skin—even when they'd deserved it—a part of my soul had fractured.

Talina stared ahead with a resigned expression. "We don't know how long Edric will be there. He hasn't made much progress this past fortnight." She fiddled nervously with her hands. "Listen, before I go, I have to put you under a sleeping spell. Commander's orders."

I wrestled myself up to sitting again. "I've been asleep for two weeks."

"But not restful sleep." She took up a syringe from the bedside table. "This guarantees proper rest."

She jammed the needle into my arm.

"Hey," I snapped. "You didn't have patient consent."

She rolled her eyes.

Talina applied a healing balm over the small insertion in my skin and wrapped it with a bandage. "You'll likely feel drowsy in a few minutes. I have to go now. Will you be okay?"

I smiled, but inside anguish ripped me apart. My thoughts spun into a wild, chaotic mess. The map was destroyed. Melvina had no way of finding the Larthalgule blade. So why had she killed Lunette?

"They surround you... always three, soon to be five. She's waiting, always watching. She wants the missing pair."

Adaline's death had never been a case of mistaken identity. Melvina had the blood of a trickster, illusionist, clairvoyant, and telepath. I was certain now that was what the grimoire was showing me. The black-veined woman needed one last blood-magic. Mine. But for what?

Talina took my hand again. "I'll be back tomorrow."

She left. Even in scrubs she looked elegant and lissom. More than a few eyes followed her out the door. Marek inclined his head only slightly, but I saw it in his face; longing and wonder. It was the quickest of glances, but it was evident in that moment that he felt the world for her, as though he was a bee and she was his pollen. Together, they had taken care of me for the past fortnight. It made sense something would develop on his part. I wondered if Talina was aware of Marek's feelings.

"You should get some rest," I suggested. "You look exhausted."

The sergeant smiled, but it was stiff and awkward. "I can't leave until my shift ends, but that's not long away. Captain Arden will be here soon to watch over you tonight."

I pinned him with a black look. "I don't need anyone watching me."

If I put an inventory together of people I wished to avoid, Jad was at the top of the list.

Marek put his hands up in surrender. "Macaslan's orders, not mine. You're not to be left alone."

I collapsed back onto my pillow, wishing I could bury myself in the sheets. "I need to speak to the commander."

I had to know what happened to Lunette's body. Did Macaslan know where Melvina and the dissent rebels vanished to? Maybe the commander would be able to make sense on what occurred with the grimoire.

But Marek never got the chance to answer.

"Zaya." A young nurse approached with a confident gait. She looked up from her clipboard, her blonde ponytail silky smooth past her shoulders.

Oh for the love of providence, why fucking now?

Smugness shone in Indree's eyes. Her shapely lips were painted in rose-red lipstick to complement the rouge on her cheeks, accentuating her beauty. Tarahik was in the middle of a crisis; how had she found time to paint her face in an entire bottle of foundation?

She raised her slender neck. "I'm the nurse taking care of you this evening."

I met her eyes coldly. "I thought Talina was the only nurse allowed to monitor me."

Indree smiled sweetly, but I detected poison in her glance. "Talina administers your medication, but anyone can watch you."

She reminded me of a blasé babysitter, annoyed at having to take care of a naughty toddler. Satisfied she needn't talk to me any further, she turned to Marek, her voice livelier and more musical, like wind chimes dancing in a summer breeze. I hated wind chimes.

Jealous rage bubbled inside. It shouldn't have been a surprise that Marek would be friends with her, but it was another painful affirmation that Indree and Jad were a done deal. I'd been a fool in Essida. When the captain had held me in his arms, I'd misread the situation. Jad had been afraid I was hurt—

nothing more. His heart belonged to this fake, snobby, breast-implanted bimbo.

It's just a stupid crush. In a few weeks, you won't even care about Jad.

So why did I have to convince myself of that so very loudly?

Indree tipped her head back and laughed at one of the sergeant's lame jokes.

Someone smother me with a pillow, please.

I closed my eyes and pretended to drift off to sleep, wishing Talina's damn spell would hurry up and work.

At last their conversation changed.

"Jad should arrive soon," I heard Marek say.

I sensed Indree's gaze fixed attentively on me. Her voice was tightly controlled. "Would you mind staying a few more minutes? It's just until I can get another soldier to replace Jad. I don't want him around her. She's a bad influence."

"Jad can't be influenced by anybody. You know that."

"But there's something about her." A heavy sigh. "I don't like that he comes here every night to keep an eye on her."

A flutter worked its way in my stomach. *Jad comes here every night?*

"They're his orders," Marek responded. "He can't help it."

"I know that, but it's… it's the fact that he doesn't mind doing it that bothers me."

"Indree, relax. Jad worries about Zaya, but it's not what you think. She's like a little sister to him."

Ouch.

"But is he an older brother to her?" That musical voice now sounded like chimes clashing together in a hurricane. "Just stay a few minutes, okay? I'll find another soldier to replace Jad."

The sharp click of Indree's heels faded into the distance.

I smiled into my pillow. At least the green-eyed monster inside me would be subdued for a little while.

CHAPTER THIRTY-EIGHT

At some point in the evening, I was shifted into a private room. The sleeping hex had been highly effective, because I hadn't woken. There'd been nothing but empty darkness with no perception of time, like that part of my life had been snatched away and was no longer mine.

I rubbed the drowsiness from my eyes to get a clearer view of my surroundings. I was lying in an enormous oak-panelled bed with a satin duvet and matching pillows. The red tapestry drapes were open, ribbons of muted light streaming in from behind dark clouds. Everything was decorated in dark timbers, the walls painted in a motif of blue skies and gold leaf. I'd thought my apartment was luxurious, but this took opulence to the next level.

"Hello, Zaya."

The voice was smooth, assertive, but I detected a hint of disapproval in the tone.

Jad sat in an armchair reading a book. The ends of his thick hair curled below his jaw, the stubble on his face suggesting he hadn't had time to shave in a while.

The back of my throat itched, like I'd been stung multiple times by bees. "You guys have outdone yourselves with the accommodation this time. Where am I?"

His eyes remained on the book. "Guest quarters. I had you moved here in the early hours of the morning. The commander will arrive shortly to speak to you. Too many people come and go through the infirmary. I couldn't risk our conversation being overheard."

"I assume she'll be answering my questions, because the list I have is endless."

He didn't answer.

I pushed my long mass of curls behind my shoulders. "I can wait here on my own. You look like hell… and I know your girlfriend doesn't want you here." The irritation in my throat sharpened. I'd wanted to sound confident, but the tremble in my voice betrayed me.

His eyes swept up from the book. "I'm not here to talk about Indree."

"Don't let her hear you say that."

He returned to his reading, but his face had lost its composure. He looked like he'd prefer to take on a round of machine-gun fire than discuss Indree.

I dropped the subject and tried not to appear too elated by this development. Jad and Indree seemed the most unlikely pair to date. Their personalities couldn't have been more different, like a lion taking a flamingo out to dinner. The idea was preposterous.

Jad's attention was absorbed in his reading. Even with his face showing visible signs of exhaustion, the captain was a striking figure to behold, like the idealised form of a Roman sculpture come to life. But there was so much more to Jad than looks, even though I knew Indree's interest in him was based solely on the physical. What did the captain see in such a shallow, conceited girl?

Jad absent-mindedly fiddled with a pendant hanging from a gold chain around his neck. It wasn't a soldier-engraved dog tag. An envious stirring swept through me. It was a promise necklace, a half sphere designed to be the moon. Linking the two halves of the pendant would complete the orb. The sentimentality made me want to vomit.

My derisive attitude reached its limit. "Nice jewellery. Did Indree buy you that?"

He sighed—the faintest sound. "It's a loyalty charm, not a promise charm. And if you must know, it belonged to my mother. It's the one thing I have left to remember her by."

I crossed my arms over my chest, feeling stupid and uncomfortable. The memories of his childhood became painfully raw in his eyes. I could only imagine the trauma the captain must have suffered when his father had died. It had left him with emotional scars that would never heal. But what had happened to Jad's mother? She'd died when he was ten. But from what?

I flinched, shame cutting deep into my conscience. "I'm sorry. I shouldn't have pried."

"No, you shouldn't have." Jad snapped his book shut. "It's my turn to ask questions. What happened that night in the detention centre? How did you end up in Shadow's Wood?"

I opened my mouth, but no response came out.

Instead, someone else's did.

"That, Captain Arden, is an excellent question."

Commander Macaslan swept into the room like a demon storming toward the gates of hell. Her face was pale and pinched, her grey eyes lethal. She stood at the end of my bed and waited.

My jaw dropped. "You're supposed to tell me what happened, not the other way around."

Did they think the pieces lay before me, a jigsaw waiting to be finished? I had no idea where to start, because I had no idea what had happened.

Jad caught my eye. "Tell us what you remember of that evening. That might be a good place to begin."

I tried to evoke a level of calm while I related my story, but I felt like a criminal under the scornful eye of a judge. I told them everything—Adaline, the cavern, the grimoire, the vision of the dam, and finally Lunette. When I finished, heavy silence fell. Would they laugh? Insist I tell the truth? Tell me I was crazy? Even to me it had sounded stupid.

Macaslan hesitated for a second, her lips narrowing into a prim, unpleasant grimace. "This changes things."

My eyes widened. "Changes what?"

"Miss Wayward, there is no memorial beyond the detention centre... nothing exists that deep in the mountain. If—"

"I'm not lying," I insisted, overcome with a fresh wave of anger.

"I never implied you were." She exhaled irritably. "Wraiths can cross dimensions. It works the same way as casters travelling by portal. When you were in that elevator and it dived, I believe the wraith took you into the otherworld, a place that exists beyond the normal plane. You are a necromancer. The grimoire showed you what you needed to see—the deaths of an illusionist, trickster, and telepath. The dam was likely a forecast of the future. This grimoire was trying to communicate something to you. Whether it transferred you to the woods in an endeavour to save Lunette or was offering you as a sacrifice to Melvina is another question."

My alarm was a cold knife through the gut. That was an option I'd never considered.

The commander rubbed her fingers along her temples. "Melvina is not deterred. Killing Lunette proved that. She's still searching for Larthalgule."

Jad rose to his feet. "But the map was destroyed. The ULD will never find the blade."

Macaslan released a shaky breath. "I don't know. There must be more to it. Something we've missed. Killing innocents for their magic suggests Melvina is preparing a dangerous spell, something Morgomoth started but never finished... something forbidden under our laws." She let out a stifled groan, her face heavy with disappointment. "I should have done more to protect Lunette. I knew she was a clairvoyant. Magic like that can make an individual unstable. Someone helped her into Shadow's Wood."

An image of Lunette's body morphed into my head. Her chalky skin, bloodless lips, and frozen eyes seemed to look at me as though demanding answers, like she blamed me for her death. "She was frightened of Tarahik," I admitted, recalling that terrifying evening when Lunette had made the prediction that had chilled my blood. "She wanted to get away from this place."

Jad crossed his arms, his voice flat. "And whoever led her into the woods must have promised they'd get her out."

My chest tightened. "So the traitor is someone Lunette trusted?"

I wished I'd paid more attention to the people she'd hung around with. I felt both angry and sorry for Lunette, because she had been a trusting fool who should have known better, and because I should have done more for her than I had. "Where is her body?"

The commander started to pace, a sure sign she was growing restless. "General Kravis had her transferred to Valdavar Tower. It's a mortuary and pathology lab… of sorts. He knows Melvina is responsible for the girl's death, but he wants to learn more about Lunette's magic and find out why it's valuable to the ULD." The rising sun outside deepened the shadows along her face. She looked like she hadn't slept in days. "My concern is now for you, Zaya."

My fingers shook violently at my sides. "Because Melvina is coming for me."

"Yes, and because General Kravis is suspicious of what you are. He's watching you." She peered out the window, squinting at the brightening morning sun. "I have only one option—putting you under house arrest."

"Excuse me?" I didn't bother hiding the defiance in my voice.

"You're not to leave your apartment, not even to go out onto the grounds. Your training has been suspended. It's the only way I can assure your safety."

"But I haven't done anything wrong."

She raised her eyebrow at me. "You will return to your apartment, where you will remain until Darius and I can figure out what Melvina and the ULD are planning. And don't bother trying to find a way out, Zaya. Binding spells will be placed in your room. Do anything to upset that magic and the punishment will be severe."

I stared, my jaw agape.

Jad's face was an impassive mask. The only sign that any of this bothered him was the flash of agitation in his eyes. "Wouldn't it be easier to remove Zaya from Tarahik? Place her somewhere safe?"

Macaslan gave an empty chuckle. It would have been insulting if it weren't underlined with a hint of fear. "Not possible. That would be the proof Kravis needs to form an investigation. The last thing we need is for the council to be involved." She moved toward the door. "I must talk to Darius and try to clear these matters up. We have to guess Melvina's next move."

I blinked at her as she slipped away. "What am I supposed to do under house arrest?"

"Not cause trouble."

And with that, the commander swept out of the room, leaving me hot with rage.

CHAPTER THIRTY-NINE

Boring.

That was how I'd describe being under house arrest. Stuck in my apartment for five days, nine hours, and eighteen minutes—not that I'd been counting—was doing my head in. I was going insane. The doors and windows were impassable, blocked by shielding charms. No matter what objects I tossed at them—weapons, chairs, the coffee table—they bounced without leaving an impact. When I beat my fists against our new front door made of galvanised steel—yes, they'd notched security up that much—an electrical current tossed me backward. I twitched and writhed on the floor until the effects wore off, then slumped on the sofa, reduced to reading cheesy romance novels Talina had brought in from the library. Counting the hours from breakfast to lunch, then lunch to dinner, was agony.

The evenings were slightly better. At five o'clock, Lainie and Talina returned from training. I'd probe them for news about Tarahik and the latest gossip of the day, but they were reluctant to share anything about the outside world, which made me think our apartment had been bugged. It was funny that after two years at Gosheniene, I'd accepted loneliness and seclusion as a way of life. But Tarahik had changed that. I'd grown to enjoy the co-dependency of the noisy, social world. Just hearing voices in the background or seeing people in the distance could console the loneliest mind, but the blocking charms had taken that from me too. Now the absence of people made my world forlorn.

On the ninth day, I couldn't face another idle hour lying on the couch. Sluggish, I ambled to my room and did the one thing a bored, unfulfilled mind could do: I crashed on the bed and slept.

When I woke, the slimmest ribbon of moonlight peeked through the curtains, cutting the monotonous dark. Outside, the night was empty and silent. There was no wind. No bugs droned. No birds chirped. None of the nightly bumps and creaks that accompanied an aging castle like Tarahik made a sound. The absence of noise was disconcerting.

I imagined Lainie and Talina asleep like sedated invalids in their rooms. Gently, I swung off the bed and tiptoed down the hall for a drink of water. On my return, the last thing my restless mind expected to find was my bedroom window open, the curtains adrift in the now frigid air, and my bed encased in ice. The fine hairs on my arms stood on end. The water in my glass had frozen.

After days of isolation, I'd longed for a visitor. In the future, I needed to be careful what I wished for. Fog swirled through the window, coalescing into a female form, as though an invisible artist had moulded a perfect ice figurine. I'd expected Adaline, but this was a new face—and not entirely unexpected.

My voice rolled into the cold air. "I'm sorry… for what happened to you."

Wearing her death wounds, Lunette was terrible to look at. Her skin was covered in white crystals, her pixie cut frozen in haphazard angles. Ice was still lodged in her throat. I knew because when she opened her mouth, it was the size of a golf ball.

Frost streaked over my bedroom walls, the temperature dropping several degrees.

I sniffed weakly. "What do you want?"

Lunette's eyes probed mine. Their colour reminded me of a bottomless black ocean, weirdly beautiful yet dangerous at the same time.

I was an idiot. Of course Lunette couldn't speak. The ice Melvina had embedded in her delicate neck would prevent it.

"Show me what you want."

She twitched a finger in the direction of the woods, just like Adaline had the first night I'd arrived. From the window, Shadow's Wood appeared haunted and uninhabitable. The tree trunks and their branches were like skeletal bodies with gnarled limbs. There was no wind, but I could have sworn the trees moved, as though their roots had sprouted from the earth, sliding like a squid's tentacles through the mossy ground.

I exhaled slowly. "I can't go in there. There are binding spells in the apartment. I can't leave."

And for some unknown reason, those spells hadn't barricaded Lunette.

She blinked hard, as though she were trying to remove water from her eyes. Her cheeks, nose, and forehead pulled into a tight frown of concentration. *"The binding spells have been taken care of,"* her voice rattled in my ears.

On cue, there was a metallic click down the end of the hallway, followed by the unmistakable creak of the apartment door opening.

Lunette began to recede with the fog, seeping into the wall like melting ice. I stepped tentatively to the window. She had manipulated space, because in the distance, she floated among the trees in Shadow's Wood, flickering in and out like an image on a hologram screen, arms raised to beckon me forward.

What I ought to have done was close the window and sleep on the couch—thanks to my bed being reduced to a wet sponge.

Uh-uh. Not a chance.

Before I could convince myself this was a bad idea, I slipped my black training uniform over my clothes, yanked on steel-capped boots, and tiptoed down the hallway. No matter how quietly I trod past Lainie's and Talina's bedrooms, every footstep was agonisingly loud. The floorboards creaked under my weight. In the silence, it sounded louder than a horn.

Without pause, I crept out the door and inched it shut behind me. Lunette had planned this escape well. Frost had been streaked like confetti across the lavish carpet, snaking around corners and twisting down staircases, leading me safely to the lobby on the ground floor without being seen. Every major entryway into the base was monitored by sentries. I remained by the staircase in the shadows, hearing a pair somewhere close, their voices carrying along the walls. I waited until their footsteps faded, then darted to the massive stone arched door, holding my breath as I twisted the lever.

Outside, the sky was dark and rainy. Mist coasted across the grounds, enveloping the landscape in a sea of cloud and drizzle. I was halfway across the lawn when my hair and clothes became heavy and soaked with rain, the night gradually colder and damper the closer I approached the woods. The stench of silt, stagnant water, and damp earth filled my nostrils, making it difficult to breathe. Lunette hovered by the trees, pale and translucent, like the outline of a painting not quite finished.

The moisture in my mouth tasted greasy. "Show me what it is you're after."

She remained impassive and unmoving. The only thing that stirred was her eyes, which peered over my shoulder.

Somewhere behind me, a twig snapped.

I twisted around, my neck making a terrible popping sound with the sharp movement. "What the hell are you two doing here?"

Talina flinched at my reprimand. She reminded me of a mouse wanting to burrow for cover. Lainie watched me with curious eyes. Slush had sunk into the girls' slippers, the ends of their pyjamas soaked in mud. They peered over my shoulder into the darkness of the trees. Of course they couldn't see Lunette.

Lainie pursed her lips. "Who are you talking to?"

"None of your business." I dared a quick look at the castle, afraid their adventure had alerted the sentries. "Why are you out here?"

Talina rubbed her arms for warmth. "We could ask you the same thing. You're meant to be under house arrest. How did you break the binding spells? And the barrier charm on the castle door? What are you up to, Zaya?"

I tilted my chin, snapping, "Go back to the castle. Now."

Lainie scowled. "We're not going to let you do something stupid." Without her pale make-up and black eyeliner, she looked young and fragile, like a porcelain doll easily shattered.

Behind me, Lunette begun to fade progressively into the trees.

My animosity flared. "Go back now."

Lainie ground her teeth. "Not until you promise to come back with us."

A sweep of light crossed the large expanse of lawn—a flashlight.

My despair escalated. "You've brought the sentries after you!"

Footsteps hustled across the lawn. We ducked as another shaft of light sped over our heads. We all knew the repercussions for being caught out of the castle at night. A weird mix of dread and apathy stirred inside me. I think each of us formed the same conclusion at the same time. We sprinted into the treacherous forest. Branches snagged at our loose hair. Thick pools of watery slush threw us off balance, the ground moist and unstable, causing traps with each footfall.

Muffled cries broke out behind us. Sporadic light shone through the woods ahead. I hauled the girls behind a fallen tree before the spotlight darted onto us.

Lainie's voice came out in a choppy pant. "You shouldn't have come out here, Zaya."

I had the maddening urge to laugh. "No, *you* shouldn't have."

I snuck a peek through the trees. More sentries had arrived. They combed the woods, advancing toward our little hideout with a speed that was alarming. These guys were trained to pursue—and they had an advantage. Low, grunting snarls first alerted me to the barghest hounds. Their enormous shapes appeared through the swirling fog, their scarlet eyes gleaming with hunger. Centuries ago, casters successfully blended the DNA of wolverines and grizzly bears with drastic consequence, creating a supreme killing beast. Frightfully proficient in running—they could outrun a racehorse—barghest hounds had an acute sense of smell and direction, making them the ultimate trackers. Their only downfall was water. For unknown reasons, they couldn't cross rivers or running streams.

Howls and yaps echoed into the otherwise silent night, the beasts' powerful muscles yearning for action beneath their thick fur. One of the hounds jerked its snout and sniffed the air. It could probably smell my fear.

My stomach ravelled into a panicked knot. Against casters, we might have stood a chance. Against barghest hounds, we needed a miracle. "We can't stay here."

Judging from the way Talina's and Lainie's faces drained of colour, the girls had already surmised that. On my signal, we crawled downhill, holding our breath every time leaves crunched under our hands and feet.

A ray of light shone down on us. "Over there!" someone shouted.

No time to be discreet. We got onto our feet and ran, dodging blindly through the trees. The hounds loped across the ground, their paws sending fierce tremors through the forest floor, rattling every bone in my body.

"Ugh!" My foot went out from under me. I'd been so preoccupied with the hounds that I hadn't seen the incline. My fingers instinctively tried to latch on to something to prevent my fall, but it was too late. I fell into a stretch of moving water. It wasn't deep—about waist height—but it was agonisingly cold.

"Zaya?" Talina's voice was a whisper from the ridge. Her head poked out from a mass of leafy bushes. "Are you okay?"

"Get down here." I kept low in the water, which stung like pinpricks.

The girls descended the sharp gradient. Growling, snorting sounds drew closer from the ridge.

"Get in the water," I demanded when the girls reached me.

I grabbed their arms and pulled them under, the three of us fully submerged. The barghest hounds would lose track of our scent in the dirty rivulet. Through the ripples, I saw the dogs standing on the ridge, howling into the night, disappointed they hadn't been able to sink their teeth into our ankles.

One second.

Two seconds.

Three seconds.

I was running out of breath. The pain was like a nuclear explosion in my chest.

At last, the barghest hounds gave up and returned to their masters.

I burst through the surface, weak and in shock, my muscles trembling in exhaustion. Lainie and Talina emerged, their pyjamas drenched, their hair mud-smeared and bedraggled. They drew in rocky breaths, shivering as they climbed out of the frigid, fast-moving water.

I scrambled out after them. "Let's find a way back to the castle. And this time, do exactly as I say."

The icy hostility in my voice made my friends cringe. They meant the world to me, but right now it took all my willpower not to drown them. Talina and Lainie had made me lose my chance with Lunette. The wraith was gone… and so was any hope of finding answers.

CHAPTER FORTY

❝Are we lost? We are, aren't we? I knew it." Lainie kicked a rock from the narrow track that ran the length of the gorge. It landed in an epic splash in the stream below. She exhaled loudly, crossing her arms over her chest.

I shot her a disdainful look. My anger was like a bushfire, sparking higher, burning brighter, until I saw nothing but red. It killed me to admit it, but she was right. We were deep in the woods and terribly lost, thanks partially to me. I'd tried to lead my friends the long way around by following the gorge—in case there were more sentries and barghest hounds on the prowl. At least, I thought it had been the long way. I knew from studying maps of the area that a tributary ran through the Tarahik grounds. I thought by following the stream, we'd come back to the castle and slip in unnoticed. Now I knew I'd misjudged. We were going the wrong way. Soon, the stream would meet other rivulets and flow into the Evanloor Falls—a cascade of waterfalls that ran into the Tarzor River below. And somewhere among that was the celestial shield. Invisible to the eye, if we stepped into its barrier, we'd be obliterated into a million pieces.

So yeah, our night was getting better and better.

My resolve fractured. "We have to go back. Retrace our steps."

Lainie's face looked stark white against the dark backdrop. "Go back? That's what you said ten minutes ago. We weren't far from Tarahik to begin with, yet here we are, lost, with no castle in sight. Explain that."

I spun around, the air tense and charged. "We wouldn't be in this situation if you hadn't followed me."

"We wouldn't be in this situation if you hadn't left the castle," she cried back.

I hated it when Lainie was like this. She knew exactly where to push my buttons but didn't know when to stop. My relationship with her was different to Talina's. We were more like sisters, bickering and hating each other, unafraid to show our feelings.

Talina rested against a tree, her face sombre and scared. She hadn't said anything for a long time. In her wet pyjamas, her extremities had turned blue, her matted hair dripping water down her shoulders. Her breathing sounded wheezy, which didn't strike me as a good sign. She reminded me of a wilted scarecrow left out too long in the weather, no longer possessing the sturdiness to stand.

Lainie tilted her chin toward me, eyes slitted and spiteful. "Look at her. This is your fault."

Cursing under my breath, I turned away. I was like a fighting bull, Lainie my matador. I had to invoke strong mental effort not to charge.

"That's right. Ignore me." Lainie tried to sound confident, but her voice shook.

Talina squeezed her eyes closed. "Lainie, please. Just leave it alone." She held on to a branch, no longer having the strength to stand on her own.

Lainie whirled on her. "You're siding with Zaya?" She pointed an accusing finger at me. "Unbelievable."

"Don't take this out on her," I snapped. I moved toward Talina and propped her arm over my shoulder, allowing her to steer her weight entirely on me. Worry clouded my brain. "She's not well."

Rage lit Lainie's eyes. For a moment, I thought she'd storm toward me and punch me straight between the eyes.

My mind struggled to comprehend the hostility between us. We argued but never fought like this. How had things gone so wrong between us?

It's the woods.

The celestial shield wasn't the only magic in this place. The woods were ancient. Who knew how many hexes and booby traps had been performed to inhibit trespassers in the ages past? The spells were messing with our heads, making us irritable. Shadow's Wood was a maze beyond our dimension, with no beginning or end. For all I knew, the trees, foothills, and streams could have sprouted legs and rearranged themselves, playing tricks on us.

An uneasy chill crept through me. "We need to stay calm. It's this place. The woods are deliberately making us lost. This probably isn't the stream we originally followed."

Laine's lower lip trembled. Her fury dwindled, evolving into tears. She looked like an afraid, lonely little girl. "Stay calm? And how are we supposed to do that? We're lost."

"We find shelter and try to light a fire. We have to keep warm," I insisted. "Keep your eyes open for anything we could use as fuel."

Already my toes and fingers were numb and fragile enough to snap. We couldn't risk our internal body temperature dropping any lower. If it did, we'd be weak and uncoordinated. Hallucinations would kick in, and our hearts, nervous systems, and other organs would shut down. We'd collapse into the mud-soaked ground and drift into an eternal sleep.

Think, Zaya. Think to survive.

For some odd reason, Professor Gemmell and the stars popped into my head.

Damn it. I'd been so stupid. The answer had been staring at me from above.

I peered toward the canopy, constellations twinkling through the gnarled mesh of leaves and branches. The gears in my brain ground into action. "We have to find a clearing in the trees. From there, we can navigate our way back by the stars."

Talina's eyes jumped to mine but with no enthusiasm. Her shoulders were hunched, her head bowed, like her neck no longer had the strength to remain upright. She reminded me of a blossoming flower reduced to a wilted stem. Hypothermia had kicked in. If we didn't find shelter soon—and warmth— she'd die.

"Come on." I trudged into the bitterly cold woods, grappling with Talina's weight.

I didn't know how long any of us had, but if Shadow's Wood turned out to be the end of us, then we'd fight until the last breath left our ice-chapped lips.

Lainie followed with heavy footsteps.

If this plan worked, I'd never take Professor Gemmell for granted again.

CHAPTER FORTY-ONE

There was no way to calculate how long we walked. The seconds bled into minutes, then hours—at least, that was what it seemed like. For all I knew, only a few moments might have passed. Every footstep was agony. An icy burn started in my legs and my chest and arms were damp and shivering. Maybe it was a trick of my eyes, but sometimes I thought faces stared at me through the dense fog. They caressed me with their wispy fingers, then, like a passing shimmer in the air, disappeared.

Thump.

Talina went down. She was as white as death on the snow-streaked ground.

Wait. It's snowing?

I tipped my head, tasting crisp air on my tongue. Enormous flakes fell from the sky, blanketing the trees in snow and vapour. The moon was not quite full and had been hidden by cloud cover for most of the evening, but now it cast eerie silvery light through the woods, making a ghostly contour out of every tree, branch, and rock.

Lainie stumbled toward Talina's crumpled body. "Up... get... up. Ground... wet. Make it... worse."

Talina remained motionless. In my medical and first aid class, I'd learnt that once your blood flow has stopped, your heart and respiratory rate has slowed down, and your body has gone numb, hypothermia is a peaceful way to leave the Earth. This didn't look peaceful. Talina's face was a frozen mask.

Tears glistened in Lainie's eyes. If she wasn't careful, they'd freeze her lashes together. "She doesn't have any strength left."

I sent a silent prayer to any divinity willing to listen. *Please help us. Please show us the way out of here. Lead us to shelter, to warmth. Don't let us die out here.*

I grew tired quickly, so it was a shock when ripples of silver radiance spilled through the trees, blinding my eyes. Lunette hovered in the light, an angel of death with blazing white skin.

Her eyes pierced mine. *"Follow me."*

I'd wanted divine intervention. Here it was.

I hooked my arms under Talina's armpits and instructed Lainie to take her legs. Lainie didn't question my new burst of tenacity. She probably couldn't spare the energy. Together we carried Talina through the woods, Lunette drifting a few metres ahead, weaving among the trees. The unearthly light that surrounded her acted like a beacon. The farther we trekked, the more spine-chilling the woods became. Where the leaves had once been glossy green, they now curled in on themselves, shrivelled and brown. I could have sworn at one stage, a tree root slithered in and out of the snow-strewn earth.

I didn't know how much time had passed when the trees became sparse and the ground sloped down to a low-lying wetland. In the centre of the stagnant water was a weather-beaten cottage with a thatched roof. The house had succumbed to peeling paint and rotten boards. If it weren't for a small peel of light peeking out from behind a closed curtain, I would have thought the place was abandoned.

Lunette pointed to the cottage and vanished.

Thank you, I thought, sensing she could hear the words in my head. The creepy mind connection I had with wraiths still gave me the heebie-jeebies, but I was coming to terms with how beneficial it could be.

Lainie's jaw clenched. When she spoke, her voice shook from cold. "Is that... a house? In the... middle... of a... moat. You're... kidding me... right?"

I found it incredible that someone lived in the woods too, but my heart swelled with relief. Sure, it resembled a witch's house, but I was grateful

Lunette had led us to shelter.

We stumbled down to the wetland. Moss-covered stones led us across the moat, which was difficult to traverse with Talina in our arms. The occasional weed drifted to the surface, appearing like the long flowing hairs of a person. I shivered and looked away, telling myself the gurgling sounds were fish splashing on the surface, not hands reaching for our ankles, which my overactive imagination immediately concluded on.

On the rocky outcrop of island, a narrow path led us to the porch. The steps were worn and uneven, with holes large enough to sink your foot through. We sat Talina in an old wicker chair and inspected the house. The windows were encrusted with grime and the gables had seen better days. The front door was rotten in places. Beneath it, bits of peeling paint had curled in on themselves like fossilised insects. Each time I took a step, the cottage constricted and groaned. The house was structurally unstable, undoubtedly held together with magic.

Before I could knock, the door opened of its own accord. Inside was a hallway lit by a single oil lamp, the end of the passage cut off by darkness.

"Hello?" My voice sounded strangled, a kind of cry and gasp at the same time. "Is anyone home? We need help."

Silence.

Lainie stamped her feet, trying to keep warm. "Maybe… it's abandoned."

I stepped into the hallway. The floorboard creaked under my weight, as though the house was sick and complaining. My scalp tingled, but this time it wasn't from the cold.

"Little Wayward, I've been expecting you," a voice called out.

Where the hall ended, a pair of yellow eyes emerged from the dark. A woman appeared, traipsing slowly as though in a funeral procession. She was robed in a cloak with an enormous crow perched on her shoulder, its yellow eyes still gleaming. I half expected the woman to unleash a scythe and transform into the Grim Reaper before my eyes.

Lainie took my hand, squeezing so tight I was certain she'd crush my fingers.

The woman pulled her hood back to reveal a skeletal face with ashen skin, so thin it looked stretched across the sharp cheekbones. My breath lodged in my throat. The woman reminded me of witches I'd read in human folk tales, vile creatures with long noses, warts, and tufts of grey hair. But it was her eyes that truly terrified me, because she had no pupils. Her eyes were colourless white orbs.

I struggled to find my voice. "Who are you? How do you know my name?"

A smile curled her crumpled mouth. "I am Macha, the Obeahwoman. And these are my woods."

CHAPTER FORTY-TWO

"Your woods?" Lainie had a wild look in her eyes, like a lamb that realised it had been led to slaughter. Her teeth were chattering so badly she could hardly speak. "Shadow's Wood… belongs to… the military… base. You're… trespassing." She transferred her gaze to me as though to say *this is entirely your fault.* I resented that look.

I fixed the Obeahwoman with a resolute stare. "How do you know who I am?"

Without pupils, Macha's eyes appeared opaque and glassy, yet somehow she watched me with burning curiosity. *"I'll answer that all in good time, little Wayward. But first, let's attend to your sick friend."*

I flinched. Macha's voice had echoed in my head, like a phantom projection whispered in my ear. I'd thought only wraiths were capable of that. Her bird studied me with keen interest. I'd heard of casters who shared a unique bond with animals. The caster could see, hear, and feel through their linked creature. It was rare magic—nothing more than a legend according to the council—but here it was. The bird must have been Macha's eyes.

The Obeahwoman disappeared into a dark doorway.

Lainie glanced at me, helpless. "We're not… going in there, right? She's… seriously weird. She's as likely… to eat us… as help us."

I shrugged. "She's an Obeahwoman. Weird comes with the territory."

I tried to recall whether Obeahwomen were cannibalistic. It didn't seem like the sort of thing you'd easily forget, which made me think they weren't. Obeahwomen were rare. To be honest, other than predicting the future and prophesising omens, I didn't understand a great deal about them, but judging by Macha, they were scary as hell.

But we had no other option.

Outside on the porch, Talina hadn't regained consciousness. Slumped in the wicker chair, her head had tilted to the side at an uncomfortable angle. We each took her arms and legs and carried her into the house.

"This is… a bad idea," Lainie muttered as we crossed the threshold.

I understood her qualms. The place was even worse on the inside. Cracks ran up the walls, the architraves chipped of paint. No matter where we trod, our feet kicked up filth.

"In here," Macha called. Her voice wasn't unkind or friendly but was underscored with a hint of impatience.

We stepped into a dimly lit parlour, making our way through dust-sheeted furniture and scattered objects. Not only was Macha an oddball but a compulsive hoarder too. The walls were lined with spell books. Crystal balls had been arranged on wrought-iron stands. A cabinet display of exotic taxidermy creatures stared with sharp button eyes, seeming to glare as we passed.

Lainie stubbed her toe and swore. "Hasn't she… ever heard… of a light? And what… is that smell?"

My nostrils were assaulted by the strange scent too. I licked my lips and tasted grime. "It's rot. The house is swimming in it."

Macha appeared in the doorway with an oil lantern, bathing the parlour in flickering light. "When dissent rebels occupied the Tarzor Plains, they kept disconnecting the power. Cleaning supplies were not readily accessible. I simply learnt to live without them."

Lainie froze. "You're… kidding, right? That was… like, twelve years ago."

The Obeahwoman's lips twisted wickedly. "And see how well I've adapted. Now, into the kitchen please."

"Kitchen" was a loose term. Tree roots twisted through the floorboards, as though the Earth was swallowing the house. The windows were tilted, their saggy shutters about to fall off. In the centre of the room, herbs, ointments, and potions were scattered across a rickety workbench. My mouth turned dry. Under the bench was a greasy black oven, perfect size for children. It didn't help that scratches had been gouged in the floorboards beneath it, as though someone had desperately tried to claw away from their doom.

"My cat likes to scratch," Macha's voice rolled through my head in explanation. She gently rubbed behind the ears of a black Bombay cat with wary green eyes. Sitting on the benchtop, the cat watched me with growing dislike. It hissed, paws splayed and claws out.

Macha rummaged through drawers and cupboards. She took out a mortar and pestle and began grinding herbs. "Set your friend down over there."

We placed Talina in a tattered armchair by the fireplace. I checked her pulse but struggled to find a beat. "What are you going to do to her?"

Macha snipped at something that looked like lemongrass. "Do to her? You make me sound like an axe murderer. I'm going to cure her. But she's very weak. It may be too late."

Guilt constricted my stomach. "Just do what you can."

Lainie nudged my arm, her voice low in my ear. "Zaya... look at the fireplace. She's cooking... something."

My eyes drifted to the hearth. I half expected to find fingers and toes brewed in stew. Instead, an inky blue substance bubbled over the sides of a cauldron. It emitted an odour oddly familiar.

"Asith potion!" Lainie's eyes nailed Macha with mistrust. "How is it... that you have— Ouch!"

Her head collided with a chandelier that hadn't been there a moment ago.

Macha's mouth tugged into a ghoulish grin, wide enough to show silver molars. "Be careful of the furniture, dear. This part of the house isn't accustomed to having guests. Most of the time the furniture does as it pleases. And to answer your question, I grow plants and herbs. Where else do you think Tarahik gets its medical supplies?"

I choked back shock. "You make the medicine?"

If Macha had the ability to roll her eyes, she would have. "Of course, silly girl. Technically speaking, it's not legal. Medicine and healing potions can only be administered by the council. But the council never supplies enough.

It's too much in demand and too expensive. Commander Macaslan and I made a deal many years ago. I supply medicine. In return, I get free lodging here."

The revelation stung. "And here I was thinking the commander was a stickler for the rules."

She'd punished me for much less.

Macha laughed a sharp, mutinous sound. "Macaslan's a stickler for common sense—which is more than I can say for the council. Run by idiot humans and caster sympathisers that place is. No wonder we haven't made any progress this last century."

Lainie had been inspecting a small taxidermy fox but pivoted around. "Are you… really that… old?"

The Obeahwoman huffed. "I see the younger generation still has no manners. Never ask a woman her age, dear. It's insulting."

Casters were known to live forty years longer than our human predecessors. Macha was frail. Her hands were shrivelled, and the skin around her eyes was dotted with brown spots. I imagined she was nothing more than tendons, bones, and veins under that robe, which—now that I had better light— looked more like a grave robe. She'd have to be over a hundred, surely.

She whisked the last of the ingredients in a bowl, inserted a tablespoon of the potion into a syringe, and then, without so much as flinching, jabbed the needle into Talina's arm. The girl didn't make a sound. Talina was so rigid and pale in appearance, she could have been a corpse laid out for everyone to pay their respects.

"We healed her just in time," Macha revealed, rubbing her hands on an apron that had magically manifested around her waist. "She'll wake in a few minutes."

The Obeahwoman dropped into a chair, exhaling a well-deserved sigh. The crow rubbed its beak affectionately along her neck. She stroked its black wings in return. "We had our work cut out for us tonight, didn't we, Bartholomew? Silly girls, getting themselves lost in the woods."

She named the bird Bartholomew?

Macha waved at us to sit down. "Take a seat. The kettle has made you tea—honey, apricot, and oolong, with a hint of dasconberries in yours. It's good for warming the heart. Good for curing hypothermia too."

At the end of the table, a brown tea service mysteriously appeared. There was a plate of stacked cookies, a lopsided teapot that unfurled a thin waft of steam, and four teacups on mismatched saucers.

"We have nothing to sit on." I didn't trust the dodgy bar stools that had been tucked away in the corner.

Macha spooned out several sugar cubes. "Nonsense. The house would never be so rude."

The air behind me shifted. Two tattered armchairs appeared, ornamented with frayed Persian cushions and matching ottomans. Fatigue had surpassed Lainie's wariness. She flopped unceremoniously into an armchair. I took a seat in the other one. It felt good to sit down. The tension in my legs unravelled, like the house was sucking the cold from my body into the ground. The kitchen was deliciously warm too, the fireplace emitting heat. Despite my clothes being damp and heavy, I felt stronger and more alive than I had in weeks. What magic was this at work?

"Tea?" Macha didn't wait for an answer and poured us each a cup.

I took a sip. It was strong flavoured and soothing.

Lainie examined her tea closely. She sniffed it, her tone testy. "Aren't dasconberries poisonous?"

Macha laughed. "To the healthy they bring death. To the sickly they replenish life."

Lainie stopped midsip, taking a moment to comprehend this.

I put my cup down. I was so nervous, my resolve started to fade. "Excuse me, Miss Macha. How do you know who I am? It appears that you had the herbs ready and waiting for us. It's almost as though you knew we were coming."

Macha took a sip of her tea, her little finger pointed out at just the right angle. In the firelight, it appeared fleshless and skeletal, the tip sharpened to a fine point. "Indeed, I did. All Obeahwomen can read minds, glimpse images into the future, and see snapshots of the past. I saw your arrival in a dream several moons ago and had the essentials prepared for days. It's a good thing too. Shadow's Wood is a dangerous place, filled with illusions and trickery. And it's wary. The trees have witnessed dark magic. It's tainted them. I've never seen them so afraid."

Lainie's hand trembled, her tea sloshing over the sides of her cup. "If you don't mind my asking, how do you know what the trees are thinking? Trees don't talk."

Macha's pupil-less eyes swivelled onto her. "But they feel. Three weeks ago, the same ice witch who destroyed Essida entered these woods. I could hear the trees crying. The wind carried their tears. Her magic still taints the area. Why else do you think it's cold and snowing in the middle of summer? Melvina Raskovitch is getting stronger."

The Obeahwoman and her bird turned to face me. A hard, intangible pressure pierced my skull. *"Melvina is after you, little Wayward. She knows what you are. She came for Lunette, but next time, it'll be you she'll want."*

My composure unravelled. I had no idea if I could mind-project with a living creature, but I had to try. *"What are Melvina and Vulcan planning? What do they need the Larthalgule blade for?"*

The Obeahwoman took up the teapot and filled another cup. *"Only your ghosts can answer that."*

A moan broke through the stillness. Talina slowly propped herself on elbows to survey her surroundings. A remarkable transformation had taken place. Colour had returned to her cheeks, her lips rosy pink. Even her eyes were bright and full of spirit. She blinked, momentarily stunned. I could almost see the wheels and cogs turn in her head as she struggled to understand what had happened. "Where are we?"

"Weeping Hollow, dear." Macha passed her a cup and saucer. "Tea?"

Lainie spat out her cookie. "You're kidding. I thought Weeping Hollow was a myth. My brother used to tell me the stories when I was young. The Weeping Witch who lived in a hollow and who cursed the Tarzor Plains was real?"

Talina delicately nibbled at her cookie. She raised a guarded eyebrow. "Didn't the Weeping Witch capture children and cook them in her furnace? That's the story I was always told."

My eyes swept to the black oven. I knew it couldn't be possible, but it looked as though it wanted to snap free of its foundation, open its wide grate jaws, and swallow me whole.

Macha sighed irritably. On her shoulder, Bartholomew shook his head. "You must not get history confused with ridiculous human folk tales," she told us. "The Weeping Witch was Queen Vivianda. When the Tarzor Plains was ravaged by war two centuries ago, King Fara of Tarahik Castle ordered she be hidden in this house. She was pregnant at the time, and the king wanted the queen safe. Protective binding spells were placed on the house so she couldn't leave."

Talina huffed. "Typical chauvinistic man."

"The war ended in a bloodbath," Macha continued. "Everyone was killed, but the binding spells never wore off this house. Over time, Queen Vivianda was forgotten. Her child grew and eventually left home, but Vivianda could never leave. Her son had many children. Whenever he visited his mother, he brought his children to spend time with their grandmother. When her family left, Vivianda could be heard weeping for miles. That is where the legend of the Weeping Witch and the children evolved."

I leaned forward in my seat. "And how did you come across the origin of this story? You seem to know it well."

Macha rested her wrinkled hand on the armrest. It was her bird that appraised me with its golden eyes. "It's been passed down through generations," Mache told me.

"You mean, Fara and Vivianda are—"

"My ancestors, yes."

"But that means you're royalty." Lainie glanced miserably at her pyjamas, perhaps wishing she'd dressed better for the occasion.

Macha scoffed. "Hardly. The Council of Founding Sovereigns took this land from my family for its geographic position more than a century ago. They own the castle and transformed it into a base when Morgomoth and his followers were on the rise. From Tarahik, the military would be able to protect the lands to the north—at least, that was the plan. Up till then, my sisters and I had been close. Not long after both my siblings married, Morgomoth's forces invaded this continent. We were forced to part ways. My eldest sister served at the Tarahik Military Base. My youngest disappeared."

My legs twitched without my permission. "Disappeared?"

An angry shade of colour rose in Macha's cheeks. "I'd left to find work in

Goondasville, a small fishing village on the East Coast. I read people's palms and gave tarot readings. I built myself quite a reputation." She rubbed a hand across her eyes, even though it was Bartholomew's golden ones that looked tired and sad. "I should have been more careful."

My hands fumbled with my teacup. "What happened?"

"Word had spread of my talent. You see, my younger sister hadn't just run away. She'd joined the ULD. She heard of a talented Obeahwoman in Goondasville and made the connection. An Obeahwoman is a powerful weapon. The ULD arrived a week later to hunt me down. I only just escaped."

"Your sister betrayed you?" Talina's expression shifted toward nauseous horror. She was close to her own sister. A family betrayal like that was incomprehensible in her eyes.

The Obeahwoman brushed a hand through her white hair. "My sister's disloyalty to me shouldn't have come as a surprise. She was much younger than me and was… different. Even from an early age, there was something wrong about her. She took pleasure in seeing others hurt. She bullied children and took her frustration out on small animals. My parents tried to help, but madness like that can't be cured." She exhaled a melancholy sigh. "In the end, after I'd spent months hiding in Goondasville, it was my older sister who came to my aid. She hid me in this house, where the spells that concealed Vivianda now protect me. I have remained here ever since. The woods answer to me."

Two pieces of the jigsaw puzzle linked in my mind. "That night when I came across Lunette having her vision, it was you I saw in the woods, wasn't it?"

I recalled the blur of shadow that had seemed darker than the surrounding trees. At the time, I thought it had been a wraith with white glowing eyes, come to destroy me.

Macha's entire posture went stiff. "Commander Macaslan asked me to keep an eye on you that evening. She didn't like the idea of you being out of the castle."

Talina and Lainie looked at me with a frown, lost in the conversation.

Macha twisted a silver ring around her finger, agitated. "Legally, the Tarzor Plains no longer belong to my family, but magically, the land answers only to us—as does Tarahik Castle and this house. They keep me hidden from the United League of Dissent."

Talina's face softened. "And your sisters? What happened to them?"

In my head, the intricate threads of the mystery weaved together. There was only one woman in Tarahik Castle who reigned like a queen, who held supremacy above others and demanded loyalty and respect. The castle answered to her like a faithful subject. Now I understood why.

Macha sat resolute in her chair. "My eldest sister is Elspeth Macaslan, commander of the Tarahik Base. My youngest sister is Melvina Raskovitch."

CHAPTER FORTY-THREE

The revelation short-circuited my brain. I pictured the faces of the three sisters, flabbergasted that such different women were related. For some reason, I'd envisioned Macaslan as a woman resigned to spinsterhood without family or love, her dedication committed to the Tarahik Base. But that preconception had been wrong. I'd never understood why she bothered to help me, or why she cared for a teenage renegade from Gosheniene. Now I knew. It was never about me. This was about stopping her youngest sister.

Macha's shoulders arched from mounting tension.

I chose my words carefully. "Melvina was able to cross into Shadow's Wood because the land answers to her, doesn't it… just like it answers to you and Commander Macaslan? No one opened the celestial shield for Melvina. She did it herself."

The embers in the fireplace sent flickering shadows across the Obeahwoman's face. "Elspeth and I cast many spells on the shields, but Melvina was stronger than we imagined. She can enter the woods and the Tarahik grounds, but not this house or the castle. As the eldest daughter, both edifices belong to Elspeth. Commander Macaslan is the sole proprietor and decides who can and can't enter the castle."

A part of my heart ached as I sensed how much this discussion hurt the Obeahwoman, but I needed answers. "How did Melvina get Lunette into the woods?"

"She didn't. Someone took Lunette from the castle and brought her down to Shadow's wood. You are right, Zaya. There is a traitor at the Tarahik Base. Someone in the castle is working with the ULD."

Talina cast a fleeting glance in my direction. She sucked in a breath. "Is this the girl you said was murdered? Her name was Lunette? I thought you dreamt that."

I struggled to keep my emotions at bay. "No. That's what you wanted to believe."

It still hurt that she and Marek hadn't believed me.

Macha rubbed at her temples. "My sister took what she needed from that poor girl and left the body. Melvina's next target is Zaya."

Lainie swivelled around in her chair to face me. "Zaya, what's going on?"

Macha's voice projected into my head, flowing to the tips of my skull. *"You must tell them. They are part of this now. You can't protect them any longer."*

My friends' faces were covered with puzzlement and fear, their eyes wide and hurt.

I moistened my lips. Macha was right. Keeping them safe was no longer a possibility. They knew too much. My chest tightened, but I took a leap of faith and told them everything from the beginning—necromancy, the ghosts, Lunette, Melvina. When I finished, the look on their faces was one I'd never witnessed before. Fear and astonishment, yes, but also relief, because now my mysterious behaviour finally made sense in their eyes.

Talina clasped a hand to her mouth. "I can't believe it. All this time you've been alone in this. That must have been so… frightening."

Lainie didn't say a word. Her faraway expression suggested she was sifting through the facts, fitting everything she knew about me with the evidence she'd seen, and liking it less and less. For a moment, I thought she'd hug me. I wouldn't have minded if she had.

The Obeahwoman tossed a log on the fire. She hobbled to the window, suddenly looking much older. A muscle twitched in her thin cheek. "As the Moon travels between the Earth and the Sun, the Sun will become darkness, the Moon into blood, and on that great and terrible day, the blackest of magic will be reborn."

Talina gave me a worried look before her eyes shot back to Macha. "I've heard that saying before. It's a prophecy, right? Marking the day evil will return? My dad told me it's nonsense and never to read into prophecies."

Macha raised her head, her blank eyes staring lifelessly. On her shoulder, Bartholomew cawed. "Your father is a fool. Prophecies are not nonsense. Everything in the universe is linked by magic. People and events are predetermined. It's constantly evolving depending on the choices made, but sometimes there is a path that must be taken. This is one of them."

The Obeahwoman waved for us to join her at the window. "Look outside. The lunar eclipse has begun. The moon is now full and has met with the sun to become a blood moon. They will travel together until the sun sets. This is a dark day. I have long believed this eclipse will mark the United League of Dissent's return to power. Everything I have foreseen, everything that has occurred, is leading toward it."

Macha was right. Outside, above the treetops, the sun was a halo of burning colour, the moon no longer a silver disk in the sky but a ruby coin in its centre. It looked like a dazzling red jewel. This was nature working with magic, the sun trying to supplement the Earth with energy and light and the moon trying to suppress it.

A cold, sick anxiety crashed over me. "I had no idea the blood moon was today."

I hadn't even realised it was morning. Secluded from the rest of the world, I'd lost track of time.

The Obeahwoman made an impatient noise in the back of her throat. "It has been brought forward. The death of Lunette Collins has spun a new, inevitable path. It's time, Zaya."

I stared at her with my mouth open. "Time for what?"

"To complete what Lunette brought you here to do."

"And what's that?"

"To raise her from the dead."

A high, disbelieving laugh broke from my throat. "What?"

The Obeahwoman furrowed her overgrown brow. "You're a necromancer. You can raise the dead. It's time you started using your magic."

My argument dissolved within me. This was what I'd been afraid of—

accepting my magic. A strange buzzing filled my head, a nervous, fluttery sensation dropping down to my toes.

There was nothing sympathetic or kind in Macha's expression. For the first time, there was resemblance to her older sister, stern and formidable. "Calm your mind, Zaya. It's time for you to conjure Lunette."

CHAPTER FORTY-FOUR

"Are you positive we need to be involved?" Lainie swallowed hard, unable to keep the doubt from her voice.

Seated beside her, Talina appeared as though she wanted to sink into the floor. The four of us sat around the wooden bench, where chicken blood, toad's feet, and bat livers had been arranged in three separate bowls, each giving off a rancid smell that made my face scrunch.

Macha struck a match and lit several purple candles placed ceremoniously around the room. Each of the wicks sizzled to life, the kitchen seeming to double in temperature. "This spell is not easy. Zaya will need something to bring her back—something she cherishes and provides her great happiness and fulfilment. And that is her friends."

Lainie blew out a sigh. "Lucky us."

In the flame light, Talina's face appeared flushed and sticky. "Bring her back from where, exactly?"

Macha combined the three ingredients into a second cauldron and stirred the strange potion. With a wooden ladle, she poured the mixture into a crystal decanter. "This is one of the oldest spells known to necromancers. It opens a portal to travel through. It's long believed that wraiths journey through a network of doorways from this dimension to the otherworld. Zaya will open a portal that will allow her to cross dimensions to Lunette's body…

and hopefully back again."

I dug my fingernails into the bench, questioning whether it was too late to slip away unnoticed. "I thought we were summoning Lunette?" Travelling through a wraith portal seemed like incredibly advanced magic—and dangerous.

Macha shook her head. "You're not ready for that. Summoning a ghost takes immense concentration. Lunette knows this. That's why she brought you here. She needed me to create the spell and link you to the portal."

Despite the overbearing warmth, a chill crawled over my arms. "I don't think I'm capable of doing what you're asking. Lunette's body is in Valdavar Tower. I'm not going to be able to magically teleport myself into a place like that. There will be security—not to mention celestial shields."

I'd heard stories of casters who'd tried to teleport themselves into buildings protected by shields. They'd been obliterated on contact. In one newspaper article, I'd read that a thief who'd attempted to rob a bank in a Free Zone had been annihilated. Only a foot and several toes remained. Anxiety expanded deep into my chest. I couldn't do this.

Macha's mouth curved into a half smile. "You'd be amazed what necromancy can achieve." She brought the crystal decanter to my lips. "Spit."

"What?"

"Your saliva is needed to make this spell work."

"That's disgusting."

"I agree. Spit."

Building enough saliva in my mouth, I spat. The potion sputtered and hissed. It smelt like cat pee, curdled milk, and unwashed socks. Lainie and Talina held their noses. Their eyes watered.

Macha popped the lid on top of the decanter with exaggerated ceremony. "Put the spell in your pocket. Lunette will need to drink this."

Poor Lunette.

A hint of excitement jumped across Macha's wrinkled face. "Now, girls, join hands. Whatever you do, don't let go."

Some of the tension in Lainie's eyes faded, replaced with curiosity. "How do you know so much about necromancy and spells?"

Macha's white eyes swivelled around in her head. It was her bird's yellow-eyed stare that looked at us intently. "Many centuries ago, the Obeahpeople were tasked with serving and protecting necromancers. Their spells are instinctive for us. Now do as I say. Link hands."

We complied, the four of us connected around the table. Talina's long nails dug into my skin, her hand tight with tension. On my other side, Lainie's fingers were cold and clammy. I sensed a combination of concern and excitement brimming on the edge of her fingertips.

"This is a protective circle," Macha informed us. "This will keep the magic bound. If anyone lets go and breaks the circle, Zaya will not be able to transport back. Now, everyone close your eyes."

Secretly, I hoped this wouldn't work. I squeezed my eyes shut and tried to banish my doubts. After all, what could Macha really do? I was the one with the necromancy—and I was so damn nervous, nothing would probably happen.

Macha cleared her throat. "Zaya, I want you to imagine Lunette. When you have a clear image of her in your mind, channel her forward. Mentally ask Lunette's spirit to take you to her body. When this happens, concentrate only on Lunette. Do not think of anyone else."

I inhaled deeply and erased all thought from my mind. The kitchen turned deathly still. I couldn't even hear the spit and crackle of the flames in the hearth anymore, or Lainie's and Talina's quickened breathing. Everything in the room had gone numb. I gritted my teeth and concentrated. In my mind, I pictured Lunette's blue eyes, her short pixie cut, and timid smile. I remembered the sad desperation I'd witnessed in her eyes the night I first met her. I wished I'd had the strength to help her then.

"Zaya?"

The voice in my head was breathy and high-pitched. It belonged to Lunette.

A cold lump rose in my throat. I'd made contact.

When I opened my eyes, my surroundings had changed. I was in a world of violent cold and painful suffocation. It was a barren landscape of snow and ice. Cold winds ran down the slopes like tidal waves. Snow pounded my body from every direction. Carefully, I trudged through the heavy snowstorm, so thick it enveloped the distance ahead. The sky and land were blurred white, making it easy to get disorientated.

Lunette's voice called out to me, panicked and alarmed. *"Don't take another step."*

I hadn't been able to see because of the snow, but now when I looked down, it was apparent I'd been inches from stepping into a crater-like void in the ground. Science couldn't be defined in a place like this, because even though it was snowing, below in the ditch the world was a fiery tomb. I'd read Dante's *Inferno* and believed it had been nothing more than an invention created to terrify and restrain our human ancestors. But there was truth in that art, because deep in this blazing pit, thousands of fallen souls screamed in anguish. They were twisted, skeletal, and naked. Trapped in a river of boiling blood, they clawed over each other like insects. The fiery canal consumed them, dissolving their bones until there was nothing left. Then, as though nothing had happened, they reappeared, their wailing screams starting again. I brought a trembling hand to my mouth. They were eternally damned to relive this scene over and over.

"Do you see what this place is?"

Lunette emerged from the swirling snow, her ghostly outline iridescent in the howling wind. She smiled, but it was sad and full of regret. "This is my purgatory," she said aloud, "the world before the final descent. It appears different for everyone. I think it has something to do with the way we die."

I'd never put faith into the idea of heaven or hell, believing the afterlife was a fable designed by our ignorant ancestors. After I'd encountered my first wraith, my philosophy had changed. Now I wasn't sure what to believe.

Lunette's vapour-like body seemed to sink from inner turmoil. "I can't move on until you know the truth. But I can't tell you here either. This place sees and knows everything. It's forbidden to tell the living any of its secrets. There are rules set in place that cannot be broken." She arched her head, as though we were being listened to even now. Her voice dropped lower. "You must resurrect me—even if it is only for a few minutes. If I'm brought back, I'm not bound to the rules." She reached out and took my hand, her fingers weightless and insubstantial against mine. "I'll take you through the portal now."

Her grasp suddenly became solid. Blistering white light burst around us, its radiance increasing until I could finally see no more. And then, like a roller coaster diving vertically down a rail track, we were sucked into a windy maelstrom to a lighted place beyond. I was too surprised to scream. My insides sloshed like water, my stomach reduced to scrambled egg. Was this sensation even real or a delusion in my head? If I was in fact sitting in Macha's kitchen right now, blindly re-enacting this event, what must Lainie and Talina be thinking?

Another flash of light brought me back to my surroundings. My feet hit solid ground. Unlike Lunette's limbo, this place was real. And creepy. My heart rate picked up as I recognised what I'd been teleported to.

Basically, the mortuary was a room full of freezers. The night staff had been busy preparing for autopsies because microscopes, various medical instruments, and trolleys were laid out, covered by clean white surgical towels. On the far wall was a sleek metal shaft. I'd seen laundry and garbage chutes at the base but didn't think this was used for the same purpose. I shivered, the rapid transportation of a body to the crematorium not something I wanted to dwell on.

"Lunette?" My voice was a prolonged echo.

No answer.

I was alone.

A hand latched on to my shoulder.

I whirled around, a strangled cry tearing from my throat.

"Be quiet," a familiar voice hissed.

In front of me, Talina's eyes smouldered like hot coals. She was fuming so badly her creamy complexion had broken out in red patches. "What the hell did you do, Zaya? One minute we're in Macha's kitchen and the next we're...." She gazed around, terror alight in her eyes. "What is this place?"

Lainie stood by the wall, rubbing her arms for warmth. "This is Valdavar Tower, right? It used to be a citadel, but now it's used as a morgue." She transferred her gaze to the steel benches where corpses lay zipped up in body bags. "Oh shit."

Talina took a firm hold of my shoulder. Her nails dug deeper than was necessary. "You teleported us here?"

My jumbled memories surfaced. Macha had said to think only of Lunette, but when I'd been falling through the portal—because that must have been what the maelstrom was—Talina and Lainie had popped into my mind. I'd unintentionally brought my friends along for the ride.

I bit my lip. "Yeah, seems like it. Sorry."

She glowered at me.

My friends' safety should have been the priority, but a more selfish part of me was happier not to be alone. There was certainty in numbers.

Talina rubbed her arms, shivering from the rising damp. "Maintenance in this place is terrible."

"It's intentionally cold," I pointed out.

I forced myself to approach the dozen bodies lying in rows in the centre of the lab, my shadow long and washed out on the corroded tiles. The light was feeble, flicking on and off. I had to get close to read the scrawled labels identifying the bagged individuals inside. Emotion crept over me when my eyes rested on Lunette's name. There was something incredibly sad about seeing her young life, hopes, and ambitions reduced to blood samples, X-rays, and dental records. I stood there for a moment to take it all in.

Talina dug her elbow into my ribs. "Hurry up with your spell. This place gives me the creeps."

My chest shrank to the size of an acorn, because of course my confidence lapsed when I was under pressure—and boy, was this pressure. I reached for the zipper on the body bag, the rasp of each tooth painfully loud in the silent morgue. Lunette's face reminded me of a porcelain doll. Her skin was white and waxy, her eyes resembling glass. Her mouth was open, just the way it had been when I'd discovered her body, only this time it wasn't packed with ice. That had probably melted during post mortem.

I couldn't believe only three weeks ago I'd found Lunette comatose in the hills. I'd tried to comfort her, to find out what was wrong. Now she was this. I was familiar with ghosts, but this was different. I didn't know how to deal with the emptiness of a body.

Praying for courage, I removed the potion from my pocket and tipped the spell down her thin throat. It oozed thick and slow, like tar sinking into the cracks and crannies of a broken pavement. It didn't take a genius to figure out something was wrong when condensation rose from her mouth. Her lips became sticky with black gunk, staining her teeth. Oily gloop seeped from her pores, dripping into the body bag where it coalesced into greasy puddles. Some of it bled onto the table, spilling over the edge.

I staggered back a step. Talina and Lainie leapt away, their cries making me want to turn and run. The necromancy potion had literally eaten Lunette. It was like watching mummified remains decompose in only a few seconds.

Lainie held her nose. "Is that meant to happen?"

The stench of acrid, bubbling fat wafted into the lab, sending a wave of vertigo through my stomach. "I don't know."

Why had I let Macha talk me into embracing my magic? Lunette hadn't deserved to die, and her body didn't warrant this treatment either. I'd wanted answers, yes, but not if this was the result.

"Look out!" Talina lunged forward, but it was too late.

Lunette's slimy hand latched on to mine, hard. Grunting, biting, snorting sounds bubbled low from her throat. She bared her teeth, animalistic and frightening. When she sat up, her movements were ungainly, as though she were attached to a puppeteer's strings.

"Lunette?" My voice barely surpassed a whisper.

The dead girl inclined her head to look at me. Inside her broken body, dried-out lungs filled with air, the sound reminding me of a balloon inflating too fast and on the verge of popping. She lifted her arm, revealing a deep gash from her elbow down to her wrist. The edge of the cut was pallid and pink, the blood crusted over. When she spoke, her voice sounded mechanical, like a trash compactor chewing up metal. "She took my blood. Now she wants yours."

My knees wobbled, my legs as sturdy as straw. Lunette's fingers burnt cold into my wrist. The gunk on her body was freezing.

I bit back the pain, forcing myself to focus. "What is Melvina planning?"

The dead girl's lips curled into a cryptic smile. "You can't stop her. The blood moon is here."

A tingle of fear crawled over my skin.

Lunette's robotic voice grew deeper, reverberating over the metal surfaces in the lab. "But you can delay the end. The cave beneath the Asrath Cliffs... that's where it waits. That's where you'll find the dagger to pierce his flesh.

The blade has been lost so long." She tried to turn her head, but the motion was stiff, as though her head would fall off and roll like a bowling ball down the lab.

I struggled against the rising panic in my chest. "*He*? Who's *he*? Do you mean Vulcan Stormouth? And are you talking about the Larthalgule blade?"

"*Him*." Her eyes turned insanely large, shining with hatred and bloodlust. The necromancy potion had made Lunette zany and erratic. It was no longer natural for her soul to be in this form. She scrunched her fingers into her hair and tore it from the roots. "He's in my head even now. Find the blade, Zaya. Kill him. Kill him."

"He's in my head even now"?

What did that mean?

The lights flickered, bright one second, insanely dark the next.

I shuffled forward. "Lunette, it's important that you tell me who led you into the woods. I need to know who I can trust and who I can't."

She didn't listen.

Something was happening inside her.

She wailed like a screeching chicken, black liquid frothing at her mouth. It was Macha's necromancy potion. Time was up.

"Lunette," I pleaded. "Look at me. Who took you to Melvina? Who brought you into Shadow's Wood?"

By *him*, had Lunette meant the traitor at the base?

She coughed and splattered. Her arms flailed at her sides, like fish flapping out of water. "Galvac Dam," she screamed. "That's where you must go. Kill him. Kill him. Otherwise, everyone meets their doom."

She fell in a boneless heap on the table, dead again.

For a long time, all I could do was stare.

Talina grabbed my arm. "We're leaving. Now!"

I'd been so absorbed by horror I hadn't heard the siren. It blasted through the lab, a high-pitched wail that stabbed my ears. A calm, professional voice boomed from a speaker in the ceiling. "Please find your nearest exit and evacuate the tower. Do not use the elevators. This is not a drill. Please find your nearest exit and evacuate the tower…"

Panic ran like spiders across my brain. If the Haxsan Guard in charge of the tower were evacuating shift workers, then that meant security knew intruders were somewhere in Valdavar.

They were preparing to smoke us out.

CHAPTER FORTY-FIVE

Outside in the corridor, voices rose above the hum of the sirens, accompanied by quick, thunderous footsteps. This was bad. Necromancy was evident on every surface of Lunette's body. Once the Haxsan Guard saw that, they'd shoot us. No questions asked.

Lainie threw herself against the door and fumbled with the latch. She slid it shut, the door locking with a resounding boom. Granted, the Haxsan Guard would easily break it down with powerful sorcery, but it still bought us a few seconds—and as it turned out, every second mattered.

A man shouted at the other side of the door. "They're in here. Get a battering ram."

The three of us instantly retreated to the back wall where the freezers were stored. Now I knew how lab rats felt—frightened, cornered, and with no possibility of escape.

The colour drained from Talina's face. "Take us back, Zaya. Teleport us. Now!"

My entire body went stiff. Macha had instructed me how to get here, but she'd never explained how to get back. My ability to think rapidly slipped away, like water down drainage.

Talina must have guessed my thoughts, because her voice turned heavy with alarm. "Are you kidding? We're stuck here?"

Think, Zaya. Think like someone who knows how to survive. There must be another way out.

And then I saw it. I didn't know why it took me so long to register the idea. I half pulled, half dragged my friends across the lab toward the strange garbage chute.

Lainie shook her head. "No way. I can't go in there."

"We don't have a choice." I levered myself inside. It disturbed me that I fit so snugly, like the shaft really had been built for the quick transportation of bodies and not soiled aprons or mucky sheets.

"This is stupid." Lainie's eyes were wet and swollen. She reminded me of a two-year-old on the verge of a tantrum. "We don't even know where it leads."

"It leads out of here," I snapped.

The explosive screech of metal against steel burst through the lab. Violent thuds hammered the door in harmony with my frenzied pulse. With a final punch, the mortuary door broke from its hinges and toppled inward.

"Follow me." I slid down the chute like a marble traversing down a maze board, quick and without interruption. Twists and bends changed my velocity at dizzying speeds. Wind rushed past my ears. Friction burned like hell on my exposed skin—and the skin I'd thought was well protected by my clothes. I moved so fast, there was no time to scream.

I plummeted soundlessly into a dumpster bin, my landing not soft by any stretch of the imagination. For a few disorientated seconds, I fought to make sense of where I was. Surrounding me were black rubberised bags. Body bags. Some were squishy, others pliant, as though the individuals inside could be moulded like play dough. I squealed and leapt out of the bin.

What the hell is this place?

My mind struggled to comprehend the large red-brick space I stood in, the walls lined with muffle kilns that emitted powerful heat, like wood fire pizza ovens, only there was no aroma of freshly baked dough. It wasn't easy to make out what I saw in the blaze that radiated from the fiery pits, but then I popped a hand over my mouth. A scalded head stared back at me. It was burnt down to the bone, eyes melted away, smiling with a sadistic, toothy grin.

My worst fears were realised.

I'm in the crematorium.

The ovens had been filled with as many bodies as could possibly fit, probably so fuel could be used efficiently. But not all the bones had deteriorated. I guess what was left would later be pulverised to a fine powder and strewn across fields for fertiliser. That was what had happened at Gosheniene when the mass graves couldn't be dug fast enough.

Screams carried from the chute. Talina and Lainie dropped into the dumpster, sending up a wave of body bags.

Talina's head emerged from the mass of bodies. She shrieked liked a howler monkey. "Get me out. Get me out."

I grabbed her arms and helped her climb over the dumpster. She collapsed in a weakened heap on the ground, the heat making her hair and skin damp with sweat. "What is this place?" Her voice was tense and hysterical.

Lainie jumped from the bin and emptied her stomach. Embers and ash swirled around us, the air too hot to breathe. Whenever I closed my eyes, my lids sealed as though melted by hot glue. We wouldn't last long in this smoke.

Through the haze, I caught glimpses of a large airtight door with a hatch wheel—the kind of thing you'd find in a submarine. I signalled the girls to follow, and we weaved through the smoke, heat blasting us with relentless force, the tips of flames licking our skin.

We reached the door, and my hope shattered. "It's locked."

I tried to calmly process our situation, but my heart pumped nervous energy into my brain, making me light-headed and weary.

Smoke continued to fill the room the same way water leaked into a sinking vessel, doubling in strength and impossible to see through. Long drawn-out coughs erupted from Lainie. A spasm of fear seized my gut. Who knew what chemicals we were inhaling in here—carbon monoxide, cyanide, nitrogen? The possibilities were endless. And then I too felt the overwhelming pain of slow, blistering suffocation. My throat burned like it had been doused in acid. There was a reason why the hatch was locked, why bodies had been left in the dumpster. This entire room was a furnace—an apparatus designed to cremate everything inside.

We can't die like this.

There had to be another way… and there was.

Why didn't I think of this before?

I closed my eyes, forcing my mind into a meditative state.

Lunette. Are you there?

Nothing.

Please. We need your help. I know you're close.

My intuition sensed her, but still… nothing.

Lunette, you helped me before. You can damn well help me now.

"Zaya?" The voice in my head sounded cool, like ice cubes cracking in water, a nice reprieve from the heat torching my body. *"You're not very good at this, are you? All you need do is ask. I can't ignore a necromancer's demands."*

I panted hard through my mouth and tasted soot. *Then take us back? Please?*

Cold fingers clutched my hand.

"Hold on," Lunette whispered in my ear.

I thrust my arm out, hoping Talina would see it in the evolving smoke. "Take my hand."

She had Lainie propped on her side. There was no time for further instructions. Talina grabbed my hand at the same time the floor went out beneath us. We were sucked into a fiery maelstrom, the pressure and wind so intense I no longer saw where the flames ended and where they began.

CHAPTER FORTY-SIX

I opened my eyes. There was an odd sensation in my head, as though my skull had shattered into fragments. I was lying on warped, uneven floorboards, my breathing sending puffs of dust into the air. Rolling onto my side, I blinked to realign my focus. I was back in Macha's kitchen, the cauldron bubbling above the crackling fire the most normal thing I'd seen in hours. I never thought I'd be so happy to see it.

A familiar voice called out to me. "I must say, you do know how to make an entrance."

I twisted around.

Macha stood in the doorway, her eyes rolling lazily in their sockets. On her shoulder, Bartholomew squawked and nibbled affectionately at her ear. The pair looked distant, like a faded old photograph lost for years, brought back to revive someone's memory.

Macha ground her teeth so hard I wondered how she didn't make her gums bleed. "Snap out of it, Zaya. Focus."

Memories resurfaced. The fire. The maelstrom that opened like a cavernous mouth beneath us. The descent into what had felt like the gates of hell.

Lainie? Talina?

I climbed to my feet, my vision swimming. Talina was slumped against the wooden bench, blonde hair streaked with ash. She rubbed at her temples, silently crying. Lainie had curled into a ball, the side of her head pressed into her knees. Her face was coated in soot, her cheeks tear-stained. The nasty look she gave me was a stab of poison to my heart. She would never forgive me for the secrets I'd held, for the horrors I'd brought on her and Talina this evening. It wasn't entirely my fault, but I doubted she'd see it that way. Our friendship was fractured, maybe severed entirely. That poignant realisation far outweighed any physical torment.

Somewhere, a siren pierced through the ageing, rutted house. It was taken up by another, then another, until every room rose to a deafening cacophony. The walls, floorboards, and windows seemed to constrict, like the house was giving in to a horrified shudder.

Talina clapped a hand over her ears. "What is that?"

Macha hobbled into the kitchen, faster than I would have thought possible for a woman of her age. "That is a level eight security alert from Tarahik. I'm linked to the base. According to my sister, dissent rebels have begun an assault on the Galvac Dam. General Kravis is sending infantry, air, and marine reinforcements at this very moment. For everyone else, Tarahik is in lockdown."

My senses went on high alert. "Lunette mentioned Galvac Dam in the mortuary."

"Galvac Dam. That's where you must go. Kill him. Kill him. Otherwise, everyone meets their doom."

"Did she now?" Macha didn't sound surprised. From the way she and Bartholomew peered through the window up to the ever-increasing red sky, she wasn't pleased about it either. Her bony fingers gripped the edge of the workbench. "Then that is where you must go."

I started to feel ill for an entirely different reason. Vulcan and Melvina were on one side of the chessboard, me on the other. The pair were about to make their final strategic move. And I was still clueless. "Lunette said the Larthalgule blade was at the Asrath Cliffs. Do you know where that is?"

The Obeahwoman turned to me. In the flame light, her ashen face looked like it hadn't seen the sun in years. "Yes, and if my hunch is correct, you've seen the cliffs too."

I shook my head, not understanding.

Macha trailed a finger along her bottom lip, deep in thought. "In the vision, the grimoire showed you Galvac Dam and the Asrath Cliffs, did it not?"

A bitter metallic taste filled my mouth—the taste of fear. I recalled the cliff face that ended in a sheer drop into the sea and the concrete arch dam that held back the ocean swell. "How do you know that?"

Her mouth lifted on one side. "Macaslan told me. We both suspected Galvac Dam had been built into the Asrath Cliffs, but we couldn't get the proof we needed. The dam is heavily guarded. The Asrath Cliffs are an ancient and sacred site. It was long rumoured that the temple of Nekros Manteia was built somewhere along the cliff face. The name is from the Greek language of long ago: 'Nekros' meaning dead, and 'Manteia' meaning divination. Translated—the Temple of Dead Divination. It was said that the temple hid a terrible power, something only necromancers could wield."

The answer surfaced like a storm surge from a bottomless ocean. "Larthalgule."

Macha clapped her hands, applauding my logic. "It's the most reasonable explanation. When the council saw fit to purge the world of necromancers, the temple was lost. It's been searched for over the centuries—most of it funded by new council members—but it was never found... or so they would have us believe."

A wave of nervous energy hit me then, so strong I had to close my eyes for a second. "And Galvac? What is it?"

"The council tell us it's a hydroelectric dam, powering energy to the provinces, but the place is a fortress. It's protected by a Haxsan Guard military base built underground. The entire facility and its surroundings are secure. No one can get near it."

My voice rose several octaves. "Because it's a ruse to disguise what the council are really protecting. Nekros Manteia and the blade."

My mind spun from all the new information. Clarence Chauvelin had known the council were corrupt, so he'd stolen the map, afraid the ULD would find it. And he'd had every reason to be alarmed. There were traitors and spies on both sides.

I sighed, dropping my hands heavily on my knees. In the end, destroying the map hadn't mattered. Melvina had pieced the clues together herself, just like we had, but she was far ahead in the game. Now she was determined to get her prize.

A hot, tormented sound broke from my throat. "I have to summon Lunette. It's the only way I can get to the temple. It's what the ghosts have wanted me to do all this time."

I had to find the blade first.

Macha's stern face crumbled. "It would be too dangerous to attempt teleporting to Galvac. The celestial shield protecting that facility will be a hundred times stronger than Valdavar Tower or Tarahik. Your magic is not yet strong enough to break shields like that."

A lump of dread rose in my chest. "Then how do I get there?"

A deep, low rumble erupted in the sky, the thunderous roar of fire-crusaders in the distance. The tremendous blast of exhausts overshadowed every other sound. Some of Macha's potions toppled and smashed on the dusty floor. The house's foundations shuddered and rattled. It sounded like the apocalypse was coming for us.

"Reinforcements to Galvac," I said, increasingly aware that I was running out of time. "The carrier-hornets will be next. I have to be on one of them."

Macha moved in a way that reminded me of an old person climbing out of a wheelchair. "Follow me. I have a way back to the Tarahik Base."

Talina leapt to her feet. Lainie remained a huddled creature on the floor, shooting daggers at me with her eyes.

The Obeahwoman stuck her hand out, barricading Talina. "No. It won't be possible for either of you to leave Weeping Hollow. This house is protected by the same spells that secure Tarahik. Weeping Hollow is in lockdown. The two of you will have to remain here."

Talina gritted her teeth. "Then how is it you have a way out for Zaya?"

The Obeahwoman drew herself forward, and Talina retreated a step. I knew from experience it was hard to comprehend the Obeahwoman's pupilless eyes. They seemed to look at you like they were staring straight through a window into your soul, assessing your worth, yet at the same time, there was nothing there but a milky white eyeball.

Macha's eyelids narrowed. "Zaya is a necromancer. The rules of magic do not always apply to her." Without any further explanation, she left the room.

The fearful glint in Talina's eyes unnerved me. "Be careful."

Things hadn't been easy between us this evening, but no matter how angry she might have been with me, she didn't want to see me wander into a war zone either. Maybe there was hope for our friendship after all.

Guilt racked my chest when I looked at Lainie. Dark rings circled the girl's eyes. Her transformation from the healthy, snappy girl of a few hours ago into a catatonic wreck was complete. Her gaze locked with mine, dark and glowering.

I shut my eyes, light-headed. There was so much that I needed to say to the pair—that they needed to hear—because there was every chance my mission at Nekros Manteia would fail. Death had never frightened me until now. In Gosheniene, I'd been surrounded by starvation and cold. I'd witnessed casters reduced to shells of their former selves, their mental state beyond repair. In the end, they'd yearned for death. I'd expected that fate too. Death was a blessing compared to the tortures of that place. But now I was afraid of the end.

Macha's shrill voice carried from the hallway. "Zaya, there isn't much time. Hurry."

I darted into the dimly lit passage, not looking back.

Macha was waiting in the hallway. She led me up a narrow flight of stairs, the banister broken in places, the balustrades strung with cobwebs. I feared the entire second level would collapse if it weren't for magic supporting the structure. On the landing, we slipped down an adjoining hallway, up another flight, into a second passage, across a hall.

"Where are we going?" I struggled to understand the enormity of the house. From the outside, Weeping Hollow had appeared a run-down two-storey cottage, battered by weather and age. Inside, the place was a labyrinth of multiple rooms, passages, and levels.

Macha took my arm and steered me around a corner. "I understand your confusion. I get lost myself sometimes. The house is constantly renovating. There are spare rooms for the prisoners."

"Prisoners?"

"Dissidents, deserters, prisoners of war—whatever you want to call them—are kept in Tarahik's detention centre in the lowest level of the base. General Kravis has supreme power when it comes to deciding their fates. Most prisoners are sentenced to death by firing squad. My sister is responsible for overseeing the executions." The end of Macha's lip curled into a razor smile. "Not all the prisoners are guilty. Elspeth sees that the innocents are transported to Weeping Hollow. I offer food and lodging until the prisoners can safely be returned to the provinces. From there, their choices are their own."

"You run an escape network?" I was secretly impressed—and amazed. The sisters had courage, sass, and daring, everything I approved of. But there was one thing I didn't understand. "How do you get the prisoners out? Everything is monitored."

Macha chuckled. "Like this."

She led me into a cavernous space carved from hewn rock. Runes and hieroglyphics were etched into the stone walls; they glowed like paintings coloured by phosphorescent inks. In the centre of the cavern stood an arch mirror, its edges encrusted with crystals. The smooth surface reflected the runes in a kaleidoscope of colours, casting a dizzying display of patterns across the walls.

"This is a portal connecting Tarahik to Weeping Hollow." Macha ran her fingers over the mirror's surface. It rippled at her touch.

Slow and careful, I edged toward the mirror. I'd heard of physical portals, but this was the first time I'd seen one. They were rare, and few casters were able to create them. It required strong sorcery and deep concentration. Portals worked like a battery. When a battery's charging amperage exceeded a safe level, it overboiled and exploded. That was how the caster brain worked with portals. Without the right level of skill or practice, the brain could end up scrambled egg in the skull.

Macha rocked back on her heels. Bartholomew hooted on her shoulder. The bird sounded… excited. The Obeahwoman scratched the creature's small head. "Elspeth has a duplicate mirror in her office. They're linked. Slip through this portal, and you'll come out on the other side." Macha gave my hand a reassuring squeeze. "You must go now. If the base is in lockdown, Elspeth will shut the portal for safety. Nothing will travel through the network."

Ignoring the warning racing through my heart, I touched the mirror. It turned into liquid metal, cold and wet. It was like submerging your hand into the cool waters of a swimming pool.

"Zaya, before you go, there is something you need to understand." Macha's voice was deep and troubled. "The path to Nekros Manteia can only be seen by the dead—or by a necromancer. If the council is guarding the temple, that means they used a necromancer to find it. They likely killed that caster afterward. Be careful, Zaya. The council will do anything to keep Larthalgule contained."

And Melvina and Kravis will do everything to obtain it, I thought dismally.

My sudden intake of air stung my throat. "Macha?"

The Obeahwoman turned around. "What is it?"

I exhaled, long and slow. "Lunette told me to kill him. Do you know who she was referring to? Vulcan? Kravis?"

Someone else?

Macha stood there for a moment, her face a mask of hidden emotion. "No. I'm afraid I don't. Ghosts don't always make sense. Lunette was likely talking about her killer." With those less-than-inspiring words, she slipped out of the cavern.

But Lunette's killer was a woman.

Unease curdled my stomach.

The Obeahwoman wasn't being honest with me, but I didn't have time to question it now. Summoning courage, I stepped into the portal. My body went limp, the energy sucked out of me. My legs buckled as though they'd turned into slushy water, my insides liquefying. I tumbled into empty space, greeted by the unknown.

CHAPTER FORTY-SEVEN

I couldn't breathe. My lungs refused to fill with air. Wind slapped at my face and played tug of war with my legs. The sensation was like tumbling endlessly through space, drawn into the thick gravitational pull of a massive black hole. What had Professor Gemmell said in class those long weeks ago?

"Portals work the same way as black holes. In the centre is a gravitational singularity, where the laws of physics terminate and magical energy prevails."

It was this magical vortex that transported mass from one point of entry to another—and what I was being sucked into right now, stretched and kneaded like dough in a pasta machine. The walls—if you could call them that—collapsed in on themselves. My momentum amplified, my body wrenched from the perilous twister.

I slammed hard onto lush burgundy carpet, the crisp scent of pine distressingly familiar. Behind me, Macaslan's gold-framed mirror returned to a smooth, unblemished surface, not at all like a machine that had just catapulted me through space and time. I took in my surroundings, noting the similarities and changes in the commander's office. The mahogany desk still stood in the centre, only last time everything on it had been neatly arranged. Now, papers were strewn across the counter, a mug of steaming coffee abandoned precariously near the edge. Commander Macaslan hadn't been absent long. That was a blessing. Dropping in like this wouldn't have been easy to explain, especially when I was under house arrest.

The grandfather clock in the corner chimed, reminding me how short I was on time. I tore out of the office, scrambling past the grinning skulls geometrically set in the tower walls—they still freaked me out—and sprinted down each level of the base, my heart beating double time. I halted at the doors of hangar bay eight. Soldiers, paratroopers, pilots, and technicians were scattered among the equipment, moving with purpose and dexterity as they prepped carrier-hornets and fuelled fire-crusaders. Even from this distance, I saw sweat on their brows, their underarms soaked. Down here was like a sauna, the engines and exhausts emitting a heat that stung the eyes and throat.

Don't be seen. Don't be seen.

But for the longest moment, I couldn't think of what to do.

Pretend you belong.

I gravitated toward an assembly of military pallets. Most of the infantry personnel were too preoccupied to question a cadet's presence, but I still didn't want to risk the chance that someone might recognise me. Certain no one was watching, I ducked behind a cargo of medical supplies and silently assessed the situation. My initial plan was to follow a squadron into a hornet, but even with their shoulders heavily weighed down by weapons, the soldiers moved too fast for me to reach them in time.

Time to activate plan B.

I devised a strategy with the least risk of confrontation and darted toward a convoy of sparrowhawks—a sort of four-wheel-drive troop carrier. The vehicles were stationed on a unit loading device, which meant it wouldn't be long till they were transported into a hornet. I chose the last sparrowhawk because it was the closest, fumbled the door open with my sweaty hands, and leapt inside.

Where I waited... and waited.

What's taking so long?

Five minutes passed, then ten. My back ached from crouching behind the seats, every muscle in my body alive with discomfort. The car lurched suddenly. I shifted my weight and kept low as the loading device hummed into motion. Tension built in my mind, an uneasiness that grew larger and darker as we approached a carrier-hornet. I did a double take to my left and barely saw the heads of cargo handlers as they propelled the device forward. There was no turning back now. The sparrowhawks travelled seamlessly into the hornet and were secured into the cargo bay. I kept still the entire time, scarcely able to breathe, afraid the slightest noise would give me away.

Alone in my secluded environment, I relied on sound. Booted feet thumped against the deck—soldiers shuffling past to find a comfortable place to stand. A dozen or so conversations dropped as the magnitude of the situation drew near. There were beeps, chimes, and clangs—perhaps the final inspection of equipment aboard the craft. Thrusters rumbled. The deck plating juddered. I leaned on my knees, giving my upper thighs a rest. It became impossible to crouch with so much vibration jolting up my bones.

I sensed the carrier-hornet taxiing down the runway, my stomach giving an unpleasant twist as the craft lifted into the clouds, my ears popping with the increased elevation. How long was it to Galvac? Minutes? Hours? I'd never had the chance to look at a map. For a long time, I sat waiting. My eyelids drooped from boredom, my brain closing off, finally resigning to sleep.

I jumped at the excessive force of the door thrust open. The soldier on the other side took a fraction of a second to appraise me before he grabbed my arm and dragged me out of the vehicle.

"You didn't learn the first time, did you?"

My despair escalated when I blinked my eyes clear and his face took form. Jad was breathing hard, his shoulders taut beneath the thick fabric of his coat. Of all the shuttles and carrier-hornets bound for Galvac, we had to end up on the same flight.

I tilted my chin. "I did learn the first time. I learnt to be sneakier."

His face transformed into a nasty glare. "What are you playing at? Do you have any idea where we're headed?"

I pulled away feebly, determined not to be treated like a kid. "I have every reason to be on this hornet."

He ran a frustrated hand through his hair.

My heart fell. There was no way I'd pull this mission off now without Captain Arden's cooperation. He needed to understand how important this was; otherwise, he'd tie me into a jump seat with a binding charm. Mission over.

I decided the best thing I could do was ease his mind. "Listen. I'm not a stowaway, all right? I'm going to Galvac for a reason."

"And that reason is?"

Willing my heartbeat to slow down and my breathing to return to normal, I gave a quick rundown of everything I'd learnt at Macha's, hoping it would appease his foul mood.

It didn't.

He shook his head, his broad hands tense as he crossed his arms. "I wish you'd come to me first... or to Commander Macaslan."

"There wasn't time." I said it with more bravado then I felt. "Please. I need to find the temple."

The veins in his neck throbbed. "No. It's too risky. After we disembark, you'll remain on the hornet. That's an order."

He pointed a finger to silence me, his word final.

I opened my mouth to argue, but a young soldier hurtled forward, snapping Jad's attention away. The young man's upper lip was damp from sweat. "Captain, we're approaching the drop zone."

The drop zone? Already?

How many hours have passed?

Despite his efforts to appear composed, Jad's jaw clenched. He gave a swift nod to two jumpmasters stationed in the rear of the plane. The pair unlocked the exit doors. The wind bit into my skin, my nose assaulted by the burning toxins of jet fuel. Sleet lashed at my face. Melvina was close.

Jad didn't stick around to question the abnormality of the weather. He moved to the rear of the plane, me tight on his heels. I was determined he would see my point, but no matter how much I pleaded, the captain wouldn't listen.

He turned to face me, the confidence and trust diminishing from his eyes. "I can't risk Melvina finding you. You shouldn't be here. You're not ready for this. You never will be."

The words were a cruel, hard slap to the face. In front of everyone, my cheeks darkened to the colour of a dying rose. Jad flashed a final look of fury at me and continued his way down the aisle.

I hung back, humiliated and resenting the decision I'd made. I should have chosen a different sparrowhawk. Damn it.

At the end of the hornet, I saw more clearly that the jumpmasters were using arm and hand signals to communicate to the rows of paratroopers waiting to jump. The paratroopers connected their static lines to an anchor cable on the ceiling, double-checked they were properly hooked, and then waited for the red light to turn green.

Wait. They're jumping into this wind?

I lowered my gaze to the window. "I can't see anything but cloud," I said to the soldier beside me. "How are the paratroopers meant to find the drop zone in that?"

The soldier had his head down, his tone guarded. "That isn't cloud cover. It's smoke. From Galvac."

He was right. I tasted soot in the air, the scent clogging my nose. Through the smog, I caught fleeting glances of the landscape below. The plane dipped. Beneath us, the sea was dark and powerful, trapping anything in its swell. Waves crashed against a towering cliff face—a vertical drop that spanned the entire coastline.

The Asrath Cliffs.

At first, I thought the small bobbing objects floating on the surface were seaweed, but as the carrier-hornet drew closer, their true shape emerged. Bodies! Dead, bloated marines were tossed and thrown through the swell like clothes in a washing machine. Two warships tilted precariously on the waves. Their propellers had surfaced, plumes of smoke rising from their hulls. The vessels had either been hit by torpedoes or bombed from the air. I couldn't tell which. Marines and sailors hung on to the guardrails. Others took their chance and plunged into the sea. They needed to swim fast; otherwise, the suction from the sinking vessels would drag them under.

I was grateful when the hornet careened to the right, cutting my view. Jad and his squadron were not on a rescue mission. They didn't have the resources to salvage casters from the water. There was nothing that could be done for the men and women in the sea other than pray the ocean took them quickly and without pain.

The carrier-hornet powered over the cliff face. Galvac Dam was even bigger than I remembered—a high concrete arch dam that stood impressively in the canyon, holding back the ocean surge to protect the reservoir on the other side. From the spillway, a monolithic tower stood like an ancient fortress, designed as though its architect had intended to pierce the sky. The dam was just as I'd remembered from the vision, only now the reservoir was frozen solid. Winter was often described as beautiful, but with the blood moon casting a misty red haze on the snow-covered slopes and mountains, Galvac's landscape resembled an alien planet.

On the ground, the Haxsan Guard struggled against the dissent rebels, their weapons sending shock waves through the landscape. The snow and ice were strewn with bodies and blood stained. Fire-crusaders bombed from the air. Warships projected cannon fire across the sea. I watched the scene with fascinated horror. I'd believe training prepared me for this, but the sound of thousands of casters screaming, choking, and dying sent a shiver through my body that would never thaw. The scenes would forever remain embedded in my memory, waiting to torment me in my vulnerable moments.

The carrier-hornet banked to the left. We soared across an expanse of snow-packed trees toward a jumble of red sand dunes and rock columns. In the red moonlight, the sand glistened like scattered rubies. A nervous energy ran through the plane. The light above the doors switched to green, and the jumpmasters signalled the go-ahead. The paratroopers jumped, accomplishing faultless parachute drops to the world below. I realised Jad's intention. It wasn't practical to disembark above Galvac, but here the soldiers could land safely. If they played their cards right and were sneaky about it, they could attack from the west, using the trees for cover.

"Captain?" The same young soldier darted toward Jad, only this time his face was sickly pale. "We're in range of—"

He never got to finish.

The explosion ripped a hole through the end of the carrier-hornet, the sound caught between a shotgun and thunderclap, amplified by a thousand volumes. The blast propelled shrapnel and debris through the cabin, each piece hitting like projectiles. Screams filled the air. A siren went off, fuelling more panic. Different mechanisms screeched and grated as heavy wind tore the aircraft apart. Some of the crew managed to secure themselves into jump seats; others got chewed up in the wreckage. I was thrown from my feet, the air current agonisingly strong. It flung me onto the jump seats. Brute force wasn't my forte, but they say when you're faced with death, the mind is thrown into survival mode. Maybe that was what gave me the strength to snag the seat belt and strap it around my waist. Jad was nowhere to be seen. I hoped by some miracle he hadn't been sucked into the gaping hole that was now the end of our aircraft.

He's in the cockpit, Zaya. He's trying to take control of the hornet.

I was kidding myself. Jad was a decent pilot, but not even he could overcome physics. And then there was the fact that the hornet was breaking apart, metal and sparks skidding everywhere on our descent. I saw faces paralysed in horror. Live wires flung free. Burning circuits and flashing lights. I wished I could have closed my eyes, but the wind kept my lids open, insisting I witness the devastation. We were falling so fast; the hornet was like a supernova through space.

The aircraft gave a tremendous roar, the underbelly screaming violently against the strain. A final high-pitched whine filled my ears as the plane made impact with the earth. It was the strangest sound, more like jets of water in a tremendous crash, shudders rippling up through my feet. I stilled for a moment, startled by what I saw. The cabin began filling with dark bubbling water. The missile had blasted us so far across the landscape that we'd literally catapulted into the sea. We were sinking.

CHAPTER FORTY-EIGHT

Screams of pain and sorrow echoed through the wreckage. No matter where I turned, I was surrounded by terrified faces, skin bruised or split, hair dishevelled, bodies horribly injured. One man's leg hung at an odd angle. Another had his arm severed. After the crash, some casters had laughed in hysterical relief, grateful to be alive. But when they saw the aircraft take on water, the initial panic returned. The fear was contagious, a virus that jumped from one caster to another, plunging the hornet into a pandemonium of kicking, shoving, and jostling, everyone propelled by the instinct to live.

My internal voice shouted for me to move, but where was there to go? And where was Jad? I couldn't leave without him.

I forced my trembling hands to unclip my seat belt. My fingers were stained with someone else's blood, making my climb difficult through the twisted labyrinth of charred metal and exposed wiring. Switchboards sparked. Bodies bobbed in the water. Two had blond hair and the other was a redhead. I took the redhead's cast-shooter from his holster. He wouldn't need it.

Examining what was left of the wide-bodied aircraft, I was thankful none of the corpses in my vicinity had black hair. My relief only spurred guilt. No one had deserved to die like this, alone and forever remaining trapped souls in underwater wreckage. Overwhelming grief caused my head to feel too heavy for my body. But there was nothing that could be done for these casters. They were gone forever. And if I didn't want to join them, I had to move.

One of the aircrew managed to prise an emergency hatch open and demanded people abandon the plane. Casters careered so fast to the exit that the different mechanisms of the hornet couldn't cope. The most frightening, unearthly sound ripped through the cabin. The walls burst in zigzag ruptures, seawater gushing in. In seconds it was up to my waist, so cold it stabbed like needles.

The airman who'd opened the door was forcing casters out of the plane. "Come on. This way. There are rocks by the cliff. You need to swim."

Swim? Was he kidding? No one could swim through the waves. At least, they could never reach the crags without a life raft, and even then, the chances were slim. I stupidly realised I should have grabbed a life jacket. The ocean was going to pummel me like spices in a mortar and pestle.

The airman took my arm with a strength that was surprising and shoved me toward the exit. "Come on, soldier. You need to get out."

Down below, waves smashed powerfully, shooting jets of water into the air. This was what I'd feared—trapped in the current and descending deeper into the abyss where no one could find me.

Jad?

Where is he?

I should have shouted for him, called out his name, but fear had hindered my ability to speak.

I can't leave without him.

The airman saw my hesitance. Stricken, he crushed his fingers into my arm, forcing me to look at him. "I'm sorry, miss, but whoever you're waiting for isn't coming. You need to focus on your own survival now."

His words left an ache in my chest, so strong it paralysed me. But he was right. No point denying the truth. Jad was gone.

I stared down at the treacherous water, which seemed to have its own storm raging beneath the surface. I didn't have long to dwell on the prospect of drowning. A muffled apology brushed my ear, followed by a painful shove. I sliced into the icy black water, my arms and legs instantly numbed by cold. Waves lashed at my body, twisting my limbs in unusual contortions. The current was going to rip the flesh from my bones.

When I finally broke through the surface, water gushed out of my mouth in implausible volume, that first breath pure elation to my lungs. I kicked to stay afloat, but the current had other ideas, pushing me precariously toward the cliffs.

Jad!

Was he being tossed around by the current too? Or was he sinking to a watery grave?

Don't think about it. You got out. Now you need to live.

But my energy had drained, my legs anesthetised by cold. In the water, they were as feeble and droopy as spaghetti. The direction of the current changed. The swell tossed me toward a dark slit in the colossal cliff, the angry sea flowing inside with unrelenting fury.

A cave.

Nekros Manteia!

It had to be.

The Larthalgule blade was somewhere in that cave.

My muscles screamed in exhaustion, but I kicked and swam with the current. I'd lost Jad. I wasn't going to lose the chance to find the blade too.

For once, the ocean worked with me, the tide sucking me into the fissure. The cave was narrow with a low ceiling, rocks jutting out dangerously through the swell. The walls were abysmally black, as though they'd been submerged in wet tar. If it weren't for dappled moonlight leaking through small cracks in the ceiling, I'd be floating blind.

After a little way in, my feet hit submerged rock. I waded through the shallow pool, careful to avoid the deeper rock ponds inundated by small fish and crabs. The air was heavy with the briny scent of seaweed and something I couldn't place. No. I knew what it was—the dank, musty odour of abandonment, like an old house slowly eaten by mould and age. No one had entered this cave in years—other than fish, at least.

A staircase hewn from rock led to the dark crags above, its edges worn by years of tidal floods. I switched on the LED mounted on my cast-shooter. The torch lent a pale cast to the cavern walls, the ceiling trellised with dark vines. The good thing about cast-shooters was that they never stopped working, even after they'd been submerged. Right now, against the dark, the weapon was my best friend.

My waterlogged boots made squishy sounds as I clambered up the stairs, a definite announcement for anyone—or thing—that lurked around a corner waiting to pounce. Where the tide hadn't reached, cobwebs extended along the walls like the ghostly sails of a shipwreck, insects fossilised in their tangled snares. I hated the grim reminder of predator and prey and couldn't deter the shiver that danced up my bones.

At the top of the stairs, the landing extended out into a huge cavern, the limestone walls transporting me to a primitive world. Figurines of ancient gods and goddesses, some of them toppled or defaced by time, were sculpted from the rock, hands held out in salvation. Along the walls stood smooth, square mausoleums. They were the colour of icebergs and were inscribed with religious texts from long ago. To my right, a natural arch in the rock face looked out toward the sea, permitting rays of smoky moonlight to leak into the cavern. The temple was beautiful but dangerous. Even the striking stalactite ceiling reminded me of pointed teeth ready to chomp down.

Alone in this place, booby traps seemed far too plausible. I grabbed a large stone and tossed it across the cavern. I'd read about ancient booby traps in rock-cut tombs. No way was I about to risk being shot by automatic crossbows, crushed by tumbling boulders, or swallowed into a deadly pit trap.

The rock hit the ground with a thud.

Nothing.

"There's no need to fear this place. The booby traps have long been disabled."

I jumped. The voice resonated across the walls in an endless, chilling echo.

A man stepped out from the shadows. He moved to a brilliant stone sarcophagus, his skin almost as white as the marble. His wavy hair fell past his shoulders, black except for a few strands of silver past his ears. There was an uncanny glint in his eyes, the irises the colour of midnight. He would have been handsome once, but now his sallow complexion gave his face a gaunt, neglected appearance, the black around his eyes more defined. Even in a tailored suit that spoke legions of affluence and privilege, it couldn't mask what must have been years of physical deterioration. I didn't think it was caused by poor diet and lack of sleep. This was the look of a man plagued by years of obsession.

"Do not be afraid." He moved theatrically, like a stage actor about to perform a stirring monologue. Yet at the same time there was something almost predatory about the way he advanced. Those black eyes sliced into mine, chiselling down to my soul. I felt exposed, vulnerable, defenceless. I imagined he saw me like a butterfly fixed in a box frame.

A well-rehearsed smile crept along his narrow lips. "Hello, Zaya. When I last saw you, you were only a girl. I hear you've become quite the soldier."

I raised my cast-shooter, clicking the safety off. "Who are you? How do you know me?"

But I had a terrible feeling I already knew the answers.

There was no fear in his eyes, just sheer determination and... amusement. "There's no need to be melodramatic. I'm here to have a civilised conversation." With a wave of his fingers, the cast-shooter flung out of my hand. It struck the cavern wall and fell into a deep fissure, lost forever. I flinched like a terrified, trapped animal. He was telekinetic!

He barked out a laugh. "And before you decide to make a run for it, be aware that the tide has come in. The tunnel you entered is submerged. There's no way out."

This wasn't a trick to keep me here. I could hear the tide sweeping in below, smashing powerfully onto boulders.

Anticipation underscored the edge of his tone. "Did you think you survived the crash out of luck? Were brought here by chance?"

Whatever composure I had left blinked out like a doused flame. He had done this. Somehow, he'd made sure I was tossed against a jump seat, ensuring I'd survive the carrier-hornet hurtling into the sea. He'd manipulated the waves and ocean current, trapping me in this cavern.

"Who are you?" I struggled from exertion and panic, unable to get the right inflection in my voice.

"You don't remember me?" There was something almost wolfish in the way he appraised me. "Then it's true. Your memories have been muddled with. Amnesia, perhaps?"

My back went ramrod straight. How did he know so much about me?

His mouth crept into another satisfied smile. "Come closer. Let me see you."

When I didn't move, he waved his hand. My feet instantly lifted from the ground. I soared across the cavern and dropped just a few metres before him. I glared. I was not some lab rat to be pricked and prodded, thank you very much.

His lip curled in distaste. "It comes as no surprise that you don't remember me. Ten years has made quite the difference to both of us."

He stepped into the moonlight.

A choked sob broke from my throat. On his lapel was a silver brooch shaped in a familiar crest—the insignia for the United League of Dissent.

A thin lather of sweat broke out on my palms. I was going to be sick.

His eyes caught mine with fierce animosity. "You really don't remember me, do you? Pity." He leant forward. "My name is Vulcan Stormouth… and I've been searching for you a long time."

CHAPTER FORTY-NINE

Cold despair inched its way up my throat. This man was a monster, a degenerate, someone who embodied the worst loathing toward humans and the casters who empathised with them. I didn't like the Free Zones. I didn't like the way the council ran the system. But I didn't agree with killing innocents—caster or human.

Vulcan studied me with cool detachment. When he spoke, his tone was as harsh and cold as the winter Arctic. "I can tell from your face that you recognise my name and the hypocrisy that comes with it."

I dug my nails into my palms, my hands clasped into fists. "You're a murderer."

His manic laughter filled the cavern. "You were always a feisty child, Zaya. That's what I admired about you. But now I find you absurdly naive. I blame the council's incredibly remiss education system and the half-truths enforced in it. They make me sound like a lunatic mass murderer, which is hardly fair."

Is this a joke?

My emotions burned into white-hot rage. I was afraid of him, but I'd be damned if I let him see it. "The only person you have to blame for your reputation is yourself. You kill innocents."

"Not true. I'm just like you, Zaya. I'm a realist. The world can't survive much longer the way it's going. Humans are a disease that needs to be removed.

They no longer have a place in this world. You used to believe that… once."

I tried to recoil, but his magic had a strict hold on me. It squeezed my chest like invisible straps. "You don't know a thing about me," I screamed, revolted by the claim.

He tilted his head, amused. "And how do you know? You don't remember your childhood."

I stood rigid, my feet heavy as concrete.

I had no memory of my early life, but I knew in my heart it wasn't possible for me to possess that level of hatred. The conviction sounded empty in my head, though. I stared into the dark pools of Vulcan's eyes, afraid of the layer of truth behind them. I couldn't deny there were occasions when dark, conflicting emotions crept through me, sometimes playing tricks on my better judgement.

I shook my head, driving away the thought. I was not like him.

The mocking grin never left Vulcan's face. "You've come for the Larthalgule blade."

It wasn't a question. He knew I'd come to destroy it.

My voice sounded whisper-quiet in my ears. "I won't let you use the weapon. Whatever you're planning isn't going to happen."

His cold, mirthless laughter pealed through the cavern. "Weapon? You think the Larthalgule blade is the weapon Melvina and I have sought for the last decade?" He shook his head, like I was the punchline of a poorly delivered joke. "Larthalgule is the key to the weapon, idiot girl." He tapped the sarcophagus. "*Here* is the weapon."

The casket was made of pure white marble, the lid resembling the earliest form of the ancient pharaohs: face gilded, dark eyes open, mouth perfectly symmetrical. The arms were crossed in a symbol of reverence, hands clenched around two sharp daggers. One blade was embellished with red serpents, the other adorned with onyx gems. Above the blades, a keyhole had been cut into the marble, directly where the heart would rest, eerily resembling a stab wound.

Vulcan looked at me, the cruel pleasure in his eyes never fading. "Inside this sarcophagus rests the caster who gave rise to the United League of Dissent… a necromancer who has watched you from the realm beyond."

My blood pounded into my head with dizzying effect.

It can't be. It's not possible.

"Morgomoth." The name tasted like poison in my mouth.

There was a hint of triumph in Vulcan's voice. "Morgomoth is the weapon. This sarcophagus is not a resting place. It's a cage, a prison to trap Morgomoth inside. The council has fed you lies. They didn't execute Morgomoth like the history books claim. He's too powerful to be killed. The Haxsan Guard bound our leader into an eternal sleep, a curse designed to keep him drifting between the realms of the living and the dead. Only one document records this tomb—the map you destroyed."

I tried to steady my breathing, but the revelation had short-circuited my brain.

Vulcan scrutinised my face slowly. "Destroying the map did hinder us for a while, but there was another way of finding the Asrath Cliffs. Your blood samples."

His voice jerked me out of my stupor.

Blood samples?

The hard lines around his eyes deepened. "After your blood made contact with the map, its magic transferred into you—a preventative way of ensuring data and knowledge is never lost. You were the carrier of a heavily desired secret there for a while." He chuckled, the tone scornful and baiting. "When you were lying in the infirmary, unconscious and recovering, our spy was able to commandeer your samples and transfer them by portal to us. All I had to do was spill your blood in the moonlight. The map revealed itself, showing the location of this tomb."

I wanted to charge at him, but the invisible barrier had me bound like a mouse in a cage.

Vulcan looked fondly at the sarcophagus. "Morgomoth is, and will remain, the leader of the ULD. I am his lieutenant. Everything I have done has been at his command." He plucked the red serpent dagger from the casket. "Larthalgule is the key that can raise the dead. Morgomoth must be awakened." His dark eyes raked mine slowly. "That is where you come in."

※

CHAPTER FIFTY

I tasted fear in my mouth. It was salty and bitter, as though a blood blister had popped in my throat. The ground seemed to slide out beneath me.

Moonlight danced across Vulcan's bone white skin, the hard edges around his lips more profound. "You will resurrect Morgomoth. Under his rule, the United League of Dissent will rise to power. The council will fall. Humans will be annihilated. And casters with mixed blood will be sterilised. We must keep our race pure, free from abnormality and illness." His voice climbed with each sentence, spittle flying from his mouth. "The inferior must be eradicated."

I trembled with rage, the blood draining from my face. "That doesn't sound like you're saving casters. That sounds like an excuse for genocide."

Fury flashed in his eyes. In one fluid movement, he advanced, locking my jaw in his grip. I felt bruises pop along my skin. "Are you siding with the council? With the Haxsan Guard? The same people who locked you away in an internment camp?" Disgust seeped through his tone.

I swallowed, the pressure on my jaw causing my eyes to water. The hairs along the back of my neck stood on end. "I'm not siding with anyone. You… the council… the Haxsan Guard, you're each as bad as the other."

I thought of Jad, Macaslan, Harper, and Darius Kerr. The group had worked hard and sacrificed much to find a way toward peace. They were mutineers, freedom fighters, revolutionists. I admired each of them. I knew whose side I was on.

A muscle twitched near Vulcan's mouth. "Your parents would be ashamed."

Coldness crept over my skin.

What did he say?

The crimson rays of moonlight made his face appear twisted and demonic. "That's right. Your parents were dissent rebels. They believed in Morgomoth's cause and were willing to sacrifice anything to resurrect their fallen master… even their daughter. That's why you're here now, Zaya—to complete the ritual. They never cared for you."

I hadn't realised I'd been crying until I lunged for him. Vulcan's force field of sorcery shattered with my fury, bursting like smashed glass. His eyes had only a moment to widen in surprise before my fist made contact with his face. He cried out, the sweetest sound to my ears. Blood spluttered from his mouth. I hoped I'd knocked out a few teeth.

"You're lying." I was about to go in for another punch when his magic suddenly took hold again, seizing my arms.

He brought his face close to mine, his breath smelling of raw meat and blood. "I underestimated your magic. Your strength is impressive." The superior glint in his eyes climbed several notches. "But you also showed me your weakness. What I said is true. Your parents and I were like kindred. I watched you grow as a child and witnessed your magic advance. In time, it became obvious to us what you were… what you were destined for. You were born into the world to be sacrificed. Fate can be cruel." He pinched my cheek with sickening affection.

Hot tears stung my eyes. "Sacrificed?"

Vulcan's mocking scowl never faded. "Oh, I apologise. I failed to explain. Morgomoth's resurrection will kill you."

He clicked his fingers. The invisible force that bound my body lifted me from the ground. It planted my feet a few inches from the sarcophagus. The coffin was even more magnificent up close. Where the stone had been painted in solid gold, coloured gems smoothed by centuries glistened. Protective spells were chiselled in ancient runes across the marble. I recognised the carvings from textbooks in re-education. Binding charms.

Vulcan leaned his arms on the casket, enjoying my discomfort. "Your parents are dead. Clarence Chauvelin killed them the night he kidnapped you."

The magic barricade pressed tighter, forcing my breath to come out in gasping sobs. Hot, choked-up tears scratched at my eyes. For a long time, I'd been in denial, but I think I'd always known my parents weren't good people. Hearing it confirmed, that they were willing to let me die, made me feel more alone and dejected than I'd ever felt before.

"My memories?" I sobbed. "Where did my amnesia come from?"

Because I no longer believed it was the work of the black-veined woman.

Vulcan ran his bored eyes over me. "Does it matter? Your amnesia was most likely caused by a spell, someone who didn't want you to remember your parents or your life with the ULD. The memories are in there, of course, just buried deep in your mind where you can't access them. My bet is Clarence did it. He was capable of magic like that." He wagged his finger at me. "Now, on to more important matters."

He brought the red serpent dagger forward. In the moonlight, dragons, snakes, and demon bodies were intertwined across the hilt. It looked like a weapon summoned from the pits of hell.

The lieutenant closed his eyes, his voice fierce and animated. "The Larthalgule blade will restore your life. Tell me what to do next."

I realised he wasn't speaking to me. He was addressing Morgomoth.

A voice boomed through the temple, raspy and hiss-like. "Get the blood."

My chest heaved. That voice. I recognised it. I'd heard it in my vision the night the grimoire had teleported me to the Galvac Dam. The voice had been deep and painful then. Now it bellowed like thunder, ricocheting across the cavern walls.

Morgomoth.

Vulcan dabbed the Larthalgule blade into four canopic jars positioned around the sarcophagus. The blade came out dripping red.

Blood! The jars are filled with blood.

His gaze transferred to mine with a wicked glint. "To provide Morgomoth the strength he needs, he must consume the blood of a clairvoyant, illusionist, trickster, and telepath—all the traits required to make a strong leader."

I stared at the dagger dripping in blood, watching in horror. The suspended moment passed. "That's why Melvina killed them?"

Four young people had lost their lives for this bizarre and sickening ritual? *Soon to be five lives*, I thought grimly.

"Their essence lives on in Morgomoth," he stated flatly. There was no remorse in Vulcan's voice.

The weight of what he was about to do slowly sank in. If the blade pierced Morgomoth's body and awakened him, the magic would transfer into him. He would be unstoppable.

The lieutenant handed Larthalgule's hilt to me. "There's no need to be afraid. All you need to do is place the blade in the keyhole, right in the heart of the sarcophagus. It will puncture Morgomoth and awaken him. It won't be painful. Your energy will leave you and pass through the blade into him. You won't feel anything."

The veins in my neck pulsed. I needed to do something. Cause a distraction. Anything. "And the other dagger?" I eyed the onyx blade still attached to the coffin. It was narrower in width and lacked the beauty of its sister dagger. Strange runes marked the weapon, but they were nothing I recognised.

Vulcan gave it a bored flick of his eyes. "That is Neathror, the bringer of death. All magic must be balanced." He returned his focus on me. "Do it. Stab the coffin."

He had Larthalgule in his hand, waiting for me to take it.

I gave a short, scornful laugh. "No."

Vulcan needed me. He couldn't threaten me with death. He couldn't beat me unconscious. We were at an impasse… and he was about to learn how much patience I had.

He fixed his steel-like gaze on mine, anger swelling in his eyes. "Then I'll make you do it."

Before I could comprehend what he was doing, his nimble fingers snatched my wrist. Too late I realised he was going to place the dagger in my hand and force me to pierce the sarcophagus. I thrashed about to loosen his grip, my mouth open to protest, but no words came out.

At Vulcan's chest, a catch of light moved like the dancing rays of sunshine, causing me to squint. At first it resembled a dog tag on a chain, but then its true shape emerged—a half-size golden pendant. The buzzing in my ears became rumbles of thunder. I'd seen that locket's other half before.

No. It's not possible.

Vulcan saw where my eyes rested and stopped fighting me. Surprise flickered across his face before his lips curled into a heinous smile. "You're familiar with my medallion, aren't you? You've seen its other half. It was a piece that once belonged to my wife. The medallions glow when they're close to each other."

You've long suspected a traitor was at Tarahik.

And it was true.

Vulcan's cruel smile was no longer directed at me. His eyes were centred on the stone stairs. "Look what fate has brought me this evening."

Pearls of sweat ran down my back, because I knew who'd stepped into the temple. I'd been standing at the edge of a precipice all this time. Now I was falling.

I turned to see Jad enter the cavern, his cast-shooter levelled on me.

CHAPTER FIFTY-ONE

My vision reeled.

This couldn't be happening. It had to be a bad dream. A nightmare!

But the cold calculation in Jad's eyes told me this was real, that I'd been deceived... made a fool of... betrayed. My stomach jumped erratically. I'd believed Jad was a hardened soldier determined to redeem all those who were oppressed. What a serious error in judgement I'd made. What a serious error in judgement we had *all* made.

Vulcan's eyes absorbed the captain down to the finest detail. "I'm forgetting my manners," he announced. "Dearest Zaya, allow me to introduce my son, Trajan Stormouth."

Horror and loathing snaked its way through my body, poisoning everything that had been strong and brave.

Trajan Stormouth?

Never had I been so possessed to curse someone, to scream the foulest and most violent spells my enraged mind could summon. I wanted to scratch at him, rip him apart. At the same time, his trickery and deception, his very presence, was an infection. I felt contaminated just being near him.

"Trajan Stormouth is dead. I know because I killed him. The death of Vulcan's son has put a target on my back."

That was what Jad had told me. A disgusting lie.

Jad—Trajan—whoever he was shook his head, seemingly rattled by my toxic glare. The grip on his cast-shooter tightened. "That is not my name. I left that person behind long ago." His jaw clenched when he looked at his father. "And I'm not here to side with you."

Vulcan's lips thinned into a narrow line. "Don't be ridiculous. You are my son. The United League of Dissent is your destiny. For once, I thought you'd seen sense. For once, you weren't a disappointment."

I turned my head between the pair.

What the hell is going on?

Had Jad meant Trajan Stormouth was dead figuratively? Had he left his old life behind and taken up a new identity? Was the target on his back put there by his own father?

Jad stared at the lieutenant, years of hatred burning in eyes. He lifted the medallion from his neck, which caught the light in a flicker of gold flashes. "I had a mother. I don't have a father."

Vulcan stared, tension blazing across his face. "If you did not come to the temple to take your place among the ULD, then why are you here?"

Jad's eyes connected with mine. It was the briefest look, but a world of communication was expressed in that single moment—concern, fear, longing. I knew because the same tumbleweed of emotions was spinning through me.

Jad averted his gaze, but not fast enough.

Vulcan tipped his head back and laughed. "Oh, I see. So that's how it is between you two, is it?"

Absurdly, I blushed.

I could tell from the way Jad's chest moved that he tried to regulate his breathing. The mental armour he wore every day was breaking. His self-control, his ability to stay calm in a crisis, had cracked.

"Jad?" I hardly recognised my voice.

Why does he still have the cast-shooter aimed on me?

The look in his eyes was foreign and frightening. "I'm sorry."

He squeezed the trigger.

The shot propelled me backward. For a moment, I was suspended in that weird interplay where time moved fast and slow, dragging out the horror and trauma. I collapsed onto the slick rocks, my head dark for a fraction of a second. When I came to, I braced myself for the excruciating pain, but it never came. There was no blood. No wound. No broken bones or missing limbs. Other than shock, I was fine.

Where is my injury?

Vulcan sneered. "A curse-breaker, Miss Wayward. My son has unbound you from my hex."

I blinked in astonishment. There were high-end cast-shooters out there that came with curse-breakers—a blast of magical energy that could destroy binding spells. The weapons were rare because they cost a fortune. At Tarahik, they were locked in a secure vault in the armoury. Macaslan had either permitted the captain to have one or Jad was better at picking locks than I gave him credit for.

I closed my eyes for a second, dizzy with relief.

Vulcan snorted. His voice choked with wrath as he glared down at me, the hard lines around his eyes deepening. "I can tell from the way you look at my son that you care for him… and that he cares for you. But don't be fooled. He is not righteous. He has secrets."

A ripple of aggravation ran through Jad's shoulders. He clicked his gun into assault mode and trained the weapon on his father. "I am not that person anymore."

"Don't try it," Vulcan warned. "I am protected by recoil charms. You shoot and your spell rebounds onto you. At this range, it would hit Zaya. And neither of us wants to see her hurt, do we?"

I squirmed. Vulcan wouldn't give a shit if I lost a finger or two. His only concern was Morgomoth's resurrection.

Jad looked as though he wanted to charge like a raging bull, but he lowered the weapon, resigned to the fact that shooting his father could have drastic consequences for us all.

Vulcan cocked an eyebrow at him. "I think your young lady is owed an explanation." He turned to me, his voice cold but brimming with enjoyment. "Trajan was inducted into the ULD when he was six years old. Back then he'd been keen to prove his worth to our followers. At such a young age, he became a remarkable soldier. His responsibility was to find inferior casters in the provinces, with the pretence of being an orphan. Gullible, they'd take

Trajan in. He would report their location back to the ULD. Late in the evening, our rebels would seize the household's occupants for extermination."

My pulse hammered, the sound reverberating through my head. I wanted Jad to contradict it, but he wouldn't look at me. Shame and self-aversion plagued his face.

My chest expanded, threatening to burst. "Inferior casters?"

Vulcan crossed his arms. "Casters who possess traces of human genetics. We call them undercasts."

"You're sick," I spat.

He shrugged at the insult. "We do what we must to protect our species. Trajan believed that once… but when he was thirteen, he ran away. I blame his mother, of course. She had her uses, but she was ridiculously soft on the boy. She filled his head with silly delusions of peace. Where Trajan should have been strong-willed, his mother made him weak."

Jad's control snapped. He stalked toward his father, voice brimming with hatred. "You betrayed her. Once she'd learnt what an extremist you'd become, she did everything to protect me from you. You experimented on me, infected me with lycanthor DNA. She hated you for that."

A slimy, bitter taste crept over my tongue. The ULD had been known to conduct their medical experiments on their followers first, loyalists like Melvina who'd volunteered and turned into a monster as a result. It appalled me to think Vulcan had willingly let his son undergo a sadistic experiment. What kind of horrors had Jad endured?

Lycanthor DNA?

The captain had abnormal strength, his agility superior to every other soldier at Tarahik, but at what cost?

Unguarded rage flared across Vulcan's face. "I did it to make you stronger. I would never have put you through that operation if it had not been successfully administered on me first. Your mother couldn't understand that."

A cold tingle of hopelessness ran through me. Vulcan had the same lycanthor DNA. I was in the presence of two men with unconquerable power. The odds of getting out of the temple were declining.

Jad stared at Vulcan as though wounded. "She made me see what you really are. A killer."

His father's eyes widened in impatience. "Don't pretend you're different from me. You are a killer too, Trajan. You just kill for a different cause."

The captain's breath came out in rugged pants. I'd seen the level of guilt play out on Jad's face whenever he'd had to kill. For him, killing left wounds that remained bruised and bleeding. And his father had just rubbed salt in them.

Sensing he'd achieved a victory, Vulcan bared his teeth in a hard smile. "After you left, Trajan, I had no idea where you were or what alias you had appointed, not until my informant at Tarahik discovered who Captain Jad Arden really was. I thought... had hoped... that when you entered the temple this evening, you'd reconsidered the ULD. But now I understand your real intention." He glanced my way. It was hard to say what he enjoyed more, tormenting his son or torturing me with the cruel, undeniable truth. "After everything that's happened, how convenient that the three of us are here together. Fate has indeed dealt a fine hand."

My attention had been fixed on the pair, so it came as a surprise when a deep groan shook the ceiling. Both men stared, their black eyes travelling around the cavern as the walls lurched and bucked.

Is this an earthquake?

The ceiling exploded suddenly in a violent, ear-splitting shriek of dirt and rock. Fissures opened, drawing the land above in on itself. The ceaseless shudders knocked me to the ground, pain driving into my knees. I blinked dust out of my eyes. Sand and soil fell from the ceiling, chips of stone pelting me like raindrops.

"Bombers," Vulcan explained, struggling to remain balanced on his feet. "My rebels and the Haxsan Guard are fighting on the surface. The magic in this temple is not as strong as it used to be. It can't sustain the explosions. We need to get this over with before the entire cliff collapses into the sea." He held Larthalgule out to me. "You know what must be done."

I spat dust out of my mouth. "Why don't you get it? I won't do it."

Lines of frustration tightened around his mouth. "Dearest Zaya, I think you should reconsider, because this time I have leverage."

Vulcan pulled a small cast-shooter from his jacket. Without hesitation, he aimed the barrel at Jad and fired. The burst of gunfire rang through the cavern, along with my screams.

The captain toppled to the ground. There was no sound from him. No anguish. There was no movement in him at all.

CHAPTER FIFTY-TWO

I screamed like a maimed animal, every inch of my body throbbing from shock. Jad remained motionless on the ground. The bullet had torn through his shoulder, blood pooling beneath him to stain the tips of his dark hair. The wound reminded me of a busted tap leaking water.

I tossed a hand over my mouth, restraining the urge to be sick. When I looked at Vulcan, my vision swayed. "He's your son. How could you?"

The lieutenant gazed down at Jad with twisted pleasure. "Quit crying, stupid girl. He's not dead. It's a flesh wound."

"It doesn't look like a flesh wound!"

Jad was grey in the face, his lips blue, the skin beneath his eyes black. If it weren't for the beads of sweat on his forehead, I would have sworn he was dead. I frantically searched for something to try and stop the bleeding.

Vulcan's voice cut through the panic escalating in my head. "I hit him with a silver bullet. It generates a comatose state in lycanthors. Trajan possesses enough of the DNA that the silver affects him." He sauntered forward, kicking his son in the ribcage to prove his point.

The captain moaned softly but didn't wake.

"See. Alive." There was no remorse in Vulcan's eyes, just cold calculation. He reminded me of a vulture right before it swoops onto a carcass. "He won't be unconscious for long. Trajan and I possess excellent healing abilities. The moon awakens us." He trained the gun on Jad again, only this time the barrel was aimed at the captain's head. "This is my final warning, Zaya. If you defy me again, I will shoot—only this time it will be with the intention to kill."

"You'd murder your son?" I shook my head in bewilderment. My heart sank like a stone. It struck me that Vulcan was far too composed for a situation like this. How many people had he threatened in the past? How many family members had he sacrificed to see his objective through?

He stormed toward me and slapped my face so hard it caused my neck to twist painfully. His fingers sank into my arm. "You will do as I say." He dragged me onto my feet, pulling me to the sarcophagus. My head swam. I fought to keep the grogginess away, but clouds of shock churned in my mind, making my movements sluggish.

Vulcan squeezed my fingers around the red serpent dagger. His breath was hot in my ear. "Stab the casket."

My courage splintered. Larthalgule's magic pulsed in my hand as though it were a living, breathing entity. This was power I'd never felt before—ancient, uncontained, dark.

The stench of Jad's blood hung in the air, reminding me time was critical. The moon might heal him, but I didn't think it would compensate for the blood he'd lost. If he woke, he'd be weak.

I will not let you die, Jad.

I fixed the blade above the keyhole.

Vulcan's voice cracked like a whip. "Do it."

Trembling, I drove the Larthalgule blade down. Vulcan had said the dagger was a key. I'd thought he'd meant that figuratively. I was wrong. Sharp metallic scrapes resonated deep in the sarcophagus. The lid lifted like a jewellery box about to reveal riches inside, powered by rusty gadgets and clogs. I closed my eyes, waiting for my soul to be ripped out of my body, to be consumed into the blade and transferred into energy and life for Morgomoth to take. But for the longest moment, nothing happened.

I peeked an eye open. Shock pounded through me. The coffin was empty.

But I heard Morgomoth's voice, deep and powerful through the cavern.

How is this possible?

The lieutenant's face blanked at the sight of the vacant sarcophagus. I shrank back in alarm, waiting for his eruption of violence. Instead, he tilted his head to the splintered ceiling and laughed. "I should have known the council would lie. They've had him locked away up there for years."

His voice rolled through my head in a slur.

"Locked away up there for years"?

What was I missing?

Vulcan slammed the lid and kicked the sarcophagus with aggressive strength, his boot denting the incredible marble. He was that strong.

A memory stirred. Lunette's voice hovered through my mind. *"The cave beneath the Asrath Cliffs… that's where it waits. That's where you'll find the dagger to pierce his flesh. The blade has been lost so long."*

I tried to make sense of her words. *"That's where it waits."* Not where Morgomoth waits. Lunette hadn't been referring to the ruler of the ULD. She'd meant the blade. But Larthalgule returned life. Morgomoth had to die, not be brought back.

My eyes settled on Neathror. The dagger's onyx gems gleamed like black snake sails. The clues ground together in my head. All magic was balanced. It made sense that Larthalgule would have a sister blade that destroyed life rather than returned it. That was what Lunette had wanted—for me to find Neathror and bring an end to Morgomoth and the ULD. This hadn't been about Larthalgule at all.

But where was Morgomoth's body?

Vulcan assessed me with his black eyes, still fuelled by obsession. "Time to go, Zaya."

Every muscle in my body coiled. "What?"

"That tower overlooking the dam supplies power to all the Athnik region. It would take an immense amount of magical energy to convert the water into electricity. That's why Galvac is heavily guarded. That's where we're going."

It dawned on me what he was saying. The dam… the military base… the secrecy. Morgomoth was a comatose shell inside Galvac Tower. The council were using him like a battery to power their equipment, guaranteeing the wealth of the Athnik region and ultimately securing their own capital gain.

The hard lines around Vulcan's jaw made it appear as though his facial bones were trying to push out of his skin. "You see what they do? The council are manipulative, scheming liars. They hate Morgomoth. They're terrified of what he's capable of, and yet they use his magic for their own self-seeking interests. I wonder how much these council dignitaries are profiting from our fallen master. And here you are, fighting for them." He spat at my feet.

My mind somersaulted. I'd been so traumatised by fear and the threat Jad's life had been under that I'd allowed myself to become soft. This man had ruined his son. He'd destroyed his wife. He'd murdered thousands of innocents for the sake of racial cleansing.

Raw, unrestrained anger sparked through every vein in my body. I slammed my hand into his face with more strength than I knew I possessed. "I'm not going anywhere with you."

The strike caught him off guard, the storm in his eyes surpassed by surprise. But it didn't impede him. Vulcan moved so fast I didn't have time to react. He yanked the Larthalgule blade from the sarcophagus and locked his bony fingers around my wrist, dragging me toward the cavern's threshold. I shrieked hysterically and tried to pull free, but his grip was stronger than an iron gauntlet. "You are coming with me to the tower where you will perform the ritual. I have no time for silly girls and their squabbles—"

He froze. I followed his gaze, taking a moment to register what was before me. Jad was gone. Where the captain had collapsed, the space was now empty except for a pool of blood that looked as thick and dark as an oil slick.

Vulcan sheathed Larthalgule in his belt for safekeeping, then removed his cast-shooter, pivoting the gun around and peering warily into the shadows. "Where are you?" His voice ricocheted off every rock and cranny, an echo that didn't seem to end. For the first time, he sounded afraid.

A blur of movement slammed into him. I let out a shrill yell and leapt back as the force hurtled the lieutenant to the ground. The cast-shooter spun out of his hand, bouncing across the rocks until it was swallowed by a fissure, forever lost in the deep earth.

Vulcan hadn't been kidding when he said the moon would revive Jad. The captain stood over his father, his eyes blazing, hands balled into fists. He was still deathly pale, which made me think this new lease on life wasn't permanent, only energy borrowed from the moon. Jad looked at his father as though he wanted to punch a hole straight between the lieutenant's eyes.

Both men ran toward each other, striking with their fists, pounding into heads, shoulders, and chests. I watched their skilful manoeuvres with amazement, stunned anyone could move that fast. They were almost graceful in the way they fought, dodging and exchanging blows, each movement like a choreographed dance.

My head caught up with me. I had to help Jad. He might have strength now, but there was no denying he was seriously injured. He grimaced each time he received a hit to the shoulder, his cry causing my own heart to beat like a trip hammer.

Where was Jad's cast-shooter? Where had he dropped it when he fell?

I searched the ground, trying hard not to be distracted by the grunts and groans as the battle raged on. I located the weapon just a few metres short of the stairwell and darted to retrieve it.

That was when things turned really bad.

A high-pitched whistling rose over the cacophony, a noise I was infinitely familiar with. Back when Gosheniene had been targeted by aerial raids, that sound had chilled me to the core. I turned to Jad at the exact moment he heard it. For the briefest instant, there was a gush of air like a tyre blowout, followed by the entire cavern ripping apart. The bomb had opened a hole in the cliff face, the conflagration sending rippling vibrations through the earth. Rocks popped up like busted floorboards. Large stones rained down. Everywhere I turned there was crumbling debris and shattered earth.

The force of the explosion knocked Jad and his father to the ground. The bedrock collapsed around them, showering the pair in dust. Vulcan was screaming. Larthalgule had tumbled from his belt. The constant quakes in the earth sent the blade hurtling down a rupture in the ground. His advantage in this game was over. He'd lost the blade.

Neathror.

I had to get it before it too was devoured by the earth.

"Zaya. Run." Jad was on his feet now. He pointed toward the stairs. The dust made it difficult to see, but I knew from the ongoing booms and splintering cracks that the steps were only moments from collapsing into the ocean. The captain was closer. He'd reach them. But if I didn't time this right, I'd plummet with the rest of the temple into the sea. So naturally I turned the opposite direction and sprinted toward the sarcophagus.

"What are you doing?" The fear in the captain's voice nearly brought me to a halt, but if there was any chance of destroying Morgomoth for good, I had to get the Neathror blade.

Dust showered the coffin. It was no longer an object of beauty but now resembled an artefact exhumed from centuries of burial. The ground split dangerously around it. I tore the Neathror blade free at the same time the earth collapsed beneath the sarcophagus. The casket crashed into the boulders below, splintering into thousands of tiny pieces, lost into the yawning hole.

I crawled backward from the edge, Neathror safe in my hot grasp. It was beautiful, magnificent, a work of art. I couldn't believe I had thought it dull in comparison to its sister blade.

"Zaya." Jad's voice sounded desperate.

It triggered an instinctive response in me. I tucked Neathror in my belt and dashed toward him. The ground was warped and uneven, but I managed to jump between the growing rifts. I was only a few metres from the captain when something hard locked around my arm.

"That blade is mine," a mirthless voice whispered in my ear.

I turned to find Vulcan standing behind me.

CHAPTER FIFTY-THREE

The cold contempt in Vulcan's eyes slashed deeper than razors.

"Mine," he said with every intention of snatching the blade from my belt. He must have guessed what I'd intended to do with it.

I kneed him in the stomach, satisfied by his small "Oomph" of pain. Fighting with Jad had weakened him. We were now an even match. A fierce battle cry tore from his throat as he charged for me. I dodged the targeted blow and finished my assault with a vicious punch to the face, sending him sprawling backward.

Maybe it was the force of that impact or fate finally siding with me, but the ground fractured beneath him into unstable fragments. He was tossed over the edge, fingers clawing into the dirt to prevent him falling, his feet kicking above the long drop to nowhere.

"Who is your spy?" I cried, realising this was my last chance for answers.

A toxic smile spread over his face. "You'll never reach the tower. This isn't the end. Casters like my son and I don't die easily. We are more like gods than casters."

My mouth tasted dry. "Who is it?"

The cunning grin never left Vulcan's mouth. "My secret."

The ground gave a final shudder, breaking apart. Vulcan was swallowed by the gaping hole, lost to the murky void below.

If watching his father fall to his death affected him, Jad didn't show it. The captain was at my side in an instant, grabbing my arm and forcing me to run. We dodged tumbling rock and pelting stone. Our cavern resembled a million jigsaw pieces crumbling apart. We dashed past the entrance just as it cascaded in a mound of rubble. Ahead, the passage was barricaded by large chunks of stone. To our left, the stairs dropped like dominos into the sea. The entire cliff face was collapsing.

Jad squeezed my fingers. "This way. There's a manhole up ahead."

We ascended the stairs to our right, each step plummeting behind us, sending up waves of grime and filth. We reached the top and entered a small alcove. I had to hold in a weak cheer when I came across the rungs that led to the manhole in the ceiling.

"Is this how you entered the temple?" I hoisted myself onto the ladder. It still intrigued me how the captain had known where I was.

"Yes." Jad climbed behind me. His movement was slow, his breathing sawing up and down from sheer exertion. A chill scraped up my spine. He was weak. The injury was taking its toll.

I need to get him to the moonlight.

But that proved impossible when I climbed to the surface—right into the heart of Galvac's battle. Both the dissent rebels and the Haxsan Guard hacked at each other with blades, hurling tomahawks into skulls, swinging maces into arms and legs. No matter where I turned, there was violence and carnage. Cast-shooters ripped holes into flesh. Bombs rained down, polluting the landscape with fire and smoke, the air rank with the stench of blood and death.

This part of the Asrath peninsula resembled nothing of what I'd seen on the carrier-hornet. The scenery had changed drastically. Snow fell in torrents, the ground soaked in slush—most of it stained red from blood. The reservoir was frozen, which meant Melvina was close. It wouldn't take her long to figure out Vulcan had failed. I had to get to the tower before that happened.

Jad made slow, painful progress out of the manhole. The air was thick with smoke and blotted out the moon. I slipped an arm around the captain and let him lean his weight on me. Running was out of the question. He was too injured. We staggered down the slope, my heart rate increasing from the deafening booms of gunfire. More of Jad's weight pressed into my body with each footfall, forcing me to stumble. His height didn't help either.

I tried to think rationally. Jad needed medical help, but this was a war zone. The makeshift hospital would be stationed away from the fighting. The only aid I'd find out here would be the field medics, and judging by the number of corpses with red crosses on their armbands, that was unlikely. I felt dizzy, unprepared for this calamity. Another bomb fell somewhere close, sending a geyser of snow over us.

The tower, Zaya. Get to the tower.

Neither the ULD nor the Haxsan Guard bombed the edifice. If the tower fell, the dam would collapse, and the mega-size tsunami that would result would wipe everything out. Hot tears ran down my cheeks, but I used what energy I had left to help Jad down the incline. His eyes were closed. He moaned something that sounded like "Leave me," but no way was I abandoning him.

"Just a little farther," I promised. I kept repeating the words, more for my sake than his.

His head drooped. The veins in his neck strained against his sweaty skin. My heart wanted to believe I could get him to safety, but my head was plagued with doubt. I hung on to his limp body and pushed the uncertainty aside. If I had to drag him to the tower, then so be it.

Smoke cleared ahead, the dam's concrete arch in sight. The bridge that ran above it was only a few metres away.

We're going to make it.

A shell hit behind us. The explosion ripped the air with violent shock waves, pitching us onto the bridge with fury. I coughed, heat scorching my throat. I wanted to curl into a ball and give in, but I needed to push my suffering aside and be strong for Jad. I slapped his cheek, determined he would wake.

"Zaya?" His feeble voice caused my own tongue to lock up.

I pulled back his coat and checked the wound. Silvery veins streaked across his shoulder like tangled cobwebs. I had to quell the wave of nausea inside me. This wasn't your average gunshot wound. The silver bullet had cursed him somehow. Even if I'd found a field medic, I doubted they'd know what to do.

"Zaya… leave." Jad spoke so softly I had to strain to hear him.

I shook my head.

Even though his face was battered by bruises, he smiled. "That blade you took… will it stop Morgomoth?"

I sniffed weakly. "I think so."

"Then find his body and kill him. The ULD will have nothing to fight for."

My heart was in turmoil. He was right. A swift slice into Morgomoth's heart would end the battle at Galvac. A hot, sickly taste slipped down my throat. Was leaving Jad the right thing to do?

His bloodshot eyes lingered on mine. "You've brought me this far. I have lycanthor blood. Moonlight will heal me."

Maybe the wound had brought on a fever and he was deluding himself. Heal? He looked like he'd been dragged to the depths of hell and torn open by demons. Healing didn't seem possible.

He blinked. He was fading fast. "Help will come to you… I promise."

Before I could ask what he meant, the taut lines around his face softened. He closed his eyes, the same way a body slackened after the final breath. His chest no longer rose and fell. He was utterly still.

"Jad." I shook him, but there was no response. I stroked his damp hair off his face and brushed away the dirt. It struck me how young he looked. So much life and opportunity had waited ahead of him, and it had been snatched away with a single gunshot. I fell into a place beyond terror, beyond anguish, beyond hope and faith—a realisation that there was nothing I could do to save him. Thick layers of ash fell onto his face and shoulders, as though nature had taken it upon herself to bury him. I knelt forward and sealed the briefest kiss on Jad's lips, a final goodbye. His lips were rough and cracked, but to me they were perfect.

With a weight that felt like an anchor holding my heart, I climbed to my feet and headed for the tower.

CHAPTER FIFTY-FOUR

Eternity. That was how long I ran across the bridge—at least, that was what it seemed. My boots slapped the frosty stone, splattering sleet up my legs. Wet, heavy snow pelted me like fists, the handrails icing over. I sensed rather than knew that Melvina was close. The awareness pestered me like an uncontrollable itch.

I reached the massive tower. It had to be three hundred metres high at least, a weird but incredible mix of neofuturistic and gothic revival. The doors were sealed. I swore at my terrible stroke of bad luck. There was no way I was getting through that industrial-strength metal. A single retina scanner was built by the door, providing access to authorised personnel only. My senses went on high alert, a warning that tingled up my spine and over my scalp. It was strange that the tower wasn't heavily guarded.

I skirted around the building and searched for another way in. That was when I spotted the service ladder drilled into the wall. It must have been for construction workers and labourers. It reached up into the storm, the tower's observation deck lost in the dark roiling clouds.

I fixed my boot onto the first rung and hoisted myself up. I made easy work of it at first, but about halfway up the tower, the muscles in my arms and legs protested from exhaustion. The fierce winds intensified, and my fingers swelled and ached from cold. Whenever I looked down, my vision swayed in and out of focus. I'd never been afraid of heights until now. One foot in the wrong place would result in me becoming a splattered mess on the spillway below.

I shoved away the depressing thought. *Concentrate on the rungs. Don't look down. Do this for Jad.*

I hooked my fingers over the metal rungs and strained my shoulders, pulling and climbing until I found traction, driving away the sounds of death and despair that raged in the battle below. I didn't let my thoughts settle on anything else until I arrived at a metal hatch that was mercifully unlocked. I forced it open, levered myself up…

And entered a whole world of trouble.

The upper observatory was a wide open glass skywalk, complete with a 360-degree view of the surrounding landscape, only every surface was enveloped in thin sheets of ice, the scenery impossible to see. In the floor lay a large shaft that travelled deep into the tower, filled with various mechanisms, pulleys, and gadgets—each implemented by magical means to convert water into hydroelectric power—only now the equipment was frozen. Ripples of light glistened off the ice. It made the tower's interior appear eerily like it was inside a frozen sea cave.

Melvina's here.

Having never retrieved Jad's cast-shooter from the temple, I had no weapon save for the Neathror blade. I dug it out of my belt, ready to stab anything that jumped out at me. Taking a deep breath, I approached the shaft. Gantries had been placed among the equipment for the workers, criss-crossing from wall to wall. At the end of the first gantry, a cold vapour rose from a glass tank filled with murky water.

No!

Not water. Formaldehyde. The creature inside the glass dome did not resemble any living specimen from this Earth. It was alien, mutated, and slimy, like a foetus preserved in a glass jar. Catheters and tubes, some of them as thick as jumper wires, protruded from the creature's body, connected to various instruments in the tower.

"Zaya," a voice boomed in my head, high-pitched and scratchy.

An internal scream wreaked havoc in my brain.

The creature was Morgomoth.

Vulcan's suspicion had been correct. The council was using Morgomoth's magic like a battery to generate power.

My fingers tightened on Neathror, my fingers slick with sweat. I descended the metal stairwell onto the gantry, determined to end this. The blade's power strengthened, throbbing like a disembodied heart in my grasp. I think it sensed a monster was present.

A flicker of black flashed at the corner of my eyes. I spun around and sliced Neathror through the air. But I wasn't fast enough. Melvina struck her fist across my face, the blow knocking me over the rail. I toppled and hit the gantry below, a sound like branches cracking exploding within me. Pain coursed through my upper left side. I knew some of my ribs were broken.

Melvina's face emerged over the railing above. She looked worse than she had at Essida. Inky dark veins bulged under her pasty skin, which was the colour of white stone. The frozen needles that made up her crown had been chipped or hacked off. I'd met only three people with eyes as dark as midnight. Jad's had shone with valour, Vulcan's with lethality, but the charcoal pools that made up Melvina's eyes were filled with murderous intent. She knew Vulcan's scheme had failed. She knew what I was here to do. And she was determined to finish me.

Melvina leapt from the railing. One foot landed effortlessly on the gantry, the other pressed onto my cracked ribs, pinning me in place. I screamed. Her foot was ice cold.

She tilted her head to look at me. "Hello, little Wayward. What blade is that you have in your hot little hand, I wonder?"

I tried to wriggle out from the crushing weight of her foot, but she only applied more force. A world of pain consumed my chest. "It's not Larthalgule. That blade is gone. It's over." I'd wanted to sound strong, but my voice shook.

She laughed, the sound like cracking ice. She took out a red-hilted blade from her black robes and brought it close to my face.

I shook with fury and fear. She had Larthalgule. "How—"

Enormous, ungainly wings unfurled from her back. They were leathery and thick, tipped with ice.

What the hell is she?

Melvina bared her teeth in a vicious smile, her black eyes full of victory. "I caught Larthalgule when it fell into the earth. I knew Vulcan would underestimate your abilities. It's time to complete the ritual, Zaya." Her talon-like fingers clasped my neck, her wings sending fierce ripples through the air as she lifted me off the gantry, hovering higher and higher. I kicked and clawed at her hands, but it was useless. The woman was harder than rock.

Our feet planted on the gantry above—the one I'd fallen from. She wrenched me to the tank where Morgomoth's comatose shell waited. "You will resurrect him," she cried in a deep, sonorous voice.

All I could think about was putting Neathror in her gut. My entire body tensed as I stabbed the black dagger into her side, right to the hilt. She howled like a wolf crying up to the moon, dropping me in an instant. There was no pain in her eyes when she looked at me, just outrage that I dared to injure her. I crawled backward, every muscle in my body screaming from the throbbing ache that consumed it.

Melvina tore the blade out with a wet popping sound that made me want to gag. Black liquid that wasn't quite blood spilled out. What the hell had those twisted medical experiments done to her? There was nothing left about Melvina that was caster. The black-veined woman was pure animalistic monster. She inspected Neathror with bored eyes and tossed it aside. It landed on the upper observatory, out of reach.

"Did you think that would kill me, little Wayward?" She wagged a finger at me as she approached in a bleeding, sloppy mess.

Stupid. Stupid. Stupid.

The first rule cadets learnt was that monsters could only be taken out by a single stab to the heart, and even then, the blade had to be enchanted with seriously powerful spells. Why hadn't I aimed for her chest?

Melvina moved fast, swifter than lightning. She caught me by the arm and flung me with a hammer throw onto the tank. Only half of me made it over. My feet kicked against the glass, my upper body hanging precariously over the water. The rail dug into my back. My poor ribcage cracked. I wondered how the bones weren't protruding out of my sides.

Melvina hovered above me, her wings beating cold undulations of air across my skin. Her face pulled back into a vindictive smile, her teeth stark white against her black lips. "If you will not resurrect him, then I will spill your blood for Morgomoth to drink. His strength will not resume fully, but in time, his magic will return and he will awaken."

She snapped my head back by my hair to expose my neck, pressing Larthalgule beneath my jaw.

This was it. She had one hand on Larthalgule, the other restraining my head. All she had to do was slice a gash in my neck and spill my blood into the tank. I squeezed my eyes shut, giving in to the inevitable.

There was sound like a meat cleaver hitting flesh. Melvina screamed.

I looked up to see the Neathror blade planted firmly through her palm. The blade protruded out the back of her hand, soaked in blood. She had dropped Larthalgule. It must have been at the bottom of the tank by now. Straining my neck to see, I blinked back astonishment. Jad stood on the observatory, his arm still raised. He must have found Neathror and flung it with enough strength that it had wedged itself into Melvina's hand.

The stunned moment passed. Using every ounce of strength I possessed, I threw Melvina off me, then tugged Neathror free from her hand and plunged the dagger into her chest. Her eyes bulged in surprise before real fear emerged. This was no normal blade I'd stabbed her with, and she knew it. The strange oil-like substance pooled from her wound, bubbling and steaming hot. She dropped onto the gantry, moans of anguish tearing from her throat. Her skin was… melting. It dripped onto the floor in fat puddles. I forced myself to watch. Perhaps Lunette, Adaline, and the wraiths could move on to a better place now that their murderer had been brought to justice. Melvina's joints went next, her arms and legs flopping around like fish out of water, writhing and squirming to find the sea. With a final high-pitched scream that shattered the ice around us, her bones snapped apart, her body liquefying into a sick black pool.

A thankful sob ripped through me. The black-veined woman could no longer haunt, terrify, or hurt me. I was free of her.

Good riddance.

My gaze flicked back to the observatory. I hardly dared breathe. Surely this was an illusion, a trick conjured to taunt me? But it was real. Red rays of moonlight spilled through the glass observatory, illuminating Jad. He struggled down the stairs onto the gantry. Relief shone in his eyes, but from the way he hunched his shoulder as he moved toward me, he was far from recovery. He'd promised help would arrive. I hadn't realised he'd been referring to himself. Willpower was truly the captain's greatest weapon.

He gripped the handrail, probably to stop himself from slumping onto the floor. A bolt of panic rushed through me. The only way he could have gotten up here was by the service ladder. He'd used too much energy.

"What are you waiting for?" he shouted. His eyes travelled beyond me to the tank. "Kill Morgomoth. Then it's over."

I was torn between wanting to run to the captain and finishing what I came here to do. The latter won the vicious tug of war. I tore Neathror up from the gooey mess that had been Melvina and approached the vat of embalming fluid.

All I had to do was break the tank and stab Morgomoth in the chest. I'd killed one monster tonight. I could kill two.

I tightened my grasp on the hilt. I had the blade ready… and then I heard the whistle.

Confusion reflected on Jad's face. I think we both registered what was about to happen at the same time. Despite the strain he was under, he ran toward me. But it was too late. The missile hit its target. The observatory exploded, a shower of flames projecting stone and steel in a multitude of directions. The force catapulted me off my feet. My back hit the glass tank. I sagged to the ground, choking on hot air.

Jad! Where is he?

I couldn't see anything in the thick swirl of smoke. The ceiling had been ripped open, the blood moon clear in the tainted sky. Before me, the gantry had been split in two, the gap impossible for anyone to jump. Jad was slumped on the other side, his body twisted at an odd angle, his arm and head hanging precariously over the edge. I crawled through stone and debris toward him, trying hard not to gag from the smoke inhalation. I reached for his hand, but it was useless. The gap that divided us was too large.

"Jad. Jad!"

He didn't answer.

I searched the wreckage around me, trying to find something I could use to prod him with. The staircase on his side of the gantry was a smouldering ruin. When he woke, Jad was going to have to find a way across the shaft so we could leave this place together. Based on where the missile had fallen, I was confident the service ladder outside the tower hadn't been destroyed, but getting down it would be an issue I'd have to resolve later. Right now, I needed to wake Jad from his semiconscious state.

Rock continued to dislodge from the gaping ceiling. A steel beam hung perilously from what was left of the roof. Each time stone, plaster, and dust were displaced, the beam would tilt a little more. If it fell, it would take out the rest of the gantry Jad rested on.

"Jad. Please. Wake up."

Something sticky worked its way into my throat—the taste of despair.

"Jad. Jad!"

No response.

But there's moonlight, damn it. Why won't he wake?

A deep groan reverberated above, the ceiling becoming as supple as wax. The steel beam hurtled down. I screamed so loud, my anguish pierced my own ears with unrelenting force. The beam smashed the gantry, rock, and stone projected in a cloud of white dust. Jad was tossed down the cavernous shaft. Gravity was relentless with its pull, spinning him rapidly among the tumbling debris. A moment later, he disappeared in the dark.

Hot tears poured down my face. For a long time, I couldn't move. Time hung suspended, the horror of what had occurred spanning for what seemed like eons.

I'd lost him. I'd failed. He was gone.

The pain in my chest burned. I'd always prided myself on my resolve, but how could anyone keep going after this? After everything Jad and I had overcome, after everything we'd achieved, I'd lost him.

Dizziness swept across my eyes. Pain finally pulled me under.

CHAPTER FIFTY-FIVE

My vision was strange, sound distant. I blinked, but everything remained a blur.

This must be death.

Grief and anguish had numbed the pain, or maybe I was so paralysed by shock, my brain could no longer register it. It took my eyes a minute to adjust to the intense light, which glared brighter than the sun. Something crackled near me. Fire! The tower was on fire. Flames licked the floor, unrolling like a red carpet. Heat drenched my face in sweat, the ash raining down from a plume of smoke in the ceiling.

At first, I mistook the *clap clap clap* for my rapid pulse pounding in my head but soon recognised it as the distant drone of a motor. Someone called my name, but it sounded like they were a million miles away. I must have blacked out again, because a second later my neck was probed for a pulse.

"She's alive." The voice sounded like it was spoken from the bottom of a well.

I managed to pry my eyes open. A familiar face came into view. Marek brushed some of the ash from my hair. "We have to go now. General Kravis ordered another missile to hit the tower. Can you walk?"

A slurred blubbering noise passed my lips. I couldn't get my words out. Thoughts wouldn't string together in my mind.

Marek plucked me off the ground and popped my arm around his shoulder. The white glare of a spotlight darted over us. I sucked in a breath, relieved to see a carrier-hornet. Marek half carried, half dragged me across the gantry to the stairs. Concrete blocks, metal sheeting, and timber obstructed our path, forcing us to take a less direct route. The tower didn't need a missile to take it down. Fire was doing fine on its own.

Marek kept repeating encouraging words to keep me awake, but his voice was too frantic to understand. The one thing I did get was "Jad made me... promise... retrieve you."

It cut a new slice of pain into my torment.

"Help will come to you... I promise."

That was what Jad had told me. But he'd never been referring to himself. He'd meant Marek.

We reached the observation deck, the floor burnt and unrecognisable. The sergeant nudged me toward the carrier-hornet. It coasted above the ruins, its huge rotor blades churning smoke, causing hot air to sting my wet cheeks. The aircraft's loading ramp was lowered. The hornet drew near but stopped short two metres. The soldiers on board must not have wanted to risk the inferno. I didn't blame them. The fires had grown to a roar, tendrils reaching into the night, as though the flames intended to burn every star in the sky. If the fire didn't get the carrier-hornet, the shooting sparks would. Marek and I were going to have to jump.

Through the smoke, I caught brief glimpses of soldiers waving their arms, signalling us to hurry. When I glanced over my shoulder, I understood why. Above the sea, a formation of fire-crusaders circled toward the tower. They resembled eagles soaring across the sky. I estimated we had about ten seconds before they released their bombs.

Marek swore under his breath. "Jump! Now!"

We leapt into the heavy smoke, caught in that bizarre moment where neither gravity nor physics was able to hold us. I landed hard on the metal surface of the ramp. I wondered if my cracked ribs would burst out of my skin for real this time. Marek rolled somewhere to my right, hidden by haze. When he re-emerged, he was sprawled face down on the ramp, his moan the only indication he was alive.

A soldier grappled my arms and dragged me from the edge. "Don't look. It'll make it worse."

Taking that advice would have been the sensible thing to do, but I slapped his hands away and looked. The carrier-hornet had travelled a fair distance from the tower, but I knew from the quick calculation in my head that it wouldn't be enough. The fire-crusaders spiralled around the structure, strategically releasing their bombs. For a moment, the entire skyline appeared cast with dazzling light before the entire tower erupted into a torrent of fire. The shock wave tossed me backward, the carrier-hornet rocked by turbulence. Someone cried out behind me, but it was the sound of thousands of people screaming on the land below that ripped me apart. The ruined edifice smashed Galvac's spillway into fragments. There was nothing to prevent the fast-moving ocean surge from taking its revenge now. A massive wave crested the reservoir. It topped trees, devoured banks, and sent mudslides down the valley, flattening everything in its path. The worst sight was the people. They were like ants wiped out by heavy rains. Galvac was their headstone now, water and sludge their tomb.

What has General Kravis done?

I was certain he'd known Morgomoth was in the tower, he and others who worked for the council. Had bombing the edifice been a last-ditch effort to thwart a resurrection or to destroy evidence of an inconvenient truth?

I dug the heels of my hands into my eyes. I'd wanted to put an end to the battle at Galvac. Instead, my actions had brought an end to lives. I cried until my eyes couldn't cry any longer. When exhaustion finally pulled me under, I willingly submitted to the dark.

CHAPTER FIFTY-SIX

Three days. That was how long doctors kept me in an induced coma while healing charms mended my broken ribs and collarbone. I'd undergone surgery twice to remove a shred of metal lodged above my hip. I didn't have any recollection of the metal stabbing me, but I had an impressive scar to prove it.

They say that moments of weakness are what make us stronger. That time heals all wounds. But I had no idea how I could regain my strength after this. Bedridden in Tarahik's recovery ward, I travelled between hallucination and dreams. I wanted everything that had occurred to be a nightmare.

During the day, I'd watch the doctors attend to the patients. Once casters started to mend, a normalcy descended on the people around me. It seemed incredible that the world had moved on—that people could smile and laugh while I was shadowed by sorrow and grief.

After a week of lamenting in my bed, someone whose name I couldn't remember came to assess my mental health. Whatever I said or didn't say obviously hadn't inspired much confidence, because after a heavily sedated sleep, I woke up in a private recovery room. The furniture was minimal, the bed, side table, and chair embedded into the floor. The bathroom was made entirely of plastic—plastic bathtub, plastic cabinets, plastic handrail. Even a hologram had replaced the mirror—not that I took much pleasure in looking at myself.

At first, I found the bathroom weird. It wasn't until I took a shower that evening and failed to find a razor to shave my legs—only waxing strips in the bottom drawer—that I realised what this place was. There was absolutely nothing in the recovery room that could be used to cause self-harm. The doctors had put me on suicide watch.

Most evenings I was sleep deprived and easily agitated. I only slept when the doctors sedated me with powerful asith potions, but they brought on nightmares that were vivid and recurring. In them, I watched Jad plunge down Galvac Tower in what seemed like slow motion, prolonging every agonising second. The yawning hole would burst forth like the jaws of a shark, swallowing me into its abyss too. But instead of falling into darkness the way Jad did, I'd plummet into freezing water, surrounded by the faces of ghostly soldiers bathed in terrible light, each struggling to breathe, reliving the horror of drowning from the ruptured dam.

I'd wake bathed in sweat and shivering, too afraid to close my eyes again. When the dreams became too much, I refused potions. Eventually the doctors chemically induced my sleep through the ventilation system, which was clever. I could stop eating, but I couldn't stop breathing. Lainie and Talina had requested to see me several times, but I wouldn't allow them to witness the miserable sight. I was cut off, flat, detached. I had no interest in the outside world.

It wasn't until I woke from one of my nightmares early one morning that I was met by a familiar and unwelcome face. I groaned inwardly.

Commander Macaslan sat perched on the chair beside my bed, her long skirt falling around her ankles. She'd accumulated several wrinkles around her eyes and mouth since I'd seen her last. Her expression reflected mixed emotions when she saw my face. "Zaya, this behaviour cannot go on. There is a facility in Denveitch that could be beneficial in—"

"Don't," I interrupted. "I'm not going anywhere… and I'm not in the mood for a lecture right now." I pulled my blanket up, shielding myself in a protected canopy.

But the commander tore it down. "You can't stay in this room forever. Captain Arden's death has affected us all. I know as your drill instructor the pair of you grew close, but this is not the way he would want to see you end up."

I pressed my hands into my eyes, not wishing the commander to witness my tears, but they trickled past my fingers, dripping down my chin. I was a sobbing mess. I couldn't prevent the sorrow pouring out. It hurt too much to deter it.

To her credit, Macaslan didn't admonish me. She stayed seated, letting my weak moment pass. "There will be a memorial tomorrow for Captain Arden. I think you should attend. It's logical to be angry, but it isn't healthy to remain so."

I fixed her with a powerful glare. "What am I meant to move on to? General Kravis murdered thousands of soldiers. Am I supposed to forget that happened? I can't pretend to be a cadet anymore, not when I want to smash a tomahawk in the general's head."

Actually, since the night of the blood moon, the Infinite Eye branded in my right hand had started to fade, peeling where new skin grew to replace it. Every day, it healed a bit more. I had deliberately defied both the council and the ULD that night. Had my decision somehow tarnished the Infinite Eye's power over me?

The commander saw my hand but didn't comment.

A look of determination spread over her face. "It will be easier if we move you to Denveitch Mental Hospital for appropriate treatment. It will give you time to heal and take you away from Kravis's interest. Senator Kerr has made all the arrangements."

Ice fastened around my heart. "Interest?"

Macaslan dropped her gaze. Reservation flashed across her face. "The general is aware the ULD planned a resurrection ritual in the tower. It's why he ordered Galvac to be destroyed. We have not been as careful as we should have. Kravis suspects you, but as you weren't officially deployed to Galvac, there is no record to support this. But it won't be long till he finds the evidence he needs."

My body went stiff with agitation. "Kravis knew what that tower really was, didn't he?"

Macaslan didn't answer.

Despite the pain in my ribcage, I levelled forward into sitting. "Did you know?"

Her gaze dropped to the floor. "You will have to be more specific."

"Did you know the council kept Morgomoth bound in sleep? That they used his power for their own interests?" My voice trembled and didn't sound like my own. It was full of accusation and anger.

Lines of exhaustion crept around the commander's eyes. "Senator Kerr suspected it, but information was so hard to obtain, we couldn't get a clear understanding of where the council were keeping Morgomoth."

"And you didn't think to tell me any of this?"

"You are far too headstrong, disobedient, and impulsive. I feared if you knew the entire truth, you'd march straight up to the general and put a spear through his chest. He has his own interests in all of this."

"And would killing him have been such a bad thing?"

She eyed me darkly. "Yes, because the last thing we need right now is for you to be hauled off to prison."

"If I'd known all the details… Jad might be alive." My voice was thick and clogged with tears. What-if scenarios kept spinning through my mind.

"And if he were alive, he'd be with Indree, not you."

Her words were a bullet in the gut. My stomach heaved. I hadn't thought my feelings were so transparent.

"That's what you must understand," the commander continued with little empathy. "Captain Arden was not yours to lose. Grieve for him, yes. Go to the memorial and say your farewell, but then move on."

Irritation bubbled through my veins like boiling water. "Do you have no feelings at all?"

A dangerous glint lit her eyes. "More than you or any of your peers could have the intelligence to understand. I have seen worse, been subjected to worse, and done worse things than you could imagine. Do not talk to me of feelings. I lost a sister. Her betrayal destroyed my family. I know perfectly well how hard it can be to move on, but I learnt to do it. And you will too." She stood and moved effortlessly to the door. "You leave in three days for Denveitch."

I swallowed back the burning in my throat. "I don't know how to move on."

Her mouth lifted at the corners, not quite a smile. "You move on with courage, Miss Wayward. Something you do not lack."

She shut the door gently behind her.

For a long time, I remained in my bed fuming, not because I was mortified by the commander's advice and everything she'd alluded to but because she was right. I'd morphed into a shadow of my former self, existing in the world but no longer playing a part in it. When I thought of Jad, of everyone who'd lost their lives at Galvac, I knew living as a miserable entity on this Earth was not only selfish but disrespectful to what they'd sacrificed.

That night, I resolved to get better and—though I didn't get any joy out of it—ate a full meal. When Dr Glatz asked later if Talina and Lainie might see me, I allowed it. Talina blanched when she entered the room. I must have been more of a sight than she'd expected, but she soon rolled onto my bed, cheerful and relating gossip like we were at a slumber party and not in the middle of a psychiatric ward. Lainie sat in the chair and produced a giant bag of lollies to share. The three of us hadn't parted on the friendliest of terms—another reason why I'd put off seeing them—but absence had set our differences aside.

We talked about the happenings and goings-on at Tarahik. There had been funerals, memorials, and services every day. Lainie and Talina both worked in the hospital, resting only when they could be spared. I questioned how they could be so positive and jovial when they looked so exhausted.

"It was hard at first," Talina admitted, "but people are starting to recover, and that makes everything worth it. Just the other day, I watched Private Davies take his first steps. He had a spinal injury. Doctors didn't think he'd walk again."

Lainie popped a lolly in her mouth. "And it hasn't all been doom and gloom. Sergeant Spiers was promoted to lieutenant. We went to the ceremony last night."

"Marek's a lieutenant?" For the first time in days, a genuine smile worked its way across my lips. I was honestly happy for him.

Lainie stood from her chair and settled onto the end of my bed. "He deserved it. Things have been tough for Marek. He and Captain Arden were close."

My good mood dissipated.

Talina's gaze shifted to me. "Not as tough as it has been for poor Indree. Did you know Indree and Captain Arden were an item? They were engaged!"

Engaged!

"It's so sad what happened," Talina continued. She dabbed at her eye. "The countess hasn't left her room since she found out. Her friends say she hasn't stopped crying, and she can't even bury Captain Arden because they never found a body. She's going to the memorial tomorrow."

I wished Talina would shut her mouth. She had no idea the pain she caused me. Selfish, vindictive Indree was the last person I wanted to think about. A monster-sized headache started to pound at the back of my eyes, my depression creeping back in.

Talina's eyebrows knitted together with worry. "Didn't you hear me?"

I flicked my gaze back to her. "What?"

She rolled her eyes. "I asked whether you had seen him yet."

I stared, not understanding.

Seen who?

Her face shrivelled into a grimace. "Captain Arden? It's just… we thought that with your talent… Captain Arden's soul… ghost… whatever you call it might have visited you."

Was she serious?

Anger overrode my patience. "Visit me to do what? Tell me he's found peace on the other side? Didn't you listen to anything I said at Weeping Hollow? Necromancy doesn't work like that."

Talina flinched. "I'm sorry. It was stupid. Forget I said anything."

Dr Glatz walked in then, announcing visiting hours were over. She couldn't have interrupted a more awkward situation. A hint of irritation slipped through her voice when my friends didn't immediately leave. "Girls. Out. Now."

She almost knocked Lainie off her feet as she pushed her out the doorway.

Talina glanced at me over her shoulder. She chewed her lip. "Will you be at the memorial tomorrow?"

I nodded. It was all I could manage.

Long after the lights had turned off for the evening, I sat in bed, sick and hot. I'd accepted Jad's death. I'd told myself he was gone. But Talina's words had filled me with hope. Perhaps there was a way to communicate with the captain and see him one last time. Maybe it would help me move on.

I shut my eyes and endeavoured to contact the spirit world.

Jad? Are you there?

Nothing.

I pictured his smile, his midnight black eyes, his wavy hair that curled rebelliously beneath his jaw.

Jad?

The room remained empty.

I burst into despairing tears.

CHAPTER FIFTY-SEVEN

Captain Arden's memorial was meant to take place in the west hall, a grand old room with stone facades and stained-glass windows, but the turnout was more than organisers expected, so the ceremony was relocated at the last minute to the auditorium. It pained me to see flags decorated with the Infinite Eye. Jad never believed in the council's symbol. It reminded me that no one in the hall really knew the captain. Not the officers, not the cadets, and certainly not the council dignitaries. They sat perched in the terraces like painted peacocks, dressed in the latest fashions and sipping from delicate champagne flutes. This was a funeral, not a frigging party. I couldn't breathe. The unfairness of it choked me. I hated them. I wanted to claw at each of their faces and make them suffer like I did.

Someone cleared their throat beside me.

I turned to see Talina. Her smile was timid, front teeth biting into her bottom lip. "I'm sorry about last night. What I said... it was thoughtless."

The tightness in my face softened. "Don't worry about it."

That was pretty much my way of saying *I'm sorry too*.

Lainie and Edric waited behind Talina. I'd never seen the pair so distant. Edric looked as though he'd prefer to be anywhere but here. After everything that had happened, I'd forgotten he too was troubled. His hair was unwashed, his face pale, the skin around his eyes hollow and cracked. He averted his eyes from Lainie, shifting to put more space between them. The worst thing about the entire aloofness between the pair was the way Lainie's face crumpled into despair. She reached for his hand, but Edric pulled away.

It was enough to bring her to tears. "I'll be right back," she whispered to us. She darted into the crowd with her head bowed. Edric didn't react. He moved away, losing himself in the throng.

I nudged Talina. "What was that about?"

I felt so disconnected from everything. It was like I'd woken from a long sleep.

Talina exhaled a sigh. "They broke up. Edric ended things a few days ago. He hasn't been right since Essida."

"I thought he was getting help for that?"

She shrugged. "I wouldn't know. He's been so distant. He refuses to talk to anyone... kind of like you."

Ouch.

I craned my neck, peering for Lainie in the crowd. "Why didn't she say anything last night?"

Talina watched me with a deepening frown. "Because last night was about you. We were there to keep you company." She smoothed back an unruly blonde curl behind her ear. "Promise me one thing. Please get better. There have already been too many others who've ended up like Edric. I don't want to see that happen with you. Lainie and I are your friends. Talk to us... let us help you while there's still time."

Still time?

I blinked at her in a daze.

She gave me a shaky smile. "I didn't get the chance to tell you last night. Lainie and I have been deployed to the Athnik region. After the dam collapsed, the entire landscape changed. There's no power. All the crops are underwater. Casters have lost their homes. There are too many sick and injured for the current Haxsan Guard responders to contend with. We leave in a few days. I don't know how long we'll be gone. Word is it could be a few months."

I glanced down at my feet, too afraid I'd cry if I looked at her. I'd pushed my friends away for days. Now they'd be gone for weeks. Why was life being so cruel?

"I'll get help," I promised. "The commander is sending me to Denveitch."

I couldn't end up like Edric, alive but just going through the motions. I had to heal and move on.

"Be careful out there," I warned her.

She had no idea what devastation she'd find in the Athnik region.

"We will." She took my hand and squeezed it. Her eyes travelled across the hall to the bathrooms. "I'm going to find Lainie. We'll both come and see you tonight, okay?"

I nodded. This time, I'd make more of an effort.

Talina left. She hadn't been absent long when a new visitor arrived.

Marek stood close, but his entire posture was stiff, his smile not reaching the corners of his lips. "Good to see you're here. I didn't think you would come. How are you holding up?" He was civil, but there was deep melancholy in his eyes.

"I'm fine," I lied. Discussing my recovery was not something I wanted to do. "I hear you're a lieutenant now. Shouldn't you be up in the terraces?"

He opened his mouth to say something, then thought better of it. "I prefer to be down here among Jad's true friends."

"But his fiancé is up there." My tone came out icier than intended.

It hadn't escaped my notice that Indree stood among the flashy dignitaries in a black cocktail dress more appropriate for clubbing. Her blonde hair hung down her back in thick curls. She kept dabbing at her heavily made-up eyes with a black handkerchief, but her cheeks weren't tear-stained like mine.

I tore my gaze away. "She's acting like she's his widow."

A widow on the prowl for her next husband, because between Indree's crocodile tears, I hadn't failed to notice how she examined the profile of every handsome man in the vicinity.

Marek tipped his head to watch Indree. I didn't miss the wounded look in his eyes. He didn't approve of her behaviour either. "This has been hard for her."

I flashed him a bold glare. "Jad never mentioned his engagement once. Doesn't that strike you as odd?"

If you loved someone, didn't you want the entire world to know about it?

Marek fixed his attention on me. "Jad was a private person."

"How long had they been together?"

Hearing the answer was only going to cause me pain, but I had to know, the same way a moth must go to the light.

Marek's eyes swept the crowd. I wondered if he was secretly looking for Talina. "Four years. But Jad and Indree had known each other longer. Indree and her father used to visit the orphanage where Jad and I were housed. Count Raminorf made considerable donations to the place. He sponsored us when we both signed up to join the Haxsan Guard. Indree liked Jad the moment she met him, but he wasn't interested in the beginning. I had to convince him that seeing her would be good for him. He was reluctant, but in the end, she made him happy." His smile faded. "Had he survived... he might have started a life with her in the Free Zones."

It was the last figurative slap I needed. The progress I'd made dissipated like a burst water balloon, leaving me hollow inside.

Marek inched closer. His voice was a whisper in my ear. "Jad made me promise to retrieve you from the tower. He put a tracker in your jacket when you were on the carrier-hornet. It was how I was able to find you."

My mind wandered back to that tragic day. The captain must have slipped the tracker into my pocket when he'd dragged me out of the sparrowhawk. Why had someone so charitable, worthy, and honest had to die?

Marek pressed his lips together. "I'm being sent to the Athnik region tomorrow. I want to do the right thing and help those in need, but I know Jad would have wanted me to take care of Indree. Would you keep an eye on her? I think she'd find comfort in your friendship."

My cheeks coloured.

Friends with Indree?

I was more likely to smother her in her sleep.

I smiled and told Marek I'd do my best to help Indree, now eternally grateful Macaslan was sending me to Denveitch. The hospital was appealing compared to the alternative.

The lieutenant dipped his head, his eyes curious and alert. "Why were you and Jad in that tower? I've been thinking about it, and it doesn't make sense—"

Mercifully, he was interrupted by the council anthem, which spared me from having to come up with an elaborate lie. The voices in the auditorium immediately hushed. When the anthem finished, the procession of speeches began. It stumped me that I was the only one in the entire hall who really knew the captain. His real identity, anyway. Trajan Stormouth had died long ago. Jad hadn't wanted any association with that past. But if the truth were ever discovered, the honour would be stripped from Jad's memory. The very casters who assembled here to pay their respects would turn away with loathing. Even a dead person could be despised. I was determined that would never happen.

Once the ceremony finished, I made a beeline for the exit. Had I known then it would be the last time I'd see Marek, Talina, and Lainie for a long time, I would have done things differently. I would have at least hugged each of them.

CHAPTER FIFTY-EIGHT

Denveitch was still two days away, but I transferred all my clothes into a suitcase, then took it out and repacked it, not satisfied with my folding. If I allowed myself to sit around useless with nothing to do, the depression would crawl back in. The white walls of my recovery room weren't succeeding in keeping me calm. I was antsy and uncomfortable. Being depressed was so exhausting.

I was folding a second pair of socks when someone tapped on the door. Dr Glatz entered carrying a package. "It's a parcel for you, dear. It arrived in today's mail. It must be a get-well gift, I think. But there is no return address, which is very odd."

I thanked her and took the package. It was small, wrapped in brown paper and addressed to me with the Tarahik address. No one from the outside world knew I was here, so who could have sent it?

Dr Glatz waited. "Aren't you going to open it?"

Most gifts received at Tarahik were from rich family or friends, so she was undoubtedly waiting for something magnificent to pop out. No one would send me anything of great significance, though. I hardly thought it was worth Dr Glatz wasting her time.

"I'll open it later."

She left disappointed. As soon as the door was shut, I tore the parcel open.

I had every expectation that inside was something from Senator Kerr. A secret message? Information on a covert mission he wanted me to undertake? But there was no letter. Not even a note or a memo of any kind. Inside was a silver bullet.

A world of confusion hung around me.

Who would send me a silver bullet?

My blood ran cold, my hand losing grip. The parcel dropped with a heavy clang. A gold locket slipped onto the floor. I recognised the rectangular pendant with a half sphere in the centre.

A typhoon of terror thrashed my head. This couldn't be possible. Jad had been wearing this locket when I watched him die.

I plucked the medallion from the floor, my insides squirming. Tucked neatly in the locket was a small mugshot of Jad, his face bruised and beaten. The number 1685302 ran along the bottom of the photo. A prisoner ID.

Jad wasn't dead.

He'd survived the fall.

And now he was a prisoner in a ULD labour camp.

Someone had purposefully removed the silver bullet from the captain's shoulder and sent it as testimony that he was alive. I recalled Vulcan's scheming smile before he'd plunged into the earth. *"Casters like my son and I don't die easily. We are more like gods than casters."*

Vulcan was alive.

And he had his son.

Misery crushed me. What was happening to Jad at that precise moment? What terror was his father subjecting him to?

I jerked upright when someone entered the room, slamming the door back hard enough that the knob went straight through the wall. Colonel Harper's blue eyes pierced mine. Something in his expression made me start. He looked… afraid. "You're leaving now. Grab your things. We need to move this instant."

The urgency in his voice startled me. "But I'm not meant to go to Denveitch till Thursday."

"You're not going to Denveitch. Not anymore." His fingers closed around my wrist. He picked my daypack off the floor and carried it on his shoulder, tugging me into the hallway. I was too much in shock to protest. My daypack only had a spare pair of training clothes, toothpaste, and a brush for my travels. Everything was in my suitcase. Somehow, I didn't think the colonel would care to turn back for it.

I slipped the locket and bullet into my front pocket, both items jabbing my leg as I walked, reminding me they weren't to be forgotten. But there was another more pressing matter on my mind. What was happening?

Screams and shouts resonated from the upper floor. Doors were slammed above. Furniture sounded as though it were being upturned. The ceiling lurched and juddered, as if it had suddenly become malleable.

Colonel Harper forced me down a flight of stairs. Beads of sweat ran down his face.

"What's going on?" I shouted, my heart racing.

"Be quiet. Keep your voice down." His grip tightened on my poor wrist. If he pressed any tighter, he'd snap the bone.

We come out to the lower level, where the passages were vacant and the rooms empty. Nobody had been down here for years. A film of dust lined the floor. There was minimal light. In my ears, my breathing sounded painfully loud.

It wasn't until we'd safely left the sounds of mayhem behind that the colonel dared to explain. "General Kravis knows you're a necromancer. He has guards searching the hospital for you. The council has given the order for your arrest."

My stomach dissolved. "What?"

Harper tugged me down another hall, his eyes alert every time we slipped around a corner. "Commander Macaslan has opened a portal. You will need to leave the base immediately."

"And go where?"

This was happening too fast. A few minutes ago, life had been a slow, miserable ache. Now it was tracking toward a hurricane of uncertainty. I hoped the commander intended to hide me in Weeping Hollow. The house was creepy but offered protection, and I found Macha's odd behaviour endearing.

Colonel Harper didn't answer. He shoved me into a room and locked the door behind him. It was a stately guest quarter, probably for families who came to care for wounded soldiers. Commander Macaslan stood beside an arch mirror, its surface rippling in a smooth maelstrom of silver. The portal didn't reveal where it led.

She crossed the room in quick strides. "There's not a moment to spare. You must leave now."

Unease surged through me. "But where am I going?"

She looked less sure of herself than I'd ever witnessed before, which only spurred my anxiety. "Honestly, I don't know," she answered. "I've opened the portal, but only Senator Kerr knows where it leads." Regret clouded her face. "Zaya, Morgomoth is missing. His body was never found at Galvac. We believe the ULD have him."

I shook my head, not believing what she was telling me. "But that can't be possible. Morgomoth died in the explos—"

Terrifying clarity struck.

Larthalgule. It had fallen into the tank. The blade had consumed the blood of a trickster, illusionist, telepath, and clairvoyant. Once Larthalgule had made contact with the water, the magic had transferred into Morgomoth. The ritual to bring him back was half complete.

Footsteps burst down the hall. The Haxsan Guard were closing in.

Macaslan shot me a stricken look. "Be careful out in the world, Zaya. Something has changed out there. Macha has seen visions of the Four Revenants."

"The four what?"

It wasn't like Commander Macaslan to be so dramatic. "The Four Revenants—otherwise known as the Four Horsemen of the Apocalypse." She sounded out of breath. "They are meant to signal a change, an unbalance in magic… an omen that terrible things are about to happen."

I recalled the evening I'd first arrived at Tarahik. I'd stepped through the threshold to find an impressive monument of four horsemen riding abreast, their faces hidden away by hoods. Each rider had carried a weapon. My mind saw the implements clearly now: a scythe, sword, axe and mace. At the time, I'd been focused on other things. Now I wondered why a monument had been built to them in the first place. What kind of power did these creatures possess?

The floor felt unsteady beneath me. "I don't understand. What does—"

"I believe it means Morgomoth will return." A flash of fear danced in Macaslan's eyes.

Someone pounded on the door outside. It sounded like a battering ram.

Harper's panicked gaze settled on the commander. "We're running out of time."

Macaslan shoved me toward the mirror. "Go!"

"What about you?" It had only just occurred to me what would happen if the commander and the colonel were found in here. "Come with me."

She shook her head, her eyes agitated but full of resolve. "Do not worry about us."

And with those final words, she pushed me into the portal.

Through a silver haze, I watched the guards break the door down and clamber into the room. Colonel Harper was forced onto his knees, a baton slammed into his back. Commander Macaslan glanced my way, her face ghostly white. Except for a hint of relief in those grey eyes, there was nothing to convince me leaving her behind had been the right thing to do. A soldier grabbed her roughly by the shoulder and dragged her out of the room.

It was the last thing I saw before I tumbled in the churning maelstrom, my world spinning into a dark void.

STAY TUNED FOR

THE FOUR
REVENANTS

THE NEXT BOOK IN THE

WAYWARD

SERIES

ACKNOWLEDGEMENTS

Enormous thanks to the Night Writers; Mark, Jane, Tom, Tommy, Stuart, Sandy, Pete, Poet Pete, Ed, Phillip, Shannon, Terry, Erwin, Tracy, Brian, and our fearless leader Gillian. I couldn't have asked for truer friends on this journey. It was your honest feedback, critiques, and passion for the story that gave me the courage to never quit. Gillian, you offer incredible support to all writers. Your guidance, faith, and enthusiasm gives us strength and bravery on our writing marathons. Thanks for cheering us on.

A big thank you to authors Ian Wynne and Tania Joyce, who read my manuscript at its early stages and offered invaluable advice on the structure and characters. Tania, thanks for all your marketing advice and showing me the path toward self-publishing, and for answering so many of my emails.

A tremendous thank you to Hot Tree Editing; Donna, Kristin Scearce, and Virginia Gaylor, for editing my manuscript and improving it a thousand times better than it was. A big shout out to Geraldine for doing a final proof read and finding those silly mistakes that only the cleverest of us find.

Thanks are due to my best friends Pierce and Alice, who read the manuscript and put up with my endless discussions on fantasy and horror. I'm sorry if I bored you... or frightened you.

And finally, thanks to my mum, who believed in me and not Mrs Sanderson. XOXO.

❊

ABOUT THE AUTHOR

From a young age, Cas E Crowe knew she wanted to be a writer. As a child, she spent her playground lunches at school creating weird and haunting stories for her classmates to listen to. An admirer of all things spooky and quirky, her grandfather recognised her unusual hobby as a gift and built her a haunted doll house to stage her stories.

Cas studied a creative arts degree majoring in design and a graduate certificate in animation at the Queensland University of Technology in Brisbane, Australia. She has worked as a sales assistant, a graphic designer, an office manager, and now pursues her dream of writing. The Wayward Haunt is her first novel in the Wayward Series, a story that spun in her mind for ten years until it was finally typed onto a computer.

Amongst Cas's likes are travel, drawing, writing, and watching movies in her pyjamas (at home, not at the cinemas). She resides in Brisbane Australia with her cat, where she is furiously typing away at her next novel.

CAS E CROWE

www.casecrowe.com
www.facebook.com/casecroweauthor/
www.instagram.com/casecroweauthor/

CPSIA information can be obtained
at www.ICGtesting.com
Printed in the USA
FSHW010154290521
81887FS